VICTOR

THE ALPHA ELITE SERIES

USA TODAY BEST SELLING AUTHOR
SYBIL BARTEL

Copyright © 2021 by Sybil Bartel

Cover art by: CT Cover Creations, www.ctcovercreations.com

Cover Photo by: Wander Aguiar, wanderaguiar.com

Cover Model: Andrew Biernat

Edited by: Hot Tree Editing, www.hottreeediting.com

Formatting by: Champagne Book Design

All rights reserved. No part of this publication may be reproduced, distributed, or transmitted in any form or by any means, including photocopying, recording, or other electronic or mechanical methods, without the prior written permission of the author, except in the case of brief quotations embodied in critical reviews and certain other noncommercial uses permitted by copyright law.

All characters in this book have no existence outside the imagination of the author and have no relation whatsoever to anyone bearing the same name or names. They are not even distantly inspired by any individual known or unknown to the author, and all incidents are pure invention.

Warning: This book contains offensive language, alpha males and sexual situations. Mature audiences only. 18+

BOOKS BY SYBIL BARTEL

The Alpha Elite Series
SEAL
ALPHA
VICTOR
ROMEO
ZULU
NOVEMBER
ECHO

The Alpha Bodyguard Series
SCANDALOUS
MERCILESS
RECKLESS
RUTHLESS
FEARLESS
CALLOUS
RELENTLESS
SHAMELESS
HEARTLESS

The Uncompromising Series
TALON
NEIL
ANDRÉ
BENNETT
CALLAN

The Alpha Antihero Series
HARD LIMIT
HARD JUSTICE
HARD SIN
HARD TRUTH
THE ALPHA ANTIHERO SERIES: BOOKS 1-2

The Alpha Escort Series
THRUST
ROUGH
GRIND

The Unchecked Series
IMPOSSIBLE PROMISE
IMPOSSIBLE CHOICE
IMPOSSIBLE END

The Rock Harder Series
NO APOLOGIES

Join Sybil Bartel's Mailing List to get the news first on her upcoming releases, giveaways and exclusive excerpts! You'll also get a FREE book for joining!

VICTOR

Philanderer.

Mercenary.

Marine.

I didn't join the Marines because I was honorable. There wasn't one scrupulous thing about me. If I saw an advantage, I took it. But serving my country turned out to be the best decision I ever made. It led me to Alpha Elite Security.

AES was the most sought-after security contractor in the world. Our reputation unmatched, we got the job done—by any means necessary. Which is where I came in. I handled AES's difficult clients, the ones no one wanted to touch. My success rate flawless, I thought I was invincible.

Then my boss sent me a cryptic text. *New client. Sensitive matter. Corporate Espionage.* Except he failed to mention the suspected spy was a terrified brunette. And the client? Her husband. Now I had one objective.

Code name: Victor.
Mission: Infiltrate.

DEDICATION

For my only child, my beloved son, Oliver.
You are, and will *always* be my entire world.
I love you, Sweet Boy, and I miss you beyond measure.

Oliver Shane Bartel 2004-2020
For my readers, thank you for being there for me. I could not have traveled this road without all of you. I am forever grateful.
XOXO

PROLOGUE

Seventeen Years Ago.

"We shouldn't do this." Her anguished voice carried over the howling wind for a split second before being swept out to sea.

"He *hit you*, Annabeth." I was right there, hiding in her closet because he'd come home early, but not even that turned out to be close enough. "You can't deny it this time. I saw him do it." Mean and drunk, he'd burst into her room, yelling shit about her books being left out. Before I could shove open the closet door, he'd delivered three hard blows and she was on the floor.

I should've done more than level him. I should've fucking killed him.

"He didn't know what he was doing," she argued without any force. "You shouldn't have hit him. It'll only make him angrier when he wakes up."

Enraged, I threw the second to last tie-down line back onto the dock. "Don't you dare try to defend him! *Not this time.*" I hoped the asshole never woke up, but then we'd have a different problem. "He's escalating, and it's getting worse." Her entire right side was already bruised, and if she would've let me take her to the ER, I'd bet every cent I had that at least one of her ribs was cracked.

Her breaths short, holding her side where she'd been punched, she shook her head. "He's my father. He didn't mean to hurt me. He never means to. You don't understand."

I stopped untying the boat and yelled at her like this was her fault. "You think I don't understand?" I was so damn mad

I couldn't see straight. "I may only be seventeen, but I understand exactly what's going on. He's beating you like he used to beat your mother before she disappeared." The incoming storm threw the boat against the mooring, and I slipped, but I still kept yelling. "He's never going to stop, Annabeth. *Never*. He's going to keep hurting you because he can!" He was goddamn Parker Stephens, famous criminal attorney. "No one is going to believe your word against his. How many times are you going to let this happen before it's too late? *How many?*" I demanded as a squall of rain broadsided us.

Huddled in her raincoat, she shivered. "You just shouldn't have hit him. He'll take that out on you now."

My shirt plastered to my chest, I swiped the water off my face. "I don't care what he tries to do to me." *Fuck him.* "I'm tired of all the shoulds, Annabeth. It's what got us here in the first place, because I should've done something a long time ago. Don't you see he's going to keep doing this? Eventually, he'll blame me or one of those criminals he defends or, hell, the gardener or pool guy or anyone at school who talks to you. Or worse, he'll blame you." He already had. He'd blamed her for her mother leaving and left bruises that time too. "Don't you see his pattern?"

"He's my father." Her hoarse voice mingled with the wind.

My anger hit a new high. "I don't care if he's the goddamn second coming, I'm not going to let him hit you ever again!"

She flinched, the boat rocked and we both almost lost our footing.

Grabbing her by the shoulders so she didn't fall, trying to be careful of her ribs, I fought to rein in my temper. "Look, we're leaving, just like we talked about. You said you wanted this." I grasped the side of her face. "You promised, Annabeth. *You promised me.* You said last week would be the last time, but here we are again, except now you're hurt a lot worse, and I can't stand by and watch this happen anymore."

VICTOR

Tears fell down her cheeks. "I'm sorry."

Fuck. "I don't want you sorry. I want you to understand what's happening." I wanted her to see where this was going. "How many more last times before it's too late?" She'd wanted to leave. She'd told me, over and over. She was terrified of him. So I'd said we'd leave, and I'd been scraping every last cent together since. Needing quick money, I'd gotten involved in some shady shit with gunrunners, but none of that mattered now. My wallet was full, and I'd be gone before they needed someone to make another delivery. "It's time, Annabeth."

"You're right." She nodded like she had to convince herself.

"Then why are we arguing? Let's get out of here." The weather was coming in fast, we needed to cast off.

"But the storm." She grabbed onto the stern line with the arm that wasn't holding her ribs as the boat rocked. "Can't we just wait a little bit? Hide in the cabin? Or the car?"

The anger at her father, at this whole situation that I'd been trying to hold in, came back full force. "Wait?" I asked incredulously as another sheet of wind-driven rain hit us. "We talked about this. Your father can trace your car. He'll call the cops the second he realizes you're not in the house. We wouldn't even make it out of the county." Her father had the cops in his pocket. He'd either spin it that I kidnapped her or that I was the one who hit her. Either way, I wasn't going to be holed up in the cabin of his boat or hiding out in her car when the police came looking.

"I don't have a car. The boat's the only way out." I grabbed a life vest and fitted it over her head. "He won't notice it's missing until we're already in the Bahamas, and we can go from there." Hell, we could fish and live off the boat until we were eighteen. I didn't care. But I couldn't live another second letting her get hurt every time her father decided he needed to hit something.

She gingerly threaded one arm through the life vest as her teeth started to chatter. "D-d-do you think he'll find us?"

"No." Yes. Eventually. But I hoped to have another plan by then. We just needed to leave now and worry about that shit later.

She glanced back up at the marina like I'd already done a hundred times. "Are you sure?"

"I knocked out the camera as we came in, your car's at the bus station and no one followed us here. Everyone's staying home because of the storm. This is the perfect time to leave." And the absolute worst. I'd only driven the boat once before, and it was calm seas. The engines were big though. I figured I could handle it or at least get us out of Miami. "But we have to go now."

The boat swayed, and thunder cracked as lightning lit up the sky.

She looked back at me. "I'm scared, Vance."

I wanted to get away from the marina. I wanted us out on open waters. I wanted us miles and miles offshore before her piece-of-shit father realized his punching bag was missing. But every single reason why I was doing this, why I was willing to leave my entire life behind, was looking at me with fear in her eyes, and I couldn't take it.

I couldn't breathe when I saw her fear.

That was why I was doing this.

All I wanted was to make it stop, and this was the only way I knew how. But if she wasn't sure, if she wasn't one hundred percent okay with this, I knew I wouldn't start those engines. It'd make me just like him if I forced her to do something she didn't want to do, and I'd never be like that son of a bitch.

Bracing my legs on the rocking boat, I cupped her face and made her a promise. "I won't let anything bad happen to you ever again. If that means I fire up this boat and we leave, then we go. No regrets. I won't look back. I already told you this." I wanted to leave it at that, but I couldn't. I had to do the right thing, even if it meant throwing myself in the line of fire. I had to give her the choice—the least feasible, least plausible, worst outcome of

VICTOR

a choice for me. "But if you want to stay and fight, then we stay. I'll take you to the police station right now. You know I will. This is your choice. I love you, Annabeth."

Her lips trembling, her eyes filled with tears, she wrapped her small hand around my wrist. "Always?" she asked.

"Always and forever," I answered, giving her the pledge we'd made to each other months ago after we'd been dating in secret because her father didn't let her go out. Even if he had, he'd never let her date a guy like me who came from nothing.

"You swear?" With pain in her voice, she stared up at me with her pretty green eyes.

Making a fist, I held out my smallest finger.

Strands of her long, dark hair escaped her hood and whipped around her face in the wind as she caught her pinky around mine.

"I swear," I promised.

The girl I loved more than life itself nodded once. "Okay, let's go."

ONE

Vance
Present Day

My head snapped left, and pain exploded in my jaw. Blood filled my mouth.

No defensive stance, I winked. "That's the best you've got, mate? A cheap shot to the jaw?" No one touched my face. Any other part of my body? Fair game. But my face? *Fuck* no. This asshole was going down—when I was ready.

He came at me again with a jab followed by a cross. My ribs took the hit, and air left my lungs. No denying it, the steroid prick was packing some force behind his punches.

Wheezing, I smiled. "My grandmother hit harder than you." Watching his shoulders, his hands, his face, I counted every fucking tell. "And for the record, by hit, I mean slap."

I let him come at me with first a left, then a right uppercut, repeating both. The fucking prick smiled around his mouth guard as he delivered the four blows, thinking he had me dead to rights.

Then he made his first and last mistake. He came at me with a textbook hook.

Leading with his right, not covering his left, he raised his arm in an arc and swung toward my temple.

I would've smiled if this wasn't so disappointingly easy. Instead, I blocked his move with my left arm as my right hand shot out.

The palm strike hit him dead center.

VICTOR

His head snapped back, his face exploded with blood and he hit the mat.

TKO.

"Right." I cracked my neck and rolled my shoulder, refraining from the unsportsmanlike move of spitting on his unconscious ass. "Apologies, I forgot. No face shots."

Ignoring the staring pricks at the private, exclusive gym that was nothing more than an excuse to beat the shit out of strangers, I left my useless opponent lying prone, maneuvered under the ropes and stepped down from the ring.

"Hey," one of the managers called. "You can't just leave him there."

"He's still breathing."

Looking like a steroid twin of the guy on the mat, the manager shook his head. "Not the point."

"Then tell me, what is? He signed the waiver, same as anyone else here." And paid a hefty sum when he did.

Frowning, the manager looked at the guy as he groaned and came to.

"Right. Good luck with that." I turned toward the locker room.

Two small hands landed on my chest as a made-up blonde planted herself in front of me and smiled. "That was impressive."

Never having seen her before, not that I kept track of the ring bunnies who liked to fuck the alpha dogs, I winked. "Love, you don't know the half of it."

"Oooh," she flirted, winking right back. "You're good with your hands *and* you're British."

Wrong. "Caught me." Literally. "Give me a chance to shower and I'll show you what else I can do with my hands."

Not half as dumb as she was acting, she tried to play me. "Over dinner? Le Saison?"

French, expensive as fuck, and impossible to get a reservation at—the little minx thought she was testing me.

Smirking, I walked into the locker room and fished my cell out of my bag. Dialing a number I knew by memory, I held the phone to my ear as the blonde strode into the locker room after me like she was staking a claim.

"Le Saison," a breathy voice answered in an accent that I knew for a fact, unlike mine, was actually real.

"Darling, it's me. How are you?"

"*Vance*," Christiane cooed. "I miss you. Are you coming in to see me tonight?"

"Of course. Table for two? Twenty minutes?"

"Ah, I hope she is beautiful." Her laugh was practiced and sultry. "Or he?"

"She, darling." I glanced at the ring bunny. "Blonde, petite." Young as hell. I'd share her.

"You always do know how to please me. And of course, come in. I'll have your table ready."

I gave her a practiced chuckle. The leggy redhead had had more than a table ready for me once upon a time. "Thank you, and what can I say? I live to please." When it got me something I wanted.

"Precisely the beauty and curse of you, Monsieur Conlon. I will see you soon."

"Right," I replied to Christiane as I eyed the blonde who'd moved closer to put her hands back on my chest. "Looking forward to it, pet."

"Oh you dirty, delicious man. Do not call me names that make me wet before you get here." Christiane gave me her sultry laugh again. "You know how I get."

I played her game. "I'm afraid I've forgotten." I hadn't. Christiane was insatiable, indiscriminate and loved pretty new toys of either sex. "Why don't you tell me."

VICTOR

"*Hungry,*" she purred right before she hung up.

Tossing my cell back in my bag, I winked at the blonde. "After I clean up, you have ten minutes to make me a happy man."

The ring bunny dragged a painted nail down my abs. "Because?"

"I'm taking you to dinner, and our table's waiting." I had no shame. She was going to work for it. Nothing was free in this world.

Her hands already drifting toward my cock, she smiled. "Le Saison?"

With practiced arrogance, I lifted an eyebrow. "Is that not what you asked for?"

Fake eyelashes and all, she fluttered like a show pony. "Why, yes it is."

I grabbed her wrist before she grabbed my dick. "Excellent. Gratitude looks good on you, pet. Remember that while I jump in the shower."

Twisting out of my grasp, she fisted the waistband of my shorts. "No need." My cock already in her hands, the ring bunny dropped to her knees in the middle of the locker room. "I'll remember it right now."

TWO

Vance

"**T**AKE MY HAND!" I REACHED OUT FURTHER AS ANOTHER GIANT wave slammed into the boat.

A deluge of water hit my back, the boat rocked steeply starboard and her hand disappeared.

"Annabeth!" *Through driving rain and treacherous waves, I blindly reached over the side.*

The boat pitched and rolled, and her head surfaced.

Coughing up water, she reached up with one hand.

I caught and grasped her thin wrist. "I got you! I got you!"

In a panic, her fingers grasped at me. "H-help."

"I'm pulling you up," *I yelled over the crashing storm as I got my second hand on her arm. Drenched, no purchase on the deck, I yanked with all my strength.*

My feet slipped, my head smashed against something and I fell to my back a split second before she landed on top of me.

Another wave crashed into the hull, and the boat pitched portside.

We slid across the deck, my head swam and she screamed.

Lacing my fingers with hers, I wrapped an arm around her waist. "It's okay. I got you."

"The bow!" *she cried, but it was already too late.*

A twenty-foot swell lifted the front of the boat, and we were suddenly vertical. Then everything went slow motion just long enough for green eyes filled with terror to lock on mine and plead for help.

"Vance, save us."

VICTOR

The slow-motion reel disappeared in a blink, and the force of the capsizing boat slammed us into the angry ocean.

My lungs filled with water, her hand slipped from mine and blinding pain lanced across my back as my flesh shredded.

My mouth opened to call her name, but the sea swallowed my tormented cry.

I jolted awake.

Panting, sweating, fear lodged in my throat as if I were drowning all over again, I sat up as the memory played on repeat in a cycle I couldn't break.

Impotence coursing through my veins, I scrubbed a hand over my face in a useless attempt to dislodge the mental image, but I was already there.

Triggered.

In my fucking sleep.

But now I was awake in my own well-deserved nightmare. Green eyes desperately pleading, drilling into the embedded guilt I never escaped, I mentally rewatched the biggest mistake of my life as her haunted cries played on an eternal repeat.

"Vance, save us."

Refusing to admit to myself that the nightmares had been increasing in frequency, I moved to get up.

A small hand landed on my shoulder, just above my scars. "You're up early."

Shaking away the hand, I stood and turned, feeling every hit from the steroid prick last night as the ring bunny looked up at me with a smile.

Her voice turned to a contrived shade of shyness. "Hi."

Taking in the half dozen used condoms on the floor, refusing to admit this was getting old, my forced smile was as practiced as it was contrived. "Time to leave." I threw on last night's pants.

Fake hurt crossed her features. "I thought you said you liked me."

Not hiding my smirk, I lied. "I do, pet. You're gorgeous and it's been entertaining, to say the least." Her dress around her waist and her legs spread for Christiane in the lady's lounge at Le Saison last night had painted quite the picture, but I had my rules. Metaphorically speaking, I didn't dip in the same pool twice and last night was a distant memory. "Now it's time for you to go." I fished a few hundreds out of my wallet and dropped them on the nightstand. "Grab yourself a cab, darling. I have to work."

Getting out of bed, she palmed the money and counted it. "Will I see you again?" Not taking offense at the offered cash, she slipped the bills into the lace bra I'd never bothered taking off her. Grabbing her dress from the floor and shaking it out, she stepped into it sans underwear without an ounce of the innocence she'd conveyed when Christiane asked for a taste of her cunt. "I think I at least deserve your number."

And there it was.

The clinginess I headed off and avoided at all cost hit me in the face just like the steroid prick last night had.

Maybe I deserved this. Or maybe I was simply losing my touch.

Either way, hard pass.

"We never get what we deserve, now do we, pet?" The sooner she learned that, the better. "Let yourself out."

Heading into the bathroom and locking the door behind me, I showered and shaved. Ten minutes later, I opened the door to a thankfully empty penthouse. Crossing the bedroom to the walk-in, I bypassed tailored suits and custom-made dress shirts in favor of jeans and a T-shirt.

Picking my phone up, I glanced at the time.

Almost sunrise.

Too damn early, but I needed to break shit.

THREE

Sabine

A NOISE SOUNDED AND I JOLTED AWAKE IN THE PREDAWN LIGHT. My heart racing, the urge to get up and run overwhelming, I glanced at my door to make sure it was still closed.

The noise sounded again.

A grunt followed by a feminine cry of pain.

Pulling the covers higher, I burrowed down and held them to my chin as if I were a frightened child.

Two more grunts preceded another cry.

I pulled the covers higher.

The telltale muffled banging of a headboard meeting a wall began to echo both in the hallway and my memory.

Willing the memory to disappear, I rubbed my thumb over my ring finger.

The banging accelerated from a steady drone to a frantic pace.

Bile rose.

Grunting.

Pleading.

"Joseph, no."

A slap sounded.

I rolled to my side.

The banging escalated.

Staring out at the sparkling predawn cityscape, I selfishly did nothing.

The banging hit a crescendo.

His groan filled me with hate.

I watched the awakening sun begin to paint the world in bright pink, red and orange hues as if everything was beautiful.

"Leave." His muffled but not muted order carried under my door. *"I have a phone call to make."*

A door opened, then closed.

Quiet sobs and bare feet padded down the hallway.

I silently prayed for a different life.

FOUR

Vance

IGNORING MY RIBS, I SWUNG THE HEAVY SLEDGEHAMMER, AND three wooden shelves splintered. Another swing, and the satisfying crack of destruction filled my headspace.

My twin brother walked down the three steps into his den with a scowl on his face. "It's early." Ronan picked up his own sledgehammer.

Translation—too fucking early. Yeah, I knew. Raising the hammer, I swung again. "It's always a good time to destroy other people's property." It's what I did best. I destroyed pretty things.

"Not when my wife is sleeping." Stepping up next to me, he yielded his hammer against an unsuspecting cabinet.

"When you ask for free help remodeling, you get what you get." I decimated another shelf.

Ronan swung again. "I didn't ask."

Laughing, my ribs killing me, I had to set the sledgehammer down. "What were you going to do? Remodel a ten-thousand-square-foot house by yourself?" Fucking Christ. "Hire a contractor. Hell, hire Christensen." The Danish former Special Forces Jægerkorpset had a dozen crews working for him. "Neil would have this place demo'd in a day." Ignoring the pain, I picked the sledgehammer up and took out another shelf. "A week after that, you'd be done with this shit."

"No one comes in the house," my brother ground out.

"Right," I scoffed. "Because a couple of contractors are going to what? Look at your wife?" My twin was a jealous fuck. Always had been. Not that he didn't have every reason to be. His wife was spectacular.

"No," he drew out with forced patience before telling me shit I already knew. "Because my wife is the largest female recording artist in history, and I'm not subjecting her to *fucking contractors*." He swung hard, and an entire section of cabinets ripped from the wall as the crash echoed through the den.

I waited until the dust settled. Then I shook my head at his idiocy. I couldn't blame him for his reasoning, but his process? "You do realize most normal people remodel their entire house before they move in?"

My brother swung again. "It's not the entire house."

"Right." Not thinking, I used the hem of my T-shirt to wipe the sweat from my face.

My twin brother's gaze immediately cut to my ribs before he glanced at my jaw and scowled.

"What?" I challenged, because that's how it'd always been between us. Contentious on my part, condemnatory on his.

Not saying a damn word, he aimed for another cabinet.

Fucking exhausted, I followed suit and swung my sledgehammer.

For the next hour, me and my identical twin broke shit and made a mess. I'd say it was our specialty, but he'd pulled his life together.

I was another story.

Not that I gave a single fuck. I didn't deserve what he had.

After the remainder of the built-ins were a pile of destruction in the middle of the room, Ronan paused and glanced from the concrete floor to the pile of carpet outside the sliders. "You took the carpet out this morning."

I picked up a bottle of water I'd taken from his kitchen before I'd come in the den. "Needed to be done."

"Did you sleep last night?"

Taken off guard, I avoided eye contact and drained the bottle of water before evading the question. "Who the fuck doesn't sleep?"

"You don't."

I chuckled and tossed the plastic bottle on top of the mess we'd already made. "Right. Because you keep an eye on me every night, baby brother."

Ronan kept fucking talking. "I'm seconds younger, and I don't have to keep an eye on you to know what I'm seeing. You look like you haven't slept a full night's sleep since high school. And before you give some bullshit excuse, remember that we both served. We both know the signs."

This time I looked him square in the eye. "I don't know what the hell you're talking about."

"Junior year, last week of school before summer break," he stated, like he knew my fucking secrets.

Rage, impotence and guilt I'd spent my entire adult life trying to control crawled up my back, and I did the one thing I never fucking did anymore.

I lost control.

Stepping into the personal space of the only living person I gave a damn about, I leveled him with a lethal look. "I said," I enunciated slowly, "I don't know what the hell you're talking about."

Identical eyes staring at me, Ronan didn't back down. "What happened on the boat that weekend?"

Wanting to destroy everything within a ten-foot radius, my brother included, I choked down self-hatred and forced a monotone reply. "What boat?"

Sanaa appeared in the doorway. "Are you two at it again?"

Searching my face like he knew my fucking life, Ronan tipped his chin as if to say this conversation wasn't over.

I snorted. "Of course not." Glancing at a woman I'd seen naked, my guilt compounded. "You're looking beautiful as always, love." I forced a wide smile.

Breezing barefoot into the construction mess in a slip of a dress, my brother's wife made a dismissive sound as she waved her hand through the air. "Stop being a flirt." Briefly holding my sweaty shoulders, she air-kissed me on each cheek before demanding, "And stop stirring the pot." Her face lit up as she passed me and kissed my brother on the lips. "Good morning."

His gaze still on me, Ronan gave me a look that said he knew I was full of shit before dismissing me and grabbing his wife around the waist. Lifting her off her feet as he thoroughly kissed the fuck out of her, he set her back down a meter away from the debris.

"Good morning." Quietly speaking in a tone he only ever used on her, Ronan touched his lips to his wife's forehead once. "Sorry we woke you."

Sanaa flushed like a woman in love. "Nonsense. The sun is awake, I am awake. I will make you two some breakfast." Her smile lighting up her face, she turned toward the steps.

His expression hardened, and my brother threw me a warning glance as he spoke to his wife. "Vance isn't staying."

Without looking back, Sanaa waved her hand over her shoulder. "Of course he is. I am making eggs."

"With peppers and onions?" I asked.

She made a derisive sound. "Is there any other way?"

"Then it's decided." I gave my brother his warning look right fucking back because I was an asshole. "The lady of the house has spoken."

Ronan waited until she was out of earshot, then he

lowered his voice. "I can guess what happened that weekend, and I see what you're doing now."

Every muscle went stiff, but I chuckled. "I can't remember who I fucked last night, but you remember a weekend almost two decades ago?"

"I remember when you became secretive junior year before a girl we went to high school with died in a boating accident. Then you showed up two days later with a blood-soaked T-shirt stuck to your back."

I opened my mouth to deny everything, but Ronan held a hand up.

"We never spoke about it, and frankly, I don't want to. You have your life, I have mine, and we both have a past. But since we've been back in Miami, I'm seeing the signs. We're not ever going to be close because I don't fucking trust you, but you're still my brother, and I know what I'm looking at."

Ignoring the hit about trust that I deserved, I smirked. "Yeah, what's that? An exact replica, except better looking?"

Dead serious, his expression remained locked. "I see guilt, but I'm not talking about the shit you pulled with Sanaa. I saw this before then." Gaze unwavering, he threw down his final accusation. "It's gotten worse."

Defensive, I aimed it back on him. "You can forgive her but not your own blood?"

"She's *my wife*."

"She wasn't when I kissed her over a goddamn decade ago, and I've apologized." A hundred fucking times.

His jaw locked, his nostrils flared and he leaned toward me as his voice went lethally quiet. "I'm not rehashing the intent behind you letting her believe you were me, nor am I having this conversation—now or ever. Do not mistake my civility for anything other than what it is."

My cell rang, but I ignored it.

Staring at me a beat longer, Ronan tipped his chin toward my ribs. "Handle your shit. My house isn't your personal therapy playground." Dropping his sledgehammer, he walked out of the den.

My phone stopped ringing, but then a second later pinged with a new text.

Pulling it out of my pocket, I glanced at the screen.

Alpha: *New client. Sensitive matter. Corporate Espionage.*

FIVE

Vance

Locking down all the shit in my head, I dialed my cell as I walked out of my brother's house.

Trefor picked up on the first ring. "Good, you're up."

Chuckling like I didn't have a fucking care in the world, I stole my brother's wife's sentiment. "Is the sun up?"

Adam "Alpha" Trefor, former Navy SEAL, owner of Alpha Elite Security, and my boss, ignored my bullshit. "We've got a potential new client, but this isn't the usual circles we travel in."

"When is anything I handle usual?" Trefor didn't hire me to be a sand-trap jockey, humping full combat loadouts as the government's off-the-books, black-ops trigger finger when they were too much of a pussy to do the job themselves. I wasn't a pay-to-play mercenary like the others at AES.

I was the last resort.

I was the guy you called when you were desperate. Or fucking stupid.

Unusual was my middle name.

"What circles are we talking about?" I didn't give a damn what it was. I already knew I'd take the assignment because Ronan's warning was pissing me off, and I needed a change of scenery.

Adam exhaled like it was the end of a shit week instead of oh seven hundred on a Wednesday. "What do you know about art?"

Fucking hell. "If you're about to upsell some bullshit assignment like Gagosian has a pretentious intern taking art home in his messenger bag, I'm out." There was the unusual, and then there was shit that was just insulting. "This is a waste of my time." I got behind the wheel of a company Range Rover.

"I'm not talking about art galleries. But the fact that you name-dropped Gagosian now has me curious."

I didn't bother telling him that all my properties had pieces from them hanging on the walls. "Spit it out, Alpha."

"Auctions."

Turning the engine over, I cranked the AC. "What about them?"

"Harrington's."

My hand on the gearshift, I paused. "*The* Harrington's?" The biggest, most exclusive auction house in the world was having corporate espionage issues?

"The one and only."

"What kind of trouble can an auction house get involved in besides stolen shit?"

"Unclear."

"Hazard a guess." I threw the SUV in drive.

"I don't have to. You're meeting with Joseph Bertrand at Harrington's corporate offices in New York at twelve hundred."

"You know I'm here in Miami." I glanced at my watch. "And who the hell is Joseph Bertrand?"

"One of the Gulfstreams is fueled up and ready to go. Zulu's waiting for you at the Executive Airport. Emailing what November pulled together on Bertrand now, but he's the last living Harrington behind Harrington's. It was his mother's maiden name."

"Right." Fucking great. "A meet and greet with a paranoid Harrington, and I don't even get to fly myself to this dick-stroke meeting?"

Trefor ignored my first comment. "Get certified, and you can fly whatever company jet you want."

What the hell did I need a certification for? "I fly helicopters without a pilot's license." Arbitrary rules never stopped me.

"I don't own any helicopters," Alpha countered.

"You own this Range Rover I'm driving. What's the difference?"

Trefor lost his unflappable edge. "*Fucking hell*, Conlon, you don't have a driver's license?"

"Not an American one." Not one in my real name anyway. "Probably not a current one either." The longest I'd stayed put anywhere was London, but I hadn't been stationary for seventeen years. The past few months helping Alpha transition the headquarters for AES from our New York offices to a new Miami Beach location was the longest stretch of consecutive nights I'd slept anywhere since being in the Marines.

Trefor swore again before issuing an order. "When you get back from this assignment, handle your shit and get legal."

I chuckled. "Legally what?"

"Conlon," he warned.

"Right," I placated. "Driver's license." I'd get right on that. "Copy that."

There was a pause, then Trefor let out an audible exhale. "Christ, Conlon. I'm fucking serious. We've been here months. Hell, you bought a place. Get a driver's license, then get your pilot's license. Zulu or I will do the flight hours with you. I need you above board on this."

I was never *above board*. "I buy a lot of places." The penthouse here was the sixth property I'd added to my portfolio of real estate I didn't give a damn about. "Doesn't mean I establish residency at any of them."

"Why not?" Trefor demanded.

Because I was still pointlessly looking for a place I could actually sleep in? Because home was a bullshit string of four letters? Because I was more fucked than he or anyone else at AES could possibly imagine? Who fucking knew? "Maybe November's rubbing off on me." I half laughed like none of this bothered me. "Living off the grid's the new cool."

Trefor didn't say shit for a full beat, then he took on a tone I rarely heard from him. "Vance," he stated quietly.

"Right," I said, stopping him before he took that train of thought any further. "Driver's license. Got it." I pulled into the underground parking garage of my oceanfront penthouse. "Let Zulu know I'm grabbing a shower and I'll be at the Executive Airport in thirty minutes."

SIX

Vance

WALKING UP THE AIRSTAIRS OF THE GULFSTREAM, I GLANCED in the cockpit at Zulu. "Lucky you. Shuttle service today."

Former Navy SEAL, Zane "Zulu" Silas, smiled at me with his aviators on like he was living his best life. "Nothing better than getting paid to fly sixty-million-dollar jets." He smirked. "Unless I get to also shoot shit."

"Last I checked, you don't need your M16 in the wonderful world of art auctions."

Zulu dropped the smile and shook his head as if in disgust. "Yeah, heard about that. Some Harrington's exec wants a babysitter." He flipped a few switches and adjusted the mic on his headphones. "Luck's all yours today, Conlon."

"Right." Luck wasn't in my vocabulary. "Close the hatch?" I glanced down the aisle at the empty seats in the main cabin and my mood lifted marginally. "Am I second chair?"

Zulu barked out a half laugh. "Nice try. Alpha already told me not to let you fly."

Fucking pussy. "Trefor needs to lighten up, and this plane needs a second pilot."

"Pilot being the operative word." He tipped his head toward the aft cabin. "November's flying second. He's stowing his shit in the cargo area. Echo's back there somewhere as well."

Christ. "November gets second chair? He's been flying for a fucking minute."

Lowering his aviators, Zulu raised an eyebrow at me. "November got his pilot's license. Legally," he added sarcastically.

What fucking bullshit. "You know I'm a better pilot than him." November's instincts were buried in a keyboard. Mine were rooted in survival.

"I'm not getting into a whose-dick-is-bigger pissing contest. Facts are facts. He has a piece of paper, you don't."

"I can get a piece of paper." I could hack the FAA.

"Don't even think about it," Zulu warned. "I said legally."

"I make no promises." Not anymore. But next time I couldn't sleep, I was hacking my way into both a driver's license and pilot's license. "Why's Echo here?" I glanced behind me. "And where the hell is he?" I closed the hatch.

"No clue. He and Blade are like chameleons. Those motherfuckers blend into the woodwork on their worst days and are downright invisible the rest of the time."

Except when Echo was at the private gym we both belonged to, then he was a goddamn beast. If you weren't terrified of him in that world, then you had zero self-preservation. Which I didn't, and hadn't on too many occasions to count. None of which I mentioned to Zulu, or anyone else for that matter. I didn't give a shit about my own mortality, but what can I say, I was a vain fucker. I didn't want my face pounded in by an unleashed Echo... again.

"I'll tell November to get his ass up here." I glanced at my watch. "I've got a meeting at twelve hundred. We need to be wheels up."

"Copy that." Zulu went back to his preflight checks.

I passed the plush leather seats I would've given my right arm to sit in as a kid, and made my way to the back of the plane.

Echo was stretched out on one of the divans in the sleeping

cabin. His gaze cut to the door of the cargo hold as November ducked his head and came out.

Lifting my chin at Echo, I sat opposite of him before glancing at November. "Zulu needs you in the cockpit."

"Copy." Nodding once, his ever-present laptop tucked under his arm, November hunched slightly to accommodate his height as he made his way to the forward cabin. He looked more like a model with his sun-bleached hair and the silver rings he wore than former Air Force with a preternatural genius for anything IT related.

I watched November take second chair. "If I hadn't seen him in action, I'd bet my bank account that pretty-boy genius couldn't fly this bird, let alone know what to do with an M4. He looks like we should drop him off in Ibiza for a month-long rager." I half laughed. "On second thought, maybe we should. Might make him crack a smile."

Echo, the cagey fuck, looked out the window but didn't comment.

"What about you? You along for the ride, or is something waiting in New York?" I didn't bother keeping up on the other AES assignments unless Alpha called me in for backup.

Echo's hardened gaze cut to me. "You took a beating last night." He glanced at my ribs like he could see through my custom Brioni suit before looking back at me accusingly. "On purpose."

Hiding my shock that he'd been there last night, I chuckled again even though every time I did, I felt the exact ribs in question that he'd just pointedly looked at. "I don't know about you, mate, but I can assure you that I never purposely aim to take a beating."

That's exactly what I did.

Every damn time.

Because then, for two fucking minutes, I could breathe without guilt.

Echo stared at me as the Gulfstream's engines came to life.

Then he sat up and said the last thing I was expecting. "Who was she?"

I forced a smirk as we started to taxi. "If I remembered the name of every woman I've fucked, I'd have no memory left."

"Cut the bullshit accent. You know damn well I'm not talking about last night."

With a locked expression so I didn't show the pain, I stretched my arm out along the back of the divan. "I have no idea what you're talking about."

Trying to intimidate me, Echo stared me down. Then he leaned forward. "I'm watching you, Conlon. Don't fucking compromise my shit because you can't keep yours together." He stood and turned toward the front of the cabin.

Too late, my instincts kicked in and I silently cursed. "You're here, why?"

Fifty pounds of muscle on me, the former Navy SEAL looked over his shoulder. "I'm your backup."

SEVEN

Sabine

"WHAT ARE YOU WEARING TODAY?" HE DEMANDED.
Startled, I flinched and looked up.

In a three-piece custom suit, his height and stature taking up the doorway, Joseph caught my gaze in the mirror. "I asked you a question."

Anxiety threaded through my nerves like caffeine, and I pulled my robe closer around me. "Good morning." There was nothing good about it. "I've laid a dress out on the bed."

With a single curt nod, he disappeared from the bathroom doorway.

Exhaling slowly, I braced because Joseph never did this. Not for a long time. He controlled every breath of my life, but in the morning, before we had to be in the office, he never checked on me anymore. Especially if he'd been previously... engaged. He expected his breakfast and me to be ready before him and waiting. Unless he had meetings outside the office, his driver took us both to work.

Work.

I would appreciate the irony of the simple word if it were not so absurd. A poor French girl who came from nothing, now living in an eight-thousand-square-foot Manhattan penthouse, wearing Dior dresses and Manolo Blahnik heels while being chauffeured to and from her own office at the most famous auction house in the world—but I did not work.

I dressed nicely, smiled when spoken to and accompanied the man who ran it all, including my life, to whatever meeting, event, party, charity, soiree, restaurant or anything else he told me to attend with him. Always by his side, always perfectly put together and *always* decorous. Even when he brutally fucked one of the house staff before dawn just steps away in his master suite, which I had slept in exactly once in seven years.

When I was not pretending my life was a fairy tale, I pretended to manage the house staff and social calendar, but in truth, I had no control over any of it. Joseph ruled all of it, including me.

Glancing down, I stared at the diamond ring weighing heavily on my left ring finger that was both my most cherished possession and a cruel reminder of why I was here. It was also a risk to wear it, but I never took it off. I could not afford to.

"You're not wearing that," Joseph barked, suddenly reappearing.

I flinched but then quickly shifted on my velvet-padded seat in front of my vanity. I had learned long ago that nervous tics, bad habits or unsightly behavior of any kind weren't tolerated. Hiding my reaction so as not to anger the very man who both made me enraged and afraid, I looked up with a steady gaze. "I'm sorry?"

Anger etched the already deep lines across his forehead. "Stop being sorry and start being appropriate. I shouldn't have to remind you what it means to be respectful and appreciative. I didn't have to take you and your problems in when you had nothing. And I sure as hell don't buy you expensive outfits to decorate the damn closet," he chastised. "Wear what I set out, put your hair down and be ready in five minutes. This is the final time I'm going to warn you today—watch your attitude."

My ever-present anxiety bled into fear because I knew this tone. Conditioned, I started to apologize. "I'm sor—" Catching myself, I stopped. "Yes, of course."

Joseph had not laid a hand on me in months, and I knew why,

but that did not mean he wouldn't at any time for any provocation. I had heard too many late nights and early mornings like today to count, and God forgive me, I'd never done anything to intervene. Not only would his attention return to me much sooner than when he eventually tired of whichever house staff was his flavor du jour before firing them, but worse, he would turn on me and our deal. The latter was what I feared most. Which was why I did not dare say anything more while he still stood, blocking the doorway.

I waited for him to retreat.

Except he didn't.

The manipulative, controlling man who'd expertly played on my naïveté and desperation seven years ago stared at my reflection in the mirror.

My heart rate accelerating, my chest tightening to the point of pain, I held my breath.

His stare castigating, he wielded his silence like a sword. A sword he knew I would fall on because he had meticulously trained me to.

Unable to stand the punishingly thick dead air that filled what should've been a safe space, I stupidly opened my mouth and spoke. "Did you need anything else?"

Staring at my reflection for two calculated breaths, he played his one-sided game of manipulation. Then, intent on shattering the already fragile morning and my very being, he dropped words as if dropping a bomb.

"Take that black eyeliner off, you look like a whore."

I waited until his back was turned and his expensive cologne was trailing behind him before I looked at my reflection in the mirror. But I did not exhale until my bedroom door was shut with purposeful force.

Studying the reflection of a woman I did not know, I pulled a tissue from a gold-plated box and gently wiped under my eyes.

When most of my makeup was a memory, I removed the small clip holding my hair back and stood, but suddenly I felt more naked than when Joseph was staring me down, trying to break me.

I could not walk into the busy corporate offices of Harrington's headquarters without a shield. Men, women, Joseph himself, the sea of offices and cubicles—all of it was a battleground, and I could not defend my position without the armor of perception. In that world, an unmade-up woman was a weak woman. I needed strength. I needed ammunition. I needed a defensive position that would keep it all at bay.

Glancing at my makeup like it was my last bastion of hope, I settled on both a win and a loss.

Picking up a lip liner and matching lipstick in a nude shade, I outlined my full lips in a color intended to cover my natural pink. Then I carefully swept the lipstick across my top and bottom lips.

Allowing myself one more glance in the mirror, I still did not recognize the woman staring back. But her makeup was in place, and while subtle enough that the enemy would not take notice, she had her armor.

Slipping my robe off, I walked into the bedroom to put on an outfit I had not chosen.

EIGHT

Vance

No way in hell was I dealing with Echo on this assignment. Or anyone else for that matter.

"I work alone," I warned Echo.

Turning to face me in a textbook intimidation tactic, Echo leveled me with a look that said I wasn't a SEAL, and he had no fucking respect for me or my process. "Not on this one you don't."

Irrationally pissed, but not letting him see it, I stood. "Let me repeat myself in case you didn't hear me the first time." Like a pretentious fuck, I straightened the cuffs of my dress shirt. "I'm flying solo on this assignment."

Echo pulled his one and only trump card. "Alpha's orders. I'm backup."

Fucking Trefor. "Right." I chuckled to cover the fact that for the second time today, Echo had taken me off guard. "Because you know so much about art?"

"Because I know how to cover your psychotic ass even when I don't want to, and trust me, I'd rather take any other assignment, so don't fucking piss me off, Conlon."

"Who's pissing who off, *Marino*?" Fucking dick.

"Nice try. You wish you knew my last name, and just to be clear, I don't give a damn if you are pissed. Alpha says your sorry ass needs a babysitter—congratulations, you got one. Keep getting your ass kicked at the gym, fuck with your pussy shirt some more. Hell, throw a goddamn temper tantrum for all I care. It's not going to change the fact that I'm your shadow on this assignment. And for the record, just like last night, you won't know I'm there." He glanced at my ribs in disgust. "Until you fuck shit up. Then you'll goddamn know."

Fucker pivoted and walked toward the forward cabin.

I had no one to blame but myself, but I was still livid. Trefor was getting a call, but before I did that, I needed to know one thing. "Why were you at the Annex last night?" I hadn't seen Echo, and while he was a chameleon when he wanted to be, he was hard to fucking miss at the gym, even if you had your eyes closed. That meant he'd purposely been trying to evade me. "You taking notes for Trefor now?"

Sparing me one of his trademark disdainful glances, Echo didn't answer. He walked toward the cockpit.

I pulled my cell out and dialed, making a mental note to hack the fuck out of Echo's records again to find out what his real name was.

Trefor answered on the first ring. "You spoke with Echo."

Barely keeping my tone civil, I laid it out. "I had one condition when I took this job. *One*. I work alone. That means, unless circumstances warrant it, I don't need backup. I also don't need a babysitter or a goddamn shadow at the gym." In this line of work, one day, I'd eventually take a fatal bullet. I didn't give a fuck. But I gave a fuck about pretending to play nice on the playground with their Teams-mantra bullshit. I didn't do group sports. I didn't do team anything. I worked alone, lived alone, existed alone. That was my goddamn cross, and not Trefor or anyone else was going to fuck with that.

"Did you read the file yet?" he calmly asked.

"I'm wheels up with an Echo albatross thirty minutes after you gave me the assignment. No, I haven't read the goddamn file yet."

"You done?" Trefor asked noncommittally.

VICTOR

"No." *Motherfucker.* "Call off Echo. I don't need backup to meet with some art auction prick."

Offhand as hell, Trefor threw down a loaded question. "How many times were you at the Annex this week?"

My muscles stilled, but my free hand fisted. Then the British accent I unconsciously hid behind came out like a fucking neon tell. "I've no idea what you're getting at."

"Three times," Trefor answered before his tenor turned to steel. "Echo stays. Read the file." He hung up.

NINE

Sabine

I STARED AT THE ROLAND MOURET OFF-WHITE, HIGH-NECKED MIDI dress that was too fitted and the wrong color to wear to the office if I wanted to be taken seriously. Disdain for Joseph polluting my mind, I directed misplaced resentment at the designer as I tugged the dress on in haste, hating it even though it was a beautiful cut.

Stepping into Gianvito Rossi heels, still feeling naked in my own skin, I walked into my dressing room and grabbed the ivory Alexander McQueen wool trench that was the same length as my dress.

Even though Joseph hadn't approved the addition, I slipped my arms into the soft material and glanced in the full-length mirror.

A seven-carat diamond on my finger, Boucheron around my neck, my dark, almost black hair I had inherited from my mother in loose waves around my shoulders before falling down my back, I looked expensive.

Bought and paid-for expensive.

Breathing deep breaths past the accelerated beat of my heart that felt ever-present these days, I grabbed my Hermès Bolide handbag and went downstairs.

Rosaline, our live-in chef and head housekeeper, stood waiting at the bottom of the stairs with a look of concern I had trained myself to ignore. "Good morning, Sabine."

VICTOR

"Good morning, Rosaline." I purposely did not glance around to see if the young housekeeper that Joseph had hired a few months ago was in sight.

"He's already waiting in the car." Rosaline, who was Joseph's age but looked much older, held out an insulated thermos. "I thought you would like to take your coffee with you. It has a lid on it." She lowered her voice. "He is not pleased this morning."

When was he ever? "Thank you, but no thank you on the coffee." Joseph didn't allow eating or drinking in any of the vehicles. He said it was *unsightly*. "I will get something at the office." It was a lie, one of many minor lies that had become part of my daily routine. Ones I told myself made my life easier, but the irony was not lost on me that easier would be not having to lie at all. But there were too many Joseph rules to follow, and no one won when Joseph was not *pleased*. Which he would not be if he caught me fetching anything from the staff break room. That, he considered beyond the pale. Which was why we took lunch every workday at one of the many expensive Manhattan restaurants in what I secretly referred to as the double intent parade. The price tag of said lunches told everyone he could afford it, and the contrived devotion to the time he carved out of his busy daily routine to take me out told everyone how pious he was.

I hated the lunches.

But on the occasions that he had an actual business lunch to attend, it was bittersweet. I would have an hour reprieve from him, but I also would go without lunch. I was not allowed to dine alone. Nor was I allowed to leave the office without one of the drivers.

Rosaline held out a small, linen-wrapped bundle. "Please, take this. You have not eaten, and this is small, it will fit." She nodded toward my purse and lowered her voice to a whisper again. "You can eat when he goes into his office."

Torn between taking the risk and offending her twice in one morning, not to mention the low rumbling in my stomach I'd grown accustomed to because Joseph liked thin women, I forced a smile. "Thank you, Rosaline." Taking the small bundle, I immediately felt the warmth of one of her fresh-baked breakfast muffins. "Blueberry?"

She smiled. "Lemon."

Bitter. Like my life. "Even better." I tucked the muffin carefully into my handbag.

Rosaline quickly scrambled in front of me and pressed the call button for the private elevator before I could do it for myself. "Have a good day."

"You don't need to get the elevator for me," I gently chided.

"I like to, and I know Joseph said you won't be home for dinner tonight, but if you need anything, come let me know. I'll be in my room." She smiled in sympathy.

Suddenly I understood. She had heard it this morning too. But the last part of what she had said worried me more than her pity for me. "Pardon?"

Joseph hadn't mentioned anything about tonight, nor put anything on my calendar. We had the big auction this weekend, and preview parties were happening every night this week around the globe where the auctions would be held, but Joseph hadn't said we were attending any of them. Which, now that I thought about it, I should have realized was unusual.

Joseph always took me to at least one of the preview parties. I knew we were going to Vienna for the main event tomorrow, but he had said nothing about tonight, and Joseph did not forget things. Ever.

Nodding, Rosaline looked concerned again. "Yes, he said you will not be dining at home this evening."

I forced a smile as another lie rolled past my lips. "Of course, our dinner plans. I had simply forgotten."

The concern in her eyes eased somewhat, and she gave a

VICTOR

small smile back that was as practiced as mine. "It's all right. We're all so busy. I won't keep you any longer. Hurry, he is waiting."

"Thank you, Rosaline. Have a good day." I stepped into the waiting lift and went downstairs.

The doorman met me as the elevator opened to the lobby. "Good morning, Mrs. Bertrand. Mr. Bertrand is already waiting." A step ahead of me, he held the lobby door, then opened the rear passenger door of an idling Bentley.

"Thank you," I murmured as I slid onto the soft leather seat.

The door closed, the driver pulled into early morning Manhattan traffic and Joseph set his paper down.

Turning in his seat, he looked pointedly at first my eyes and hair and then at my coat. "I did not lay that out."

Summer was over. "There's been a chill in the mornings." Instead of defending my choice, I smiled. "I hope you like it?"

Tall, stately, and in shape from his weekly sessions with a personal trainer, Joseph was a man of stature and wealth. He dressed impeccably, had piercing blue eyes, salt-and-pepper hair and a defined jawline, but he would never be attractive. Not to me.

Giving me a dismissive nod, he picked his paper back up.

Ignorantly emboldened, I opened my mouth. "Rosaline said we are not dining at home tonight, but I did not see anything on our calendar."

"Our calendar?" he challenged, looking for a fight. "*I* have a calendar. *You* have a calendar." He looked over his paper at me. "Tell me, Sabine, if you are too ignorant to keep up with the simple task of tracking a calendar, let alone during one of the busiest seasons Harrington's has ever had, what are you good for?"

Dropping my gaze, I pulled my handbag closer to me like armor.

It was the wrong move.

Like a burst of air freshener, an invisible scented cloud of lemon filled the car as I inadvertently squeezed my handbag.

Joseph sniffed the air in disgust. "What is that god-awful scent? It smells like cleaning supplies."

Anxiety rippled across my nerve endings like a sudden blast of winter chill. "Pardon?" *Oh God*, the muffin.

His entire countenance stilled.

Then, focusing his glare on me, he pressed the button that raised the privacy screen between us and the driver. "You heard me."

Alarm shot through my veins and my instincts were screaming at me to flee, but I did not have that option. I never had that option. So I did the only thing I could do. I lied. "I do not smell anything."

"It's something on you," he accused, deliberately folding his paper in a slow, calculated maneuver I recognized.

Fear raised the hair on the back of my neck. "I am sure I do not know what you are talking about."

His voice turned lethally quiet. "Give me your purse, Sabine."

"Joseph—"

"Now," he barked.

I handed over my Hermès.

With a single glance, Joseph found and fished out the linen-wrapped offense. His face creasing with ugly rage, he leaned toward me, and his voice turned to a steely calm that terrified me more than when he yelled.

"*Breakfast?*" Crushing the muffin in his hand, he threw it on the floor. "You're disrespectful, insubordinate, ignorant *and* late, and you think you deserve to eat?" He grabbed my wrist in a punishing grip. "*In the Bentley?*"

Tears sprung and pain radiated. His hand crushing my small bones, I was sure he would break my wrist. "Joseph, please," I begged.

"Please what?" he demanded.

Refusing to implicate Rosaline, knowing how much worse

this could get, I did what he told me not to do. I apologized. "I am sorry."

Twisting my arm, he roared as he forced me to my knees. "What did you say?"

Hitting the floor of the car, praying he did not break my bones, I did not dare reply.

He squeezed harder. "You're *sorry*?"

Pain radiating, I could not hold my tongue. "Yes." I was sorry I had ever met him. Sorry I had ever fallen for his false charm. Sorry I had been so naïve and afraid and desperate, but mostly I was sorry for ever trying to sell my mother's jewelry.

Evil glinted in his eyes. "You're going to have to do better than that."

Desperate, afraid, and in pain, I made the only choice I had at my disposal in the moment. Choking on bile, I reached for his zipper with my free hand.

My head snapped to the left as the slap echoed through the vehicle a split second before fire exploded across my right cheek.

"Do you think I want a worthless whore touching me?" Joseph shoved me away at the exact moment the car braked to a short stop.

My head hit the door and I fell back on my ass as I grabbed my throbbing wrist.

"Don't you *ever* disobey me again," Joseph threatened before giving me a dismissive sound of disgust. "Straighten yourself up."

As always, the driver opened Joseph's door first.

Smoothing a hand down his tie and buttoning his suit jacket, Joseph threw an order at the driver as he stepped out of the Bentley. "Make sure she pulls herself together before you let her out."

"Yes, sir." The driver shut the door.

A moment later, the partition went down, and without

looking at me, the driver handed me a perfectly pressed white handkerchief.

With a shaking hand, I took it and dropped it in my handbag, where there were half a dozen more just like it.

Then I gingerly pulled back the left sleeve of my coat.

Angry, red and already swelling, my wrist painfully throbbed.

Sucking in a stilted breath, I hit a new low.

Punished. Over a muffin.

TEN

Vance

S ILENTLY FUCKING FUMING, I PULLED UP MY EMAILS ON MY PHONE AS we took off. The Gulfstream lifted effortlessly, and I got even more pissed off that I wasn't in the cockpit.

Not that I gave a particular damn about flying, but it was one more distraction in my arsenal. Not to mention sixty-million-dollar private jets were a far cry from the military transport I'd experienced in the Marines, let alone the wrong side of Miami that Ronan and I had grown up in.

If humility was in my vocabulary, I'd recognize how lucky I was to be flying at thirty-five thousand feet in luxury. But humility would've implied I wasn't arrogant, and that trait I had in fucking spades.

Opening the email on Bertrand, I quickly scanned the file. Fifty-two, unmarried, a list of pretentious degrees from even more pretentious schools followed by a bullshit curriculum vitae. Zero interest in his publications on art authenticity, I pocketed my cell and stood.

Too early for alcohol, not that the time of day usually stopped me from doing what I wanted, I needed something to counter the lack of sleep that was catching up. In search of caffeine, I bypassed Echo as he stretched out in one of the leather seats in the forward cabin with his eyes closed. Making my way to the galley, I reached for the coffee pot.

Empty.

Disgusted and in the mood for a fight, I shoved the pot back in place and turned on Echo. "Did you read the file?"

"Did Alpha assign me to this mission?" Echo countered, eyes still closed, head back, hands laced over his stomach.

"Client," I corrected as I dropped into a seat across the aisle from him. "This isn't the Navy. We don't have missions."

Turning his head, he opened one eye, lifted his eyebrow and looked at me like I was dumber than shit. "Mission, babysit. Client, Bertrand. Objective, don't kill you." Closing his eye, he leaned his head back again. "I read the fucking file."

"Right." Prick.

"All in, all the time." Not for the first time, the fucker spouted one of his SEAL doctrines. "Something they forgot to teach you in the Marines."

Seventeen years ago, I would've lost my temper and acted rashly or told him to fuck off. Then a single moment changed everything. Now I fought differently. Hell, I fought an entirely different battle. One I didn't let anyone see because I deserved to fight it alone.

"You're right." My chuckle was well-practiced. "While you were busy getting drowned in BUD/S, I was fucking your girlfriend." I stood. "Time well spent, I can assure you." I aimed for the cockpit.

"Heard that's your MO," Echo stated.

Assuming he was talking about the shit between me and Ronan, I wasn't surprised he'd heard about it. My brother worked for a personal security firm in Miami, and half of the former Marines working at Luna and Associates knew half the guys on AES's payroll. Hell, we'd done jobs together, rumors spread. But I was surprised he knew the why of it.

Not taking the bait, I glanced back at Echo. "Modus operandi, you can say it. Or is that too big of a word for you, SEAL?"

"The only thing too big here, *Marine*, is my dick."

VICTOR

"Ah. Beyond reproach and to humbly serve," I paraphrased. "Glad to see you take your SEAL ethos to heart."

"The execution of my duties will be swift and violent," he quoted without hesitation before adding threateningly, "*guaranteed.*" Closing his eyes again, giving me the proverbial finger, he dismissed me.

Almost respecting him, I made my way to the cockpit.

"Making friends again, Victor?" Zulu asked, using the call sign I'd been given when I joined AES.

"What's the point of being a lone wolf if you play nice?" I wasn't here to make friends.

Zulu smirked. "Rule number one, never piss off the baddest motherfucker on your team. You'll need him one day."

Too bad I didn't give a shit. "Maybe, maybe not." I glanced at my Patek Philippe steel-banded watch. "What's our flight time?"

"Touchdown's in one hour, twenty-six minutes," Zulu answered.

"I scheduled a car service. They'll be waiting," November interjected. "If traffic's normal, you'll make the meeting time."

"Right." Car service. Which meant me and Echo in the same vehicle. "Harrington's has valet, I assume?"

November glanced at me. "Yes."

"Excellent." I pulled my cell out. "I'll arrange my own ride. Echo can use the service." I dialed.

"Prestige, Manhattan," a woman answered.

"Gigi, please."

"May I tell her who's calling, sir?"

"Vance."

"Oh, of course, Mr. Conlon. My apologies, I didn't recognize your voice. Let me put you right through."

"Thank you."

"Oh, you're most welcome, Mr. Conlon," the woman flirted. "Please hold."

A moment later the line was picked up again. "Vance, darling, how are you?" Gigi asked in her polished mix of sultry professionalism.

"Excellent, pet. I need a car at Teterboro in an hour. Can you accommodate me?"

"Always," she shamelessly insinuated. "Let me see what I have. Are you in town for pleasure?"

"Only if it's yours, darling."

Her laugh sounded as practiced as mine. "As much as you'd probably enjoy that, I'm sure my fiancé would not."

"Pity."

"For you," she teased. "All right, I have a Rolls-Royce Wraith, the Ferrari 488 you like, and I have a McLaren 720S."

"The atrocious gold McLaren? Darling, please."

"Why, Mr. Conlon, are you insulting my memory? I remember your preferences. All of them," she added flirtatiously before switching back to her business voice. "The McLaren is black, of course."

"That'll do. Are you bringing it for me?"

"So you can convince me to leave Gerard?"

"You're too good for him. Not to mention the appalling alliteration your two first names make."

"So he tells me, the first part that is. The latter I'm quite fond of."

"You would be." I chuckled. "See you in an hour."

"I never said I'd be your personal delivery girl."

"And yet you never miss the opportunity to see me."

Her laugh came through the line again. "Who's appalling now?"

"I prefer inappropriate, pet." I hung up.

November turned in his seat and stared at me.

"Problem?" I shoved my cell in my pocket.

Zulu shook his head. "Don't answer him, November. That's just asking for it."

November ignored Zulu. "I already made the arrangements."

"I made different ones."

"I always make the arrangements," November reiterated.

Smiling, I clapped him on the shoulder. "Right. Appreciate it." AES wouldn't run without him. We all knew it. "Minor adjustment this time. Don't worry, I'll bill the client."

Despite sitting in the cockpit of one of the most coveted private jets, November took off his headset, grabbed the laptop that was leaning against his chair, and made to get up. "Excuse me," he clipped.

I stepped back.

No eye contact, November walked past me toward the aft cabin.

Zulu spared me a glance. "Is there anyone you don't piss off?"

I glanced back as November calmly took a seat and opened his laptop. "I didn't piss him off." Taking the second chair he'd just vacated, I put on the headset. "Besides, November's untouchable. He doesn't get angry." The cool bastard was unflappable.

"Yeah, you did piss him off, and he absolutely does get angry."

"What does that take? An EMP?"

Incredulous, Zulu turned to look at me. "Tell me you're joking."

"I'd never joke about an EMP," I deadpanned.

"Jesus, Conlon." Zulu shook his head.

"What? Should I now be worried about him hacking into the NSA and adding my name to the terrorist watch list because I arranged for my own transportation?" I could unhack that shit anyway. November had been teaching me all his tricks, and I'd learned a few on my own. Shocking what you could accomplish when you avoided sleep.

"Christ. I don't know if I feel sorry for you or just think you're fucking stupid. All I'm going to say is watch your back."

I laughed. "November was a Cyber Surety specialist in the Air Force. What's he going to do? Hack my bank account?" I only kept a mid-six-figure balance in my US-based bank account anyway. The majority of my money was offshore, the rest in crypto currency and real estate.

Zulu banked the plane east. "You have it wrong. He wasn't a specialist. November was a Cyberspace Operations Officer, and not just any officer, but *the* Cyberspace Operations Officer. At the Pentagon," Zulu added. "Besides, that was before, and if you tell anyone I told you this, I'm denying the fuck out of it."

"Before what? Becoming everyone's right-hand man at AES?" If I hadn't met November, I'd wonder why he'd leave a career like that in the military. But what I did know of him, hacking and secrecy was his religion, and illicitly banking money for a rainy day was his mistress. The latter of which would've been highly frowned upon when collecting a government paycheck.

Leveling us out, Zulu turned and looked at me. His aviators hiding his eyes, I could still tell he was giving me a look. "With all the shit you hack for fun, you're telling me you don't know?"

"Don't know what?" I made a mental note to search November's background again.

Zulu focused his attention back out the windscreen. "I lied. I will say one more thing, not that I'm holding my breath it'll make a difference, because you have no self-preservation."

"I have plenty." I didn't. "Including a healthy dose of respect for Echo and staying out of his way." Except for when he was at the Annex.

"Echo's got nothing on November."

I laughed. Hard. "Right."

Not cracking a smile, Zulu seemingly changed the subject.

"Why do you think Alpha, me and the Team were sent into Bosnia?"

The infamous Bosnia mission. The one they all talked about by name but never gave any details about. One I'd unsuccessfully tried to search for intel on. "No idea."

Zulu's gaze drifted a moment before he looked back at me with the heavy weight of war in his expression that no man ever wanted to carry. "It was a hostage recovery mission." Zulu inhaled, but then he stopped talking.

Knowing better than to ask, I waited.

Shaking his head, he finally exhaled. "Everything that could've gone wrong, did. Our intel was fucked, our comms got scrambled, we HALO'd into the middle of a terrorist hotbed and lost overwatch the second we were boots on the ground. Total ambush. They knew we were coming, and they were prepared. One of the best brothers I've ever served with lost his life when he shouldn't have. Next to losing Bravo, it was the worst fucking mission of my career." Zulu adjusted our altitude and heading. "Then twenty-two hours in, low on ammo and out of options, we finally breached their compound to recover the hostage." He glanced out the side window for a moment. "Except when we got inside, there were no tangos left to recover the hostage from." Zulu's throat moved with a swallow. "Covered in blood with eight dead terrorists at his feet, the hostage was the only man left standing." Zulu looked back at me. "November was that hostage."

ELEVEN

Sabine

THE DRIVER CLEARED HIS THROAT. "DO YOU NEED ME TO CIRCLE the block?"

Still staring at my wrist, I gently pulled my sleeve down and sat back on the seat. "No, thank you. I just need a moment." Smoothing my dress, my wrist hurting with every movement, I pulled a makeup compact from my handbag. Checking my face in the little mirror, I assessed the damage.

There was some reddening, but I knew from experience that it would be gone in a few hours. Applying powder as gently as possible, I made a choice. The same choice I'd made seven years ago.

"I am ready to go inside." Closing the compact, I tucked it back in my purse.

"Of course, ma'am." The driver got out and opened my door.

Without looking at him, without looking at anyone, I let my hair fall forward over my face and walked into the lobby of the high-rise that Joseph's company owned. The guards ushered me through security, and I pressed the call button for the elevator with my good hand.

For once, I rode the lift alone, but my reprieve was short-lived. The moment I stepped onto the top floor, Joseph's secretary, Norma, was waiting.

"Sabine, good morning." Eyeing my cheek, she paused infinitesimally, then met my eyes again and continued as if nothing was amiss. "Joseph is requesting that you go over your schedule in your office this morning. He also said he would like for you to wait for him there." Rattling off her boss's directive like it wasn't a scolding reprimand but a perfectly reasonable request, Norma handed me a printed sheet of paper. "I took the liberty of printing the rest of your week's agenda. He has a busy schedule this morning, but I'm sure he'll be with you shortly."

Knowing full well he would not summon me until our scheduled lunch time, I took the paper. "Thank you, Norma."

"No problem. Will there be anything else?" Always in a rush because Joseph kept her occupied with everything I didn't do, Norma gave me the courtesy of a raised eyebrow.

Knowing better than to ask Joseph's secretary for an ice pack for my wrist, let alone for anything that would take away her time from Joseph, I merely smiled. "No, but thank you."

"Anytime." Norma turned and was already halfway down the hall before I made it to my corner glass office.

Closing the door behind me, my wrist throbbing, I stepped behind my desk and set my purse down before I glanced at the printed schedule.

As usual, every day, from one to two o'clock, lunch was blocked out with Joseph.

Today at three p.m. was a staff meeting about the event this weekend.

After that, noted in bold and taking up the time slot from four in the afternoon on, there were three words that had not been there yesterday.

Miami. Preview Party.

For a brief second, I allowed myself to break. Closing my eyes, fighting tears, dreading the extra time trapped on the private jet with Joseph followed by an evening of smiling until my face hurt as much as my wrist was hurting now, I thought about leaving.

Just putting one foot in front of the other.

Walk to the elevator, take it downstairs, exit through the lobby, then simply disappear into the crowded hustle of New York.

I could do it.

Joseph would not look for me.

He would dissolve our deal, do as he threatened a thousand times, then move on. A week later, I would be replaced with the next young woman stupid enough to believe his lies.

It would be simple for me to leave. But it would not be safe.

I looked down at the ring on my left hand.

And I would not be the only one who suffered.

Taking a deep breath, I let it out slowly.

Then I shook away useless daydreams and took my seat in my leather office chair at my overly expansive desk. Behind me was a skyline view I could have only dreamed of as a child. In front of me, well-dressed people were rushing about, working for a company that had a century's worth of prestige.

Protecting a past I found harder and harder to bury, I opened my laptop and logged into the internal servers. Pulling up the files that contained the daily submissions, I went for the folder that Joseph had approved for me to look through.

The jewelry files.

All the necklaces, earrings, rings, watches and brooches that people wanted Harrington's to sell at auction. The family heirlooms that made me sad to see pawned off. The pieces that had once been worn and loved by deceased relatives, or simply coveted for what they represented. Pieces people hoped to trade for old debts and new dreams.

This was my job at the world's most prestigious auction house.

I decided what jewelry we would sell.

Then I attended the live auctions, wearing said jewelry, because this was my penance. Punishment dished out by a man who imposed no such duty upon himself for his actions, but

VICTOR

wholeheartedly believed in it for others. Every submission was a daily reminder of who I was when I had walked through the door of Harrington's Parisian office seven years ago with jewelry that wasn't my own.

    I was desperate then, and I was desperate now.
    I was also hurting, exhausted and hungry.
    Nothing left to do, I opened the first file.

TWELVE

Vance

Seven minutes late, files in hand, Joseph Harrington Bertrand strode into his office. "AES, I presume."

"Victor," was all I offered.

Tossing the files on his overly large desk, the sharp-faced, middle-aged man peered at me with narrowed eyes. "Victor," he stated. "No last name?"

"Right." I smiled. "I'm not here to make friends."

"This is my company, and I'm not here to incite suspicion by introducing a new employee posing as a wannabe pop star with a singular name," the stodgy fuck argued, emphasizing *employee*.

"Is that the cover you're going to assign me? Employee?" Not only was he an asshole, he was an idiot. "Security consultant works fine."

"Your dossier didn't say that you were British."

My dossier didn't say anything. I didn't fucking have one. "I'm not." He'd find nothing about me online or otherwise.

Crude, dismissive and with far more money than class, Bertrand gave me the full weight of his suspicious stare. "You speak like it."

I spoke like many things, none of it representative. "Shall we get down to business?" I already hated this prick. "Or would you prefer I muck about on my own, rattle some cages?" Amping up the accent on purpose, I aimed to piss him off. "Or perhaps I merely ruffle some feathers, see what flits about." The sooner I was done with this asshole, the better.

"This isn't a game, Victor."

It was always a game, especially with pretentious fucks like him who threw their weight around. "Never insinuated as such." I nodded at his files. "I'm sure you have business to get back to. Why don't you tell me precisely why you called in AES?"

"I called Adam Trefor," he corrected.

This prick was lucky I was still here. "I can assure you I have the full weight of Alpha Elite Security behind me." One more line of bullshit from him and I was walking out. AES didn't need the money or whatever irrelevant problem he thought constituted an emergency.

Exhaling loudly for effect, Bertrand dismissed me with a shake of his head before jabbing the intercom on his desk phone. "Get Sabine in here."

Sabine? Nothing in his files mentioned a woman by that name. I would've remembered.

"Yes, sir," the older woman sitting outside his office placated.

"Sabine?" The name rolled off my tongue like sex.

"Wife," Bertrand grunted.

Hiding my surprise that this asshole was married, let alone that we'd failed to find it, I made a mental note to ask November how the fuck he could've missed this. Before I could conjure up what type of woman would marry this egotistical prick, the air shifted and my gaze cut to the open door.

My heart fucking stopped.

Thick, dark hair cascading over her shoulders, haunted blue eyes, and lips so lush, I wanted to devour them—a brunette appeared in the doorway.

Dressed in all white like an angel, she was stunning.

Absolutely stunning.

At least twenty years Bertrand's junior, lightly clasping her right wrist with her left hand in both elegance and fear, she halted on the threshold and met my blatant stare.

Jesus.

She was exquisite.

So damn exquisite, but there was something familiar in her haunted eyes. A familiarity that stood out in stark contrast to her expensive clothes and rigid stance.

I knew that stance.

I knew it in every nightmare and waking regret, and if I had even an ounce of self-preservation, I would've looked away. But her throat moved with a swallow, and I could practically taste my visceral reaction to her on those lush lips, and I wasn't moving.

As if she could read my self-destructive intent, she inhaled sharply.

Then Bertrand shuffled some papers, and her gaze immediately trained on the asshole.

Except, she didn't meet his eyes like she had mine. She didn't even look at his face. Focusing on his left shoulder, she exuded a submissiveness so damn palpable, my thoughts turned singular.

I wanted this woman.

Every gorgeous inch. Including that mouth. *Those lips.*

My cock stirring, my palms itching to touch her smooth skin, I wanted to take her away from him.

Then she spoke, and her voice rattled my entire fucking existence.

"You needed me?"

Fuck me, she had an accent.

French. Subtle. Bred.

Never looking up from his desk, Bertrand barked at the exquisite creature. "Don't just stand there. Get in here and shut the door."

It was instant. Instinctual and deep-seated, as if I knew this woman and she belonged to me, a protectiveness I never experienced anymore reared its head, and I fucking saw red.

No longer willing to walk away from this assignment, I moved. "Sabine, have a seat." I pulled a guest chair away from her asshole husband's desk.

Her gaze wary, she glanced at me as she took a tentative step forward. "I am afraid I'm at a disadvantage. I do not know your name."

Bertrand snorted. "No disadvantage. His name's Victor. You heard me, shut the door."

Graceful, moving like she didn't know how to disturb the air around her, she closed the door, then came toward me. A second before she gave me a slight dip of her head in acknowledgment that I was still holding the back of the chair, I smelled her perfume.

Christ.

If you held a gun to my head, I wouldn't be able to place the scent. Not one single fucking adjective except perfect as her coat parted and her fitted dress showed every luscious curve, including her Oscar-worthy breasts.

Taking the seat, she crossed her legs. "Thank you, Mr. Victor."

Drowning in a whole new world of dark possessiveness I didn't know existed before two goddamn seconds ago, I didn't even manage a smile. "Of course, love."

Forcing myself to let go of the back of her chair, I glared at Bertrand in silent warning to check his shit. This asshole didn't deserve this woman, and he was lucky I wanted more information.

Zero awareness of what I was capable of, Bertrand scowled at me. "Her name's Sabine."

Cataloging every mistreatment he was throwing at her, I filed them away. Then I smiled down at the beautiful creature and winked. "My apologies, Mrs. Bertrand."

"Malcher is my last name," she corrected.

I glanced at Bertrand.

His glare focused on his wife, his left eye twitched.

No longer giving a single fuck about Harrington's, Bertrand's problems or corporate espionage, I was now here for her. I would listen to what this asshole had to say, but then I was going to uncover every single offense he'd committed against her that'd put the fear in her eyes, and I was going to give it back to him. Tenfold.

Taking the seat next to her, I leveled the asshole with a look. "Shall we get started?"

THIRTEEN

Sabine

My intercom buzzed, startling me as Norma's voice came over the line. "Sabine, Joseph is requesting that you come to his office."

My heart rate skyrocketed, and my stomach dropped. I looked at the clock.

Twelve-oh-nine.

It was too early for lunch.

"Sabine?"

"My apologies. I am here. Do you mean now?" Of course she meant now, but Joseph never called me into his office. As much as I wanted to ask what it was about, I would not put her on the spot, not that she would tell me anyway. I knew Harrington's was having their largest auction to date on Saturday. All the employees had been planning this for over a year, but I had been left out of it. Relegated to lunches with Joseph and jewelry acquisitions, Joseph had made it a point to tell me several times that jewelry wouldn't be a part of this important, art-only event.

"Yes, immediately," Norma insisted.

With dread heavy on my shoulders, the growing sense of unease I had been trying to ignore all morning grew. "Of course. I am on my way." I didn't want to go. With the auction looming, Joseph even more on edge than normal, I wondered how much more I could take, not that I had a choice.

"See you soon," Norma replied with her usual brisk efficiency before disconnecting.

Gently rubbing my still-throbbing wrist, I slipped my feet back into my heels before I stood and smoothed down my dress one-handed. Taking two deep breaths, I made the short walk down the corridor.

Sitting outside Joseph's office at her desk, Norma nodded her approval for me to enter.

Inhaling one more time, I stepped into the doorway, but then I froze.

The most handsome man I had ever seen stood on the other side of Joseph's desk.

Taller than Joseph by inches, muscles straining against the sleeves of his expensive, custom suit, his piercing eyes weren't green or brown but almost amber as he took me in with the most penetrating stare I had ever encountered.

Rendered immobile, as if he had the power to capture and hold me with his mysterious eyes alone, I stood caught in his gaze and did something I never, ever did.

I stared back.

The sharp angle of his jaw, barely hidden under a day's growth, looked like he had been caught running late, but I suspected it was probably purposeful. As purposeful as his meticulously cut suit and the slightly longer length of his silky dark, almost unruly hair that was defiantly disordered on top but neatly controlled on the shorter sides. As if there were two distinct sides to his personality, dark disorder and controlled dominance, his hair mirrored the depth and dichotomy of the two colors of his eyes.

But it wasn't just his eyes or the darkly ominous beauty of him that was so stunning.

With his stare intently focused on me, it was his presence.

He was so commanding and dominant, and so unreservedly

disarming, that for one impossible moment I drew in a sharp breath and forgot who I was.

Then Joseph angrily shuffled papers on his desk.

Anxiety I had not realized had momentarily fled came flooding back, and I focused my downcast gaze on Joseph's shoulder before barely finding my voice. "You needed me?"

Never giving me the respect of eye contact unless he was reprimanding me, Joseph did not look up as he issued one of his usual, brusque commands. "Don't just stand there. Get in here and shut the door."

The handsome stranger immediately moved. Pulling one of the guest chairs away from Joseph's desk as if to protect me, he spoke. "Have a seat, Sabine."

Have a seat, Sabine.

Profound but quiet, and so darkly dominant, his voice rippled across my skin like a blast of desert heat. British? American? I did not know. No words for the penetrating warmth flooding my body as a tingling sensation both caressed and alarmed my nerves, I shivered.

Distrustful of both myself and the stranger, I barely glanced at him again when all I wanted to do was stare. "I'm afraid I am at a disadvantage. I do not know your name."

Joseph snorted. "No disadvantage. His name's Victor. You heard me, shut the door."

Scarcely aware of my feet moving, I closed the door as Joseph ordered, but then, as if drawn to this commanding man like he could save me from my life, I was walking toward the chair he still had a grip on.

With his eyes tracking me and my breath gone, a runaway thought filled my head. One that was so outlandish, and so dangerously foolish, I did not want it to form. I willed it not to take shape. But just like this stranger's inexplicable hold on me, with his enigmatic, amber eyes, I could not stop it.

What if this dominant man had been waiting for me to come into his life as much as I was waiting for him?

As soon as I thought it, I dismissed my insanity.

But I could not stop myself from giving the handsome man a slight nod in appreciation for still holding the back of the seat he was offering me despite Joseph's clear animosity toward him.

"Thank you, Mr. Victor." Sitting, I crossed my legs, and then it happened.

His intoxicating scent blindsided me.

Like a summer night in the fourth arrondissement of Paris. Rain-wet cobblestones, mystery, musk, anticipation, sandalwood—all of it raw and sensual and wrapped in forbidden masculinity. He smelled like the perfect capture of the illicit affair between dusk and night. He smelled like haunted memories.

But he looked like salvation.

I wanted to lean toward him and tuck myself into the space between his sharp jaw and crisp shirt collar. I wanted to tangle my fingers in his ink-black hair. I wanted to be so impossibly close to him that his commanding dominance crushed my fears.

Then he spoke again. "Of course, love." His deep voice furled around me like cigarette smoke after nightfall, embracing me in a heated trance.

I wanted to drown in him.

Breaking my reverie, Joseph bit out a scowled retort. "Her name's Sabine."

The darkly handsome man smiled down at me and winked. "My apologies, Mrs. Bertrand."

Without thought to the consequences, as if Joseph were not even in the room, I stupidly, foolishly, let the truth slip past my lips. "Malcher is my last name."

The man, who I could not bring myself to call Victor in my mind because it did not fit, looked at Joseph. As if taking in my slip of tongue like he was angling for a kill, every muscle in his body stilled like a predator's.

Joseph, arrogant or unaware or both, did not even glance at the man still standing behind my chair like he was protecting me. Instead, Joseph glared at me in a warning I knew all too well as his left eye twitched like it did when he was very, very angry.

Unafraid of my husband, the stranger took the seat next to me. "Shall we get started?"

Joseph may have missed it, but I did not.

The look in the man's eyes as he sat next to me was unmistakable.

Mr. Victor was a thousand times more dangerous than Joseph Harrington Bertrand.

FOURTEEN

Vance

EMANATING ANGER AT THE BEAUTIFUL WOMAN NEXT TO ME, THE asshole spat orders at her. "Sabine, Victor is here to do an assessment of our security measures, both internally and externally. I expect you to coordinate with him, get him whatever he needs and keep your mouth shut. This is not open for discussion. You will not tell anyone what he is doing here, you will not ask him questions, and you will not withhold information from him. If pressed by any employees, Norma included, I'm going to trust that you're not too damn incompetent to either defer any questions or default to Victor. If you can't handle that, then I will permit you to say he is here for added security for the preview parties and auction this weekend." The fucking piece of shit leaned forward, intimidating her further. "But if you give one single more word of explanation other than that, we are going to have a problem. Do you understand me?"

Without hesitation, as if this fucking prick spoke to her all the time like this, she nodded. "Of course."

"Good. Leave. Victor and I have business to discuss."

Gracefully standing like she was unaffected by every abusive word this asshole said, she gingerly clasped her right wrist. "I will be in my office."

"Check your schedule like I told you. We're leaving at four for Miami, then Vienna after that. I didn't see you pack a bag."

She nodded again as if he hadn't just insulted her five fucking times in the past two minutes. "I will take care of it." Turning slightly toward me, but not offering her hand, she gave me the slight dip of her head again. "Nice to meet you, Mr. Victor. My office is just down the corridor."

I wanted to pick her up and haul her out of here, but not before I lunged across the desk, grabbed Bertrand's fucking head and slammed him face-first into his own pretentiousness.

Having sized up Bertrand two fucking seconds after his wife walked into his office, I knew exactly what this piece of shit's unforgivable agenda was. Making the conscious decision not to stand to say goodbye to her, because doing so would only give this bastard ammunition to use against her, I remained seated.

But fuck did I want to stand.

I wanted to stand and put my mouth to her ear. Then I wanted to make this woman a promise. If it was the last thing I did, I was taking Bertrand down, but not before I took her the fuck away from him.

Inhaling to calm down, I held her pretty blue-eyed gaze and gave her the only assurance I could in the moment. "I will find you."

With barely a nod, her and her scent floated out of the room before she quietly closed the door behind her.

Looking back at the fuck across from me, I gave Bertrand fair warning. "Where I come from, men don't speak to their wives like that." Trefor's client or not, this asshole was done.

Snorting in ignorant dismissal, he shook his head. "Because you seem to be as stupid as your bullshit name, I'll give you the benefit of my decades' worth of running a successful business empire." Glaring threateningly, the prick leaned toward me like he'd leaned toward his wife when he was berating her. "Women have their place," he bit out, punctuating every fucking word before sitting back up. "Now, if you're done letting your dick rule your emotions and have any clue how to do the job I hired Trefor for, we can get down to real business."

Reminding myself that I'd learned a long time ago that bad shit happened when I got mad, I instead cataloged every word this prick said, and mentally added nails to his coffin. "Right." I raised an eyebrow. "Business."

Grabbing one of the files in front of him, he tossed it across his desk. "Look at these. Now."

Purposely pausing for a beat, I picked the folder up and scanned the three pages before tossing it back on his desk.

"Did you even read the reports?"

"Advance notice leaked on upcoming auctions, breached intel on winning bidders, price controlling. Armored transport routes hacked and security systems bypassed at multiple locations." I'd fucking read it.

His hand fisted on his desk. "Every breach originated from my wife's computer. The last one as recently as yesterday."

Hiding my shock, I wondered if he was that obtuse, or if she was that good of an actress. The latter only made my respect for her compound. "What did she say when you confronted her?" If she had orchestrated all of that, I only wished her success in her endeavors.

"Do I look stupid enough to confront her?" Standing, he pointed at me. "This is why you're here. Get evidence on her I can take to the district attorney and *fix this*."

Taking my time, I stood. "Who did you tell about this?"

"Again," he ground out. "Do I look stupid? No one."

"Those reports came from somewhere." He wasn't only a fucking asshole, he was ignorant as hell. I didn't give a shit how long he'd run his business. At this rate, he'd run it into the ground. Not that I gave a damn.

"My security supervisor alerted me to the armored transport and location breaches, which is why I've already fired our usual contractors and hired new ones for this weekend's upcoming event. The head of IT told me about the rest," he clipped.

"Two people then." Internally. Who the hell knew what he'd said to his old security contractor. "How many others did they discuss this with?" This was already too far gone to contain. He should've seen what was coming and called AES after a single one of those incidents listed in his report, not five. This was a planned attack in the making, and his auction house was going to get hit hard.

Bertrand's nostrils flared in anger as he leaned both hands on his desk. "They work for me."

I casually straightened my tie. "Meaning?"

"They're loyal."

"Right," I mocked with a generic smile. "Then I'll get to it. To be clear though, you want AES to investigate your wife, deliver hard evidence of her activities, which, in your estimation, should be more than the brief files you shared, and ignore the five security breaches already in play."

"That's exactly what I said. I've handled the breaches. Now you have seventy-two hours to handle her. Harrington's largest auction to date is on Saturday, with a global, five-venue, live-streamed, twentieth-century art sale. With auctioneers in Hong Kong, Vienna, Paris, London and New York working simultaneously, and an estimated quarter billion in sales, I don't need to tell you how many moving parts there are. I will not allow for any more transgressions. I expect you to do your job, which includes watching her in Miami tonight as we attend one of the preview parties, then in Vienna on Saturday where we'll be conducting the main venue from. My jet leaves today at four for Miami. You got yourself up here, I'll assume you can get yourself back in time for this evening's event. Once we conclude in Miami tonight, we leave for Vienna. You can find your own way there or travel with us for that flight. Either way, your job is to ensure she does nothing further. Then I expect you to wrap this the hell up. But understand, once you get the hard evidence I need, I'll be the one who personally deals with my wife. Until then, it shouldn't have to be said, but I'm spelling it out for you anyway. Be discreet. I will not have any of your actions tipping off a single person here that we have a problem. Understand?"

I understood perfectly. The fuck wanted fabricated evidence on his wife so he could get rid of her. I also didn't need three days, let alone a single fucking minute to figure out he'd either manufactured everything on those three pages or, more likely, had someone coming after his entire outfit. Either way, even if there was a remote chance she was behind this, no way in hell would I hand him his wife on a silver platter after what I'd just witnessed.

I could all but guarantee that the breaches he already had, if they were real, combined with five global locations and a quarter of a billion at stake, only spelled out one thing. This auction was FUBAR. If he'd seriously wanted a chance at containing this, he would've needed an AES team already in place at each site. Not that I was going to clue this piece of shit in about any of it.

I'd already decided on my assignment here, and she had black hair and blue eyes. No fucking way was I going to leave Sabine Malcher open to an all-out war perpetrated by this bastard.

Feigning compliance, I answered the prick. "I understand perfectly. You want proof, by any means necessary, that your wife hacked and leaked intel, breached your internal security measures and sabotaged your company in the process." He was out of his fucking mind.

"*Discreetly*," he repeated.

"Right. Discreet." Fucking asshole. I took a step toward the door.

"Victor," the prick clipped.

I spared him a glance.

The fuck gave me a warning glare. "If you make one move to alert my wife that this is coming, I'll have your head."

Heads were going to roll all right, but it wouldn't be mine or hers.

A shitstorm the likes of which he'd never seen was about to hit his company, and there was no way you could convince me that his wife, let alone by herself, was orchestrating and executing a multi-location, global hit from an internal, easily traceable computer. Bertrand was barking up the wrong goddamn tree, but one thing was for sure.

He had enemies. Cunning ones.

Which made me smile wide. "Is that a threat?"

Eyes narrowing, puffing his chest to make up for the fact that he'd never picked a fight with a man because he was a spineless fuck who preyed on women and subordinates, he tried to intimidate me. "Yes."

Excellent. "Do you know the last line of the Navy SEAL ethos?" Two could play this game.

He snorted condescendingly. "You're telling me you were a SEAL?"

"No." I was telling him I was going to destroy him—after I took his wife away from him. "But in this situation, it's apropos." I leveled the fuck with a warning look he was too stupid to pick up on. *"I will not fail."*

Whatever was coming, his company was going to get hit hard.

But I was going to hit him harder.

FIFTEEN

Sabine

My heart beating too fast, my breath short, I stood with my back to my office door as I blindly gazed at the skyline of New York, willing myself to calm down. *Breathe, Sabine, breathe.*

But no matter how many breaths I took, his scent, the way he had stared at me with his mesmerizing eyes, it would not leave me.

I could not afford these wayward thoughts any more than I could pretend my life was different, let alone that I had a way out. The man rescuing the woman only happened in movies. Or rather, it had already happened, and that man was Joseph.

I needed to remember that.

Accept it.

But before I could, the soft push of air and scrape of glass over carpet sounded as my office door was opened. Sensing his presence without even having to glance over my shoulder, my whole body reacted as if I had a sudden sunburn. Hot, cold, fire, there was no escape from the burning chills.

"Mr. Victor," I preempted, not turning to face him because I was afraid to see him again.

"Ah. I thought I was quieter than that. What was my tell, love?" he casually asked with a very slight British accent.

I made the mistake of inhaling deep, and suddenly I was back there—in my past, where hope lived. But I was also here, with a man who smelled like everything Joseph was not, and I wanted to weep tears of self-pity.

Instead, I turned and faced the only man I'd taken a second glance at in more years than I could count.

Midday Manhattan light bounced off the sea of sparkling skyscrapers and hit his face. He was even more handsome than when I first saw him, and I took a moment to study his striking features.

No guile, no smile, no movement, he calmly stood and stared back at me with a stillness I was not expecting from a man who looked like him.

I did not want to look away from his unusual eyes or unruly hair or perfectly fitted suit. I did not want to understand why he was letting me study him without speaking. I just wanted to breathe him in and forget who I was. But the longer I did that, the more it would matter later when I was hidden in a penthouse, staring at life from the other side of my choices.

Turning back toward the window, I considered how to answer his question, or if I should answer at all. The truth was telling, but lies were hard to keep stacked in neat piles, and my piles were slipping all over the place.

So I told him the truth. "You did not have a tell. I heard the door open, and I knew it was you because no one except Joseph comes into my office, and it is not one p.m. yet."

The air shifted again. Then he was standing next to me, sharing the view as if it were a stolen moment between intimate lovers.

"What happens at one?" he asked, his voice deeper and quieter than mere seconds ago.

I did not want to torture myself. I tried to stop it, but what little willpower I had left after seven years of Joseph was no match for this man. Errant thoughts broke through my defenses, and I imagined if this was what he would sound like in bed, whispering in my ear, saying my name.

Inhaling to clear the thoughts, I only buried myself deeper when I took in a lung full of his scent. "Lunch," I answered absently, wondering how he smelled both like rain-kissed ancient cobblestones and exotic, masculine sandalwood.

"Every day?"

Too late and too intoxicating to stop them, I gave in to my rebellious mind and its disobedient thoughts. "Yes." What would a meal with this man be like?

"So you are the trophy."

Startled out of my own musings, shock—an emotion I had not allowed myself to feel in seven years—broke past my defenses.

Before I could argue or take mock offense because it was expected of me, as carefully, painfully, repeatedly drilled into me by Joseph, this stranger turned toward me and spoke as openly as he had behaved when he had let me look at him.

Frank and without any intonation that I could grasp onto, he laid out the ugly truth of my life. "He doesn't treat you like a trophy wife."

"Mr. Vic—"

"I think it's time," he interrupted. "Shall we have our first secret?" The smile that touched his full lips was reserved, but no less arresting than what I imagined him to look like if he had smiled in full.

"First?" I foolishly asked.

The smile disappeared and the serious version of him returned, but this time, it came with an intensity I was not prepared for. "Vance," he dominantly stated.

"Pardon?"

"Our first transgression." He did not wink, he did not

smile, he did not playfully banter. "Now you know my real name. Is Sabine yours?"

I flushed.

Not from the question or what he was saying, but from the way my name filled his parted mouth before it crossed his lips with a deeper tone than every other word I had heard him speak.

I flushed because I wanted to hear it again.

Over and over.

At night. In the predawn morning. In the bright sunlight. On the streets of a faraway place I barely remembered.

I wanted to hear him say my name over and over until I believed it was my life and not what I was living.

"Vance," I whispered, tasting his name like he had tasted mine.

Commanding dominance hardened his features, but his voice quieted. "Your real name," he ordered, but not in the threatening way Joseph gave me orders.

This order, I wanted to answer. I wanted to answer anything this stranger asked of me. "Sabine Malcher is my real name."

"You didn't take his surname."

"He never married me," I admitted, trenching the widening hole under my feet.

"Is that another transgression or common knowledge?"

Unwisely not objecting to his use of the term transgression, I gave him even more ammunition Joseph could use against me if he found out. "Everyone believes I am his wife."

Vance looked back out at the view. "Including him."

It wasn't a question, so I did not answer it.

Instead, I took the moment, wondering how a brief conversation with a complete stranger was the closest I had felt to another human being since the day I lost my brother.

As if he knew I was bathing in his presence and physical closeness, he did not speak for a moment, he simply let me be. As the seconds grew longer, I began to feel comfortable in my own skin.

But then he burst the false reprieve of security I was silently building around us, and he told me why he was really here.

"He thinks you're responsible for multiple incidents of corporate espionage within the company."

My body froze, but my mind, my heart rate, they swirled into a frenzy.

It was happening.

SIXTEEN

Vance

I MADE A CALCULATED MOVE THAT WAS NOTHING EXCEPT SELF-SERVING. "He thinks you're responsible for multiple incidents of corporate espionage within the company."

Still as a statue, her expression unreadable, she merely nodded as she stared at Manhattan's skyline.

I wanted this woman, more than I'd wanted any woman since my worst mistake. But in that moment, I wanted something more. I wanted in her head.

"You're not surprised." It wasn't a question.

Her gaze locked on the view when I wished like hell it was on me, she didn't answer for a beat. "I was surprised to meet you."

"Did we meet?"

Like I was hoping it would, my comment made her turn to me. "I know your name, you know mine. We have met."

"I met Bertrand, but he doesn't know my real name."

"Why is that?"

The more I got her talking, the less she showed fear. Which was the reason I said what I did next. "Because I'm going to take you away from him."

For one second, she didn't react.

Then the fear in her eyes didn't only come back, every tell in her body language broadcast what I saw the first damn moment that piece of shit Bertrand spoke to her.

She stepped back. "Mr. Victor—"

"Vance," I corrected.

"Mr. Vance, I think you need to leave. Joseph will be here any moment to pick me up for our standing lunch date."

Bullshit.

No fucking way was I letting him take her out after the accusation he threw down not five minutes ago. "It's Vance, no mister, unless you want to get formal and call me Mr. Conlon. And maybe Bertrand is coming to take you to lunch, but maybe I'll give him an excuse as to why you can't join him today."

Her left hand went to her right wrist, and she took another step back. "He always takes me to lunch. It is expected."

"Do you always do what's expected of you?"

"Of course. He is my…." Turning her head, dropping her voice, she left the lie unsaid, but she also did what I was expecting.

She walked right into it.

Concealing my anger toward Bertrand, I kept my tone even, nonthreatening. "Do you always do what he tells you to do?"

Nodding once, she stared at the closed computer on her desk. "Of course. He is the owner and president of Harrington's."

I drove it home. "Always?"

Favoring her wrist, she looked up and met my gaze, but not before I saw her inhale. "Yes."

Closing the distance between us, I took her right arm just below the elbow and pushed up her sleeve.

Flinching, she tried to jerk away from me as panic pitched her voice. "What are you doing?"

Knowing what I would see didn't stop the consuming rage that coursed through my veins.

Red, swollen and freshly bruised, her wrist looked fucking crushed, and I knew who goddamn did it.

Years of training, even more years of concealing my own damn rage, I held her arm and kept my voice low and even.

"Joseph Bertrand is going to pay for this, one way or another. And trust me, love, when I make a promise, I keep it." I released her.

Stumbling back as she frantically pulled her sleeve down, she put half the fucking office between us as she backed into a corner. "Y-you're here for security. Not for me."

"Correction. I *was* here for security. Now I'm here to do a much more important job."

"Joseph hired you." She glanced around the office and at her computer again. "To find out who is leaking secrets."

"Not leaking, hacking," I corrected.

"You said he told you it was me. You said I am a spy." Every new word out of her mouth was coming faster and with a heavier accent. "You are supposed to give him what he wants."

"I said corporate espionage, not spy, and those were his words, not mine." Her compounding fear only confirming my suspicions further, I hated Bertrand all the more. I was going to enjoy the fuck out of taking him down. "And mark my words, love, no way in hell am I handing you over to him, trussed up on a silver platter."

She crossed her arms protectively around herself. Then she threw herself under the bus. "You do not know that I did not do it."

My jaw ground tight, and I fought not to fucking fist my hands. "Are you telling me you're so afraid of him that you're willing to go down on felony charges for crimes you didn't commit?" I changed my mind. I wasn't going to take Bertrand down. I was going to kill the son of a bitch.

"Maybe I did do it."

Reining in anger I knew better than to direct at her, I leaned against her desk and tipped my chin toward the wall of glass separating her office from the hallway. "Does your office door lock?" Rhetorical.

She glanced at it.

Reaching behind me, I picked up her laptop. "Do you take your computer home at night? Does he allow you to remove anything from the premises?" Also rhetorical.

Her gorgeous throat moved with a swallow.

I nodded at the purse sitting on her desk that was big enough to fit a lot of female shit, but not large enough for her laptop. I drove another point home. "Do you have a cell phone that he doesn't pay for?"

She still said nothing.

"Black hat or white hat, darling?"

"I am not wearing a hat."

"Footprinting, scanning, stack fingerprinting?"

She frowned.

"SQL injection, sniffing, flooding, rogue servers—stop me when any of this sounds familiar." She had no fucking idea what I was talking about. If she was Bertrand's hacker, I was going to retire from AES, become a talent agent and sign her as my first client.

She turned away from me. "I think you should leave."

"You're right. I should." I should've fucking walked out the second that asshole Bertrand dropped this entire shit show in my lap, because when it blows up in his face, he's going to point at Trefor and AES and blame us for his own stupidity. "And you should come with me, but do you know what I absolutely hate, pet?"

Her gorgeous blue eyes met mine.

"*Should.*" I said it exactly as I meant it, like a goddamn noose. "The moment you add that word into your vocabulary, you're no longer in control. Can, will, have, do—all of those actions are acceptable as a choice made by oneself. But should? No, darling, I *shouldn't* do anything anyone else tells, expects or demands that I do. I either choose to do them…" I pushed off her desk. "Or I don't."

Fucking Bertrand came down the hallway and strode into her office. "Sabine, the car is waiting."

Crossing my arms, I kept my gaze locked on a woman I'd be smart to walk away from, but I never did the smart thing. "Sabine's not feeling well. She's leaving for the day."

Bertrand turned on me. "I'll be the judge of what my wife does or doesn't do."

Fully aware I was adding fuel to the fire he'd no doubt attempt to take out on her, I ignored his bullshit. I didn't intend to have her in the same goddamn residence as him by close of business, let alone on a plane with him where who knew what the hell he would do to her. "I have my car. I'll take her home. You said she needs to pack a bag." And leave this prick.

"Mr. Victor," the asshole bit out. "If you had been doing your job the past half hour, then you would be aware that my wife escorts me to lunch every day. Standing reservation. Nonnegotiable."

Taking my gaze off her, I stared the fuck down. "Not today, she doesn't."

Looking like he was going to have an aneurysm, Bertrand glared back at me.

I smiled. "Just doing my job." I casually picked up her laptop. "Discreetly."

Bertrand pivoted and aimed for the door, but not before firing one more shot of his abuse at her. "Wait at home until the driver picks you up for the flight." He walked out.

Grabbing her purse, I handed it to her. "Ready, love?"

SEVENTEEN

Sabine

With a hint of a smile that I was not sure was real, he tucked my laptop under his arm and picked up my purse before holding it out to me. "Ready, love?"

In all the years I had known Joseph, I had never, ever seen anyone stand up to him.

My stacked piles of lies slipping further, my fears bled out before I could hold them back. "You do not know what you have done."

"Quite the contrary, darling." His smile broadened. "I know exactly what I've done." He slipped the strap of my purse over my good arm. "But I suggest we get moving before I have to very *un*discreetly show the owner of Harrington's exactly what I think of the way he speaks to his wife."

"Vance," I whispered like I had a right to say his name.

His expression immediately turned as serious as when he had first walked into my office. "I know, love." His hand landed on the small of my back. "Asking you to trust me is not only premature, but from where you're standing, I would imagine it's downright offensive." He gently guided me toward my own office door but paused before opening it. "I can recite my résumé, tell you I was in the Marines, confirm that I work for Alpha Elite Security and that AES is the largest government military contractor in the world. I could assure you that me and all of the other former SEALs, Marines, Rangers and Special Forces men I work with not only have security clearances and experience downrange, but are the most elite group of trained mercenaries you'll ever meet. I can also tell you that you're incomparably safe with me or any one of them. I could say all of that and more, but I'm not here to insult you with facts that won't change who Joseph Bertrand is."

I stared at his green and amber eyes as I inhaled the scent of hope. "Then what are you saying?"

"I'm explaining to you that I know exactly what I'm doing, and if you choose to walk out this door with me, I will not only make you the promise of safety, I will personally guarantee it."

The trace of hope was crushed by my reality.

He was right. None of his guarantees changed who Joseph was, or more importantly, why I was with him. "I think you make a lot of presumptions, Mr. Conlon." Presumptions that interfered with his grand gesture and bold promise. Still, I irrationally and desperately wanted to trust him, but doing so would be an even bigger mistake than trusting Joseph all those years ago.

"I am neither presumptuous nor ignorant, Miss Malcher. Experience affords me more than intuition and honed instincts. Bertrand hid you from AES when he requested our services, and I've witnessed firsthand his behavior toward you. I'm not making assumptions, I'm looking at facts."

"I...." Joseph hid me? "I beg your pardon?"

"In this instance, I'm not going to make you beg for anything." After flashing his hint of a smile again, he lowered his voice and held me captive in his intent gaze. "I'm going to tell you exactly what I'm looking at." He let one whole breath linger between us before his voice went even quieter. "I'm looking at a beautiful woman living in fear."

An unfamiliar warmth flushed across every inch of my flesh as if I were naked but coated in hot sunlight. I wanted to reach for this man. I wanted him to touch me just to feel the sensation of his fingers coasting across my skin. But I couldn't be that woman. I didn't have the luxury of careless desires.

Forcing myself to ignore the fluttering low in my belly and the way his voice had dipped when he'd called me beautiful, I focused on the truth. "You cannot save a woman who does not need saving." I'd made this choice.

The side of his mouth briefly tipped up in a way that I was certain was practiced. He winked. "Why don't you let me worry the details, love?"

I said the most honest thing I could. "You are playing a dangerous game."

"Crossing the street in Manhattan during rush hour is dangerous." His half smile made another appearance. "And leaving Harrington's corporate offices on my arm would be downright scandalous." His serious side came back. "But I'm not exactly asking you to do that." He held my gaze for a heartbeat. "Unless you prefer it that way."

Traitorous emotion I dared not name bloomed in my chest for two whole seconds before I choked it down and said words that made me sick to think about, let alone push past my lips like I believed them.

"Mr. Conlon, you may think you are playing a game, but this is my life. And while I appreciate that you have a job to do that Joseph hired you for, I am not going to assist you in making my relationship with him collateral damage. I know I did not do what he is thinking I did, and in time I am sure he will realize the error of his ways. Just as I am sure you are capable of finding the real culprit to assist Joseph in finding the truth. But in the meantime, I would prefer that you do not use me to facilitate whatever kind of entertainment you think you are engaging in here. I can take care of myself, and any preconceived notions you have about my life, Harrington's, Joseph, or our relationship, it is none of your business."

Watching me as closely as he had in Joseph's office, Vance took in every word I said, but he did not immediately respond.

His eyes unwavering, his expression unreadable, his chest steadily rising and falling, he stood perfectly still.

Then he brought his lips to my temple and feathered the faintest of kisses against my skin before he whispered, "I will never play games with you or your life, Sabine Malcher."

Straightening, he pulled his cell phone out, dialed and held it to his ear as he scanned the corridor outside my office.

EIGHTEEN

Vance

I WAS AN IDIOT TO THINK IT WAS HER SCENT THAT WAS GOING TO BE the determining factor that drove me over the edge.

Protecting that fucking piece of shit Bertrand was.

Pulling my cell out, I dialed Echo.

The bastard picked up on the fourth ring. "Problem?" he mocked.

"This is Mr. Conlon. I'm coming downstairs. Can you please bring my car around?"

"Using your real name? You're either losing your touch, or wait, let me guess, you spied a hot piece of ass, it's now love and you're giving up your bachelor ways," Echo hazed.

Fucking prick. "Five minutes would be fine," I replied.

"Get your own damn car, I'm not the fucking valet," Echo clipped.

"Right. The black 720S," I added, waiting for Echo to clue the hell in.

Echo snorted. "Did you get fired already?"

"I appreciate it. We'll see you soon."

"*We*." Echo sighed, but then he finally relented. "All right, Conlon, I'll play along, but this better be fucking important."

"Thank you, we're heading to the elevators now." I hung up and glanced at her. "Let's get you home."

She dropped the closed expression she'd taken on when she

accused me of playing games with her life and frowned. "You really are taking me home?"

Hopefully only long enough for her to pack a bag and get her the fuck away from Bertrand. "Unless you'd prefer to go somewhere else?" Then I'd buy her all new shit.

The frown stayed as her gaze drifted to the view out her windows, but when she looked back at me, her expression was locked again. "What do you think you're doing?"

Getting her away from Bertrand. "Removing you from the current situation." I didn't give a fuck what she said in her little speech. It was all lies.

Leaking tells, she covered her injured wrist with a protective hand and looked past me. "So you can do what?"

"My job." My new, self-appointed job. One I was sure AES wouldn't get paid for. "Is that all right with you?" It was a bullshit question because I wasn't asking for permission. I was getting her out of here no matter what, but I wasn't blind to the look in her eyes. She needed an excuse to walk out, and I was giving her one.

"Yes, of course." She nodded briskly like she was on board, but not before I saw the flash of disappointment in her eyes that said anything but.

I opened her office door. "After you."

She glanced at her laptop that I was holding, but she didn't comment as she gracefully moved past me.

Not overstepping, even though I wanted to put my hand on her back, I didn't touch her as I walked beside her to the elevators. Every damn employee we passed noticed us, but all of them pretended to look away. Not one of them said a word to her, which only compounded my hate for Bertrand.

Hitting the call button for the elevator, I glanced behind us. I was half expecting Bertrand to show his face, but I had the fucking pussy's number. He wouldn't risk creating a scene he couldn't control the outcome of, and if he was smart, he'd know by now that I wasn't someone he would be able to control.

The lift arrived and I ushered her inside. When the doors closed, I turned. "Is it always like that?"

"Like what?" Her gaze averted, she wouldn't look at me.

Fuck this. "Do you need me to put my mouth on you to get your attention?"

Her head whipped up. "Excuse me?"

That was more like it. "I'm not going to tell you to look at me when I speak to you because I don't want you to mistake my preferences with the way that piece of shit treats you. I'm nothing like Bertrand, but I will tell you that I prefer for you to look at me when you speak to me."

Every ounce of her composed expression fell the fuck away, and her face paled. "So you can control me?"

"No." Fuck no. Submission in the bedroom aside. "So I can see your gorgeous eyes and read your expression and hear all the words you don't say to me."

She blinked.

"I told you I'm not playing a game with you, Sabine."

"Yes," she blurted.

I backtracked. "Yes, it's always like that in the office?"

She nodded.

"Has he expressly told the employees not to speak to you?" That fucking dick.

"I do not know."

But she suspected. I could see it in her eyes. "Why are you with him?"

She looked away again. "He is not all bad."

Bullshit. "Sabine," I warned.

The elevator stopped and the doors opened. She glanced at me before stepping out. "I do what I must."

Scanning the lobby, nothing stood out, but suddenly

something was kicking at my instincts, and I'd swear we were being watched. No longer giving a shit about touching her in public, I put my hand on the small of her back and led her toward the valet.

"Just so you know, love, I'm not dropping that statement indefinitely, but for now I'll let it slide." I glanced behind us as we exited through the revolving doors, but I didn't see anything suspicious.

Echo stood at the curb with the McLaren in front of him and a valet to his left who looked like he was about to piss himself.

I bypassed the valet and nodded at Echo. "Excellent, thank you."

Not making a show of it, but nonetheless scanning Sabine from head to toe, Echo nodded as he opened the passenger door of the 720S.

Sabine glanced from Echo to the McLaren to me. "This is your car?"

Echo snorted.

"For the time being, pet." I helped her inside and shut the door. Then I glanced at Echo. "Sabine Malcher. She's Bertrand's wife. He's accusing her of over five counts of corporate espionage, but none of it's adding up."

Echo raised an eyebrow. "You have got to be shitting me. There was nothing listed about a wife."

"I know. I need background ASAP, and something major's about to go down with his company. This is a coordinated attack across their global locations, but Bertrand has his head in the sand, not that I give a damn because he's abusing her."

Echo glanced at the car as his expression hardened. "Fuck this."

"My thought exactly. I don't give a damn if Harrington's goes up in flames at this point, as long as she's nowhere near when it happens. I got her out for now, but I need intel before the piece of shit leaves the office today at sixteen hundred hours."

"Copy. I'll get November on it. What else?"

"I think we were being watched in the lobby, but I can't confirm it. Stay and follow Bertrand if he leaves, see if he picks up a tail. I've got her laptop. After I drop her at home, I'll see what I come up with. If I strike out, I'll bring it to November."

"You're taking her home?" Echo asked, incredulous.

"For now. Tried to convince her otherwise, but she's fucking terrified of the prick."

"That's reason enough to pull her," Echo argued.

"Agree, but I'm not going to take her choices away, not yet, not until I can figure out what's going on and make sure that fuck Bertrand doesn't implicate her in any of his bullshit." I was hoping like hell I could convince her to walk before I was left with no choice but to pull her. "Give Zulu a heads-up, we'll be heading back down to Miami this afternoon. There's a Harrington's event this evening."

"Copy." Echo handed me the key fob. "What's the event?"

"A preview party for one of their upcoming auctions, after which Bertrand wants me to escort them to Vienna to—quote, unquote—keep an eye on her."

Echo snorted. "Sounds like a setup."

"That's what I'm aiming to find out. Let me know immediately if Bertrand leaves."

Echo tipped his chin.

I walked to the driver's side, got in and put the laptop behind her seat.

Sabine looked at me, then glanced back at Echo. "Do you know him?"

"Just the valet, love." I didn't fucking enjoy lying to her, but the less she knew right now, the better. "Where am I going?" I

VICTOR

knew Bertrand's address, but I was hoping like hell she'd give me any other location.

She rattled off that fuck's penthouse address. "You spoke to the valet for a long time."

Revving the engine, I smiled at her and winked. "Just a few words about the car, darling. Everyone loves a McLaren." I pulled into midday Manhattan traffic.

NINETEEN

Sabine

THE CAR WAS NOT HIS, IT DID NOT SMELL LIKE HIM, AND THE HUGE man dressed in all black was most definitely not a valet. I did not know what was going on, but I did remember what he had told me upstairs.

"Joseph hired your company?"

Driving too fast for the amount of traffic, Vance glanced over his shoulder and changed lanes. "Not my company, I don't own it, but yes."

"Alpha Elite Security?" I clarified.

He changed lanes again and made a turn too fast, but the car only seemed to glide around the corner. "Yes."

"AES is a private military contractor?"

"And security contractor, yes."

Then that man standing outside at the valet was most definitely someone Vance knew, probably someone he worked with. Joseph had a whole security team for both Harrington's and for us when we traveled, and while I did not know any of the particulars, I did know one thing. The security men never worked alone.

"Why would Joseph hire a military contractor to accuse me of using my computer to give away company secrets?"

Vance stopped at a red light and gave me his penetrating gaze with his beautifully haunted eyes. "One of the many questions I'd like answered."

Alarm spread. "Are you going to ask him?"

"No. But I promise you, I will find out."

Forcing myself to take a calming breath, I reasoned that there were only two ways Vance would find out about what I was protecting. And that was if either Joseph or I told him. I knew so little about the inner workings of Harrington's that I did not know if Joseph actually was involved in any illegal business practices or if he was simply planning on blaming me for corporate espionage to get rid of me. But either way, reputation meant everything to Joseph. He would never tell Vance what I was hiding.

In response to Vance's reply, I merely nodded, but then I went back to the man standing outside Harrington's. "That man was not a valet. He works with you." For some reason, it made me feel better to know that Vance had not come to Harrington's alone.

Vance had the decency to look apologetic for a brief moment before he stepped on the gas and turned his attention back to the road. "The less you know about what I'm doing, the better it will be for you."

"But the more you know about me, the better it will be for you."

With a quick glance, he smiled ruefully. "A tragic double standard, I'm afraid."

I did not reply. I leaned back in the seat that felt designed to cradle and watched Manhattan slip by. Not for the first time since a few minutes after noon, I wished more than anything that I had met a man like Vance instead of Joseph when I was nineteen. Maybe my life would have turned out differently. Maybe—

I stopped the thought and pushed it down deep with all of the other regret.

Vance took another corner, driving toward the penthouse like he knew the streets of New York City as well as he knew anywhere. "You've gone quiet on me, darling."

"I am always quiet."

"Now or before?"

Before. I knew what he meant—before Joseph. But there was also before I lost my brother and before I lost my parents. It did not matter if he was asking about one or all of them. I did not have an answer, so I changed the subject. "If you are British, then how did you serve in the Marines? Or did you mean the Royal Marines?"

"I'm not British, love. Hopelessly American, but I lived in London for a while after I served in the Marine Corps."

That explained why I could not exactly place his accent when I first heard him speak. "Did you like London?"

"The weather was atrocious."

In another life, his comment would have made me smile. A tall, muscular, former Marine calling weather atrocious seemed so frivolous. "You do not like rain?" I loved the rain. I loved even more how Vance smelled like the best part of fresh rain on ancient streets.

He took another turn, getting us closer to the penthouse, then his voice got heavier and turned a shade of quiet I imagined I understood. "I used to like summer afternoon thunderstorms."

The impulse to touch him, to rest my hand on his, it was so strong in that moment, but something told me he would rebuff the gesture, not that I was brave enough to make it. "That does not sound like London weather."

Inhaling, he let it out slowly before answering. "No."

"Where are you from?" I could not imagine him from anywhere, and yet he seemed to fit everywhere.

"Where are you from?" he countered effortlessly like this banter, this whole conversation was not weighted by circumstances.

"France," I answered vaguely.

"Florida," he answered equally as vaguely as he pulled up in front of our building.

"I think I would prefer living in Florida over London." I had only been to Miami and London proper, but white sand beaches with dazzling blue water would always be my preference over a bustling city with chilly weather.

Putting the fancy sports car into park, Vance studied me a moment. "If you like sun, humidity and lightning year-round, then you'd love living there."

I would love anything that was not Manhattan or New York or Harrington's or anywhere Joseph or his auctions or offices were. "I have been to Miami." Exactly six times, Joseph had taken me to the tropical paradise where he had a huge house in an expensive zip code that we never utilized unless there was a Harrington's event that justified traveling down there. "It is beautiful."

Vance stared at me a moment longer. Then he asked the question I had been waiting for. "Before I take you upstairs, do you want to tell me why you're still with him?"

I looked out the window at the imposing glass and steel highrise that had an address more enviable than a bank account with seven figures. Lulled into a false sense of security within the confines of the expensive car with a man who inexplicably made me feel safe, I thought about it.

Did I want to tell him?

Surprising even myself, my answer was an immediate yes. Yes, I wanted to tell him. I wanted to share the burden. I wanted someone to tell me I had made the right choice. But none of that was reality.

Telling him and trusting him were two different things, but neither negated the fact that this was not only about me, which was the real issue. One I had been avoiding thinking about since he had told me in my office that Joseph was accusing me of terrible things, because it was petrifying.

If Joseph would hire a military contractor to produce evidence that I was committing corporate espionage, then he could, and would, do any number of things I never imagined him to be capable of. I knew I could not trust Joseph's word, not that I should have in the first place, but now the stakes were so much higher, and I could go to prison.

Would Joseph even honor his original promise to me after that?

Of course he wouldn't.

Not to mention I had aged far beyond the young women on staff at both Harrington's and the house that he liked to go after. I was no longer young enough for Joseph Harrington Bertrand's particular tastes, but it was too late for him to simply kick me out.

Almost seven years ago, right after Joseph had moved me in with him, he could not get the board members of Harrington's to vote to expand their business. So he had added me to the board of directors and told me how to vote. I had barely been given a chance to see the documents I had signed, let alone read them. I did not know any of the particular legalities except that board members served a term of ten years and Joseph had promised that at the end of my term, I would be compensated. He had even said he'd set up a bank account for me, but since he controlled everything, including the finances, I had never been given access to it.

I did not even have access to the jewelry he had gifted to me over the years. Minus the diamond on my finger and the Boucheron around my neck, Joseph kept all of my jewelry locked in a safe in his master suite.

If I could just hold on a few more years, I would have money and hopefully it would be enough to undo my mistake and start new somewhere far away from here.

Telling Vance "Victor" Conlon could jeopardize that.

But if Joseph was using him to get rid of me, then I was already exposed.

Calm and quietly reserved, but no less commanding, Vance's deep voice broke the cocooned bubble of silence around us that I had been stretching out.

"Do you know what I think?"

Turning to give him my attention, because he had told me that was his preference, I looked at him. But I did not just look.

I studied everything about him.

The casual way his left arm draped over the steering wheel, with his suit jacket and shirt cuff riding up just enough to show an elegant but masculine watch. The strain of the fine wool stretched over his biceps. The curl of hair that seemed to go rogue over his forehead even though he had most likely combed his hair back this morning. The color of his eyes that changed hues depending on his expression or surroundings. The confidence with which he carried himself—not like he had something to prove, but as if he were equally comfortable in a custom suit behind the wheel of a luxury sports car as he would be on the battlefield with a gun in his hands.

I studied all of it because I had never met anyone like him.

When I did not reply, he answered his own question. "I think you're wondering if you can trust me."

Trusting him would be reckless and rash. It would also go against everything I had sworn to myself I would never do again after my first night under Joseph's roof. "I have learned that it is best not to trust anyone."

"Poignant and telling, but also intelligent. I'd be lying if I said I thought differently."

"Then why are you asking me to trust you?"

"I didn't ask you to trust me. I told you I'm not playing a game with your life or circumstances, and I told you I know exactly what I'm doing. I also said that if you chose to walk out of Harrington's with me, that I would personally guarantee your safety." His tone softened. "You did, so I am."

I stared at him for a long moment because I did not understand him, this great dichotomy of a man. If he did not trust easily, then why did he trust that I was telling him the truth about not doing what Joseph accused me of? "Joseph hired you for a job, but you are, in effect, doing the opposite. Why?"

His penetrating gaze, which all at once unnerved me and made me feel things I did not think were possible, faltered, and he looked out the windshield for a moment before turning back to me. "The truth?"

"Please."

His expression hardened, and suddenly he looked much more like the Marine he said he had been than the polished, suited man from a security company who made pretty promises. "I hated Bertrand the moment I met him. Then you walked in and I saw a situation that made me despise him more. I wanted to decorate his pretentious desk with his blood, then pick you up and carry you out of there. And I would have, except for one small detail, love. I'm not that man anymore. I don't lose my temper. I don't lose control, and I do *not* get mad." His voice dropped to a lethally quiet warning that was more terrifying than if he had shouted it. "I get even."

A storm of emotional reactions broadsided me all at once, but as fast as it had come into being, it settled, and I realized two things. I did not fear him, not like I feared Joseph. I knew this man sitting next to me would never lay a hand on me in anger, but I also saw something in his eyes.

He was withholding the why.

"You are not telling me the whole truth," I accused because I had nothing more to lose. "You have no reason to get even with Joseph. You have never met him before today." There was more to Vance's story. There was something he was not saying that gave him the reason why he was how he was, and I needed to know.

The seriousness to him that had been taking up all the air in the small sports car only moments ago evaporated like smoke, and he winked. "A man needs a reason to play the hero and rescue a beautiful woman?"

For the second time today, he elicited a feeling of hurt from me. "You said you were not playing a game with me." He had promised, but then he winked and practically made a joke out of my circumstances.

His expression instantly locked down. "I'm not."

The defensiveness in his tone, his words, his actions, it suddenly struck me. I was right. He was hiding something. "Then tell me the whole truth." I did not simply want to hear it, I needed to hear it. I desperately wanted to trust him, but I did not know him. Like an addict wanting a fix, I rationalized. If he could tell me this one thing, this one reason, then maybe I could trust him. Maybe I could tell him my whole truth.

But he had to go first.

He had to be the one to break this wall between us because God knew, I was not strong enough.

Except Vance Conlon did not say anything.

His amber eyes that looked more green than brown right now held me captive, while outside, all around us, Manhattan was alive with rushing traffic, honking horns and impatient people. Steam rose from the streets, the sun glinted off windows, the city was all moving parts and pieces, but inside this car, everything was still.

We were still.

His gaze holding mine, my heart stalled for his answer, my breath holding itself in—the moment turned into a lifetime.

Then, deep and resonate, his voice landed on me like hope before his words broke me into pieces. "You remind me of someone I used to know."

TWENTY

Vance

NO CHANGE IN HER EXPRESSION, HER QUESTION WAS IMMEDIATE. "Did you love her?"

I didn't answer. I couldn't. The fucking admission rattling around in my head on repeat, I'd already said too damn much.

Averting her eyes, she grabbed her purse with her good hand. "I understand. Thank you for the ride." Her voice laced with disappointment like I'd just failed some test, she reached for the door handle.

Fuck.

Careful not to hurt her, I grasped her elbow. "Wait. I'll open your door and walk you up." I was right, I'd just failed some test she'd given me, but I had no fucking idea why because I'd already shared with her more than I'd ever shared with anyone about my past. I didn't say her name. I didn't speak of or about her. I didn't ever fucking sully her memory by tarnishing it with my shit.

"I do not think that is a good idea." Crisp, accented, and dismissively polite, her French upbringing came out in her tone.

"Fortunately for you, bad ideas are my specialty." I smiled, but I knew it would have no effect. I was already in the doghouse, but hell if I was going to let her go upstairs alone. "Wait for me, love." I got out of the car, and the doorman for her building was on me.

"You can't park there, sir."

"Not parking." Amping up the smile, I palmed a hundred

VICTOR

I already had ready in my pocket. "Just bringing Miss Malcher home. She's not feeling well today. I'm sure you can keep an eye on the McLaren while I run her upstairs and make sure she gets inside okay." I held the bill out to him.

"Oh, of course, sir. I'm sorry to hear Mrs. Bertrand is under the weather." He stashed the hundred. "Should I call Mr. Bertrand?"

"No need." Disloyal prick. "He's the one who told me to bring her home. If you don't mind, I don't want to keep her waiting."

"Oh sure, sure." He stepped back.

Opening the passenger door, I held my hand out to her. "Ready, love?"

She took my hand, but she briefly looked at the doorman. "Good afternoon, Louis."

"Afternoon, Mrs. Bertrand."

Hearing him call her that made me grind my fucking jaw. "Right. This way."

"Sorry to hear you're not feeling well." The prick held the door. "Get better soon."

"Thank you, Louis."

Rushing her through the door, I led her to the elevator, but I didn't lose the doorman.

Hitting the call button before I could, he waited until the doors opened, then he leaned inside, swiped a card that was attached to his belt by a retractable keychain and pressed the button for the penthouse. "There you go, Mrs. Bertrand."

She smiled without making eye contact, and the doors closed.

I scanned the ceiling for a camera and found two. Turning my head away from them, I glanced at her. "Do you have your own access card, love?"

"No." She watched the floors tick higher.

Shocking. "Louis always swipes for you?"

"Or one of the other doormen."

"Right." Of course, they did.

The elevator stopped and opened directly into the foyer of a penthouse I never would've dreamed of walking into as a kid, let alone imagined being able to afford. Not that I gave a damn about money anymore.

Bringing her back here was a bad fucking idea. It would've taken me less than two seconds to overpower the doorman, take the card key and get into the place. Bertrand's security was a joke, and she had no protection here.

Before I could tell her to pack a bag, a woman in a uniform rushed out of a hallway.

"Sabine, what's wrong? You're not at lunch with Joseph?" Looking guilty, she stopped short when she saw me. "Oh. I'm so sorry." Bowing her head, she actually fucking stepped back. "I'll be in the kitchen if you need me." Quicker than she'd come in, the older woman retreated.

Fuck this. I was done.

No way in hell was I leaving her here.

Stepping in front of her, it took every ounce of self-control I had left not to touch her or go back downstairs and beat the fuck out of the doorman for sport. As pissed as I was at Bertrand for the bullshit fear and manipulation tactics he was using on this beautiful creature, including the intrusive doormen, I'd be lying if I said I didn't want to touch her more than I wanted the rush of a fight. Which was a fucking first in so long, that I refused to acknowledge it.

Instead, I lowered my voice in case Bertrand had cameras in this place and spoke so only she would hear. "We need to talk."

She looked up, and her gaze locked onto mine.

Then shit went still.

Dangerously still.

Eyes locked, sexual tension thick, fuck my head up, I couldn't remember a more beautiful woman, *still*.

Without thought, my hand slid to the side of her face, and her eyes closed.

Jesus. "Sabine—"

The muted sound of a cell phone ringing interrupted me, and she flinched before stepping back and reaching frantically into her purse.

"Leave it," I ordered.

"It is Joseph." Rooting around in her bag, she shook her head. "I cannot leave it."

"You don't know it's him."

"Yes, I do." Her hand came away with her cell. "He is the only one who has the number."

"Don't answer that," I warned, close to losing it.

Her eyes met mine, and like a fucking switch had flipped, the fear was back in them. "He knows by now that you are here, that you came upstairs."

I took the phone from her and answered the call. "Bertrand. Problem?"

"Put Sabine on, *now*," the asshole barked.

Like hell. "Something I can help you with?"

"Last warning, Victor. Put her on, and if you answer her phone again, it'll be the last thing you do as an employee of Trefor's."

"Right." I smiled reassuringly at the woman cowering in front of me. Then I hit a button on the cell. "You're on speaker, and she's here. Now you have us both on the line. What can I do for you?"

For one victorious beat, the surprised fuck didn't answer. But then he lost his shit and aimed at her. "How many times have I expressly told you that you are forbidden from letting anyone into the penthouse, Sabine? *How many?*"

My instincts kicked in, and I didn't give her a chance to answer. "She didn't let me do anything, Bertrand." I took a seemingly casual glance toward the living room, and that's when I saw the piece hanging in the middle of two other paintings. "I brought her up to make sure she was safe." Jesus, I'd been so caught up in her, I hadn't seen it before. "But if you want to speak about your doorman, his lack of security, and the access card to your home he leaves hanging off his belt on a keychain anyone can take from him, then I'd be happy to give you an assessment. Complete with recommended new security measures to ensure you and your wife's safety, of course. Fingerprint scanner access would be a good place to start." Fingerprint scanners were the bare minimum this fuck needed with the priceless Picasso he had hanging in plain sight in his fucking living room. No wonder he didn't want me up here.

"Put. Sabine. On. *Now*."

The fear in her eyes switched to resignation, and she reached for her phone.

That resignation only adding to my determination to take this asshole down no matter how fucking rich he was, I didn't give her the phone. "As I said, she's standing right next to me. She can hear you."

TWENTY-ONE

Sabine

Holding my cell phone and a smile that did not reach his eyes, Vance spoke to Joseph like he was a child. "As I said, she's standing right next to me. She can hear you."

"Give her the phone!"

Vance's smile dropped, and he winked at me as he completely ignored Joseph's directive. "I'm actually heading back to Miami now on one of AES's corporate jets. Since I have plenty of room, I'll take Miss Malcher with me and make sure she gets to the event on time. We'll see you there."

Joseph's full-blown yell turned into a biting tone. "Who the hell do you—"

"Think I am?" cutting him off, Vance finished Joseph's sentence. "Right now, I'm the man you hired to keep an eye on your wife. So unless you need anything else, we have a flight to catch."

"You fucking idiot, you're fired!" Joseph roared.

"Right," Vance countered calmly. "AES appreciates your business. As per our contractual terms, we reserve your retainer and wish you the best of luck in your endeavors."

"You fucking bastard, my security is calling the police! When I get to the penthouse, my wife better fucking be there, or I will have your head!"

"As I said, best of luck." Vance hung up and pocketed my phone. "Now's a good time to pack a bag, love."

Anxiety making my heart pound wildly, I tried and failed to

swallow. "Vance." The single word came out like a plea when it should have been an admonishment for what he had just done.

My phone started ringing from his pants pocket, but he ignored it. "I'm not leaving you here, pet. It was never going to happen. I would apologize, but I'm not sorry. You're coming with me, and once I find out what's really going on, we can reevaluate."

Stunned, my entire existence imploding, I stared at him as my cell stopped ringing, then started again. "Are you going to answer that?"

He raised an eyebrow. "Are you going to pack a bag?"

"I-I can't leave." Oh God, could I? Could I trust this man and tell him the truth? I almost believed I could. He had stood up to Joseph, said all the right things and was offering me an escape. I had been dreaming of an escape for more years than I wanted to count. Maybe this could work… or maybe Joseph was already undoing his promise to me, and the consequences were unraveling faster than my thought process. *Oh God.*

"You can, love. Packed bag or not, that's up to you. I'm happy to buy you all new clothes and whatever else you need if you prefer to travel light."

My cell rang again, then a different ringtone added to the mix. I should have been infuriated at him. He had pushed over my house of cards. He had ruined what I had been holding together, but shockingly I was not angry. Even more shameful, the only word that seemed to come out of my mouth as I stood there completely distressed was his name. *"Vance."*

Holding my gaze, Vance reached into his suit jacket pocket and pulled out his own phone as it too kept ringing. "I know, love. And trust me, I understand your concerns, I do, and we'll discuss them later, but I'm not taking no for an answer. What's the name of the woman on your house staff?"

My mind reeling, I answered without thinking why he was asking. "Rosaline."

"Thank you, pet." He nodded once before raising his voice. "Rosaline!"

With both cell phones still ringing, Rosaline appeared almost instantly as if she had been standing around the corner.

Her cell in her hands, she looked sheepishly at me. "Mrs. Bertrand, Mr. Bertrand would like a word." Skirting around Vance, she walked toward me, holding her phone out.

Before she got to me, Vance intercepted her and snatched her cell. Ending the call, he handed it back to her. "Rosaline, please go pack Sabine a bag. Essentials will do, but hurry."

Her eyes going wide, she looked between me and Vance.

"Now, please," Vance calmly stated with authority as my cell started to ring again from his pocket.

"But what about Mr. Bertrand?" Rosaline asked in fear. "He said—"

"I'm perfectly aware of what he said, and I'll handle him, but I suggest you think about packing your own bag after you pack Sabine's and consider getting a new job." He pulled a business card out of his pocket and handed it to her. "Call the number listed and ask for Maila if you need help finding alternate employment. I'll give her advance warning that you may be reaching out."

To my shock, Rosaline took the card and hurried toward the hall leading to my bedroom without another word or even a glance in my direction.

Words were out of my mouth before I knew what I was saying. "You cannot do this." He already had. I knew it. He knew it. But I was still so stunned, the woman I had become over the past seven years came out and put up the front that she was supposed to.

"It's already done, love." His eyes on me, he answered his cell. "Victor. Right. Understood." His gaze drifted. "Change in scope… No." He glanced toward the elevator. "Copy that." Hanging up, he pocketed his cell and stepped in front of me as the elevator doors opened. "Don't even think about it," Vance warned the doorman.

Looking angry and determined, Louis stepped off the elevator. "No, *you* don't think about it, Victor. Mr. Bertrand wants to speak to his wife, and he insists that you leave now, without her." He reached in his pocket.

Faster than I had ever seen one of Joseph's security men move, Vance had Louis's arm pinned behind his back as he slammed his face into the entryway wall. "I can assure you I don't make idle threats. If you want your arm to remain in one piece, you're going back downstairs, and you're not going to disturb Miss Malcher or me again, not even to hold the lobby door. Questions?"

"No," Louis bit out.

Not letting go of Louis's arm, Vance used his elbow to press the elevator call button. The doors slid open, and Vance simultaneously threw Louis inside and grabbed the keycard off his belt.

Using the side of his fist, Vance hit the lobby button before shoving the keycard into his pocket.

Louis glared at Vance. "Mr. Bertrand's going to hear about this."

"Excellent, make sure you tell him I have the keycard, and I'll be giving it to Miss Malcher," Vance retorted as the elevator doors slid shut. Turning to me, he calmly straightened his cuffs. "You okay, darling?"

I should have demanded my phone back and told him to leave before he did any more damage, but for the first time in as long as I could remember, I was looking at someone who had stood up for me.

Before I could stop myself, reckless words I had never spoken aloud came out of my mouth. "Joseph has something on me." It was as close to the truth as I felt safe saying in that moment, which was more than I ever thought I would say out loud to anyone.

For a brief, reaffirming second, a look of sincerity crossed

Vance's face, and his voice softened. "I figured, love." Then the moment was gone, and his gaze focused over my shoulder as his expression locked down. He stepped around me. "Is she all set?"

"Yes, Mr. Victor." Rosaline pushed the larger of two rolling suitcases toward him. "She will have enough for a short while."

"Thank you." Vance nodded at the smaller suitcase she had not pushed over. "And yourself?"

Rosaline's face flushed, and she looked down as she clasped her hands. "I thought I would leave with you two."

"Rosaline," I whispered in shock. She had been with Joseph since before I had come into his life, and even though she was kind to me, she had always been loyal to him. In fact, I had always wondered if she was in love with him, or had been at one time. "Are you sure?"

The woman, who I had watched be subservient to Joseph for years, squared her shoulders and looked directly at me. "Yes. This is something I should've done a long time ago."

"Excellent," Vance interrupted. "Shall we?" He took my suitcase, rolled it toward the elevator and pushed the call button as his cell made a buzzing sound then rang.

Rosaline stepped beside me, silently looping her arm in mine.

Vance frowned as he glanced at his phone, but then he swiped his thumb across the screen and answered it as he had before. "Victor."

Standing close enough to him to hear the yelling that was coming from the caller, I involuntarily shuddered at the sound of Joseph's anger.

Rosaline squeezed my arm. "It's okay," she whispered. "I think this Victor is a good man. If he can get me a new job, he can get you out of here too."

She did not understand, but it was not her fault. "Thank you, Rosaline," I quietly responded, but I knew what Joseph was going to do. He was going to do what he always did. He would make it so that none of us walked out of this penthouse.

"I'll get back to you." Vance hung up and looked at me as he spoke to the older woman holding my arm like a life preserver. "Rosaline, give Sabine and me a moment, please."

The elevator doors opened and she glanced between us before looking back at Vance and shocking me for a second time today. "We have to leave now before he comes back."

"I understand." Vance held my gaze as he replied to Rosaline. "Take the lift or give us a moment," he quietly ordered.

Rosaline turned and walked back toward the kitchen.

Vance let the elevator doors close before he spoke. "He wants to negotiate."

TWENTY-TWO

Vance

LOOKING DEFEATED AS HELL, HER SHOULDERS SLUMPED. "He is lying." She glanced toward the hall where the older woman had gone. "Joseph does not negotiate. He threatens and he bullies until he gets what he wants. He has probably already called the police." She looked back at me. "You should go. I will stay, but please, take Rosaline with you."

I didn't know if I was more impressed with her bravery or angry with her for being stubborn. "First, I already told you, I'm not leaving without you. I can handle Bertrand and whatever he throws our way. I'd feel more prepared if you told me what he has on you, but right now, my priority is getting you out. Understand that doesn't mean I walk away once I get you out the door. I'm following this through. I'll make sure the threat's eliminated, then I'll get you set up somewhere safe." Most likely at my penthouse in Miami because I was already out of my fucking head, and I didn't want to walk away from this woman.

"Set up like Rosaline?" she asked.

"Yes." If that's what it took to get her out of here of her own free will. "Second, you were half right. He doesn't want to negotiate per se, and he did threaten, but it wasn't about calling the police." I knew he wouldn't the second he'd threatened it. If he did, he'd have to explain why he had a priceless stolen painting in his living room, which I could give two fucks about. I was more concerned with watching her face closely for any change in expression or tells as I gave her the rest of it. "He said if you're at the Miami event tonight and Vienna the following day, then you can walk away—his words, not mine—*free and clear*." Which was a fucking setup, but I still didn't know what he was after.

Inhaling sharply, she turned away from me.

"Sabine?"

"I should call him," she murmured. "I should speak with him."

"I've already spoken with him, and I've told you what he said." At least the pertinent details, the other ninety percent I wasn't going to fucking repeat because she didn't deserve to take any more of his bullshit. "But if you feel the need to hear it for yourself, we can call him." On speaker, because no fucking way was I giving him unfettered access to her under my watch.

"Fine." She turned to face me, and the same damn look of resignation as before was back, haunting her gorgeous eyes. "When do we leave for Miami? You said thirty minutes?"

Goddamn it, I needed to talk to November. "What does he have over you?"

Ignoring me as if I hadn't asked the question, she gave me more closed-off bullshit. "I am going to do what he asks, and while I cannot stop you from doing what you are going to do, I would prefer it if you did not stop me from doing what I am going to do."

Fuck, this woman was fierce in her stoicism. I forced a smile. "Well played, love, using my own tactics against me."

"I can assure you this has nothing to do with you."

"I know." That was both the allure and the problem of it. I didn't need a shrink to tell me I was out of my mind. I knew I couldn't save this woman to exonerate myself from my past. The last person she needed at her back was me, but here I was. "Does this have to do with the stolen art hanging on the wall?" I tipped my chin toward the living room.

"Pardon?" She followed my glance, then frowned. "Oh, no, that is a replica. A very good one, but nonetheless an imitation."

"Right." I glanced at her ring and took a wild stab. "Is your diamond fake too?"

She covered the ring with her right hand. "When do I leave for Miami?"

Fucking hell, I didn't know if she was covering for that asshole or actually believed his lies, but the fact that she was willing to walk blindly into this trap wasn't sitting well. "I can't in good conscience recommend you do this." I didn't even know if it came down to it, if I would physically let her walk back into that asshole's web.

"I understand, but if two events mean a clean break and he drops this investigation, then so be it."

"I can guarantee that nothing about this will be clean." And Bertrand wasn't going to drop shit. She knew who the fuck she was dealing with. "He has no regard for your safety or well-being. At a minimum, he'll pull something over on you, and the fact that I can't anticipate what that is because I don't have all the details has me far more alarmed than if he went to the district attorney with his trumped-up allegations of corporate espionage."

Her gaze drifted past me, but she didn't respond.

"I need to know exactly what I'm protecting you from." I knew pushing the issue was the wrong approach with someone like her, especially with what she'd clearly been dealing with for years. But this was what I did. This was what Trefor had hired me for.

I fucking pushed.

I unraveled. I peeled back layers. Then I flushed out secrets.

Stripping people back to their motivations, unveiling what made them tick—it cut to the chase. I'd get to the bottom of what she was hiding. Everyone I'd ever met was driven by one of two things, money or love, sometimes both. I suspected she was no different, but the devil was in the details.

Details she still wasn't giving up.

Switching up my tone, dominant, controlled, but low enough not to frighten her, I used her name. "Sabine."

She looked up at me, and for two seconds, I thought I had her.

Then her eyes and her expression shut down. "No charges have been filed. I have done nothing wrong. There is nothing to protect me from." She turned her back on me. "Rosaline!"

The woman instantly appeared from around the corner. "Are we leaving now?"

"Not exactly," Sabine replied. "I am going to Miami with Joseph for the preview party, then on to Vienna for the live auction."

Rosaline blanched. "But—"

"All is well." Sabine put her hand on the other woman's shoulder. "I am going to quickly pack what I need for the two events, but I suggest you leave with Mr. Co—" Sabine stopped herself and corrected. "With Mr. Victor."

Fuck this. "Nice try, pet, but I'm not going anywhere without you." I looked at the older woman. "Do you have somewhere safe to go?"

Rosaline glanced at Sabine, then back at me. She nodded hesitantly.

I pulled my cell out and dialed.

November answered on the first ring. "Echo filled me in, and I'm working on it, but Alpha's been trying to get a hold of you. The client's blowing up his phone, leaving threatening messages. What happened?"

"Later. I need a driver sent to the penthouse ASAP."

"What happened to the McLaren?"

"Nothing. This isn't for me. Pull Echo back, and let Zulu know we need to be wheels up in thirty. We're heading back down to Miami with a plus one, and I'll need you and Echo tonight." I was all about working alone, but in this situation, if I couldn't get her to change her mind, then even I wasn't arrogant enough to walk into that fucking party with her without backup. "I'll update you on the rest in-flight."

"Copy," November replied as he typed on his laptop. "Car's en route. Filing a flight plan now. The Gulfstream will be ready when you are. Do you want me to arrange to have Prestige pick up the McLaren at Teterboro, or are you handling it?"

I told myself I was remembering Zulu's warning and not stirring the proverbial pot, but in truth, I had a sudden aversion to any woman in my past colliding with the woman standing in front of me. If that didn't spell fucked, I didn't know what did, but I didn't have time to dwell on it. Bertrand could show up any second, and I wanted Sabine out of here before that happened.

"I would appreciate an assist on that, and send the driver into the lobby for pickup."

"Copy and consider it done. Driver's downstairs. I'm relaying pickup instructions now." November hung up before I could thank him.

I glanced at the older woman. "A driver's waiting downstairs in the lobby. He'll take you wherever you want to go."

She looked at Sabine.

Sabine nodded.

"Then it's settled." I hit the elevator call button. "Don't speak to the doorman, and leave your phone here." I fished out two of the three grand I had in large bills in my wallet and handed them to her. "Have the driver make a stop to buy a new phone before you have him take you somewhere safe. Once you're settled, contact the woman I told you about, but under no circumstances do you call Sabine, Bertrand or any other staff member from here. Understand?"

Clutching the money, she nodded with the same fear in her eyes I'd seen in Sabine as the elevator doors opened.

"You'll be all right," I assured. "Just remember, clean break."

Tears welled and she nodded. Then she turned toward Sabine and hugged her before quickly getting on the elevator. As the doors closed, she looked at me. "Thank you."

Sabine waited until we were alone. "Joseph is not going to forget this. Rosaline has been with him longer than I have."

I watched her for a moment, wondering if she knew.

"I see that look," she accused.

"What look is that, pet?"

"First, you are calling me *pet* now instead of *love*, and second, you are either assuming she was once involved with Joseph or asking yourself if I see what has been right in front of me all along. Most likely the latter, and you are judging me for it."

I wasn't judging shit. "I'm in no position to cast judgment on you or her. Trust me, love, I'm saving that for Bertrand. But otherwise, you're right. I'd bet my life he went through her before he spied a younger, prettier punching bag."

She dropped her head. "He does not punch me."

"Doesn't he?" Repeatedly, every goddamn way he could. "What do you call the fresh bruising on your wrist, the fabricated paperwork to put you behind bars, the way he speaks to you?" Every damn hit he was taking at her was fueling my rage, but I didn't have time to hash this out here, nor did I want to. I needed to get her the fuck out of here, find out want she was hiding, then decide if I was going to let her attend that goddamn party in Miami. "We'll revisit this later. Go pack what you need. I have to make a call."

Without a word, she turned toward the hallway.

I dialed Trefor.

He answered on the first ring. "You never call me when you're on assignment."

VICTOR

I watched the curve of her perfect ass as her heels quietly clicked across the marbled foyer before she disappeared around a corner.

"You never text me, demanding that I do," I countered.

"I've never had a client call to say he's pressing kidnapping and assault charges against you for taking his wife, as well as aiding and abetting a felon."

I glanced at the painting again. "Didn't know there was a wife, and the bastard needs to pick a side. She's either his wife, or she's a felon." I didn't know shit about art other than what I liked, but there was no way a prick like Bertrand would hang a fucking replica in his living room.

"The problem is none of us knew he had a wife, so we don't know what she's capable of."

"The problem is Bertrand," I corrected. "Not her."

"Echo filled me in, and from what we know so far, I don't disagree, but November's working on gathering more intel. So far, there's no legal documentation, at least not in the States, that says he's married to her or anyone else, and November's still coming up short on her background."

"He may not have married her, but she's been living with him for almost seven years, taking his shit, complete with fresh signs of physical abuse."

Trefor exhaled audibly. "Understood. What do you need from me?"

"I need to find out what Bertrand has on her that's making her stick around, and I need that intel yesterday."

"There's not always a reason in domestic situations," Trefor cautioned.

I refrained from telling him to fuck off. "There is in this one. Bertrand's demanding she attend a preview party in Miami tonight and the live auction in Vienna on Saturday. Then he says he'll let her walk, free and clear."

"She agreed?"

"She's packing a bag as we speak."

"You think he'll follow through?"

"Not for one fucking second." Something was going to happen at one of the events, I'd bet my life on it. "Bertrand said if I don't deliver her to his private jet at Westchester by oh four hundred, then his attorney is locked and loaded, ready to press charges on all counts of espionage, and I'm being thrown into the mix for everything he mentioned to you."

"Christ," Trefor muttered.

"If I can't talk her out of going, I want Echo and November at the party with me tonight. Then, depending on what happens, I'll need a team on standby for Vienna."

"Done, but for the record, any other woman, you would've already removed her from the situation and done damage control postcoital."

"I'm not fucking her, Alpha," I warned.

In a rare show of emotion, Trefor laughed. "I'm Alpha now?"

"Fuck you," I bit out.

His tone sobered. "What's really going on?"

"I just fucking told you what's going on. Tell November she's French and to start with the Harrington's Paris location seven years ago. Then we need to get into Harrington's main servers and find out what the hell is going on."

"Copy that. Can I ask one more question, or are you going to bite my head off again?"

"This isn't me biting." Not even close. "If I was going to bite your fucking head off, you wouldn't see it coming." Just like Bertrand won't know what's hit him until it's too late.

"I'm well aware. All I need to know is if you're solid."

"I'm going to ignore the fact that this is the second time in twenty-four hours that you've questioned my judgment."

"Then I'm going to ignore the fact that Sanaa called Maila this morning."

"What the fuck for?" They weren't friends, they were acquaintances.

"Coffee."

"You're saying that or your woman said that?" I didn't have time for this, but I also didn't need my brother's wife talking shit about me to my boss's woman, which would invariably get back to Trefor.

"Both. Maila left thirty minutes ago for your brother's house to meet Sanaa. I'm guessing this has more to do with why Echo called me last night than two women having coffee."

Fuck me. I never should've shown up at my brother's before dawn. "So your woman and my brother's woman are having coffee, and Echo is a fucking pussy gossip. Your point?"

"Don't underestimate women."

"Never have. Never will." Not again.

Trefor was quiet a moment. Then, "I know you won't." He hung up.

Sabine walked into the foyer with a second suitcase. "I am ready."

Taking in every gorgeous, reserved inch of her, the truth stared back at me with piercing blue eyes.

I hadn't only underestimated this woman, I was already in over my head.

Too damn late to turn back now, I smiled. "Excellent, love. Let's go."

TWENTY-THREE

Sabine

HE SMILED AT ME.

He accused Joseph of beating me and Rosaline, all but said he was going to kill him, then he sent Rosaline away with spy-like instructions about safety, and now he was smiling?

This did not fit. Something else had happened.

"What is wrong?" Instead of packing, I should have listened to his phone call. All I had heard was him angrily say what sounded like a man's name.

Taking the handle of my rolling suitcase from me, Vance pushed it toward the elevator where the other suitcase Rosaline had packed for me was waiting. Pressing the call button, he avoided looking at me as he replied, "Did I say something was wrong, love?"

This man was a stranger to me. I had only met him hours ago, but for reasons I could not explain, I knew him. I could already read his expressions and the slight nuances in his tone. I noticed his different smiles and how his posture was sometimes perfectly still but he was even more alert. I had also noticed that, the drive over notwithstanding, this was the first time he had not looked directly at me when he had spoken to me.

That was how I knew the smile he had just given me was different. His body language was different too, but I could not pinpoint exactly why. All I knew was that sometimes he was undressing me with his eyes, and other times, it was as if he were looking right through me.

I could not figure out if he thought he was saving me because he wanted to sleep with me, or if he simply had picked a side and Joseph was not it. Maybe I was reading entirely too much into this, but I swore I'd gotten a few, true glimpses into the man who was Vance Conlon. Other than those rare, brief moments, the rest of the time I was looking at a man so guarded, so closed off, that no one or nothing could break through his steel exterior.

And I still was not sure how he knew about my wrist.

I had had years of practice hiding it.

I hid it so well, most days I believed my own lies.

No one knew that Joseph took his anger out on me, and yet, this tall mystery of a man in front of me had figured it out within seconds of meeting me.

Studying his handsome face and the almost neutral expression that was in direct contrast to the storm rioting in his gaze, I knew he was hiding something. "You did not have to say anything, I can see it in your eyes. Something is not right."

He gave me his fake smile again, but this time it was laced with sarcasm. "Love, the only thing *not right*, besides Bertrand being a complete bastard, you not telling me what he has on you, and me stupidly contemplating taking you to the party, is that we're still here."

As if on cue, the elevator doors opened.

Vance held his hand out for me to enter first. "Let's remedy the latter, shall we?"

Reminding myself I had already made my choices, I walked into the elevator.

Vance wheeled both my bags in after me and pressed the button for the lobby.

As we started to descend, the same thoughts that had been plaguing me while I had been packing dresses for both Miami and Vienna returned. I did not know if I would ever come back to the penthouse, or if I had a home at all after this. I didn't even know if I cared. As long as the reason why I had been here in the first place remained intact, I told myself I could live with whatever came next.

That was all that was important.

Do these last two things for Joseph, maintain his image, or whatever other reason he had for wanting me at both places, and I could think about the after later. I could worry then if Joseph would keep his promise. I could contemplate what Vance had said about the painting in the living room. I could do something about the ring on my finger, and I could maybe, possibly ask the handsome stranger next to me for help if Joseph did not keep his word.

I could also think about what it had felt like when that same handsome stranger had stepped in front of me in the entryway and stood so close I could feel his body heat blanketing me in desires I had buried so long ago, I did not have a name for them anymore.

"You're telegraphing, love."

"Pardon?"

Glancing at me, heat filled his eyes and he winked. *"Pardon,"* he repeated, before lowering his voice. "Very French, very attractive. Keep that, pet."

The switch. This side of him I understood. Flirtatious, suggestive—I knew what men wanted when they behaved like this.

"What do you know about French women?" The question, while asked casually, was anything but. I foolishly wanted to know. I wanted to know if that someone I reminded him of was French. I wanted to know not if she was beautiful, but how beautiful. I wanted to know if she held his attention like I could never hold Joseph's. At least not the kind of attention a woman wants from a man.

The smile that touched his face a moment before the elevator opened to the lobby wasn't one that reached his eyes. "Oh,

VICTOR

pet, a gentleman never tells." Stacking my smaller suitcase on top of the medium-sized one Rosaline had packed for me, he nodded toward the lobby. "When you step out, stay to the left, love."

Following his directions, I avoided eye contact with Louis.

Vance came out of the elevator immediately behind me and blanketed my right side. With one hand on the small of my back, his other maneuvering my bags, he put himself between me and an angry-looking Louis.

Louis stood, but before he could come out from behind his desk, Vance stopped him. "Stand down, mate, no need for repeats. I can assure you I won't be as gentle as last time."

"Give the card key back," Louis demanded.

Vance let go of the suitcases to push the door open for me before glancing back at Louis. "Right. Not happening."

"I'm warning you, Victor," Louis growled. "You give that card key back or I'm reporting it to Bertrand."

"The fact that you haven't already speaks volumes about your incompetence." His hand still on my back, Vance gently but firmly ushered me out of the building.

A minute later, after opening my door and stowing one suitcase in a front trunk and one at the back of our seats, Vance was behind the wheel and pulling away from the curb.

"What are you going to do with the card key?"

His attention on the traffic, Vance spared me a quick glance. "That's what you're worried about?"

I was worried about so much, and had pushed everything down so deep for fear of falling apart before Joseph's party, let alone Vienna, that now my nerves, my anxiety, they were taking up new purchase. Past being on the edge, smaller details were exploding into disproportionate importance, and all I could think about was the card key. Being blamed for it being stolen. Punished for Louis's incompetence. Reported to the authorities for being the thief of it. Rationally, I knew it was a simple matter of deactivating the card key, but in my head, it was a sudden and insurmountable problem.

"Yes," I admitted.

"Right." He shook his head once, but he did not say anything else as he pulled the card key out of his suit pocket and handed it to me.

Taking it, I tucked it inside my purse, then leaned back in my seat. Preoccupied with having a card key for the first time, it took me a few minutes before I realized Vance was not heading back toward the office. Nor was he heading in the direction of the private airport where Joseph and I flew in and out of. "Where are we going?"

Glancing over his shoulder, he changed lanes. "Airport."

"Which one?"

"Teterboro."

"That is not where we usually fly out of."

"I understand."

No, he did not understand. "We fly out of Westchester." More than the anxiety already gnawing at my empty stomach, alarm spread. "Joseph will be expecting me." I had heard what he'd said on the phone to Joseph earlier. I heard Vance tell Joseph he would fly me down to Miami, then Joseph promptly firing him. I understood that they had spoken since, and Joseph was now saying he wanted to negotiate, saying I could walk away if I did this. I understood all of that.

"Will he?" Vance asked nonchalantly.

"Yes," I replied firmly. "I told you I would do what he asked. Take me to the proper airport." What I did not understand was why Vance was ruining this. Joseph would never let me walk away if I did not get on his plane and do what he said.

"Right," Vance said seemingly absently as he pulled his cell out, dialed and put it on speaker.

Two rings and Joseph's angry voice came through the line.

VICTOR

"Were my instructions unclear? Are you fucking stupid? You were supposed to give the access card back to the doorman and get her to the goddamn airport. Do you want to go to jail with her?"

"Did you pay me to do a job?" Vance casually asked.

Joseph practically crawled through the phone line, his anger was so loud. "The only reason I haven't hung up is because Trefor assured me that you weren't a complete fucking idiot, but I'm warning you, Victor, if you so much as—"

"I'll take that as a yes," Vance stated, cutting Joseph off. "Miss Malcher will be at the party tonight as requested. She's being flown down to Miami on one of AES's corporate jets with proper security."

"My *wife* flies with me. Four p.m. Westchester. I already gave you these instructions."

Vance didn't budge. "You also hired me to do a job. Do you want it done?"

"I don't know what the hell kind of stunt you think you're pulling, but this stops *now*," Joseph practically yelled.

Still holding the phone, Vance skillfully took a corner. "I have her laptop, I have her phone and I have her surrounded by AES security measures, none of which I can control if she's on your plane."

My stomach plummeted.

Vance stepped on the gas, and his voice turned lethal. "You came to me with a problem, Bertrand. You wanted a specific solution. I told you I always deliver. Do you want me to do that or not?"

All the air left my lungs.

In a sheer panic, I reached for the door handle.

TWENTY-FOUR

Vance

Fucking livid, taking it out on the gas pedal, I knew what the hell I had to do, had to say, but I goddamn hated it. "You came to me with a problem, Bertrand. You wanted a specific solution. I told you I always deliver. Do you want me to do that or not?"

If she wasn't going to listen to me, then she needed to hear what this piece of shit was going to say. He wasn't going to let her go. He was going to throw her to the fucking wolves, and it was past time she heard it directly from him.

But before Bertrand could incriminate himself, she was reaching for the fucking door.

Dropping my cell, grabbing her arm, holding the wheel with my knee, I hit the lock button. "Answer the question, Bertrand. Yes or no?"

"*Yes*," the asshole ground out as she struggled against my hold. "Get me the goddamn evidence to put her away, but you better make sure she's at that party tonight, or I'll do a hell of a lot more than call my attorney and your boss. *I will ruin you.*" The fucking prick hung up.

Wrenching out of my hold, she turned in her seat and crossed her arms around herself.

Grabbing my phone from the center console, I checked to make sure the call was disconnected then I shoved it back in my suit jacket pocket. "Sabine."

Her shoulders shook once, but she didn't make a sound.

Fuck. "Look at me."

She turned even more toward the window.

God damn it all to hell. Slowing down, I changed lanes. "Sabine, listen to me."

"No," she barely whispered before giving me exactly what I deserved. "You are just like him."

Hitting the gas, I cut across traffic, swerved onto the shoulder, and slammed on the brakes.

I didn't give a fuck about traffic, cops, or even Bertrand. But I goddamn cared about the last thing that had come out of her mouth.

Grasping her chin, behaving like the piece of shit she'd just accused me of being, I turned her face toward mine.

Not flinching or pulling back, the most beautiful woman I'd ever laid eyes on met my enraged glare. Then she fucking gutted me.

No anger, no hatred, she stared at me with one unmistakable emotion in her stunning crystal-blue gaze that I could not handle.

An emotion that haunted me to my fucking core.

Hurt.

"Sabine," I rasped as my past came at me like a goddamn tsunami.

Her eyes welling, her body trembling, she whispered the one question that I couldn't fucking answer. "Why?"

Too much of a coward to tell her this had nothing and everything to do with her, I gave her a different truth. "I'm not a good man." I wasn't even close to honorable. "You deserve better." Two minutes ago proved exactly that.

It also proved I hadn't learned a damn thing from my worst mistake. But for once, instead of looking for a barrel to stare down or picking a fight that would inflict pain I knew I deserved,

I wanted something else. For the first time in seventeen years, I wasn't looking to take a beating for a past I couldn't fix.

I was looking for redemption.

Cupping her face, staring down my own weakness, I apologized. "I'm sorry." I had no right to lose my temper with her. "You need to know that I have no intention of handing you over to him, not figuratively, not physically. I could've picked a better way to convince you to trust me."

Because that's what this was about.

I wanted this woman to trust me.

Fuck, I wanted her to trust me, but how the hell was I supposed to do that when I didn't trust myself around her?

"Trust?" Pulling out of my grasp, she turned toward the window. "I will never trust you. Take me home."

Reining in anger at my own damn stupidity and hers, I opened my mouth and made shit worse. "And where would that be? Because I heard the same conversation as you."

Abruptly turning back to face me, her dark, luscious hair fell over her shoulders in a cascade I wanted to wrap around my fist.

"You did that," she accused, finally pissed off. "You made him angry. You made this situation worse. You made him want to break his promise to me."

Now we were getting somewhere. Calm, but firm, I asked the question. "What promise, love?"

"I am not your love!"

Ill-timed and inappropriate, but not giving a damn, I smiled.

"Don't you dare smile at me, Mr. Conlon."

I dropped the smile. "It's Vance, and while you may not be mine, you're absolutely lovely." Risking the move because I wanted to touch her, I tucked a strand of her hair behind her ear. "And for the record, I prefer your anger over fear, sorrow or hurt any day. Anger I can handle, pet."

"But the others you cannot?" Still pissed, she snapped the question at me.

"The truth?" If this little bird could show me her anger, then maybe I could show her mine.

"You have been lying before?"

"No." Evading. "But having seen you fearful, knowing his intent and witnessing his treatment of you." I nodded at her wrist. "This is no longer about me simply handling your emotions." We were way beyond that. "This is about me planning."

Her voice went quiet. "Are you saying you are going to hurt him?"

"Would it make you walk away from him if I said yes?"

She faced the window again. "We already had this conversation."

"No, we didn't, not this exact one."

"There are no shades of my decision. It stands."

Fuck, I wanted to dominate this gorgeous woman. "I'm asking you to look at me." I wanted to get her on the mats, have her throw everything she had at me, and I wanted to fucking feel it. But more than my own screwed-up shit, I wanted to see her goddamn fight for herself.

Doing as I asked, she turned and gave me her eyes. "You are asking for much more than my attention when you speak to me."

"You're right." I hadn't even kissed the woman, but I wanted everything with her. "I'm asking for your trust."

In a move I should've seen coming because I'd left myself wide open, she set a trap using my own damn negligence. "If you had wanted me to trust you, then you would have taken me to Westchester. Since you are unwilling to do that, then take me to Joseph's home in Miami."

Outmaneuvered by both her seeing right through my bullshit and another piece of missed intel, I didn't have much of a choice. If I wanted to get her on the Gulfstream and get her the fuck out of here, there was only one way to play this.

"Fine," I agreed, pulling back into traffic.

"Thank you," she politely murmured.

I didn't reply.

In a few hours, she was going to hate me again. She could have exactly as much time in that prick's house as it took for him to get his ass down to Florida. Then fuck consequences, I was pulling her out.

Physically if I had to.

TWENTY-FIVE

Sabine

Vance did not speak another word as he drove us to the airport in New Jersey.

Pulling up next to a black sedan parked in front of a private jet that looked fancier than the sports car we were in, Vance turned off the ignition.

The back passenger door of the sedan opened, and a beautiful woman got out. With a seductive smile, she walked straight toward the driver's side of our car as a man, almost as muscular as Vance, came down the stairs of the private jet.

"Wait, love." Grabbing my laptop, Vance got out of the car and shut the door behind him.

As he spoke to the woman, the man approached them.

Vance handed the handsome but austere-looking man my laptop, and he retreated back onto the plane without acknowledging the woman.

The woman barely glanced at the man before looking back at Vance with her flirtatious smile as she touched his arm.

Vance said something else.

The woman threw her head back and laughed.

A pang of jealousy I was not expecting broadsided me, and I had to look away. Before I could process the sinking feeling in the pit of my stomach, Vance was opening my door with a serious expression. "This way, love. Let's get you on the plane."

I glanced between him and the woman still standing on the

other side of the car. I wanted to ask who she was, and I wanted to know what he had said that had made her laugh. I wanted to tell him to not let her on the plane. But mostly, I wanted this awful, stomach-turning, sudden nausea to go away, right along with the woman, because I had never felt like this and I hated it. I hated the other woman touching him and laughing, but I could not say anything about it because I had no right to, which was a worse thought than her touching him.

My mind unraveling, I grasped at the only solid thing I had left of my life. "My bags?" The mere few possessions that, until a moment ago, I had no attachments to because they were all props purchased by a horrible, cruel, dishonorable man who was trying to blame me for crimes I did not commit. But now those bags represented the last tangible part of my life that I had.

"I'll get them." His tone gentle, his hand held out, Vance gave me the full weight of his attentive gaze.

All at once, I knew I'd made a horrible mistake.

I should have trusted this man from the very beginning, but it was too late for that now, and I had to follow this through. Joseph may or may not keep his word about letting me walk away *free and clear*, but I kept holding on to the one thing that he had not done yet. Joseph had not yet broken his original promise. At least, not that I knew of. But that was the crux of all of this.

I would not know if he had.

All I knew was that time was running out—for me, for the deal I made, maybe for the promise Joseph said he would keep.

Slipping my purse on my arm with the injured wrist, I hesitantly took Vance's offered hand.

Vance's gaze briefly cut to my wrist, and his eyes narrowed.

Except I barely noticed it because the moment my hand landed in his, a wave of a thousand tiny shivers raced across the back of my neck and down my arms, electrifying all of my senses. And just like when he had tucked my hair behind my ear, my stomach dipped. It was everything I could do not to audibly catch my breath.

I needed distance from him.

But Vance Conlon did not step back.

Towering over me, ignoring the woman and the busy airport all around us, he lowered his head and locked his gaze on me. Warm and intimate, his breath touched my face a second before his quietly concerned voice erased the tangible space between us. "Your wrist?"

I was not thinking about my wrist.

I was not even thinking about Joseph or Miami or the laptop or how much trouble I was in if this all fell apart.

I was drowning in this man and his masculine scent that smelled more like home than my best memories.

I should have told him I was fine. I should have stepped back. I should have insisted he take me to Westchester.

But I did none of that.

I looked into his amber-green eyes, and I gave away a piece of me I did not have to give by showing a side of me I could not afford to show. "Who is that beautiful woman?"

As if unconcerned by my question or that I was asking it at all, he answered immediately. "Her name is Gigi, her fiancé is Gerard, and the only beautiful woman I'm looking at is you."

The dip in my stomach turned into a fluttering storm as he called me beautiful, but that storm did not stop the tightness in my chest. "You made her laugh," I accused.

The back of his fingers barely coasted across my cheek before he brushed my hair from my face like we were intimate lovers and he touched me all the time. "Would you like me to make you laugh?"

Would I? Did I know how anymore? If I said yes, would he think I trusted him? There was no good answer to his question, but the woman I used to be wanted to give him the carefree response.

As if reading every vulnerable thought going through my mind, he cupped my cheek and gave me a smile I had not seen on him before. Unassuming, wary, it barely crested his beautifully full lips. "How about I start small?"

"Meaning?"

"I make you smile first." With a wink, he released my cheek and grabbed my two suitcases before tossing the car key to the pretty woman. "Thank you, Gigi."

She caught it midair and smiled at both of us. "Anytime, Mr. Conlon." She nodded at me. "Mrs. Bertrand."

One hand on the bags, his other on my back, Vance paused and glanced at me as his eyebrows drew together. "Since you asked me who she was, I'm assuming you've never met Gigi before?"

"No." I would have remembered her.

"Right." His frown deepened before he glanced behind us and called out to the other woman. "*Gigi.*"

About to get into the sports car, she stopped and walked toward us instead as the black sedan pulled away. "Yes?"

"How do you know Miss Malcher?" Vance demanded.

The woman's smile dropped, and she blanched as she looked at me. "Oh, I'm so sorry. I just, I mean, I assumed because…." She glanced at the ring on my left hand. "Well, my apologies. It's a lovely piece of jewelry by the way." She smiled sheepishly. "Anyway, I've seen you lunch frequently with Mr. Bertrand at the Gramercy. My office isn't far from there. I've also caught a few auctions at Harrington's and saw you with him. I'm sorry again for the assumption."

When Vance said nothing, I answered her. "There is nothing to apologize for."

The woman smiled. "Do either of you need anything else?"

Still frowning, but now looking angry, Vance ignored the woman and turned me back toward the private jet. "Let's go, love."

I walked up the airstairs.

TWENTY-SIX

Vance

I DIDN'T KNOW IF I WAS MORE PISSED THAT A WOMAN WHO RENTS CARS who'd never met Sabine knew her as that fuck's wife, or the fact that we missed her existence in the first place. More than that, shit was adding up, and every new piece of the puzzle was pissing me off worse.

Following Sabine's sweet ass up the airstairs not helping with my mood, I issued her orders like she was my goddamn subordinate the second she stepped onto the plane. "Through the galley and take a seat. Buckle in." I stowed her bags as she wordlessly did as I said, taking the closest seat.

His gaze on Sabine as she adjusted her seat belt, Zulu stepped out of the cockpit. "Hey."

I lowered my voice. "How much lead time do we have over a flight leaving Westchester for Miami at oh four hundred?"

Zulu glanced at his watch. "Couple hours, maybe." He looked back at Sabine. "Why?"

"Just wondering how long I have before I commit murder." That fucking prick Bertrand.

Zulu focused on me. "What's going on?"

Instead of reining my shit in, I stupidly kept talking. "Not one goddamn person at AES knew Sabine existed, but a single glance and Gigi not only knew her, she called her Mrs. Bertrand. *Gigi*," I repeated, my hands going to my hips.

"So? Everyone knows Harrington's, and Gigi knows everyone because she fucks everyone."

"Exactly," I bit out.

Zulu stared at me a beat. Then he grinned. "You think Gigi fucked Bertrand."

"How the hell else would she know about Sabine, and wipe that goddamn smile off your face or I'll do it for you."

Zulu laughed. "I'm writing this shit down. The great Vance Conlon falls for a married woman and is pissed that her husband cheated on her. Wait. That is why you're angry, right? Not the other way around, that Bertrand fucked your Gigi?"

"Gigi's not my goddamn anything, and now I'm planning two murders."

Zulu laughed harder as he slapped me on the shoulder. "Tell November to get his ass up here. Echo's one minute out and we need to be wheels up."

"I need November to work on her laptop. I'll take second chair."

"Negative, handle your client." Zulu tipped his chin toward Sabine. "You may not currently notice the tension radiating off her like she's about to toss her cookies because you're too damn busy being a jealous dick, but I do. Go calm her down. I don't need some woman puking at thirty thousand feet, no matter how beautiful she is." He retreated into the cockpit.

Echo took the airstairs two at a time before stepping aboard. "We all here?"

"Yeah." I glanced back at Sabine as she studiously looked out the window.

"Good, closing her up." He secured the hatch, then knocked against the open door to the cockpit twice. "Zulu, cabin secure."

"Copy that." Zulu started the engines. "Get November up here."

"Ten-four," Echo replied before glancing at Sabine and

lowering his voice. "No movement. Bertrand was still in his office when I left, but something's up."

Dragging my attention away from her, I looked at Echo. "What kind of something?" Did she put two and two together about Gigi and her fucking piece of shit *husband*?

"The kind that had a dozen private security rent-a-cop dicks coming and going, doing perimeter checks and not letting anyone use the valet service after you left."

I mentally went back over the event list Bertrand had rattled off to me in his office. "He told me to get her down to Miami for the preview party. There was no mention of an event in New York tonight. Why would he need extra security there?"

"Don't know. Delusional paranoia?"

His sarcasm wasn't that far off the mark. "You're sure it was for Harrington's?"

Echo leveled me with a look. "For the record, this is me giving you one fucking pass, but this will be the last time I put up with you questioning my shit. I'm not the one picking fights for sport so I can take a beating. It's Harrington's. I watched the elevators. The dicks were coming and going from the top floor, and before you ask that next question, the answer is no."

Fucking prick. "I didn't ask anything else." Not yet, but if someone noticed him, he would be useless to me tonight at the preview party.

"I'm telling you anyway. No, no one noticed me. That's what I mean when I said rent-a-cop dicks. They weren't trained. They weren't watching their backs. They had one objective with myopic vision, and not one of them looked twice at me. When I tell you something, listen to what I'm saying."

Fucking Teams guys. "You mean learn to speak Echo?"

"If that's what it takes."

"Hey," Zulu interrupted as he backed the plane up. "Was I talking to myself? Get November up here. We're cleared to taxi."

"Take second chair," I ordered Echo. "I need November."

"No fucking way. I'm not a flyboy."

"Get comfortable being uncomfortable. Adapt and overcome," I quipped, spouting SEAL mottos as I moved past Echo, giving zero fucks that it was known throughout AES he hated to be in the cockpit. "And for the record, flyboys are Air Force. The Navy has aviators."

"Conlon," Echo barked.

Christ. "What?"

"I know what a pilot is called, asshole, and you fucking owe me for this."

"Right. I'll be sure to remember that." I walked to Sabine. "Can I get you anything?"

Turning away from the window, she glanced up at me, then looked away again. "You lied to me."

I sat. "About?"

"He wasn't a car enthusiast."

Ah. "No, he isn't. Echo works for AES."

"Echo?"

"Yes." All of us at AES went by our call signs, some leftover from our service, others inherited along the way. I had no fucking idea why I'd given her my real name, except that it'd felt like the right thing to do, and I didn't regret it. "Echo was my backup. Zulu's the pilot, and November's working on your laptop."

"My laptop," she repeated, still staring out the window.

"Yes. Bertrand indicated all the security breaches originated from your laptop." The clock ticking until we touched down in Miami, I needed to talk with November.

Her right hand covering her left wrist, she pulled her arms closer toward herself. "And Alpha, who is he?"

So she'd been listening to my conversation with Trefor. "The owner of AES."

"Alpha, Echo, November, Victor, Zulu," she quietly listed. "All the phonetic alphabet."

And the military alphabet. "It would appear so," I answered vaguely.

"You were angry when that woman recognized me."

Zulu taxied to the runway, and the engines whined as he gave them more thrust.

Sitting in the seat facing her, I used the time to secure my seat belt to formulate my response. "I was angry, but not at you."

"You were mad at Joseph."

With no intonation in her voice and her eyes directed toward the window, I didn't know if I wanted to shake the fuck out of her or grab her and kiss her until she gave me a goddamn reaction that wasn't as tight as her dress.

Tired of this bullshit, I turned the tables. "Why do you think I'd be angry with a man who provokes your fear, abuses his dominance and will over you, and uses physical force with intent to harm?"

Zulu lined up the Gulfstream for takeoff.

She didn't so much as blink at what I'd accused Bertrand of. "That is not why you were angry with him in that moment."

Right. "Isn't it?"

"No." She turned and met my gaze. "You think Joseph slept with that woman, and I think you slept with her."

The Gulfstream's engines came to life and the plane took off.

TWENTY-SEVEN

Sabine

I turned to face Vance exactly like he had said he preferred, and I said something I never, *ever* would have said to Joseph, not unless I wanted to pay for it. "You think Joseph slept with that woman, and I think you slept with her."

The private jet's engines roared, and I was pushed back in my seat as the plane took off.

His eyes, still more amber than green in the muted light of the plane's cabin, held me captive in his intense gaze.

Afraid of what he might say, terrified he would confirm my suspicions about him and that woman, angry that I was so jealous I wanted to cry, I bottled everything up and turned toward the window because that was what I did.

I hid.

I let everything important go.

I never spoke my mind.

I pretended. I compartmentalized. I survived, and I did it to feel as safe as I could.

But this didn't feel safe.

I saw Vance's anger, and it felt a thousand times worse than when Joseph was angry, and yet, it was not fear I was feeling. It was hurt.

Horrible hurt.

"Sabine."

My heart skipped a beat, but then it came alive at the way he said my name. Like I was something to be cherished, someone to be valued and taken care of—someone he respected.

Out of the corner of my eye, I saw him lean forward, and I wanted to lean back to protect myself from something that I could not stop from happening, but it was already too late. My heart was reaching for him, and he was reaching for me.

Two of his fingers gently touched my chin, but he did not apply pressure, not like Joseph would have. "I'd like you to look at me, love. I want to see your eyes when I speak to you."

In the intimacy of the private jet's cabin, I could almost imagine we were alone, but we were not. There were three other imposing, large, muscular men on board who looked nothing like the men Joseph hired as security. These men were all intimidating, and they had an air about them that said they were as lethal as they were handsome, especially the tallest one he called Echo. But he was not who I was nervous about.

The man with the unusual eyes who had taken my laptop and who was now sitting behind us—there was something about the way he had looked at me when I had walked aboard. Staring directly at me like he saw things I could not see, he had made me nervous.

I did not want him to hear this conversation.

And I knew he could hear us. As sure as I could hear some of what the pilot had been saying to Vance before we had taken off. I knew it before the man he had called Zulu had said it. I had suspected right away when the young, beautiful woman had called me Mrs. Bertrand that she knew Joseph. Not only was she his type, but I'd had seven years of fielding those exact same scenarios.

The accidental meeting of women Joseph had slept with.

I had crossed paths with dozens of women like her, and maybe I should have been upset by it, or even ashamed, but I told myself the same thing I had been telling myself since the first time it had happened. It took the pressure off me.

It gave me a brief reprieve.

And sometimes, on a very rare occasion, those women had put Joseph in a good mood, and I had benefitted. A quiet evening, a nonconfrontational conversation, a surprise gift, a moment to breathe without fear, I had selfishly taken every one of them.

If Vance wanted me to look at him and show him any kind of remorse or anger over it, I could not do it. But maybe, this once, I could look at a man and give him the truth.

Except it would not be without consequence.

Nothing about this Marine turned mercenary would leave me without consequences. The cost would be my heart, and the penalty would be a life I could never have.

Knowing that, I still made the decision. I started to turn my head.

Dominant and commanding, yet respectful as if he knew every second of the self-imposed hell I had been living, Vance's fingers grasped my chin and he took over my decision.

He turned me to face him.

But the moment his beautiful, complicated eyes met mine, I knew I had made a grave mistake.

His thumb stroked across my cheek with the gentlest, most possessive caress I had ever received. Then Vance Conlon broke my heart.

"I did sleep with her."

TWENTY-EIGHT

Vance

I ADMITTED THE TRUTH BECAUSE I DIDN'T WANT TO LIE TO THIS WOMAN. "I did sleep with her. I've slept with a lot of women." But not one of them mattered to me right now like she did.

Her face fell and she dropped her gaze, robbing me of her eyes.

"Don't look away," I selfishly demanded, lifting her chin. "I'm not going to lie to you, and I won't insult you with platitudes, but, love, I am asking you for something else. Something that doesn't have to do with either of our pasts."

"Which is?" she quietly asked.

Not telling me to fuck off, politely or not, or giving me a dozen other responses that would've been justified, this elegant, beautiful woman showed me again how much I didn't deserve to be having this conversation. Let alone the fantasies I was having of stripping her, not naked, but as bare as she was right now.

She couldn't be more vulnerable in this moment if she'd tried, and I didn't believe for one second that she fully understood that. It was what made her so absolutely exquisite.

"I'm asking for trust," I admitted.

Like a fucking sunrise, she lifted her head, and her gorgeous eyes met mine. "Your list of conquests is not how to get it."

That mouth.

Those eyes.

This woman.

If she only knew how true the fourth word in her sentence was, she wouldn't be upset. "You're right." Conquests weren't exquisite. "But telling you the truth is."

"Like you told me the truth about the man you call Echo?"

"That was before," I argued.

"Before what?" she demanded, holding her own against me in a way she didn't with that asshole Bertrand, which stupidly made me feel fucking special to her.

"Before I had you on this plane with your bags packed." Because that was a victory I wasn't going to ignore.

"Vance—"

"I need you to listen to me." Leaning closer, I focused on her eyes but I wanted her mouth. Hell, I wanted any piece of this woman I could get. "This started the moment I laid eyes on you, Sabine." Glancing my thumb across her cheek, I stroked under her bottom lip and wondered how long it would take me to unravel her. "I think you know that."

November appeared in the aisle beside me. "A word?"

Not letting go of her, not taking my eyes off her, I answered November. "In a minute."

"It's important," he insisted.

Pulling out of my grasp, Sabine turned back toward the window. "Go."

I stood and spared November a glance. "Back of the plane. Wait for me."

November retreated.

Raising the table between the two seats, I leaned over and crossed a goddamn line because I was out of time. Grabbing her chin, I brought her eyes to me. "I meant every word I said, and I'm still going to mean it no matter what I find on that computer. But I told you, I'm not him. That means I'm not going to take from you. I'm not going to hurt you, and I'm not going to force you to do anything you don't want, no matter what. That includes

VICTOR

my advances. If you tell me I'm imagining this, or that it's one-sided, then no hesitation, I back off. You tell me to walk slow, I'll keep pace. You tell me you want Bertrand out of your life this second, consider it done. No matter what you choose, I made you a promise and I'm going to keep it. I *will* protect you. Full stop."

Lake-blue eyes framed by dark lashes stared back at me, but this woman said nothing. She didn't so much as blink.

Not trusting her silence any more than I trusted her secrets, I issued a demand. "Give me something, love."

Nothing.

No response.

"Right." Fuck. *Fuck*. Already up to my neck in this, I wanted to take her silence as a win, but I wasn't stupid enough to think her lack of response was a victory any more than if she'd actually said what I'd wanted to hear. "I know I've put you in an impossible situation." But fucking hell, that was exactly what she'd done to me. "However much I'd like to think I'm your better option, I won't pretend that I know exactly what it's like to be in your situation. Think on it." My hands tied, I switched gears. "In the meantime, what would you like to drink, or should I choose?"

This time she did answer. "Water, thank you."

She looked like she needed something stronger. Hell, I needed something stronger. "We have wine, red or white."

"I have not eaten. Water is fine, please."

Christ, I was an asshole. "Of course."

Taking off my suit jacket and tossing it on a seat, I went to the galley. I grabbed water, a glass, some prepackaged snacks, a sandwich, two napkins and two instant cold packs out of the first aid kit before returning to her. Dumping the water, glass and food in front of her, I activated both cold packs.

"May I see your wrist, love?"

She glanced at the food, then looked at me.

I held up the cold packs. "This will help, promise."

Averting her gaze, she gingerly placed her left forearm on the small table.

That I did take as a victory. "Thank you, pet." Taking her hand and carefully pushing her sleeve up, I placed the cold packs on the top and bottom of her wrist, then wrapped one of the cloth napkins around them and gently rested her wrist back on the table. "Once you eat, I'll give you some anti-inflammatory medicine."

"This is fine, thank you."

It wasn't fine. I should've taken care of her wrist the moment I saw it. "I'll refrain from making a comment about that little *f* word." Opening the water, I poured her a glass. Then I opened the sandwich and placed the napkin next to her. "Eat, love. I'll be back in a minute."

Knowing I wasn't going to like one damn word of whatever November had to say, I walked toward the aft cabin and took a seat across from him.

November looked up from her laptop, but he didn't say shit, he just stared at me.

Fuck. "That bad?"

He glanced over my shoulder, then back at me. "You like her."

My muscles tensing, I filtered my response. "What's not to like? She's beautiful and she's in trouble."

"That's your prerequisite?"

Fighting for patience, I inhaled. "Considering this is the longest personal conversation we've ever had, I'll bite." I wanted whatever intel he'd found, and I wanted it yesterday, but one thing I'd learned about November was that when he didn't want to speak about a particular subject, you waited. "No, it's not a prerequisite. In this instance, I just happened to get lucky. I told you mine, now tell me yours. What'd you find?"

He turned the laptop around. "Nothing at first, until I dug deeper."

I glanced at the screen and skimmed.

Then I stopped short.

Pulling the laptop closer, I read it again.

Sabine Malcher. Twenty-seven. Father, janitor, dead. Mother, housekeeper, dead. Brother, construction worker, dead. All within months of each other. One after the other. Then a nineteen-year-old Sabine walks into the Harrington's in Paris and seemingly never came out.

Jesus Christ.

I looked up at November. "Any of this strike you as odd?"

"All of it is odd." November rattled off the stats of her background from memory because that's what he did. If he read something once, he remembered it—word for word. "Father, deceased, aged fifty-three. Mother, deceased, aged forty-eight. Brother, deceased, aged twenty-seven. October twelfth, February twenty-eighth, March fourth. Traffic accident, car accident, motorcycle accident."

I'd known November long enough to understand how he thought. He was a genius. Literally. Numbers were his love language and inconsistencies were the bane of his existence. I knew he'd seen what I saw, and statistically, Sabine's background was quite the anomaly, but I was looking at the bigger picture. "I'm talking specifically about those photos of Sabine walking into Harrington's in Paris seven years ago and nothing on her since." No paper trail, no passport renewal, no driver's license, no lease, no property, no cell phone, no bills in her name, no bank accounts, nothing. It was as if the last image of her caught by a Harrington's security cam was the last evidence of her existence.

"Maybe they're not all dead," November stated.

It hadn't crossed my mind, but it was now. Maybe this was what she was hiding. "Did you look into their deaths?"

November stared at me, but he wasn't seeing me as he rattled off more stats. "Father, hit and run, crosswalk, no reliable witnesses. Death certificate, burial plot, paper trail on funeral expenses. Mother, auto accident, brake failure, older vehicle. Death certificate, burial plot, no paper trail of burial or funeral expenses. Brother, motorcycle accident, downed power line, accidental beheading. Death certificate, cremation, no funeral, no burial plot. All of which, including her background, was hidden under enough layers of encryption not to be coincidental."

What the fuck was going on? "When did she walk into Harrington's?" I scanned the screen again.

"Which time? She went twice in one day."

I toggled between the pictures then noticed it. The lighting was slightly different in the first few pictures. "What day?"

"March fourth, seven years ago. First time was ten-thirty-six a.m. Second time was four-fifty-one p.m."

Jesus Christ. "The day of her brother's death." I zoomed in on one particular picture in the second set of images.

"Bookending her brother's TOD," November corrected.

I glanced at November. "What time did he die?"

"Accident report states his body was found outside city limits, on a stretch of country road just before thirteen hundred hours."

"Coincidental?"

"Do you want the hypothetical or real answer?"

I didn't bother answering November. "Fuck, this is stacking up." Shaking my head, I focused on the screen. "What the hell was she doing?" I asked absently as I zoomed in further on an image in the second set.

"Selling jewelry."

The photo was grainy, but I could still see it. Her ankles, both of them, were bruised all to hell like she'd been restrained or put up a good fight.

Exiting out of the photo, I looked at November. "You're sure?"

He turned the computer around, typed, then turned it back

to face me again. On the screen was a picture of the ring she currently had on her left hand. "She's wearing that now."

I'd noticed. "She was trying to sell it?"

November gave a clipped nod. "That and four other diamonds, loose, same cut, almost exactly like the one set in the ring. I found an old Harrington's file that logged the inquiry on the pieces—one ring, four loose diamonds ranging from five to eight carats, but there was no appraisal, and no sale or auction was ever recorded."

So Bertrand took her jewelry in exchange for what? Fucking keeping her? Covering something up? Blackmailing her? "What do we know about the ring?" Why the fuck was she bruised to hell when she'd walked into Harrington's? And how the hell had a nineteen-year-old from a working-class family come up with five diamonds?

"It looks like it could be vintage." November turned the computer back around and started typing again. "I've not seen it up close, but the design and cut of the diamond are similar to a piece made almost a century ago by a well-known designer from a famous jewelry house. There were supposed to be a dozen rings made in a limited run, but the designer passed away before that happened. So the ring could be authentic, but more likely is a replica."

Replica. Right. Just like the fucking painting hanging in Bertrand's living room. "Estimated value?"

"I don't know what the ring would go for because it's never been up for sale, and there's no recorded owner of it, and no trail on it other than the photo in the original advertisement by the jewelry house. But I'd estimate the diamond alone is worth half a million."

Enough to kill for, or be killed for. "Twelve rings you said?"

"Yes."

I leaned back in my seat. "So they would've needed twelve large diamonds."

"Assuming so."

"What do you think the value would be if you had all eleven of those diamonds and the ring?"

November glanced at me. "You mean if she had them."

I shrugged. "Or if the jewelry house was still holding on to them."

"They aren't, or they aren't advertising that they are. I already checked." November's gaze drifted for a beat. "As for all of the diamonds, minimum six, seven million. To a collector, who knows?"

My guess was at least ten million, especially if the ring was part of the deal. "Did you look into Bertrand's financials?"

"It's on my list. I checked Harrington's, and they aren't as flush as you'd expect. They're spread pretty thin, but they're not in danger of going under. Bertrand's used a lot of capital over the years to grow the business to include all of their current locations."

It didn't surprise me that the fuck had spread the Harrington's brand too thin. "Bertrand said there would be a quarter of a billion in potential sales at this weekend's auctions. What's Harrington's cut on that?"

"Thirteen percent."

I did the math. "Roughly thirty-two million gross, or twenty-one million net after taxes. Add in five global locations and overhead and I'm guessing profit would be half that."

"At best," November agreed.

"That's not much compared to the value of those diamonds if they were in one person's hands and sold under the table." And Sabine presumably had five of those diamonds at one point. "Makes me wonder what happened to the other seven diamonds." Which I could've asked her about, and I would, but not yet. Bertrand was definitely setting her up for something. The only question was what. I needed more intel and a solid plan to extract her.

November glanced at me. "I'm more interested in who was watching me trace the hack on Harrington's servers after looking into the allegations you said she's being accused of." He turned the laptop to face me again. "None of which originated from this laptop or New York."

I scanned the screen.

Halfway down, I saw it. Then I fucking stared, seeing the same exact thing November had seen. The pieces started falling into a pile of shit so deep, I didn't have a roadmap for this, let alone a compass. Not that it mattered. This assignment didn't just implode, it went FUBAR.

"Jesus." I looked at November. "French military intelligence? Why the hell would they hack an auction house in New York to plant a bogus trail of corporate espionage? Unless…." *Fuck.* "Is she still a French citizen?" Christ, was she DGSE?

"Two years ago she became a US citizen, and DGSE wouldn't leave a trail if they had planted evidence, but they were definitely in Harrington's servers."

I exhaled, but only marginally. "Could this be about someone in her family? The brother?"

November turned the screen around, typed and faced it back to me.

I stared at a whole new level of fucked. "You should've led with this."

"I don't have confirmation that these photos are her brother."

"But you know what the hell this is." I pointed at the grainy photo on the screen. "*This* isn't supposed to exist. That rogue, black-ops company of Legionnaire mercenaries was supposed to have been taken out by their own government. All of them eliminated when they went freelance."

Nothing in November's expression changed. "There're a lot of off-the-books military operations that aren't supposed to exist."

"Those fucks may have started out as soldiers, but they weren't military," I argued. "Loyal to no country, they went after the money. They didn't give a fuck what terrorists they got in bed with."

November didn't say shit.

"Jesus. How the fuck is she tied up in this?" I toggled back and forth between some of the photos of the brother November had dug up. "Please tell me you covered your tracks after you found this shit." I had more questions than answers now, but I did know one thing. If Bertrand was on to any of this, he'd have a host of shit to hold over Sabine's head, let alone implicate her on.

"I never leave a trail." November turned the laptop back to face him, typed something, then shut it down. "We need to talk to her."

No wonder Sabine wasn't walking the fuck away or saying shit. I'd be goddamn cagey too if I was her. Stolen diamonds could fund a hell of a lot of bad shit, and stealing them would've been right up her brother's alley. Using Bertrand to fence them with Sabine as either a consolation prize or leverage wasn't only fucked, it was FUBAR if those mercenaries were still alive. You can't fight men who have a death wish. I should know. Fuck. *Fuck.* "Do you realize what we're potentially looking at?"

"Yes," November stated in his usual monotone.

"You've seen this before?" Christ, of course he had. This was what he'd done in the Air Force. Hell, what he still did, but under a fake identity even I couldn't hack no matter how many times I'd tried. But this shit we were looking at now—*fuck*, this was bad.

"Yes," was all November admitted to.

My sleepless night and everything else catching up to me, I scrubbed a hand over my face. "Okay, I'm not asking for details about your experience with this, because I know you can't tell me, but how deep do you think this is?"

November stared at me a beat before his usual stark expression locked down. "Deep." He stood. "I alerted Alpha. He'll be waiting when we land." He grabbed her laptop. "We're out of time. I'll question her."

"The hell you will." No fucking way. "I'll ask what needs to be asked, and nothing more. If she is in the dark on this, we're not dragging her into it further with information that could put an even bigger target on her back."

For the first time since I'd met the quiet hacker, November showed me the man behind the story Zulu had told me.

Leveling me with a lethal look, he fucking unloaded. "Find your objectivity and do it now, or you'll be on the floor of this plane in one point three seconds." Without waiting for a response, he aimed for the forward cabin.

"Are you threatening me?"

Turning back to face me, November dropped his voice. "No, I'm making you a promise. If you don't get some perspective, I'll leave you conscious but incapacitated so you can watch me do what you're too emotionally compromised to accomplish."

Rage flooded my veins. "Right." Already tasting blood, I relaxed my posture and took in every inch of his. One hand holding her laptop, the fucker was insane if he thought he had me. I would level him faster than he could drop that computer, which I was betting he wouldn't do because I knew what made him tick. "That's your kink? Watching others do what you can't?" Every asshole I'd ever met projected. "You think you can take me down, tie me up, and make me watch?"

The fuck didn't even blink. "This isn't like any of your previous AES assignments. Attempting to handle this how you do everything else will get the woman killed. I'm stepping in. Work as part of the team or stand down."

"You're a team player now?" I asked, aiming to insult the one person at AES who should've understood working alone.

Instead, Nathan "November" Rhys threw the dig right back at me. "I'm the team player who's going to question the woman in trouble who's sitting by herself while you feed your psychoses." Lowering his voice even further, he aimed his final blow. "Then I'm going to do what you're currently incapable of. I'm going to help her."

November walked to the front of the cabin and took the seat across from Sabine.

"*Fuck me*," I muttered before following the asshole.

TWENTY-NINE

Sabine

BARELY ABLE TO EAT PAST THE KNOT IN MY STOMACH, I HAD MADE it only partway through half the sandwich when November sat down across from me. As he placed my laptop on the table between our seats, Vance perched on the arm of the seat across the aisle.

"Miss Malcher, I need to ask you a few questions." November spoke in a low voice that was so austere it frightened me in a way Joseph never had.

I glanced at Vance.

His eyes darker and more somber than mere moments ago when he had caressed my face and told me he wanted my trust, Vance crossed his arms and gave me a slight lift of his chin. His biceps stretching the seams of his dress shirt, his intent stare gave nothing away.

I looked back at the man across from me.

I was not ignorant. I knew what they were doing. Vance had not gotten answers from me, so now it was November's turn. Learning a long time ago it was better to seemingly agree to play along than offer resistance, I gave consent. "All right."

Opening my laptop, November typed for a moment, then turned the computer so the screen faced me. "Is this you?"

I looked at a picture that filled the whole screen. In a dress I no longer owned, with an expression that made my heart hurt, I looked at another lifetime. "Yes."

Reaching around the computer with a large hand, November's long finger touched a key as if he knew where it was in his sleep. The image changed. "And this?"

I glanced at myself leaving Harrington's in Paris seven years ago. "May I ask where you got these?"

"Answer the question, please." November clicked again.

A level of panic I did not know existed crawled into my body, tightening every muscle as I stared at my past self entering a tenement block in the nineteenth arrondissement. "Yes, that is me. What is the point of this?"

Ignoring my question, November clicked and the image changed again, but this time it was not me. "This is your brother."

Anxiety threatening to stop my heart, I did not look at Vance. I did not even look at the man across from me that I had foolishly underestimated when I had first gotten on the plane. I stared at what I had lost, and I answered even though his last statement was not a question. "Yes," I whispered. "That was my brother."

Another depression of his finger and a new picture appeared.

This time, the man across from me said nothing.

He did not have to.

My sharp inhale of breath gave me away as I looked at an image I had never seen, one that the possibility of had never crossed my mind. "No," I barely breathed as shock collided with disbelief.

November clicked again.

Another image.

He clicked again. And again.

Picture after picture, I stared.

Speechless, dismayed, dread crawled up my throat.

November's finger kept hitting that dreaded key as impossible images filled the screen. The uniforms, clothing, they changed, but the man in them did not, and I wondered how I could have been so naïve.

VICTOR

"Stop." This could not be true. "This is not possible." That was not my brother. It couldn't have been. "Henri was a construction worker. He worked hard." My voice broke. "He drove a motorcycle." He did not carry guns and kill people. "That, those pictures... No." I reached to close the laptop to make the images stop, but my mind was already putting together the pieces of a horrible picture I had willingly overlooked.

A warm hand closed over mine.

"That is not my brother," I uselessly protested before stupidly trying to defend a man I suddenly realized I never knew. "Henri, he had—" Holding back a sob, I barely stopped myself from saying the one thing I could never, ever say.

"Sabine." Vance's hand tightened on mine.

"He had what?" November asked, his stark gaze penetrating. "A family?"

My mind reeling, barely holding it in as the ramifications of this fell down around me like rubble, I partially lied. "I was his family." My brother had lied about everything.

"Where is the ring from, Miss Malcher?" the man across from me demanded.

"November," Vance clipped. "Enough."

He did not stop. "The other four diamonds, where did you get them?" he asked, his voice growing colder, deeper.

I flinched, then fear froze every muscle in my body.

"I said enough." Vance slammed the laptop closed, grabbed it and handed it to November. "Find me something I can use before we land."

His eyes on me, November stood before finally walking to the back of the plane.

Vance grabbed the food and water off the table and dumped them in the small galley before stowing the table that was between our seats. Then he sat down and took my hands in his. "You didn't know."

They knew about the diamonds. *Oh God,* they knew. But Vance, he was not asking about that right now, so I did what I had always done when I panicked. I tried to shove it all down and focus on one thing in front of me.

Vance.

Asking about my brother.

Did I know?

Did I know?

"*Non.*" I shook my head. "I was told Henri died while on his motorcycle. There was a downed power line across the road. He was going too fast, and he must not have seen it in time. It was an accident." A horrible, unimaginable accident, and I could not bring myself to look at a body with a separated head, so they had shown me his wallet and a picture of his clothes. "I identified him barely an hour after the accident." Then I had told myself over and over it was an accident.

Vance did not say anything, but I saw it in his eyes. Pity.

I hated pity. "Those pictures, what was Henri doing?" Was anything I thought I knew about my brother true?

"We're working on it."

Taking my hands out of his, I turned toward the window. I did not want to ask, but I had to. "Does Joseph know that Henri was part of…?" I did not even know what Henri was. In a Legionnaire uniform in one image, all black in another, in fatigues in another, all of them looked like images taken without his knowledge, like he was in combat. Except the photos that showed him with his gun, standing over bodies, those were not pictures of war—those were evidence of murder.

I looked back at Vance. "What was he?"

Vance stared at me for a long moment, then he told me what I already knew. "The data on your laptop was purposefully planted."

"What does this have to do with Henri?" I demanded. "Why were you showing me those pictures of him?"

VICTOR

"The planted evidence traces back to a particular source."

Money was always tight growing up. We could barely afford cell phones, let alone laptops. "I never saw Henri with a computer, and he has been gone for seven years, so I hope you are not suggesting he was the source."

Still leaning forward in his seat, Vance stared at me.

Every nerve on edge, I wanted to grab him and shake him and demand he tell me what he was not saying. "What source?"

His arms resting on his knees, Vance threaded his fingers together. "DGSE—French intelligence."

"I...." The impossibility died on my tongue, and I blinked.

"Sabine." Grave, unwavering, his intensity focused on me. "You need to tell me everything. Now."

THIRTY

Vance

Fear suffocated her voice. "I do not know anything about that."

She was either the world's best actress, or she actually didn't know the severity of the fucking pressure plate she was standing on.

I didn't know if I was more alarmed that she might not have actionable intel I could work with, or pissed at November for his bullshit.

Wanting to reach for her, my fucking hands laced to keep from touching her, I started with the only tangible thread I could pull at. "Where did you get the ring and diamonds you walked into Harrington's with?"

Her eyes averted, she hesitated a fraction. "They were my mother's."

I watched her face for tells. "Where did she get them?"

Her gaze dropped to her lap.

"Sabine," I warned. "The time for withholding critical information is long gone."

"My brother," she confessed before looking up, but her eyes didn't meet mine. Her gaze focused on something else, she looked past me. "He said he found the ring at a demolition construction site where he was working, and no one claimed it." Her voice dropped to barely a whisper. "I was young. We were poor. I wanted to believe him, and my mother loved the ring, but my brother had said it would be dangerous if she wore it out of the house because of where we lived, so she never did. I did not know about the diamonds until after she passed, and I went looking for the ring to sell it… to pay for a funeral service." Her throat moved with a swallow. "I found the diamonds with the ring in her jewelry box."

Reminding myself why the fuck I was here, I ignored the bullshit her brother had fed her. "Where are the diamonds now?"

"Joseph took them," she said, confirming my suspicion.

"But you kept the ring."

"It was my mother's favorite possession." She absently stroked the expensive jewel. "After finding the other diamonds, I did not see any reason to sell the ring." Her throat moved with a swallow. "Joseph was not pleased, but he let me keep it."

Let her. Fucking bastard. "Did you know the value of the ring and diamonds?"

She stared at the ring. "Not really."

"Did Bertrand mention their origin?" With his background, if anyone would know where they came from, it would be him.

Perfectly still, holding her composure, she looked up, but then she did what she'd been doing since I'd met her. Remaining reserved as fuck, she dished out a single serving of benign truth. "You have to understand, I needed money to lay my mother to rest. I was not thinking about where the diamonds had come from, only how much I could get for them."

"One of the diamonds would've been enough." With a lot to fucking spare.

"Joseph did not want just one, he wanted them all as a set. In fact, he asked me if I had more, and frankly, he did not believe me when I said no."

Of course the self-serving asshole didn't, but at least now we were getting somewhere. "Bertrand didn't mention anything at all about where they came from or their origin?" No fucking way her brother had found those diamonds. He'd stolen them, and Bertrand was probably holding that over her head.

"All Joseph said was that the set would only go for twenty-five thousand euros because there was not proper documentation that they were not stolen. He said he would not put them up for auction because of that, but he would take them off my hands, pay me up front, and try to find a buyer. I needed the money, so I took it."

"The ring alone is worth fifteen times that," I pointed out.

"I was young and desperate. I did not realize what they were worth until much later."

"Did you confront Bertrand about it?" Maybe this was as simple as him trying to get rid of her before she demanded reparations for the jewelry he essentially stole from her.

In a rare show of emotion, anger flashed in her eyes. "What would you have had me say?" Her tone turned condescending, and fuck me, it shouldn't have been sexy. "Joseph, you house me, feed me, clothe me, but please, since I have changed my mind, I would like you to give me the current market value of jewelry I willingly gave to you seven years ago in exchange for a deal I already took and money I already spent." She turned back toward the window and dropped the sarcasm for her usual reserved tone, but this time, her accent was thicker. "Of course I did not confront him about it."

Not wanting to hurt her, but needing to speed this up, I stepped on the pressure plate under her. "Do you want to know the statistical anomaly of losing your entire family within that short of a timeframe?"

"Do not patronize me, nor pretend to understand that level of grief. I will not sit here and listen to it."

Under any other circumstances, I would've been fucking thrilled that she was asserting herself. "I'm not doing either, love. I'm asking if you suspected their deaths were anything other than accidents." The more I thought about it, the more I believed her brother wasn't actually dead, but I was still missing how all of this tied into her now.

Her beautiful but haunted eyes met mine. "I took my mother to the hospital to identify my father's body. I saw the car after my mother's accident."

"Did you ever see your brother's body?"

"I buried him."

"He was cremated," I quietly corrected.

The color drained from her face. "What are you accusing me of?"

"Did you see his body?"

It wasn't a bull snorting before charging, it wasn't even a steroid gym fuck telepathing his next swing with his muscle movements. This was subtle and controlled and mannered, but make no mistake, Sabine Malcher was suddenly irate, and she was aiming at me.

Her back straight, her hands stacked, her eyes laser-focused on mine, she doused me with her own brand of fire. "What would you like me to tell you? That I was nineteen, alone, and could not bring myself to look at a decapitated body the authorities said was my brother? Or that I did not have a job or money and the only thing I could afford after my parents' deaths was the taxi fare to Harrington's? How about how I thought I only needed money for my mother's funeral when I tried to sell the diamonds, so I did not negotiate a better deal, and then my brother died, and I did not have enough to properly bury him? Maybe you would like me to confess to going to the cemetery in the middle of the night, digging into the dirt with my bare hands, and then pouring my brother's ashes in a shallow hole above my mother's remains. Would you *prefer* I look at you as I tell you that? Would you like to *see my eyes* when I say I had less than a week before the police would come to evict me from the apartment where I had lived my whole life but could no longer afford to stay in because the rent had not been paid since my father passed? Or how I did not have the luxury to keep any of the items in that apartment because I had nowhere to take them, and no one to take them to?" Her chest rose with a fury-induced inhale before she carefully enunciated her next words, owning every damn one of them. "I was alone, Mr. Conlon. I made choices."

"What did Bertrand offer you?"

"I already told you," she bit out angrily. "Twenty-five thousand euros."

"After that?"

"Everything I already told you."

She hadn't told me shit. "Say it."

"He bought me, is that what you want me to say? I am bought and paid for with a penthouse in Manhattan, the clothes on my back and the restaurants he takes me to. And I stayed all these years because at any moment he could tell the authorities I tried to sell him stolen diamonds. Is that what you want me to say?"

Not one fucking bit, but she was lying about what he had over her, and I was feeding an anger I had no claim in but was taking ownership of anyway, so I asked the next question like a goddamn martyr. "And the bed you slept in?"

Fury emanating off her, her jaw tight, she aimed. "Why don't you say it?"

"Would you like me to?" I challenged.

"You seem to have all the answers."

"Only one matters. Do you want to hear it?" It wasn't a question. I was throwing down the gauntlet, but if she were smart, she'd see it for the lethal warning that it was. I fucking fed off high stakes and even higher risks. Every breath I took was for control. The beast in me lived for this kind of challenge, and she had no idea who she was stepping in the ring with.

VICTOR

"You will do it anyway, so say what you will," she flippantly replied, sealing her own fate.

"Ask," I demanded with total fucking dominance.

For three seconds, she didn't move, she didn't blink.

Then her posture changed, her expression steadied and she fucking unfurled. "Say it."

I didn't hesitate. "He robbed you, imprisoned you and abused you." Leaning to her ear, I dropped my voice. "Now he's going to pay for that. Painfully."

THIRTY-ONE

Sabine

"ASK," HE DEMANDED.

The anger simmering in my veins halted like water hitting a dam, and I froze.

I could not breathe, I could not think, I could not move.

Perverse and twisted and sick, seductive awareness was spreading across my body and settling low in my belly before I could comprehend what this man was doing to me.

As if he held the keys to my anxiety, as if his voice alone was made to shelter my fears, he blanketed me in his dominance, and all I could do was utter two words.

"Say it."

Threatening and low and so thick with controlled aggression that I could taste it, he listed every transgression another man had committed against me like he was the judge raining down the gavel. "He robbed you, imprisoned you and abused you." His hands tightly clasped between his knees, leaning his tall, muscular frame toward me, he closed the distance between our seats and brought his mouth to my ear. Then he lowered his voice and murmured a murderous promise as seductively as if he were telling me he was taking me to bed. "Now he's going to pay for that. Painfully."

The shiver of sin shuddered up my spine, and for one impossible moment, my heart, my soul, they wept with relief.

But then every broken piece of my mind clamored together

VICTOR

like an angry mob thrust at a chain-link fence keeping them from their fight. All the years of slung insults and put-downs and shameful abuse fused together en masse to battle the wrong side of the war until humiliation escaped across my lips.

"Joseph is not the enemy." I was.

I was my own opposition, and there was nothing this man sitting across from me could do to change that. Joseph could die. I could go to jail. A country I used to call home could brand me a thief and I would still sit here, alone in my quest, keeping a promise I made seven years ago because this was not about my life.

It was sacrifice, and I knew no other way.

"Sabine." Dark and ominous, the only man who had ever tried to help me said my name like a curse, and suddenly I was thrust back to a memory I tried to never, ever think about.

"Sabine!" Henri yelled as he flew into the apartment, slamming the door behind him. "What did you do?" Grabbing my arm tightly, he shook me. "What the hell did you do?"

Tears sprung, and I quickly used my thumb to turn the diamond ring on my finger to face inward so the jewel was hidden. "What do you mean?"

"I told you the ring was to never be taken out of the apartment!" Anger contorting his face, he spit his words at me. "Now you go and do this?"

"I-I don't know what you mean." Shame slid down my cheeks.

"You liar! Where are they?"

Pulling my arm out of his grasp, I tried to hide my hand as I stepped back. "Stop it. I don't know what you are talking about." I had never lied to my brother, but Maman was gone, and she deserved to be buried like Papa, and this had been the only way I knew how.

Zeroing in on the hand I was hiding, Henri grabbed my wrist. When he saw the band on my finger, his fury escalated to rage. "Who did you show this to?"

"No one," I lied again.

"WHO?" Henri demanded.

I cried. I cried for my Papa. I cried for my Maman. I cried for the life I'd had and lost, and I cried because nothing would ever be the same again. But mostly I cried because I was ashamed. "I wanted to bury Maman. I showed a man at Harrington's." My lips, my voice, they quivered. "I asked him how much money he would give me for it. That is all. I did not sell it." Not the ring, but the diamonds, they were already gone.

Like a tree falling in the forest, my brother dropped to the chair Papa had sat in every day after a long day's work. His head fell to his hands, and his voice came out in a strangled rasp. "Do you know what you've done?"

I silently cried harder.

Henri picked his head up and looked at me in utter defeat. "Now they know what I have, and they'll come for me. They'll kill me, Sabine." His voice turned to pure anguish. "They'll kill Julien."

A useless whisper passed my guilty conscience. "I'm sorry. I-I did not know. I just wanted money to bury Maman."

Abruptly standing, Henri looked at me with sheer hatred. "I'll get the money to bury Maman, but if something happens to Julien, this is on you."

"What about Chantel?" A boy needed his mother.

"Why do you think I left her?" he bit out in anger before storming toward the door.

"Wait!" I cried, needing to tell him, but when he glanced over his shoulder, I could not make the rest of the words come out.

"I don't have time to wait. Because of you, I need to go make sure they are safe. Stay here and do not answer the door." Henri's expression turned murderous. "And whatever you do, do not touch the rest of the diamonds. That is the only thing I have left to bargain with."

Vance grasped my chin. "Do you hear me?"

Blinking away my past, I looked at the eyes of a man who was not my brother. "Pardon?"

Lines drew together between Vance's brows. "We're out of

VICTOR

time. When this plane lands, we're exposed. Whoever hacked Harrington's did it with a purpose in mind. Bertrand wants you at the event tonight for a reason. This is coming to a head, Sabine."

"I do not care." My life did not matter.

The side of his jaw clenched, but the rest of his expression remained perfectly composed. "You need to tell me all of it."

I would never tell him.

My brother was dead because of me.

I would not be responsible for them dying as well.

THIRTY-TWO

Vance

I FINALLY SAW IT.

The same damn thing I saw every time I looked in the mirror.

I couldn't believe I'd missed it before, but I was fucking seeing it now. Blatantly staring me in the face.

I was up against a wall.

She was going to protect her secret. Take it to her grave if she had to.

Self-sacrifice came in every damn shape and size imaginable, and I'd tried them all. Pain was my drug of choice. I was an idiot not to realize she was doing the same damn thing. Which only made me angrier. This woman, no matter what she thought she was responsible for, she didn't deserve this.

I was beyond redemption, but this exquisite woman wasn't.

I didn't believe in a damn thing beyond death and pain, but maybe this woman was put in my path because I would understand her fight. I would fight for her. But the only way I saw forward right now was something I had never done, never even considered.

It seemed so goddamn simple.

Tell her my truth.

Show her mine, hope like hell she shows me hers. Then I could do something about it.

Fuck.

VICTOR

Standing on a cliff, I stared at time I didn't have, a woman I couldn't fix and a past I'd never escape.

Taking her good hand, thirty-five thousand feet above the ground, I fucking jumped. "The woman I said you reminded me of?"

Blue eyes the color of the ocean that fateful night landed on me as Sabine Malcher lifted her head and gave me her beautiful gaze.

I gave her a piece of me no one had. "I made a mistake."

THIRTY-THREE

Sabine

"The woman I said you reminded me of?" Both of his strong hands holding mine like he was protecting me, his deep voice quietly shattered me. "I made a mistake."

My heart stalled.

His expression stoic, his voice steady, his hands warm, only his chest rising and falling gave him away. "I was seventeen and stupid."

I was nineteen and stupid.

"I thought I could be the hero."

I thought I was doing right by my mother.

"Every mistake I could make, I made."

I'd made more.

"She deserved… better."

My heart ached. For this woman he spoke of, for whatever happened to her, for him, for my brother, maybe even for me. The whisper escaped, revealing too much. "I'm sorry."

"Not as sorry as I am," he gravely acknowledged.

I had no words.

He had more. "I had seconds to make a decision. Two choices, two sides of a losing coin." His eyes were no longer amber and green but honest and raw. "In the end, I picked the wrong side." He looked at me like he knew my darkest secret. "I think you know something about that."

I did. *Oh God*, I did.

His nod knowing, he pulled one of his hands away from mine only to gently swipe at the tears I did not know were falling down my cheek. "I tried like hell to bury my mistake, but blame isn't a forgiving game, is it?"

My past stuck in my throat, I barely shook my head.

"I know, love." He reverently cupped my face. "But I'm asking you. Don't fall on your sword." His thumb gently stroked the side of my face like he understood my shame. "Let me help you."

I gave him the most blatant honesty I could. "I do not deserve your help."

"I don't know anyone who deserves it more."

That could not possibly be true. "You do not know what I did."

"You're brother's death wasn't your fault."

I sucked in a sharp breath and tried to pull my hand back.

Holding tight, he did not let go of my hand or my face. "You were nineteen. Your parents were gone. You didn't make his motorcycle crash. Tell me what happened. Give me all the details. Let's make this right. You and me." His hold on me tightened. "You have this chance now, Sabine. Take it."

Choking down my own grief and guilt, God help me, I selfishly wanted every word of redemption he was offering. I wanted it more than my next breath. But if I took that breath, I risked theirs.

I could not, would not do that just to appease my own culpability.

Leaning closer, his fingers threaded into my hair. "I see it in your eyes, love." He touched his forehead to mine. "I'm not Bertrand, and I'm sure as hell not anyone's salvation, but I can protect you. I can protect what you're protecting. Give me the reins."

"Vance," I whispered, his name the most intimate word to ever cross my lips.

"Let me do this."

My voice thick, I barely breathed the hint of what I was trying to protect. "I cannot risk their lives."

His chest rose with an inhale, and he took my face in both hands. "Whoever it is, they're already compromised." Leaning back just enough to hold my gaze, he gave me the one reality I never wanted to come true. "Remaining silent may not save them."

Crushing guilt robbing me of all breath, I spoke of the one thing I swore to myself I never would. I gave him my secret. "My brother had a girlfriend, Chantel Blanchet." *God forgive me.* "They had a son." My voice broke. "My nephew. Julien." Tears fell like my now empty promise. "They are in Italy, hiding from whatever my brother had gotten himself into."

His eyes on mine, my secret now in his hands, he merely nodded once. Then the former Marine turned mercenary abruptly stood and walked to the back of the plane.

Seven years of impossible responsibility crushed me, and I doubled over on myself.

Panicked, no breath, the shame came to the surface.

I killed my brother.

This was going to kill his son.

I had a choice. It was the wrong one, and I was making the wrong one again, but I was out of options, and this was too close. Oh God, this was too close.

What have I done?

A tattooed hand holding a glass of amber liquid appeared in my field of vision. "Sit up."

Holding my roiling stomach like it would hold me together, I looked up at the scary man from the valet stand outside Harrington's.

"Drink this," he ordered in a dark voice that was more frightening than his appearance.

Was he listening? "Did you hear?"

"I hear a lot of shit."

"Because you are a soldier?" Was my brother ever a soldier? Did he ever help anyone? Was he all bad?

"I'm what I have to be. Drink." The huge man held the glass closer.

With shaking hands, I undid the seat belt that was suddenly making me feel claustrophobic, and I took the glass. "Do you know?" I stupidly asked like he could possibly know that I was talking about my brother.

Unlike Vance's sinuous movements in his custom suit, this man moved like every flex of his muscles was the conscious calculation of a predator. Lowering his massive body to the seat across from me, he never took his eyes off me. "I know a lot of shit. Like when a woman needs a drink."

Drowning in guilt, I looked away. "I know nothing." Not seven years ago, not now. I was not strong. I was not smart. I had not made one right decision. Everything falling apart, I brought the drink to my lips with shaking hands.

Inked fingers grasped the bottom of the glass and held it steady as he tipped it up. "You held the line."

I took a big swallow, and fire burned a path down my throat and added to my churning stomach. My grip still unsteady, I lowered the drink only a fraction. "I do not know what that means."

"You protected them." He did not let go of the glass. "Drink again."

"*Non*." I took another swallow with his assistance. "I failed them."

"We've all failed at something."

"Not like this." My hands trembling, my stomach burning, I could not drink anymore. No amount of alcohol could dull this pain.

As if he knew I was done, the man Vance had called Echo

took the glass. "Not telling us would've been a bigger mistake." He stood.

I was desperate. I had to ask. I had to know. "Did… did you see the pictures?"

He looked down at me with an expression so hardened that I wondered how much the men on this plane had seen. How much they were concealing, holding in. How much my brother had seen, or if he had ever been like them at all.

"Ask," he commanded.

"Ask what?" I whispered, but I knew what.

"What you want to know, specifically."

"You are going to tell me if I do?" Vance had not told me. November had not either. Why would this man who was not even a part of the conversation that flattened my entire existence tell me the truth?

Remaining perfectly still, no change in his locked expression, this beast of a warrior stood over me without so much as a single breath showing in a rise of his massive chest as he said nothing.

I asked. "Was my brother a soldier or… something else?" When I was a teen, I had heard stories about the secretive, deadly military unit that had gone rogue, but never in my wildest imagination would have thought my brother was a part of that. I had believed him when he had said he was a construction worker who went where the work was. I never questioned his long absences or his muscular physique.

"He made choices," Echo stated cryptically.

Choices. Was that what this was? Too many choices, too little life, too much bad, not enough good—it was all too much and too heavy a burden to carry and protect anymore, but I had to ask. "Did he kill people for profit?"

"Did you?"

A sudden and horrific reality broadsided me.

Oh God.

Henri was dead, and I had made money. "Yes," I whispered, hitting a bottom I never imagined I could surpass seven years ago.

The man named after a mere reflection of sound did not judge me. He did not even say a single word. He merely nodded once as if this was how life was.

Suddenly in the aisle beside us, Vance clipped out a terse command aimed like a bullet at his coworker. "Leave."

His gaze focused on me, Echo downed the rest of the drink he had offered me as if making a point. Then, calm and measured, without any sense of urgency, he turned and made his way back to the cockpit.

Vance waited until the beast of the man was safely out of earshot before he took the seat across from me. His stare as intense as the man who had just walked away, but an altogether different nuance of intensity, he leaned his arms on his knees and locked his hands together. "They're not in Italy."

Unlike Echo, Vance gave me glimpses into himself, and there was no mistaking what I was seeing. I saw it in his eyes. He knew where they were, and it was not good.

Anxiety swirling into fear, I asked the question. "Where are they?"

He paused for a single heartbeat. "Vienna."

THIRTY-FOUR

Vance

Once I'd had the names and given them to November, he'd impressed the fuck out of me.

Two minutes.

Two goddamn minutes and he found where her nephew and his mother were. Or rather where they had been. New names, new identities, carefully crafted with some skill, but not enough that November couldn't find them. The woman and her kid had crossed into Austria exactly one week after those photos of Sabine walking into Harrington's in Paris with bruises on her ankles had been taken.

Then the woman and the kid had fucking vanished. They were either dead, or the woman was a level ten paranoid with skills beyond most trained CIA operatives and was living completely off the grid. Either way, November was doing his thing, but we were looking at a snowball's chance in hell at finding her now unless Bertrand was holding more damn cards than he'd let on.

"The intel we have isn't recent, so we can't definitively confirm she and your nephew are in Vienna, but when you put it together with Bertrand's demand that you accompany him there, I think it's more than coincidental."

Her shoulders deflating, she exhaled. "I am sure there is a reason for Miami too."

Good, we were finally on the same page. "Does your nephew's mother have any more diamonds?"

"I do not know."

"Is there anything being auctioned that isn't listed in the promotion for the event?"

"There usually is, and it is usually a well-guarded secret, but Joseph never divulges that information to me ahead of time. That is part of the promotional hype and client anticipation that drives engagement for the larger auctions. I cannot imagine this particular event will be any different, especially since Harrington's has never done a simultaneous global auction like this before."

I could look it up or ask November, but we were about to land, and I needed to cut to the chase. "How often are the withheld items jewelry?"

She thought for a moment. "Usually they are high-ticket items, something in the high seven figures, or even eight figures. If it were to be jewelry, it would have to be something unique."

Yeah, something unique like the one-of-a-kind ring on her finger and the eleven diamonds that never made it into a limited-run production. "You gave Bertrand all four diamonds seven years ago?"

"Yes."

"Do you know what he did with them?"

"I never saw them again, and he never mentioned it, so I assumed he sold them."

Not yet he hadn't. "Then what happened?"

"Pardon?"

"There's a long line from point A to point B. Seven years ago you had diamonds worth millions, now you're a woman choosing to live in fear."

She blinked. Then her voice dropped to a shocked whisper. "Millions? In dollars?"

"Yes." I laid it all out. "We think the ring you're wearing is a vintage, one-of-a-kind design from a well-known jewelry house, by a famous designer. There were going to be twelve rings made in total and sold as a limited run before the design was retired, but the designer passed away after making only one ring. Presumably there were eleven diamonds waiting in the wings for production. I think you had four of them, and that's what you gave Bertrand. However, if the whole set was recovered, all eleven diamonds combined with your ring, that would sell for an estimated ten million."

Still as hell, she stared at me.

"I'm assuming you didn't know?"

She barely shook her head.

I had to ask. "All the years working at Harrington's, you never looked up your ring?"

Exhaling, she shook her head again. Then she started talking. "I wanted to, but I neither wanted a record of my searches on the company laptop, nor did I want to draw attention to the fact that I was looking up a piece I wore every day."

Which led me to my next question. "You never take it off?" I wouldn't put it past that fuck Bertrand to have a replica made and swap it out on her.

"No, never," she adamantly insisted. "I may have been naïve, but I am not ignorant. I always kept the ring on, and have always had it in my possession."

She paused, but then she finally told me the rest. "He offered me the initial amount I told you about. What I did not say was that he also wanted the ring, but I refused to sell it. I may have been nineteen, but I'd had a lifetime of experience with my brother and men like that." She shifted in her seat. "Men who put money before everything else. I had seen it in Joseph's eyes. The ring was significant in some way. I did not know if that meant it was significant in value or history, and at the time, I did not care. I needed the money, but I said I would only sell the diamonds." She looked me in the eye. "That was my counter offer."

Fucking hell, I knew where this was going. "He didn't accept it, did he?"

"No, he did not." She shook her head at the memory. "He said I was insane."

Of course the asshole did. Then he probably used that shit to his advantage. She was exquisite now, the years had made her even more so, but she was a stunning, innocent beauty back then in those photos, and Bertrand was a fucking predator. "He said twenty-five thousand euros and you. Then he'd let you keep the ring."

With a clipped nod, she confirmed it. "Yes, and he promised he would also keep the secret of my brother's theft and his child's identity."

"You agreed." She'd had to, he'd backed her into a corner, but fuck, I couldn't think about what he had done to her those first days he got his hands on her, let alone in the past seven years.

"I did. By then I knew my brother's girlfriend needed money to get away, and I had to protect my nephew."

Shoving down anger, I focused on what I needed to know. "How did you transfer the funds to her?"

Sabine's head dipped again, but this time, the color drained from her face. "I actually did not know where she was or how to find her. I was not even sure if she knew Henri was… gone." Her hands smoothed at her dress. "I had to ask Joseph for help." Her voice quieted. "He found her."

Jesus, fuck. "Please tell me you didn't carry twenty-five thousand euros in cash across Paris by yourself." I was staring at her, virtually unharmed physically, minus her wrist, but that still didn't make me any less pissed at the thought of her putting herself in that kind of danger under those circumstances.

When her gaze met mine, guilt was written all over her face. "I would have if I could, but I did not have a choice. Joseph would not tell me where she was. He insisted on taking her the money. He said it was for my own safety." Her eyes welled. "I did what I had to do so Chantel could get the money and get herself and Julien safely out of the country."

And Bertrand was weaving the web the whole goddamn time.

"I know what you are thinking," she accused.

No, she didn't. "Did you see him hand her the money?" No fucking way would he have handed over that amount of cash just to get in Sabine's pants. If the nephew's mother was still alive, I guarantee Bertrand screwed her over in some way.

"I am not that foolish. I insisted on going with him to take her the money."

Foolish wasn't the word I was going to use, but I had to ask. "When was the last time you had proof of life?"

She looked at me for a long time, then she played a game I knew so damn well, I could write the book on it. She tried to reason with her guilty conscience by justifying her actions. "That was part of the deal—I would not see her again."

"Your deal or Bertrand's?"

Her cheeks reddened. "His, but he had a point. Whoever had come after Henri could go after her, and if I stayed in contact with her, that would put me at risk. Joseph said that he could protect me as long as I was with him, and Chantel and Julien would be protected as long as they disappeared and no one knew where they went."

"How charitable of him."

"What was I supposed to do?"

Go to the police, the DGSE, hell, anything except get in bed with a piece of shit like Bertrand, but what choice did she have back then? She was one hundred percent spot-on, she was young and alone.

Keeping my tone in check, I asked the next question. "Were you ever in contact with her again?"

Sabine inhaled like she was the one fighting for patience. "I know you think I made mistakes and that I could have done many things differently, but I am not going to justify my actions to you, same as I would not expect you to justify yours to me when you were seventeen years old."

I didn't lift my head, but I looked at her. Really fucking looked. And for the first time, I understood something I hadn't when this exquisite beauty stood in Bertrand's doorway nursing a fear seven years deep.

She'd sacrificed everything for a child that wasn't her own.

She gave herself willingly to a viper so another could live.

She was a goddamn warrior.

She was the same as every Marine I'd ever met.

Hell, she was stronger.

And she was so fucking beautiful, I didn't deserve to sit across from her.

What the fuck had I ever done in the name of sacrifice? For atonement?

Nothing.

I'd covered my tracks, walked away and never looked back at the carnage I'd left as I'd wallowed in self-fucking-pity for seventeen goddamn years.

"I'm in no position to judge. I'm trying to figure out what the hell Bertrand's going to do next, because believe me, he has something up his sleeve, and no way in hell am I letting him come after you."

"This is not about me."

Was she fucking blind? "This is exactly about you."

"No, it is not," she corrected. "It is about money. It is always about money for Joseph."

She was fucking blind. It was about possessions, control and feeling like he had the upper hand over everyone because he was a sick son of a bitch who got off on abusing everyone around him. Money was only a catalyst for his narcissism.

Not touching her last statement, I focused back on what I needed to know. "Can you think of any valid reason he wants you in either place?" Because he could've forcibly taken the ring from her at any time.

Inhaling deep, she looked up at me with resignation. "Are there extradition laws between America and France?"

Fucking hell. "Why?"

Her right hand went to her left wrist. "I killed a man."

I was expecting something like this, but I sure as hell wasn't expecting the casual way she delivered the admission after holding everything else back. "Seven years ago in self-defense?"

Her throat moved with a swallow, but she said nothing.

"I saw bruises on your ankles in the security camera images taken of you walking into Harrington's in Paris seven years ago. I'm guessing whoever your brother stole the diamonds from, or your brother himself, tried to stop you from selling them. Either way, it looked like you put up a fight."

"I was wrong," she abruptly interjected.

"About?"

"You are not presumptuous."

"No, I'm not." I figured shit out, and I'd already realized this woman wasn't going to speak until she was ready. This time, I didn't ask for details. I waited.

Nodding slowly, she rubbed her wrist gently. Then she started talking. "I never went without growing up, but we were very underprivileged. I believed Henri when he had said he found the ring because it felt like a win in a world full of losses. He loved Maman, and he wanted her to have something nice, even if she could only enjoy it at home." Her shoulder lifted with an air of acceptance before she looked out the window. "I should have known it was stolen. It was not the first time my brother brought trouble home. He was always looking for ways to make money quickly. He said he did not want to work hard his whole life like our father and have nothing to show for it."

VICTOR

Grasping her chin, I brought her face back toward me. "What kind of trouble?"

Her gaze drifted past me. "The usual, I suppose. Small things at first, then drugs. When my father found the drugs in his room, he told Henri he could join the military or move out. Henri left, and we did not see him for a long while." She shook her head, then looked back at me. "When he reappeared, he did not only come home with muscles he said were from his construction job and the ring for Maman. He came home with a shy young woman holding a new baby."

"Your nephew."

"Yes. My brother was beaming. He was so proud, so happy, but the woman, she looked scared. Henri wanted us to meet his son, and we were all excited, but then it fell apart when my mother asked where they were living. She insisted she come help, make dinner, tend to the infant, let them get some rest. They both looked so tired. But my brother got cagey. Next thing I knew, he was rushing the woman and Julien out the door, saying they had to get home so the baby could nap. My father stopped Henri, and they had words. He told Henri to be more respectful of our mother, and Henri got angry. He pushed Papa against the wall." Her eyes filled with tears. "Then he was yelling that Papa was the disrespectful one as he pulled a wad of cash out of his pocket and threw it at my father, telling him to take care of his own family, before he slammed the door in his face. Two weeks later, my father was gone." Her voice dropped to a whisper. "Then Maman and Henri." She looked at me as if pleading for me to understand. "You have to understand, I did not care about life after that, especially my own, but I could not let anything happen to Julien."

THIRTY-FIVE

Sabine

HE HAD TO UNDERSTAND.
He had told me he'd made a grave mistake. He had implied he was responsible for a young woman's life.

He had to know the kind of guilt and grief that came with that, but now, the look in his eyes as he watched me confess my sins, he did not look like the compassionate man who had told me about his past.

He looked angry.

Joseph-level angry.

"Conlon, November," the pilot called from the cockpit. "Final approach."

Without a word, Vance leaned over and secured my seat belt.

On edge, needing to catch a single breath that did not smell so intoxicatingly forbidden and masculine and dominant, I asked for the only escape within my reach. "Do I have time to use the restroom?"

"Yes." Not giving me any eye contact, Vance undid my seat belt, then stood and went toward the cockpit.

Even more anxious, I walked to the rear of the plane.

Sitting in the conference area, two laptops open in front of him, November typed simultaneously on both computers as his gaze moved from one screen to the other. "We're about to land."

In other words, sit down and buckle in. "I understand."

He looked up from his computers. "Do you?"

"Does she what?" Vance's body heat covered my back a fraction of a second before his voice coasted over my shoulder in a lethal demand.

A tremor swept across my body. "It is all right. I will be quick."

"Take your time." Moving past me, his glare on November, Vance opened the restroom door for me.

Hurrying inside and securing the door, I washed my hands and stared at my reflection. Dark hair, light eyes, cheekbones my mother said made other women jealous, I knew I had been blessed by no act of my own. Men had always found me pretty, but it was my mother who had taught me early on to never give anything away.

She had said a proper French woman was a reserved woman, and that beauty came from being gracious.

Looking at the woman in the mirror, I felt as if I had failed my mother in every way.

A knock sounded. "We're about to land, love."

Inhaling deep, I opened the door. "I'm sorry."

Towering over me, blocking the aisle, Vance's height almost to the very top of the cabin, he didn't move back. "What did I tell you?"

Fearful of seeing anger in his eyes, I looked past his shoulder. "You have said many things."

"*Fuck.*"

The curse was so sharp and unexpected from him that I met his gaze.

His eyes weren't angry as I feared, they were worse. They were a storm the flavor of which I knew well. Self-hatred.

Grasping my chin, he did not speak his next words, he cut them from stone. "I will never hurt you. You do not *fucking ever* have to look past me in fear. Understand?"

Tears welled.

His tone turned rougher. "*Understand?*"

I fought an emotion as unfamiliar as his declaration. "Yes."

"Good." Taking my hand, closing the restroom door behind me, he led me to a couch-type seating area in the rear of the plane, behind where November was sitting with his back to us. "Sit."

I had no sooner taken a seat in the corner and Vance was pulling out a seat belt and buckling it for me.

"Thank you," I murmured as he sat directly next to me and buckled himself in.

His muscular arm draped over the back of the seat behind us, and he faced me. Then his amber-green eyes studied my face for a moment as if he were looking for something.

The plane tilted, and he started with a non sequitur. "I meant it when I said I wasn't an honest man."

I had no reply because I did not know where he was going with this.

"In fact," he continued. "Before I enlisted and became a Marine, I was similar to your brother." Watching me closely, he paused for a moment. "I've done many things I'm not proud of."

Hadn't we all? I gave him his own words back to him. "I am not here to judge you."

"I appreciate that, pet." His expression turned deadly serious, and his voice darkened. "The thing is, I feel responsible for you." Brushing my hair off my shoulder, his fingers played a seductive dance down the back of my neck before possessively grasping my nape in a firm hold. "I haven't felt like this in a long time." He inhaled deep. "But I'm not sure that's a good thing for you."

His touch sent a shockwave through my system that was as strong as the sting of his words that were hurting my soul. But exactly as every other time this man had given me his full attention, the rest of the world disappeared and my heart beat in a new rhythm—one that was all at once frightening yet familiar while it stole my breath and made me feel as ethereal as a sultry, tropical breeze.

The air suddenly humid between us, I dared to ask about the woman he had said I reminded him of because I refused to focus on the other part of what he'd said. "A long time, as in not since you were seventeen?" I wanted to be her. Naïvely, selfishly, I wanted to be the woman this man gave everything for.

His expression grave, his hold on the back of my neck tightened. "No," he forcibly rasped as the plane's engines whined and we pitched forward.

Gravity pushing me toward him, I braced against his strong chest.

As if he'd planned this, as if he had been waiting for this moment, he brought my lips to within a hair's breadth of his, and he angled me exactly how he wanted. "You are *not* her."

Vance Conlon kissed me.

THIRTY-SIX

Vance

MY TONGUE SANK INTO HER MOUTH, AND THE PLANE TOUCHED DOWN. Like an addict, I took.

For one mind-bending second, she gave.

Her breath, her mouth, her body.

Leaning into me, my kiss, my addiction—I stole her moan and fucking swallowed every ounce of her submission.

She wasn't perfect.

She was goddamn exquisite.

Then Zulu reversed the thrust, the plane braked, and she pushed at my chest.

Her lips wet from my kiss, she looked at me with every ounce of mistrust I deserved.

I was a bastard, but no way in hell was I apologizing. "You felt that, same as me, so know this." I skimmed the back of my fingers across her soft cheek. "I'm going to protect you. You're going to walk away from Bertrand. Then I'm going to show you how a real man treats a woman. But before all of that can happen, it's going to get uncomfortable. In five minutes, the owner of AES is going to walk on this plane, your life is going to be on display, and me and the men I work with are going to chart a plan of action with or without your consent." Grasping the back of her neck, I held firm. "All I'm asking is that you trust the single moment we just shared."

Saying nothing, she stared at me.

I fucking forged on. "If you get scared, remember how this

feels, right here, right now. My hands on you. My taste on your lips. My promise to keep you safe." Goddamn, I wanted to kiss her again. "That's all you need to focus on." The plane came to a stop. "Let me handle the rest, all right?"

Her chest rose with an inhale, her eyes held steady, and minus the flush across her cheeks, she remained as poised as if I'd never kissed her.

I fucking thought I had her.

Then she opened her mouth, and with quiet reservation, she gutted me.

"That is not a question, nor is it a choice."

Adrenaline coursing, my dick hard from kissing her, I wanted to throw her over my shoulder and walk the fuck off this plane and out of this life. I wanted to give every damn thing I had just to strip this woman of the expression on her face right now. But the airstairs were already down, Echo and November were coming this way, and I was out of goddamn time.

I was always out of time with her.

Instead of reacting how I wanted to and telling this beautifully broken woman that I was her only goddamn choice, I didn't so much as blink. "After Vienna, you'll have whatever choice you want, pet."

"I know what it means when you call me pet."

Thrown, I hesitated only a second. "Good, tell me later. For now? Your choice, Sabine." I leaned toward her ear. "Your decision." Brushing my lips to her temple once, I released her and undid our seat belts.

November sat across from us and opened his laptop.

Echo took the seat next to him.

Trefor came aboard, walked down the aisle and held his hand out to her. "Miss Malcher, I'm Adam Trefor. I believe we have a lot to discuss."

THIRTY-SEVEN

Sabine

A MAN WITH JET-BLACK HAIR AND THE STARKEST BLUE EYES I HAD ever seen came down the aisle. In an expensive custom suit, with his tall, muscular frame, he held his hand out to me. "Miss Malcher, I'm Adam Trefor. I believe we have a lot to discuss."

I did not want to discuss anything with him.

Despite his manners and composed countenance, he had an air about him of not only dominance but lethality. Unlike the man named Echo, who moved with raw energy and barely constrained power, Adam Trefor was hiding his deadly skills behind an expensive suit, a six-figure watch, and a brand of fine Italian boots that I would not even know the name of, let alone recognize, if I had not been living in the world of Harrington's for the past seven years.

Make no mistake, this Adam Trefor was not a man I wanted to ever go up against.

My nerves still singing from every caress and word Vance had said, I shook Mr. Trefor's hand, but it felt like a betrayal to the man sitting next to me. Thrown into a new world where I only wanted to be around one man who smelled like the home I never had and kissed like his life was mine, I aimed for distance from Mr. Trefor's comment. "Mr. Conlon may have a lot to discuss with you, but I am not sure I will have much to add to the conversation."

Casually taking a seat across from me that his men had purposely left for him, Mr. Trefor nodded once. "Understood. Then I'll start by telling you what I know." Leaning his forearms on his knees, he steepled his fingers. "We believe Harrington's is about to come under a coordinated attack. Someone within the French intelligence community or someone impersonating them planted a trail of supposed corporate espionage. That trail led to your laptop. Harrington's internal security and IT team brought it to Bertrand's attention. Bertrand contacted AES, retained us, then requested that we provide him with evidence to implicate you."

I blinked.

Then I had to tell myself and my racing heart that I already knew this.

Every word this man was saying was exactly what Vance had told me right before he had kissed me, made me promises and turned my horrible world completely inside out.

I did not blame him. I couldn't. I had created this path.

But until this very second, it had not sunk in how utterly unrecoverable my life was. Not that it was a life worth living, but I had been enduring it for one single reason. A reason I'd had no contact with, nor seen in seven years.

Drawing in a deep breath, I realized what I had to do.

I told Mr. Trefor the truth. "I do not know anything about an attack against Harrington's or what Joseph is planning to do. I also do not know why Joseph has chosen to implicate me in false crimes now, but he does have true incriminating information about me. If he wanted, he could go to the authorities right now. He would not even need the laptop I use at work. Seven years ago, I gave Joseph stolen diamonds in exchange for cash so that I could give the mother of my brother's son money to disappear. In the course of events leading up to that, I killed a man who came after me for the diamonds."

Without looking up from typing on his laptop, November

interrupted my confession. "I need the date and location of that altercation and the name of the assailant if you have it, otherwise his description."

Fixated on the word *altercation*, I gave the address of the apartment I grew up in, the date I would never forget and the description of a man that was etched into my conscience.

"Had you ever seen that man before?" Adam Trefor asked.

I shook my head. "No. I did not know who he was, only that he showed up at the apartment after my brother's accident, demanding the diamonds. When I tried to close the door, he lunged, and we both fell. He grabbed my ankles, and I reached for a knife my father had kept by the front door for protection." Bile rising, I tried to rush through the next part. "The man hit me, and I stabbed him, but he did not let go, so I just… kept stabbing." The memory, the fear replaying like it was yesterday, I tried to push it all down and keep my voice even. "When he stopped moving, I dropped the knife. Then in a panic, I went back to Harrington's."

"Just to confirm, this is the afternoon of the same day you sold the diamonds to Bertrand?" Adam asked.

I tried to swallow down guilt and shame. "Yes."

Adam nodded. "Walk me through that first meeting with Bertrand, please."

Rubbing my sore wrist, wishing I did not have to speak of any of this, wanting Vance's touch for comfort but not daring to reach for him, I did as Adam asked. "When I walked into Harrington's that morning, Joseph Bertrand was walking out. Not knowing who he was, I accidentally ran into him. When he saw my face, he asked if I was okay, and I blurted out that I had jewelry I needed to immediately sell. He took me to his office, told his secretary not to disturb us, then he closed the door, poured me a drink and asked to see what I had. I showed him the diamonds."

Next to me, Vance audibly inhaled.

Adam glanced at Vance before looking back at me. "That's when Bertrand purchased them from you?"

"Not exactly. He asked for proof that they were not stolen, and when I said I did not have it, he was quiet for a long moment. I thought he would tell me to leave or report me. But then he asked to see the ring I had on my finger. When I said it was not for sale, he tried to negotiate a deal for the diamonds and the ring. I held firm, and he finally offered me twenty-five thousand euros for the diamonds but said I would have to come back the next day for the funds if I wanted cash. I agreed, left the diamonds with him and went home. Then I got a call my brother had been in an accident, and you know the rest."

"Yes, thank you." Adam nodded. "Lastly, can you please tell me what happened when you went back to Harrington's?"

"I asked to see Joseph, but the receptionist said I did not have an appointment. I told her it was urgent, but she made me wait almost an hour before walking me back to his office." I had been so young, so stupid. Joseph had not even looked up from his desk when he had told me to come back the following day for the money. "When he finally saw me, he asked why there was blood on my hands. I…" I cleared my throat. "I told him. Then said I needed the money immediately." I had wanted to get money to Chantel and warn her. I owed her nothing less. "Joseph told me to go home, clean myself up and meet him at his hotel bar later."

November stopped typing and looked up.

Echo and Mr. Trefor were already staring at me.

Vance pinched the bridge of his nose as he muttered a curse. *"Jesus fucking Christ."*

Mr. Trefor spoke to November while staring at me. "November?"

Looking at me for a second longer, November then focused back on his laptop. "No security cameras in her tenement block or surrounding buildings. No homicides reported on that day, in that district, matching that description. None reported the following week either. Unsolved cases…" November trailed off as he continued to type. "None matching that description or timeframe."

Mr. Trefor spoke directly to me. "Did you go back to the apartment?"

"Yes."

His expression locked, he stared at me for a second. "What did you do with the body, Miss Malcher?"

"Nothing," I admitted. "It was gone when I got home, and the floor had been cleaned of all blood. I assumed Joseph had… taken care of it."

"To be clear, you told Joseph Bertrand there was a body in your apartment?"

"Yes."

"November?" Mr. Trefor asked again.

November typed furiously. "No outgoing calls that afternoon from either his cell or his Paris office. Security footage shows a chauffeur service picking him up at eighteen hundred hours and various traffic cams track the limo to his hotel, where he walked through the lobby fourteen minutes later. Elevator footage shows him going to his suite. At nineteen hundred, he took the elevator to the lobby and walked into the bar. Six minutes later, Miss Malcher walked through the lobby to the bar."

Adam looked at me. "Miss Malcher, what did Bertrand say to you at the hotel bar later that evening?"

"He told me he did not have the money yet. Then he said it was not safe for me to walk around with that amount of cash, and he offered a bank transfer before saying we should have dinner. I declined and asked for the diamonds back, but he said he had already sold them."

"Alpha," Vance practically growled.

"I know." His eyes on me, Mr. Trefor tipped his chin at Vance. "What happened next, Miss Malcher?"

VICTOR

I glanced at the four dominant, highly trained former military men staring expectantly at me, who were all here because of my actions, and for the first time in my life, I was not sure if anything I had done for the past seven years was worth it.

I did not deserve this.

I did not deserve to have any of them risking their lives for me.

I knew my nephew was an innocent life caught up in all of this, but I could have saved him a different way. I could have done so many things differently.

Swallowing down regret, I answered Mr. Trefor. "I made a deal."

Mr. Trefor did not react. He did not even ask what kind of a deal. Patiently waiting for me to say more, his fingers still, he stared.

Not daring to so much as glance at Vance, I elaborated. "I told Joseph I would have dinner with him if he gave me the cash and helped me find my sister-in-law so that I could give her the money. Joseph agreed." But not before he added his own list of demands, none of which I told the men in front of me about. I casually shrugged as if I were not lying and the truth was arbitrary. "I had dinner with him, and the next day he came through on his promise. Together, we took the money to Chantel, and she left the country with Julien."

Adam Trefor nodded once. "That was the end of it?"

"Yes." No. It was only the beginning. Joseph had agreed to pay for my Mamam's burial for a price that cost me my innocence and began my decent into hell, but we were not here to discuss my life or what I had been through.

Adam Trefor tapped his fingers together as his focus shifted. November stared at his laptop, but his hands were still. Echo remained silent, his gaze locked on me. And Vance, I did not want to look at him, but this time, I could not stop myself. His posture stiff, staring straight ahead, the man who had passionately kissed me looked like he wanted to kill someone.

"Miss Malcher." Adam Trefor focused his attention back on me. "Here's the situation. On the books, Bertrand is the one who hired us. He's en route, and he wants you by his side at the preview event tonight. Since he's threatened legal and criminal action if you're not in attendance, then that's what we're going to do."

"No," Vance immediately interrupted.

Adam held a finger up to Vance. "As far as I'm concerned, we're dealing with the present situation, and that's his allegations of corporate espionage."

"She's not responsible, Trefor," Vance ground out.

"I understand that," Adam calmly replied. "But we're going to deal with the facts that we have. Until we know what actions, if any, Bertrand has planned against Miss Malcher, we're going to operate inside the wire. It's a controlled event, invite only, and we already have the guest list. This gives us the opportunity to tip the scales, so focus up. You, me, Echo and Ronan will be in attendance. Miss Malcher will be safe."

Vance abruptly stood. "*Ronan?*"

Adam spared him a single glance. "He's taking Sanaa."

"Not happening, Trefor, and you're not calling the shots on this," Vance warned in a lethal tone. "We've got homicides covered up as accidents, missing bodies, blood diamonds and foreign intelligence agencies hovering. All of it circling an auction house primed for money laundering with potential ties to a known mercenary ring of former Legionnaires. Neither woman should be anywhere near this."

My stomach dropped, and my head spun. "Joseph is a money launderer?" *Blood diamonds?*

Adam said no at the same time Vance said yes.

Echo smirked and stood. "I'm going to do perimeter checks

at the event location. Sitrep at seventeen hundred. Don't call me if you two need a referee."

"I'll be in the office." November closed his laptop, grabbed mine and followed Echo off the plane.

The pilot stepped out of the cockpit and came down the aisle. Tall and handsome, he was less rugged-looking than Echo but had the same presence about him as all the other men who worked with Vance.

"Zulu," Adam stated in greeting.

"Alpha." The pilot nodded at me before glancing at Vance, then looking back at Adam. "I'm grounding this plane for maintenance. I need to know sooner rather than later if I'm filing a flight plan for Vienna and if we're taking another one of the 650s or your Falcon."

Vance muttered a curse under his breath. "We don't know what's going to happen tonight. The flight plan can wait."

"Vienna's nine hours and forty-five minutes of flight time. Our entire fleet's been in the air this past week. Like it or not, one of you needs to make the call now so I have time to pick a plane, complete any needed maintenance, do my prechecks, refuel and restock."

Adam stood. "We're going through with the plan. Prep the Falcon."

"That's announcing your involvement to every intelligence agency circling this thing," Vance warned Adam.

"Whether it's one of the Gulfstreams or the Falcon, it doesn't matter. If they check the tail numbers, they'll know it's AES." Adam buttoned his suit jacket.

"I said you, not AES," Vance corrected.

"Exactly," Adam countered before holding his hand out to me. "Miss Malcher, nice to meet you. I'll see you tonight."

"Mr. Trefor." I shook his hand, but I had the distinct feeling I would regret it.

THIRTY-EIGHT

Vance

"Wait here a moment, love," I ordered Sabine before grabbing my jacket and following Trefor off the Gulfstream.

The heat of the south Florida sun hit me with both a punch of humid lethargy and familiarity, but it did nothing to dampen my rising anger. "Alpha," I clipped.

Trefor stopped at the open driver door to one of the company's Defenders. "I'm Alpha again?"

"You're fucking acting like it." I didn't for one moment forget this was his company, his clients, his rules. But I wasn't a subordinate to anyone. He knew that when he'd signed me on.

Zero tell in his expression, Trefor did what he always did. He didn't say shit. He waited for you to sink your own ship.

Which apparently I was aiming to do. "We had one deal." Like a fucking pussy who'd already lost the battle, I held a finger up. "One goddamn condition of me coming to work for you when I know every other asshole at AES came in with a list. One," I reiterated.

"Why are we in Florida?" he casually asked.

"For the client event tonight." Why the fuck else did he think we were here? "That's not the point."

"Before that?"

Motherfucker. "Nice try. I'm not walking into your mindfuck

VICTOR

games." If psychoanalyzing people were an Olympic sport, Trefor would own the gold.

"It's not a game, and you already did," he calmly stated.

Bullshit. "The only point of this conversation is that I work alone. Always have, always will. Regardless of the two times I've requested backup, tonight included, working alone means I call the shots on all of my assignments, and I'm calling it on this one now. I don't care how much goddamn security we have at that party, I'm pulling her out. Tell Ronan to stay the fuck away as well."

Trefor continued as if I hadn't said shit. "We're in Miami because we're both from here, it logistically made sense to relocate the company headquarters and your brother's here. You don't live in a vacuum. You don't work in one, and you've never operated in the field or on a single assignment without the support of AES on your six. Drop the fucking bullshit, Conlon. I don't know what's going on in your head, but it's affecting this assignment, and more importantly, it's affecting you. We all saw what November dug up on this. You want to pull the wife? Then do it. But understand that if you make that move, every illegal thing Bertrand has his hand in stays covered up, and his wife will go down for whatever bullshit he's concocted because he'll make sure of it. So make the call, or don't, but stop feeding me a line about working alone until you can actually handle it. That means no November, no pilot, no shadow on your six and zero fucking resources besides your offshore bank accounts."

Goddamn it. "I never said I had offshore bank accounts."

"You didn't have to. November already told me when he did a thorough background check on you when I hired him, because unlike you, I don't work alone. And for the record, I'm not your secretary. You want to relay a message to your brother? You call him." Trefor got behind the wheel and shut the door.

Two seconds later, I was staring at taillights.

"Motherfucker," I muttered.

"He has a point."

I turned to face Zulu. "Who the hell invited you to the conversation?"

Zulu grinned from behind his aviators. "Three-foot world, my friend. Three-foot world," he spouted, giving me one of his SEAL philosophies before turning toward the Gulfstream's airstairs.

"I'm not a goddamn SEAL, and this isn't the Teams," I called to his retreating back.

Stopping at the top of the stairs, Zulu glanced at me. "No shit, and no shit." Zulu stepped aboard the plane.

I wasn't a team player, and no speech from Trefor or anyone else was going to change that, but fucking hell, Alpha had valid points.

Pulling my cell out, I dialed.

Ronan answered on the third ring. "What?"

"You're not taking Sanaa to the Harrington's event tonight."

Pause. Then, "Security's arranged, she wants to go. She wants art for the new house."

"Joseph Harrington Bertrand is my new client. Do not take Sanaa anywhere near this." It was the best advice he'd get out of me.

For five beats, Ronan said nothing.

Then my twin surprised the fuck out of me. "Understood. Need help?"

"No."

Ronan didn't say shit.

Fuck. Inhaling, I rephrased. "No, thank you."

"Sitrep?"

Ronan wasn't a talker, he never had been. Sometimes I wondered, between the two of us, who kept shit locked up tighter. So I understood the olive branch he was extending by asking a one-word question, but I no more wanted to discuss this fucking assignment than I wanted him to take Sanaa to the damn event tonight.

"I don't know if this line's secure," I evaded.

"Since when has that stopped you?"

I shouldn't have been pissed. He was right. I fed off danger like he fed off calculated control. He avoided risk, I aimed for it. But not this time. "This is different."

"What's her name?"

"Who?"

"The woman you're protecting."

"Who says I'm protecting a woman?"

"I do."

I hated the rumors about identical twins I'd been fed my entire life, but I had to admit they were true. We knew shit about each other, even when we didn't want to.

"Sabine," I admitted.

"Sounds French."

"She is." Or was. Fuck, what did I actually know about her? Nothing real. Not what she ate for breakfast or what she smelled like when she slept or what her eyes did when she came. All of which I wanted to know. Badly. Except I wasn't that guy. I didn't do domestic. I didn't stay in one place. I didn't even commit to a vehicle, let alone a residence. I had no damn right making this woman promises, but I couldn't stop myself. I hadn't felt a damn thing in the vicinity of my heart since I was seventeen years old, but something had awoken when she'd walked into that office.

A better man would've handed this assignment over to anyone else at AES and walked the hell away before this ended in a fucking firestorm.

But I wasn't a better man, and no way in hell did I want to go back to my pre-Sabine world.

"You speak French to her yet?" Ronan asked.

"No."

"You should, your accent's better than mine." A beat of silence passed, then, "I'll be there tonight." Ronan hung up.

I scanned the tarmac of the private airport, then felt it.

Knowing she was there like I knew that asshole Bertrand was going to pull something, I turned toward the Gulfstream.

Standing at the top of the airstairs, the breeze blowing her hair, stood a woman who made me not want to fight in the ring anymore.

THIRTY-NINE

Sabine

I stared at a man I watched change before my very eyes.

The composed, confident, dominant man in his custom suit and expensive watch who was polished and flirtatious was now arguing with all his friends and holding a weight on his shoulders that I put there.

I was so tired of being exhausted, but I could not do this.

I could not do any of it.

I wanted out, except not like this, not at the expense of anyone else. Enough lives had been ruined.

I had listened to Mr. Trefor. I had heard every word he had said to Vance. He was right about one thing. I was going to the event. But I was not going to hide anymore. I gave them Julien's name. If anyone could protect him and Chantel, it would be these men. They were nothing like the security that Joseph hired when he needed it. These men were capable, articulate and intelligent.

They would find a way to unravel this mess.

But I was done.

I would take whatever Joseph wanted to dish out this one last time, and I would live with the consequences. Then I would be done with him. None of these men understood what Joseph was capable of. Joseph Harrington Bertrand would never set his ego down and let me go simply because Vance decided he wanted to remove me from the situation. That would never free me.

Inhaling the humid southern air that felt more like home than New York ever had, I walked down the stairs.

His gaze intent, hot wind whipping his hair in every direction and pressing his shirt against his impressive physique, Vance stood with one hand on his hip, the other holding his jacket. I did not know if he looked more boyish with his hair like this, or more intense with his muscles straining his shirt.

Tracking me as I walked toward him, Vance did not take his gaze off me.

Willing courage, I met his beautiful eyes that sparkled with flecks of gold in the direct sunlight and wished I had any other life. "Please take me to the house in Coral Gables."

His stare unwavering, he pulled his cell phone out, barely glanced at it to dial, then held it to his ear. "Can you handle the luggage? Copy. Thanks." Hanging up, he pocketed his phone. "This way."

He did not touch me, and we did not speak as I followed him through Miami Executive Airport's terminal and out to an adjacent parking lot. Reaching into his pocket again, he came away with a key fob and aimed for a brand-new Range Rover.

Opening the passenger door, he did not offer his hand.

I got in, and he simply closed my door, circled the front of the SUV and got behind the wheel.

Tossing his jacket in the backseat, turning the engine over, he adjusted the air-conditioning, but then he sat back and looked at me. "You don't have to do this."

Yes, I did. "I am not doing anything I have not done dozens of times. Preview events are as much about meeting the clients as the clients getting an advance showing of what is going up for auction. Joseph likes me to mingle, so that is what I will do." Sitting next to him, smelling the earthy musk of his cologne that was laced with dominance, I did not know if I was trying to convince him or myself that I needed to do this. "You said yourself that

Joseph was laundering money and that there were other agencies after him or involved with whatever is going on with these security breaches. Frankly, I do not care. If Joseph is going to blame me, he will find a way no matter what you say or do. He operates one step ahead, he always has. Before he called your company in, he already had a plan of how he wanted all of this to go down. Regardless, it does not matter. I am not walking away now. Even if I wanted to, I couldn't. If I did, he would know something was wrong and he would change his course of action. Then no one would be able to catch him or the people behind this."

"You know what I think, pet?"

I already understood the nuances of his speech. Pet meant he was angry or did not believe me, love meant he was trying to come across as sincere and darling was reserved for outright flirting. He had used all of them on me. At first, I was flattered. Now I was telling myself he did this with all women because that was the train of thought I needed to hold on to. Not his promises or the way he kissed or the look in his eyes when he stared at me.

I focused on his question. "I do. You think I should not go. You want to *pull me out*. And you think when you call me pet, I do not notice what it signifies."

"I think there's something you're not telling me. I think you're recklessly ignoring the offer I made you, and I think you know exactly what it means when I call you pet," he quickly countered, rattling off arguments for every one of my statements.

But I could not argue with this man.

I did not know how.

I had spent years perfecting my façade, but it was as if he saw right through me and knew every fear I held onto like they were my own personal life preserver. "Since we are at an impasse, I think we are done discussing this."

"What impasse is that, love?" he pushed. "The one where I protect you?"

"Protect me?" I asked, incredulous. "What exactly do you think you are going to do, Mr. Conlon?" Anger I had been holding down for so many years came alarmingly close to the surface. "Declare a bruise as a lifetime of abuse, justify it to inappropriately kiss me before you steal me away from my life, dump me in a hotel and walk away, job done?" My voice rose with every word of my misplaced resentment and mistakes I made seven years ago. "Then you can collect your dirty money, wash your hands of this assignment and move on to the next victim you pretend to save?" I regretted the last words before they were out of my mouth, but it was too late to take them back.

Anger mirroring my own tightened his jaw, and his nostrils flared. "First, I'm not taking one goddamn cent from that bastard you're protecting, and second, if that's what you think of me, then we truly are at an impasse, *pet*." Throwing the SUV into reverse, he backed up too fast before shifting into drive and pulling out of the parking lot.

FORTY

Vance

I WAS A SELFISH BASTARD.

I'd called her pet because she'd called me on my shit, but that wasn't what was cycling through my head on fucking repeat, making me want to hit something.

The next victim you pretend to save.

I wanted to hate her, every exquisite inch, but she was right. I had been inappropriate, inappropriate as hell. I didn't think for one second before I kissed her what the consequences would mean for her. I wanted it, so I goddamn took it.

Now, we were exactly where she said we were. But it wasn't just a damn impasse, it was a dangerous deadlock. I wanted to pull her out immediately, but what the fuck was I going to do then? Take her from that asshole and move her into my penthouse? Give her another cage to live in?

I wouldn't fucking do that to her.

No matter how much I hated it, because I didn't actually trust a goddamn soul, Trefor was dead-on. I needed a team behind this, and I needed to do my damn job. I wouldn't make the same mistake I'd made seventeen years ago.

Pulling my cell out, I dialed, but I let the call go through the SUV's speaker.

Echo picked up on the fourth ring. "Already told you, I'm not your referee, motherfucker."

"You're on speaker," I warned him.

"Fucking perfect."

Asshole. "I need a sitrep on the residence."

"Already done. Gated, two house staff, no on-site security."

Fuck. "We need to remedy that, off the radar."

"Good copy."

As much as I hated the asshole, Echo would follow through, so I didn't question it. I moved on to the next problem. "The venue?"

"Complete cluster. Three ingresses, four egresses. Balcony, kitchen, restrooms, stairwell and lobby access points. Sightlines from three dozen vantage points, and I haven't even mentioned the fifty yards of unpatrolled oceanfront access. That's just the shit I found in the first few minutes."

Christ. "Hired security?"

"Haven't seen them yet, unless you count the extra valet pricks standing around holding their dicks."

I glanced at the clock on the dashboard. "They're cutting it close."

"Or they don't give a fuck."

I glanced at Sabine. "How soon before these preview events are the items brought in?"

"I am not part of the security team, but it depends on the venue. Usually, right before the event, armored transport brings the items in for display and the guests have an hour to view them. Then the armored transport leaves with the items before drinks and hors d'oeuvres are served."

"Echo?"

"I heard. I'll get November on it."

"Copy, I'll meet you back at the office."

"Yes, boss," Echo said sarcastically before hanging up.

Taking the bridge onto the barrier island, I scanned the rearview mirrors. Every passing minute, my instincts were kicking up a notch. "Have you stayed at this house by yourself before?"

"I will not be alone. Your friend said the house staff was there."

"That's not what I was asking, and he's not my friend." Bertrand would touch down in a little over an hour, and I was already losing my shit about her being alone with him.

"I am not a mind reader, Mr. Conlon. If you have a specific question, then ask."

Mr. Conlon. I fucking deserved that, but goddamn I hated it. Focusing up. I laid it out. "AES will have someone on the outside, but I'm asking if you think you'll be safe with the current staff that's there now. Is there anyone you trust on the inside if a problem arises? If not, are you comfortable calling me from your personal cell phone, or would you prefer an untraceable one?"

Staring out the window, she didn't answer right away. Then she both surprised and alarmed me. "I would prefer the untraceable cell phone, please."

That one statement saying more than I wanted to currently hear as I was driving her into enemy territory, I handed her my cell.

Taking the phone but not putting it in her purse, she stared at it like it was on fire. "What are you going to use? How will your men contact you?"

"I'll grab a new phone and text you so you have the number. As far as everyone else, I don't give a damn."

Taking a deep breath, she placed the cell on her lap. "Vance—"

"I'm Vance again?"

She hesitated. "I am simply asking, how you will get a hold of your coworkers or anyone in your contact list if I have your phone?"

"Look," I demanded.

"Pardon?"

"Look at the contact list."

"I do not need to pry into your personal—"

"Look at the phone, Sabine."

Just like she got when that asshole Bertrand yelled at her, she shut down, but she did pick the phone up and swipe. "There is no lock screen?"

"Contacts," I repeated.

She swiped again.

I glanced at her before taking a corner. "There doesn't need to be a lock screen."

She frowned. "You have no contacts in here."

"No, I don't." I turned down her street. "Look at the call history."

Her fingers moved gracefully over the screen. "It is blank."

"There're no contacts because I memorize the numbers I need to know. There's no call history and no text history because the phone has a program loaded on it that wipes it clean every few minutes." Another trick November had taught me. "Same with the browsers, if you need them."

"Why—"

"Once I text you, memorize the number."

"Okay," she quietly consented.

"If you need me, you don't hesitate. You call, you text. I will be here in fifteen minutes, max. If it's an emergency, text me nine-one-one, and our guy on the outside will get to you within two minutes and stay with you until I get here. Whatever it is, you call or text."

"I am sure I will not need to." The phone grasped in her hands like a lifeline, she looked out the window. "But thank you."

Goddamn it. "I'm serious, Sabine. He doesn't get to put a hand on you again. If you think it's escalating, if you so much as *feel* threatened, don't hesitate. Make the call. There's no such thing as a false alarm in this situation, understand?"

She nodded.

VICTOR

Pulling up to the gate, I lowered the window. "What's the code?"

"Nine twenty-eight," she replied, her voice small and quiet.

My hand hovering by the keypad, I hesitated. Then I punched in the significant numbers and put the window up. "Your birthday."

Surprise in her expression, she glanced at me, but she didn't ask.

I pulled through the gate. "I saw it in your file."

"My file."

"Intel November pulled on you."

"I see."

She didn't.

I drove up to the pretentious house. "Nonnegotiable—when I text you, reply."

"Will you do the same?"

Jesus. Just when I didn't think this woman could gut me any worse. "Of course."

"All right." She slid the phone into her pocket.

I glanced at the house. "I know you don't want to hear it, but I'm going to say it one more time." I turned to her. "If you come with me, I'll get you out. I'll stay by your side until you disengage from Bertrand, until we find your nephew and his mother, and until whatever fuckery Bertrand pulls with the Feds or whoever else is over. I'll stand between you and whatever he has aimed. I will not leave your side until you're safe."

Her head down, her left hand on her right wrist, she spoke so damn quietly, I barely heard her. "Then what?"

In front of the asshole's house, no idea if there were security cameras aimed at us, or if he gave enough of a damn to watch them if there were, I didn't touch her. I wanted to, *fuck* I wanted to, but I wasn't going to give that piece of shit one shred of ammunition to use against her.

"Sabine, look at me."

No hesitation, she gave me her eyes.

"Then you get to make your own choices."

Inhaling sharply, she quickly turned toward the window. "Thank you for the ride, Mr. Conlon."

I took the hit like a blow to the chest, but I didn't show it. "You're welcome, Miss Malcher." Releasing her seat belt, I unbuckled mine. "Wait there. I'll walk you in."

She reached for the door. "There is no need."

"Your safety is my *only* need." I got out of the Range Rover.

FORTY-ONE

Sabine

"Your safety is my *only* need."

Dropping his sentiment like a bomb, the wreckage of my resolve to stay distanced exploded all around me as he got out of the vehicle, leaving nothing but his trail of rain-wet cobblestones and sandalwood-scented promises.

The full force of everything I had ever wanted but never had decimated me.

I did not want to get out of this vehicle.

I did not want to go into an ostentatious house full of art I hated with memories I hated even more.

I wanted to stay in this vehicle and smell the heady combination of forbidden masculinity and hope. I wanted to leave this place behind. I wanted to fly away and never look back. But my door opened, and there it was.

The two proverbial sides of the losing coin he had mentioned as he held his hand out to me.

One decision was bad.

The other was worse.

Even though I had only had sex with one man, I was not ignorant or inexperienced in the world of powerful men. I knew what kind of a dominant alpha Vance was, maybe more than I knew what Joseph was capable of. Vance was not offering me a life with him, not that it wouldn't be utterly insane to even consider it if he were. This former Marine turned mercenary was only offering what he knew how to offer.

Protection.

And he was offering it with every method of coercion in his arsenal.

Holding his hand out for me, his eyes intent on mine, he played his role so well I wanted to believe him. I wanted to lace our fingers and fall into the escape he was offering. Even more insane, I wanted to believe it would be the life I had always dreamed of—when I used to allow myself those kinds of wayward thoughts.

Except this was reality, I did not have a choice, and my role was already written.

Taking his hand, playing my part, I stepped from the SUV. "Thank you."

Not letting go of me, he leaned down like he was going to tell me a secret, but instead, he ushered in another dose of reality. "Your luggage will be here shortly."

His voice, his breath on my skin, his scent—*oh God, the way this man smelled*—I stood there stunned into silence, allowing myself one single heartbeat of a willing suspension of disbelief.

Me. Him. *Us.*

Inhaling every intoxicating thing about him one more time, I straightened my spine, my will and my resolve, then I pulled out of his grasp and stepped toward my prison.

"Your purse?"

His cell phone in my pocket anchoring me, I had forgotten one of the props of my sham of a life. "Yes, of course." I turned to reach for it, but at the same time, so did he.

Our heads came together, our gazes locked and my heart completely stopped.

Staring at amber-green eyes I could not imagine never seeing again, taking in full lips that had touched mine, knowing how the shadow dusting his angular jaw felt against my cheek—I drank in every beautiful, stoic inch of him as the memory of his kiss flushed my cheeks.

I wanted him to kiss me again. I *willed* him to.

But like all the other parts of my life that no longer fit together, he did not close that final puzzle piece of distance between us, and neither did I.

As fast as we had accidentally collided into this electrified space that existed between us every time we got close, he pulled back, coming away with my purse in his hand.

I could not help but think how Joseph had never, in all the years I had known him, ever picked up my purse—until the day this man had walked into my life.

The stark contrast of the men alarming, I reached for my Hermès handbag. "Thank you."

"I've got it." His gaze already scanning the front of the house, the driveway and the grounds beyond, he put his free hand on the small of my back. "How many security cameras are in front, love?"

Heat radiating from his palm, I could not think. Were there any security cameras here? "I am not sure, but knowing Joseph, probably a few."

"Do you?" Vance scanned the side of the yard leading down to the intracoastal. "Know him?"

I had never known Joseph, but I had always thought I had known what he was capable of. "Apparently not."

Guiding me up the front steps, Vance paused in front of the ten-foot-tall etched-glass and mahogany double front doors. "Were you ever close?"

My back stiffened, and it struck me.

Vance had never asked me about Joseph. Not if I loved him or if I wanted to leave him or any intimate details. It was as if he had taken one look at me, decided what he wanted, picked a course of action and executed it.

In fact, he had never asked me what I wanted at all.

He had assumed.

Or maybe he had not assumed at all. Maybe the thought of what I wanted had never crossed his mind. Maybe he was exactly like Joseph, and that was why he was asking. And make no mistake, I knew what he was asking.

He wanted to know if I was currently sleeping with a man more than twice my age.

Blatantly ignoring him, knowing it would be unlocked because Joseph would have had Norma alert the staff that we were coming, I opened the front door.

FORTY-TWO

Vance

DEFIANT, PURPOSELY IGNORING MY QUESTION, SHE WALKED INTO an unlocked, unsecured house.

Trying not to have a fucking coronary, I shut the door behind us and stepped in front of her. My hand up in the universal gesture to stop, I took in the entire open-plan entry and living area in one sweep. "Wait here. Does the staff usually come to meet you?"

"Not me, but they do for Joseph."

Of course they fucking did. "I'll be back in a minute." I caught her gaze and repeated myself. "Wait."

Cursing myself for not leaving her in the Range Rover, doors locked until I cleared this fucking place, I aimed for the sounds I heard coming from a kitchen.

Two women, one older, one a cheap imitation of a nineteen-year-old Sabine, had their backs to me as I walked into the kitchen. "Excuse me," I barked.

The younger one jumped about a foot as she dropped a pot then spun around.

The older one calmly turned and looked at me like she gave zero fucks that someone had walked in on them. "Can I help you?"

"Anyone else in the house?" I demanded.

"No," she answered while the Sabine look-alike bit her bottom lip and checked me out. "And you are?"

"Security. Why was the front door unlocked?"

"Security for who?" she countered.

"Miss Malcher. The door?"

"Clearly I left it unlocked so you could waltz into my kitchen and demand answers to your questions," the older one quipped. "Now, if there's nothing else, I have meal prep to tend to."

"A meal for who?" After the event, if shit didn't go completely FUBAR, we were flying to Vienna.

"I'm going to assume you've met *Miss Malcher*," she hazed.

Narrowing my gaze, I eyed her. "For the record, I appreciate the attitude." The question was if she would stand up to that asshole Bertrand if Sabine needed help. "But I seriously hope you're not about to insult Miss Malcher."

The older woman smirked. "No, but I am about to feed her. You too if you play your cards right. Now if you'll excuse me, I have work to do." She turned back to her meal prep. "And *for the record*, you might not be awful either."

The silent one, still wide-eyed, quickly turned back around to help her companion.

"Right." I chuckled without humor. "*Not awful*. Lock the front door after I leave."

The older woman stirred something on the stove. "Aye, aye, Captain."

Leaving them to it, I did a quick walk-through of the first floor, checking any doors and looking for security cameras, before making my way back to the front of the house.

Standing exactly where I left her, Sabine's gaze tracked me as I walked across the foyer.

Not stopping, already having scanned the foyer for internal security cameras, I walked right up to her and braced my hands on either side of her head. "You never answered my question."

"Pardon?"

"You know what I'm talking about."

She looked away.

Grasping her chin, I brought her gaze back to mine. "I need to see your eyes for this conversation, love."

"Do not call me that," she whispered, eyes averted.

"Look at me, Sabine."

Her chest rose with an inhale, and she gave me what I asked for.

I repeated my earlier question. "Were you ever close to him?" Was I off base about any of this?

She blinked.

I fucking asked. "Do you love him?"

Turning, she made to escape under my arm. "I am not talking about him. This is absurd."

"Highly unusual, maybe from your perspective, but not in my line of work." I talked to all kinds of people. "I ask the hard questions." I dealt with murderers, kidnappers and terrorists. Bertrand didn't come close to topping the list of deplorable human beings, but he fucking topped my personal list.

"That is not what I am talking about."

I knew exactly what the hell she meant, but I pushed anyway, driving the fucking point home. "Isn't it?" The singular truth was that she was avoiding the question.

A foot away from me, she crossed her arms and gave me a look. One that said I was full of shit and I could take a fucking hike. A look that she completely underestimated. Whether she knew it or not, that look conveyed everything she wasn't telling me.

Add in the fact that she felt safe enough with me to give me attitude, and I was taking the win because I saw it in her eyes. She gave a damn what I thought, not Bertrand. So as absurd as she'd claimed this conversation was, it was happening, and I wasn't finished.

I stepped in front of her. "Have you ever met someone and

thought, deep down, where it counts, that you know them?" Because I hadn't, but I fucking *knew* this woman.

"I do not know you," she immediately retorted.

"I know you."

Something close to anger flushed her cheeks, and the front she put on for that fuck Bertrand and everyone else in his world slipped further.

"Do you?" she asked incredulously. "Do you know anything about me besides what I look like, what I am wearing, where I live or what I do at work? Because you have not asked," she accused before her voice morphed from anger to hurt. "You have not asked me the simplest of questions."

Leaning closer, caging her in, I smelled the subtle fragrance that was an expensive perfume, but more, it was the woman behind it. The warrior who started her day by putting on a designer dress and heels, not knowing what kind of hell was going to be unleashed on her. But she got fucking primed, showed up and did what she had to do because that's who she was. This woman was living with a conviction sentenced by the draw of absolute shit circumstances, and she still fucking showed up.

"I don't need to ask the simple questions, because I know you, pet. And if you recognize the nuances in my speech like you claimed you do, then you heard my tone when I said pet, and you know exactly what it means in this circumstance." I cupped her cheek. "You know I'm staring at an extraordinary woman that, despite absolute untenable circumstances, shows up every day of her life and takes the deplorable behavior of a man so goddamn beneath her he doesn't deserve to breathe her same air, let alone lay one word of anger on her. So if you want to lie to yourself and say I don't know what kind of woman gives up her own safety to protect a child she met once, then go ahead, pet, tell yourself that. Do what you have to do, because unlike him, I won't hold it against you. I know damn well what I'm looking at, and it's a woman living in fear but doing it with every ounce of bravery she has."

She sucked in a sharp breath, but I wasn't finished.

"You want to know why I'm doing this? You want a reason why I'll take a goddamn bullet for you if that's what it takes to set you free?" I leaned closer. "There is no reason." Dropping my voice, I enunciated every fucking word of the truth. "It's simply the right thing to do." Holding her blue-eyed gaze, I gave her the rest of it. "But make no mistake, I'm not doing this because of what I *see*. I'm doing this because the woman holding her head up to fight another day is just like me." Grasping her jaw, my palm on her throat, I brought my lips to hers. "I see you, Sabine Malcher, and I fucking know you—all the parts that count." I slammed my mouth over hers.

She didn't hesitate, not one fraction of a second.

Opening up like she was as starved for me as I was for her, she gave me permission to kiss her as much as if she'd said the words and asked for this. She knew. I knew. And sinking my tongue into the sweet heat of her mouth was never going to be enough for either of us.

Tasting her once but then pulling back before the kiss even started, I dropped my hold on her. "I'll be back for you in one hour. Be ready."

Without another goddamn word, I forced myself to walk out.

If the truth didn't convince her to take a fucking chance with me, nothing would.

FORTY-THREE

Vance

Scanning my thumbprint, I walked into AES's secure headquarters on the top floor of a Miami Beach high-rise. Bypassing the empty reception desk that was just for show because all of our support staff was remote and hidden behind firewalls even I couldn't hack, I went straight to the command center.

About to scan my fingerprint again to gain access, I was stopped by Alpha's woman.

"Vance, do you have a minute?"

"Not now, love."

Alpha stepped out of his office. "Her name is Maila, and if she asks you for a minute, you give it to her."

"Adam," Maila quietly chided. "I've got a handle on this."

Out of patience, I turned. "Instead of getting a handle on this, whatever *this* is, maybe you should get a handle on him." I looked at Alpha. "I'm perfectly aware of the name of the only female operative at AES who also happens to be a former CIA agent. I also know where she shopped last week, how she likes her coffee, and what the fuck she wants to talk to me about right now, but at this moment, while I'm in the middle of a time-sensitive case, I don't have a minute to spare, let alone explain a term of affection to you. Live with it."

Trefor's tone went low and lethal. "Lose the *affection*, gain some respect." Glancing at his woman, he tipped his chin and walked back into this office.

I turned and pressed my thumb to the scanner outside the command center.

"He's not wrong," Maila said to my back.

The door clicked and I pushed it open. "He never is." I walked in.

The blessed woman followed me. "I saw Sanaa."

"Good for you." Scanning the war room for November, I spotted him in his usual corner behind four monitors and three keyboards.

"She said Ronan's worried about you."

Halting midstep, I spun. "Do you know why I call you *love*?" I didn't wait for an answer. "Because I like you." She was impenetrable, stood her own against Alpha and made everyone's life at AES easier, but she didn't get my fucking nuances.

"You use that pet name with every woman," she calmly countered with no intonation.

"No, I differentiate," I corrected. "There's a significant difference." But so far, only one woman seemed to have picked up on that. "The difference in this instance is that my affection for you is directly linked to the fact that you don't get involved with my personal life."

Well trained by the CIA and life circumstances I wouldn't wish on anyone, she didn't even blink. "Understood." She turned.

"That's it?"

She glanced over her shoulder. "Respect is a two-way street."

I winked. "Understood, love."

In a rare show of emotion, she shook her head.

I made my way to November. "What have you found on the breaches?"

"Nothing good."

"I think I may know why Bertrand wants to get rid of her." I just couldn't figure out why he'd gone to such elaborate lengths instead of just kicking her out on her ass sooner.

"Seven years," November stated, coming to the same conclusion I had.

"Right. She'll be his common-law wife soon, if she isn't already. She'll get half of everything."

"I thought the same thing, and she would have been if New York state recognized common law marriage, but they don't. I did find something else though. She's on the board of directors at Harrington's. There's also a bank account set up in her name, with Bertrand as the beneficiary. Regular deposits have been made that indicate she's earning a salary, but otherwise, the account hasn't been touched." November kept typing. "There's no security footage of her at the bank and the account was opened online after she was made a board member."

"I'm betting the account setup was Bertrand's doing." If she'd known she had money, she probably would've left.

"Most likely."

"Why make her a member of the board, besides the advantage of a second vote he could manipulate?" She hadn't mentioned she was on the board.

"Don't know." November glanced at me. "But she's not the first woman he's kept around. He has a history of this. There's a string of them before her, all young, all the same scenario, with the exception of becoming board members. They move in, work at Harrington's, disappear off the radar financially, then he ends the relationship. Rinse and repeat." He glanced at me. "But she's lasted the longest. By a significant amount."

"How significant?"

"Before her, he usually upgraded every year."

I stared at the financial records on the screen. "How did he end the other relationships?"

November removed his hands from the keyboard and turned

in his chair to face me. "He has several offshore accounts, and there are coordinating twenty-grand withdrawals that match his dating history, but a different offshore account caught my attention. Other than the opening deposit, it's never been touched—with only seven exceptions. Every year, for the past seven years, it gets fifty grand poorer. Cash withdrawals. There's also this." Reaching back, November's index finger hit his keyboard.

Images of young women, all in dresses and heels, flashed across the screen. Blonde, brunette, redhead, short, tall. They had nothing in common except two things. Not one of them was over twenty-five, and every single one had on the same necklace Sabine was wearing.

"The fucking cheap bastard's recycling."

November nodded once in acknowledgment before spinning back to face his setup.

"So what makes her different?" I knew what was so damn special about this woman, I felt it the second I laid eyes on her, but Bertrand didn't. "Why has she lasted longer? Bertrand could've kicked her off the board. And what the fuck is that account about with seven annual withdrawals?"

"Working on it."

"How solvent is he?"

November glanced at me. "How solvent is he or how solvent is Harrington's?"

"Both."

"He's sitting on eight figures in property and company equity, but his personal accounts barely total a quarter of a million in cash between all of them."

So the fuck had spread himself and Harrington's thin. "Makes that potential ten million from a sale of the entire collection of diamonds combined with her ring much more of a motive."

"If the other diamonds exist."

"And if he could get them, depending on who has them.

What about the nephew's mother? That could be why she's been off the grid."

"Possibly. I'm looking for a trail on the rest of the diamonds, but so far, there's nothing."

"Keep looking." If her brother had gotten his hands on four of them, I was betting the other seven were out there. "Going back to the fifty grand annual withdrawals from Bertrand's offshore account, could he be purchasing one a year?"

"Each diamond is worth ten times that, and why not buy them all at once?"

"If the nephew's mother has them, maybe she isn't aware of the value, or maybe Bertrand's blackmailing her? Fuck, maybe she's spreading it out, who the hell knows? But it makes more sense than anything else."

"Possibly," November replied noncommittally.

"It still doesn't explain why Bertrand would set Sabine up. He's concerned enough about his reputation to show her off every day for some bullshit standing lunch date, so why smear her name and Harrington's by implicating her?"

"That's what I meant by nothing good. I can't find a trail to those hacks that lead back to anyone on Bertrand's staff or any of his security or IT contractors."

"You're sure DGSE isn't behind it?"

"They're definitely involved. They've got malware on Harrington's servers that has been there for years, but they're not behind the breaches he's accusing her of."

Fuck. "I don't like walking into this with an unknown third party involved." I glanced at my watch. "We're running out of time." The event started in less than an hour. "I need to know who the hell I'm protecting her from." And what they'll be coming at us with.

November glanced at me. "Not exactly your assignment."

"We're back to this bullshit again? You think I give a single fuck about what that asshole hired Trefor for?"

"No."

"You mentioned it for a reason." November didn't waste his breath.

"You're in deep."

"I'm always in deep." My safety wasn't my priority. "That's what Alpha pays me for."

"This is different."

No fucking shit. My head a goddamn playground for psychiatrists, misplaced redemption just out of reach, a woman I couldn't get off my mind—this wasn't just different. It was the perfect storm. Maybe, finally, I'd fucking go down with the ship. Except I wasn't sure I wanted to go down anymore. And that wasn't a place I could afford to dwell in, for too many reasons to count, none of which November needed to know about.

"She's the one in danger, she's the one I'll protect." Simple fucking truth.

November spun in his chair and, without any change in facial expression, managed to look at me like I was full of shit. "You have a moral compass now?"

"Right." Fuck this. "You were speaking to Maila," I accused.

"About?"

Itching for a fight, but reining it in, I kept my composure. "I don't have time for a coffee chat. You want to gossip, find Echo. You two can wax poetic about moral compasses and being deep." Fuck November. "In less than an hour, I'm walking into a compromised event with no intel. Do your job, or don't. I don't give a fuck." Pissed, I aimed for the exit as the door swung open.

His usual smirk in place, Echo walked in.

"Why the hell aren't you watching the house?" I'd promised her someone would be on site.

"Sent Blade." Echo eyed me like I was losing my shit. Which

was equivalent to stepping in it for him. "What the fuck is wrong with you?"

"Blade," I deadpanned. That fuck was completely insane.

"You got a problem with it? You go sit on the house." Echo looked past me to November and tipped his chin. "You get what I need?"

Suspicion flared my already-lit fuse. "He's neck-deep on my assignment. What the hell do you need from him?"

"None of your fucking business." Echo purposely shoved past me. With a smirk, he shook his head at November. "I see he's still got his dick in his hand over the brunette."

I didn't think twice.

Jumping Echo, I took the motherfucker down. Twenty pounds of muscle on me, the former SEAL hit the floor as I pinned his arm behind his back and slammed one knee between his shoulder blades. "What did you just say to me?" Out of my goddamn mind, I didn't notice he wasn't fighting back until the asshole laughed.

Then he turned his head and grinned. "I'm gonna enjoy the fuck out of this, jarhead."

Echo moved.

No regard for the arm I still had pinned, he flipped, arched and kicked himself upright.

I lost my grip on him, and in the next second, my face was slammed into a desk.

Game on. "You're going to pay for that, motherfucker."

"Whatsa matter, grunt, don't like getting your pretty face hit?" Grabbing the back of my shirt, he threw me against the wall. "Is that better? Your pussy ass needs a fair fight? Is that why you only step into the ring at the Annex?"

I wasn't a match for a six-six Navy SEAL. But I had one goddamn advantage. Rage. "Maybe I am a pussy, but my dick's not in my hand now. What's your excuse?" Slamming my head back into his, my elbow hit his ribs before I spun and kneed him in the balls.

Then it was all-out war.

He fucking threw me, my back crashed into monitors, I leveraged my fall and went for a tackle. We took out a desk, he hit the floor, I landed three strikes, he cut more. Punch after punch, equipment smashed, fists collided with cartilage, we destroyed the command center.

I was intent on killing him, he was fucking me up for sport, and neither of us was going to give in first.

My fist slammed into his jaw. He threw an uppercut into my already-bruised ribs. I kicked out his legs, he grabbed me in a headlock, and I twisted as we hit the floor.

The control room's door flew open, and Alpha yelled, "Echo!"

"Party's over. Night night, grunt." Echo reared back with a right hook.

Before his fist made contact with my face, he was yanked off me.

Pinning both his arms behind his back, Alpha unleashed. "What *the fuck* are you two doing?"

His shirt ripped, Echo winked at me. "Playing chess."

"*Goddamn it.*" Releasing Echo only to shove him back two feet, Alpha pointed at him. "You fucking know better." His finger aim came at me. "Bertrand touched down ten minutes ago. You need to be handling your shit." He looked between both of us. "This is coming out of your salaries."

"I got something," November interjected.

Alpha's ire zeroed in on November, who was standing in a corner, holding a laptop with one hand while typing with the other. "Why the fuck didn't you stop this, Rhys?"

"Not my fight." Still typing, November didn't look up from his screen.

"What did you find?" I demanded.

Alpha leveled me with his glare. "No. You're on fucking cleanup duty." He turned to Echo. "You too."

"Can't." I swiped the blood dripping from my mouth with the back of my hand. "I have a party to attend. November?"

He glanced up and surveyed the room as if seeing the destruction for the first time. "Armored transport company hired to bring in the art and babysit it tonight had a last-minute employee change in their roster this afternoon."

"Because?" I demanded.

Still looking around the room, November frowned. "Stomach flu."

Bullshit. "Did you run background on the replacement?"

"Yeah," November answered, but then he didn't elaborate as he stared at his second-favorite workstation, desk overturned, monitors on the floor.

"*November*," Alpha snapped.

"Sam Smith, age thirty-two, no priors, no credit history, no bank account." November looked up. "His passport is French."

Goddamn it.

"Fuck." Alpha looked at me. "Clean up, escort her to the party." He glanced at Echo. "Create a diversion that gets Bertrand to the event early so Conlon can get to the wife. Everyone on comms. November, you're point." Alpha glanced at Echo, then me. "Work together and fucking focus up. Both of you," he warned before aiming for the exit.

I followed.

Grinning, blood covering his teeth, Echo dropped his voice as I passed. "Pussy."

"Dick."

"See you at the party, Lover Boy."

FORTY-FOUR

Sabine

The cell phone that I'd been glancing at every other minute silently lit up with a text.

Are you okay, pet?

Nerves fluttered in my stomach, and I glanced over my shoulder to make sure Joseph was not nearby. Then I typed a quick reply.

Yes.

The three dots appeared, and another message came in.

That doesn't sound very convincing.

I elaborated.

I am fine.

For a whole minute, I sat there, staring at the screen, but he did not reply. Forcing myself to set the phone down, I started to tuck it into my purse when the screen lit up again.

You're more than fine. You're beautiful. Did you memorize this number?

Heat rushed to my cheeks, and I quickly read the number twice then repeated it in my head.

Another text came in. *Darling?*

For the first time in as long as I could remember, despite the circumstances, despite my life, despite the here and now, the sides of my lips tipped north.

I typed a reply. *I memorized it.*

His reply was immediate. *Good girl. Now wait three seconds and call me.*

If I was not holding the phone and staring at it, I would not have believed what I saw next.

The texts and the number that they had come from disappeared off the screen.

Standing up from the vanity in the master bathroom, I glanced out into the bedroom. Then I closed the bathroom door, but not all the way because I had learned seven years ago about the repercussions for closed or locked doors.

Moving to the far corner of the bathroom by the window, I dialed the number I had memorized.

He answered before the first ring. "Hello, pet."

Deeper, darker, his voice was even sexier over the phone. "Hello."

He chuckled. "No reprimand for calling you pet this time?"

"No."

His tone turned serious. "I know Bertrand showed up a few minutes ago. How are you holding up?"

I had not been separated from Vance for more than an hour, but it felt like a lifetime. My stomach hurt, my wrist was sore, I was hungry, tired and out of sorts, but his voice seemed to make everything better, which only scared me more.

"I am fine." I did not tell him that Joseph had already shown up in my room, yelled at the cook to remove my meal, then threatened me to behave at the party before storming out.

"Right," Vance stated flatly. "I'm going to let that lie slide because we don't have much time, and I don't want you to get caught on the phone. But you need to know, pet, this is going to get worse before it gets better. We haven't found your nephew, we're still tracking who was behind the security breaches, and I don't know what will go down tonight. As much as I want to pull you immediately, I'm not going to take that choice away from you. Not now at least. But it bears repeating. If you're ready to walk, I'll be there in ten minutes."

"I thought you said it would take you fifteen minutes to get here."

"With Bertrand on-site, it's now ten."

I closed my eyes against the welling tears. "Thank you," I whispered.

He paused a moment, then his voice deepened. "You never need to thank me for protecting you."

"What can I thank you for?" Because I may not know him intimately, or even on a personal level, but everything he had said to me in the foyer, it resonated. There was something about him, about us, that felt like we knew each other, like we were connected in a boundless, limitless way without beginning or end, just as if it were always there, waiting. In all my life, I had never experienced anything like it.

I had no name for it, and I was terrified of this connection that had seemed to already grow deep roots, but I also wanted to run toward it. I wanted to grasp on and desperately hold this intangible feeling that did not make any logical sense, but was there as surely and as intimately as a part of my own body.

Vance's chuckle was reserved and so very seductive. "Oh, darling, how I would love to give you a thousand reasons to thank me right now. All of them sordid and inappropriate and will give me far more pleasure than you can possibly imagine, but we'll wait for that, yes?"

For a single heartbeat, I could not breathe as I felt both weightless and stricken by a current that tingled at every one of my nerve endings. Heat flushing my entire body, I held the phone tighter. "Are you asking me or telling me?"

"Oh, pet." His voice went deep and gravelly like the wet cobblestones he smelled of. "You have no idea, do you?"

"About?"

"How absolutely, stunningly beautiful and submissive you are."

The ethereal feeling of butterflies floating all over my skin evaporated. "A submissive woman is not a strong woman."

"*Au contraire, ma chérie.*" He switched back to English. "In time, I will show you exactly how wrong that statement is."

His French was near perfect, as if he had been speaking it his whole life, but it was also a short turn of phrase that was not uncommon. "When did you learn to speak French?"

He chuckled again, but this time it was more playful. "I tell you I'm going to show you how gloriously submissive you are, and that's what you ask me?"

I hesitated as the butterflies came back. "Yes."

His tone turned serious again. "Is that a question or a statement, because you hesitated, love."

Briefing closing my eyes, I soaked up every second of this conversation. His attention to detail, to me, his mannerisms, his voice, the way I was imagining how he would be looking at me if he were here right now. And more than anything, I loved that I could hear the smile in his voice when it had been missing since we had touched down this afternoon. I knew what we were up against, but this brief reprieve with him, it was exactly the soothing balm my soul needed.

"Statement," I decided.

It was his turn to briefly pause as I heard him inhale, then let it out slowly as if he were about to tell me something no one else knew.

"My mother had twin boys, one of which was unruly and prone to getting into trouble, especially when she wasn't around. Her solution to keep her twins out of trouble was to have them learn a foreign language." He half laughed, then switched back to talking about himself in first person. "Countless CDs later, I was proficient enough to impress the ladies, which only spurred my commitment to attaining the perfect accent."

I did not know which part of his reveal to digest first. "You are a twin?"

"I am. And before you ask, I'm the better-looking one."

"Fraternal?"

"Identical."

I laughed.

His voice turned quiet. "Oh, darling. Your laugh is exquisite."

I blushed. "Thank you."

"No, thank you."

Neither of us said anything for a brief moment.

Then, the Marine turned mercenary cleared his throat and his tone went all business. "I'll see you in half an hour. Call if you need anything before then." He hung up.

Tucking the phone away in my small Judith Leiber crystal-embellished clutch that matched the emerald-green Monique Lhuillier sleeveless dress I had on, I smiled as it vibrated with a new text.

Pulling it back out, I looked at the screen.

One last thing. When he tells you it's time to leave for the party, stall. Tell him you're not dressed, you need five minutes.

Instead of nerves shooting through my system like an adrenaline rush of fear, they danced in dangerous anticipation. Anticipation I could not afford. I quickly typed a reply.

Why?

His reply was instant.

Trust, love.

No longer smiling, I put the phone away.

FORTY-FIVE

Vance

EXPECTING IT, I WAS STILL PISSED WHEN I SAW BERTRAND'S number light up my cell.

I waited for four rings before answering. "Bertrand."

"What the hell are you doing, and why did I have to call Trefor to get your new phone number because you didn't answer any of my calls on the old one? Where's my evidence? You've had all goddamn day."

"Right." Ignoring his comment about my new cell, I made a mental note to block his number from the phone I gave Sabine. "In a rush now, are we? I thought you said I have seventy-two hours." I tossed the ice pack I was holding against my jaw back into the freezer.

"That was before I got a call that there's a problem at the venue. This better not be something she's behind."

"What problem?" I asked dryly, stepping into a pair of Santoni dress oxfords.

"I'll handle it."

I bet he would. "Right then, see you there." I slid my VP9 into a shoulder holster.

"Pick up Sabine on your way," he ordered. "I didn't have time to wait for her. Make sure you're both there in time for the preview event. Understood?"

"Copy that." I grabbed an extra comm for Ronan and shoved it in my suit pocket.

"Don't give me your military bullshit, just do what you're paid to do. And let me remind you, after the event, we're leaving for Vienna. You'll fly on my plane."

Fucking hell. "And let me remind you that you said to find my own transport. Which, under the circumstances, if you want me to continue to do my job, it's safer for you to have her on an AES jet where I can monitor and intercept her cell communications."

Bertrand snorted in disgust. "If you'd already been doing that, we wouldn't be having this conversation because this problem would've been handled by now. Do your fucking job, Victor." He hung up.

I dialed Trefor.

He picked up immediately. "Echo's got Bertrand en route to the venue with some fabricated problem. You on your way to pick her up?"

"Leaving my penthouse now, but we have another issue. Bertrand wants me on his plane for the Vienna leg. I countered with bringing Sabine on the Falcon. It's a no-go."

Trefor didn't say shit.

"You there?"

"I'm here. I'm just processing that she went from his wife to Miss Malcher to Sabine and now you're calling because you can't... what? Control the narrative?"

Sore, tired and fucking frustrated, I let shit slip. "I'll kill him if he lays a hand on her."

Trefor sighed. "Look, I'm working this through back channels, November's on it, we'll find the nephew and his mother, we'll work the problem. As far as tonight, Vienna, stick to the woman, stay in your three-foot world, then you can pull her the second the auction ends and do whatever the fuck you want to Bertrand because you will anyway. Until then, keep it tight. But

I have a feeling you won't be dealing with Bertrand for long. Neither will she."

Trefor had security clearances I didn't, and he was honorable to a fault. I knew he wouldn't tell me, but I asked anyway. "What aren't you telling me?"

"I can't say, but the French aren't the only ones who've had their eye on Harrington's and Bertrand."

"Feds?" If he was looking at hard time, I might spare the asshole's life so he could enjoy living behind bars.

"No comment."

It was. Fucking good. "You always know how to cheer me up." I grabbed an extra magazine for my 9mm.

"Christ. Just don't kill him on the flight to Vienna."

"Right. I'll keep that in mind." I wouldn't. "In the meantime, keep sweet-talking me, and one of these days I just might listen to you."

"The day you listen to me is the day I fire you."

I chuckled. "Because you'll know I've turned into your whipping boy?"

Trefor's tone turned lethally quiet. "No, because I'll know you lost your edge."

"Understood," I replied, equally serious.

"Good. See you at the party." Trefor hung up.

I texted Sabine. *On my way, pet.*

Her reply came a few seconds later.

All right.

I was still staring at it, trying to decipher the tone of her reply when another text came in.

Echo: *Fucknut took the bait, you can put your dick down and go pick her up.*

Against my better judgment, I typed a reply.

Me: *I wasn't holding my dick, your mother was, but copy that, on my way.*

VICTOR

Echo: *You may have some balls after all, Lover Boy.*

Shoving my cell in my pocket, I walked out the door.

Ten minutes later, waging an internal war, I was pulling up to the Coral Gables house. Lowering my window, telling myself I would not touch this woman tonight, that I'd keep my head in the fucking game and keep it professional, at least until I got her through tonight and Vienna, I reached to punch the code in.

"All's quiet." Blade stepped from the shadows of the awabuki hedge bordering the property. "Target left fifteen minutes ago."

"Client," I corrected.

"Officially or unofficially?" Blade asked, his gaze scanning first left then right.

"Both. Bertrand's the client." I didn't know who the fuck I was trying to convince, Blade or myself. Bertrand was the client but not my objective. I'd protect this woman tonight no matter what, even if that meant from myself.

In cargos and a black T-shirt, Blade said nothing. He fucking stared at me.

My resolve to keep it tight for one goddamn night already slipping, I glared back. "What did Echo tell you?"

"That you have your dick in your hand over some brunette and the client is now the target and the suspect wife is now the client."

"Right." Asshole. "Paraphrase next time." Antagonizing Blade was a hundred times more suicidal than taking on Echo, but one comment about her and I was already losing my shit. "She's not his wife, and I'm late picking her up."

"I'll be outside the event."

Fucking great. "You're not on comms."

"I hear you."

Pissed at myself, at that asshole Bertrand, at the impotence

I felt over this whole damn situation, I antagonized Blade further. "You didn't check in earlier when November cued us all up."

"I didn't need to."

Right. "And I thought I was a lone wolf."

Blade's vacant gaze held steady on me, then he reached over and entered the gate code. "Woman's inside, untouched."

Not bothering to question how he knew the code, my head fucked six ways from Sunday, I pulled through the gate.

FORTY-SIX

Sabine

The cell phone Vance gave me pinged with a new text.
Coming up the front steps, love. I'll let myself in.
A flurry of nerves danced in my stomach, and I re-checked my reflection in the mirror. This time I had on eyeliner and eye shadow and a warmth to my cheeks that was not entirely from the text I had just gotten.

With my clutch under my arm, I held the hem of my dress, and hurried downstairs as the front door opened.

Then I stopped short.

In a dark blue suit and a deep violet shirt unbuttoned at the neck, Vance stepped into the foyer.

He was so handsome, my heart stalled, then started beating as erratically as when I first saw him.

With his hair slicked back, the angles of his face stood out even more as he took me in from head to toe. His eyes more green than amber in the evening light, he met my stare with a heated gaze. "You're stunning."

His voice alone, deep, rich, and reverent, made me want to rush toward him and fall into his arms. But nerves I had never experienced with any man before kept me rooted on the bottom step, holding onto the banister for support, as a blush swept up my neck and across my cheeks.

Almost forgetting my manners, I managed a shy response. "Thank you. You look lovely."

One of his eyebrows arched teasingly. "Lovely?"

"Handsome," I amended.

"Right." Inhaling deep, he strode across the foyer toward me but then stopped two feet away. A frown creased his brow, and his voice went quiet. "I have a problem."

Alarm spread. "Joseph?"

"Entirely different problem." His gaze cut to the gold cuff on my right wrist before he met my eyes again. "I told myself I wouldn't touch you."

Just like his different kind of problem, a different kind of alarm settled in my chest. "Oh." I did not want to think about him never touching me.

"Right," he said even quieter, searching my face.

I said nothing. Any words I let slip at that moment would be too revealing, and I could not afford that luxury until I knew Julien and Chantel were safe.

"That's another problem," he added.

"Pardon?"

"That look in your eyes. The one I unintentionally just put there with my admission. I apologize." Stepping back, he glanced at my wrist a second time. "Shall we?"

"Please, stop."

His gaze focused on the single suitcase I had left at the bottom of the stairs. "Stop what, love?" He reached for the handle. "Is this all you're taking?" He still did not look at me.

I stepped off the bottom step and closed the distance between us. "I prefer eye contact from you as well."

His gaze immediately cut to mine.

"Please stop worrying about my wrist." As I was about to tell him I was fine, I noticed a shadow on his jaw that had not been there an hour ago. "Do I need to worry about what happened to you?"

He smiled, but it was muted. "No."

"I will anyway," I admitted.

He shook his head, and the damper on his smile lifted to make room for a taste of irony. "The feeling's mutual, love." He gestured toward the door with an open hand. "After you."

His suit jacket opened briefly, and I saw it. "You are armed."

His expression locked down. "Always."

Everything in my mind shifted to a place I did not want it to go to but could not stop. "In New York?"

"Yes."

Oh God, he was lying. "You took your suit jacket off on the plane. You did not have a gun strapped to your shoulder then." I had told myself he was not violent. He was protective and a hero. Yes, dominant and alpha and controlling, but I never, not once, suspected him of being violent, and now everything was shifting. The bruise on his face, the gun—*oh God*.

"No, I didn't." His eyes on me, he lifted the hem of his left leg a few inches to reveal a glimpse of another gun strapped to his ankle.

I sucked in a sharp breath as the familiar pinpricks of fear erupted across my entire body. "It is only a preview party."

"Then I won't have to shoot anyone."

The sinking feeling in my stomach grew to insurmountable proportions. "Do you do that a lot?"

"Define a lot."

"Vance," I barely whispered as my voice broke.

"You're making this very difficult not to touch you, love."

I stepped back.

I did not want him to touch me. I did not want him to be like Henri. I did not want him to have a job where he had to carry two guns and shoot people because that was not a world where he would be safe, where I would be safe. "This, this is—" Choking on the words and the thought, I could not say it.

"This is what protecting you looks like," he said, finishing my words with a steely resolve that was not in my prevue before yesterday.

Or before Joseph accused me of terrible crimes, I had to remind myself, but it did not help. I was afraid. Except that fear had a very different distinction than the one I felt for an infant I had not watched grow into a child, and suddenly, I did not know if I could do this.

"Are you afraid of the guns or what I'm capable of doing with them?" he asked, as if knowing the trajectory of my thoughts.

I tried to swallow down the anxiety rushing up my throat. "I—"

"I'm not Bertrand."

I shook my head. "I did not say that."

His stare intense, his muscles straining his suit jacket, he looked every bit the fierce warrior who had served his country. But then something shifted in his expression, in his eyes, and he was on me, quick and silent and lethal.

His hands taking my face, his eyes holding me captive, he read my fear as if I had spoken it. "I am not your brother, and there is only one innocent victim I have ever hurt. I will *not* hurt you."

"I am frightened."

"I know," he said simply, poignantly.

"You are not giving me reassurance."

"I'm not going to lie to you."

Feeling both as if I had nothing and everything to lose, I spoke my truth. "Your world scares me."

"My world is your world."

I desperately tried to inhale every nuance of how that statement could be perceived, but he had said it with the same hardened resolve and locked-down expression as when he had spoken of his weapons—without apology, without emotion and with complete alpha dominance.

I thought I had known this man, but I knew nothing. The

once-nostalgic rain-wet cobblestone and sandalwood musk of his scent that had lured me into a sense of rightness and made me feel as if I was coming home—it now smelled like the danger hiding in darkened shadows.

For seven years I had been frightened of Joseph, afraid of what I knew he was capable of. I thought I knew what true fear was.

Oh, how naïve I had been.

Stepping back from the mercenary in front of me, from his hold, I willed my voice to hold steady. "We should go."

FORTY-SEVEN

Vance

SHE WAS AFRAID OF ME. Every damn inch of her gorgeous body was radiating with it, but it was her eyes that fucking killed me.

Pulling out of my grasp as if I would hurt her, she stepped away from me and completely shut down. "We should go."

"There's that word." I fucking hated it.

"It is time to go," she amended without an ounce of life in either her voice or her eyes.

It was fucking time for me to end this bullshit, put my hands on her and kiss the fuck out of her. But I'd made a goddamn promise to myself that for one party, and one single fucking flight, I wouldn't touch her.

I wouldn't scare her. I wouldn't push her. I wouldn't flirt with her. I wouldn't do a damn thing that even hinted at the insane, possessive thoughts clouding my judgment. I'd do exactly as I promised her.

I'd protect her.

From Bertrand, from her past, from whatever storm was brewing—and from me.

I'd do my damn job.

Then I'd told myself the reward would be in Vienna. After the last gavel strike ended the auction, I'd steal her away. I'd take her anywhere in the world. I didn't care where, anywhere she wanted to go, as long as it was with me. Then I'd show her exactly how my hands on her felt. Pleasure, want, need, and yes, pain—the kind of torturous ache where I withheld her orgasms until I drove her over the edge, making her crave no one and nothing but me.

I couldn't wait for the sweet fucking agony and pleasure of what I knew would be explosive between us.

I'd told myself that was when I'd earn her trust and make her mine.

But I'd been a goddamn fool.

This woman was never going to trust me. Not my touch, not my word, not what I did at AES. And she'd never fucking understand the Annex.

The irony was I would've given it all up for her.

One fucking kiss, and I would've walked away from my life for her.

I never thought fate would screw me twice in one lifetime with this kind of mindfuck, but here I was, staring it in the face, drowning all over again, but this time in blue eyes, and there was no mistake.

I knew what I was looking at.

No choice, I grabbed her suitcase. "Right." Walking to the door, I held it open. "Let's get you to your party."

FORTY-EIGHT

Vance

TWO GODDAMN HOURS. Two fucking torturous hours of watching that son of a bitch put his hands on her and play a fucking game of pretentious bullshit like he didn't treat her worse than a goddamn dog behind closed doors.

The hired security fucks had come and gone. The French passport prick had stayed outside with the armored transport. Miami's elite, dressed to impress, drank and stroked their own dicks with the bullshit size of their wallets that said they could and would spend bank on shit paintings, and every single woman in the place hit on me, Ronan, Alpha and Echo like it was a champion sport.

I fucking hated every second, and I didn't just want a drink, I wanted a whole goddamn bottle. Then I wanted to pound Bertrand's face in until he begged for mercy.

If all of that wasn't torture enough, she kept looking in my direction. Every goddamn chance she got. But it wasn't me she kept looking at. Sabine was staring at Ronan because my twin, unlike her, had fucking stood within arm's reach of me all goddamn night.

Except for the two times she'd come within speaking distance of me. Then Ronan had dropped back like he knew I'd fucking level him if he spoke to her.

November's voice came through comm. "Armored transport

VICTOR

cleared the property. All guards accounted for. Guest list vetted. Force protection level normal."

"Copy," Ronan quietly replied next to me before Alpha and Echo acknowledged with the same response from their positions across the event space.

Ronan discreetly turned his head and turned off his comm. "You haven't spoken French to her."

"I didn't fucking speak to her at all." She was too goddamn busy sticking to the asshole that'd hired AES to put her in jail, like she didn't give a damn what he did to her.

"The British accent is slipping, and you're swearing. You've spoken to her twice since you've gotten here."

I didn't count asking her if she wanted a drink one time, water another, as speaking to her. "Your point?"

Ronan turned to face me. "The last time I saw you like this was seventeen years ago."

I glared at my exact replica. "Fuck off."

I smelled her perfume a split second before I heard her intoxicating voice. "Hello."

Ronan sidestepped me and held his hand out before I'd turned the fuck around.

"Ronan Conlon. Nice to meet you, Miss Malcher."

She shook his hand but then glanced at me before speaking to him. "Vance said he was a twin."

Pissed as hell, I aimed my misplaced anger at both of them. "Don't let the façade fool you, darling. He doesn't usually shake hands, and he isn't polite."

Ronan immediately fired back. "Apparently my brother doesn't suffer pretense. Feel free to ignore him. I do."

A second's worth of shock widened her eyes before she quickly recovered. "Yes, well, all the same, it was lovely meeting you, Mr. Conlon. I hope you enjoyed the pieces on display this evening."

"Lovely," I replied dryly, aiming the insult at her.

Her gaze cut to me, and I saw the exact intended reaction I'd wanted, but it felt like shit.

"I'm not here for the art," Ronan stated.

She looked back at my brother, and her voice quieted. "Oh, my apologies, I did not realize you work with Vance."

"I don't. I work for another security firm here in Miami, but my attendance this evening isn't work related."

Sabine glanced at me again.

I smirked. "He's babysitting me, love."

"Yes, well, if you'll excuse me." She turned heel and practically ran in the opposite direction.

Ronan didn't hesitate. "I see you're still consistent. You fucked that all to hell."

"Screw you."

"Go after her. I've got Bertrand."

"Again, screw you."

My brother glanced at me and said all he needed to say with a single look.

Goddamn it. "Fine. Cover me." I took one step.

Ronan caught my arm.

I glanced over my shoulder.

"She's afraid," he warned.

"I know." Fuck, I knew.

He nodded once and dropped his hand.

I turned my comm off and went after her.

FORTY-NINE

Vance

I FOLLOWED HER TO THE LANAI.
Standing near the end of the outdoor bar, looking at the ocean, she was no longer favoring her wrist, but twisting the cuff she'd used to hide the bruises around and around in an anxious tell.

Her long hair loose around her shoulders, her full lips painted a neutral shade as if to hide them, dark makeup around her eyes—she truly was exquisite. But fuck, the things I could do with her nervous energy. I was hard just thinking about it.

Hell, I'd been hard all night. And pissed off, which was my problem, not hers.

As if sensing my presence, she glanced up, but then quickly looked away and tucked one hand into the other. "Did you come out here for a drink?"

"Drink?" Right. "No."

Glancing back at me, her eyebrows drew together in a tempting display of confusion before she hid it. "Fresh air?"

"Closer." I winked.

No smile, no acknowledgment of my insinuation, she moved like she had the first time I saw her in Bertrand's office. As if she were floating, she headed toward the far end of the bar before continuing toward the wide concrete railing that separated the sand from the lanai. Stepping into the shadows, her dark green dress blended in with the night. If it weren't for the faint click of her heels, you'd never know she was there.

Except I knew.

I saw her.

I smelled her.

I felt every ounce of her disquiet, and I wanted a taste of it.

Hell, I wanted all of it.

Feeling the hits I'd taken from Echo, unable to stop thinking about her under me, I watched as she reached with her slender arm and gracefully drew her hair over one shoulder, then turned her back to me. Her movements both practiced and fluid, she performed the seductive dance as if she'd done it countless times. Probably for that asshole Bertrand.

But the real problem was that she didn't know how seductive and how damn alluring it was, which only made me want her more.

I glanced at the bartender. "Two scotches, best of whatever you have out here."

"Yes, sir." He moved down the bar to retrieve the liquor and pour the drinks.

When he came back, I slid three hundreds toward him. "Take a break. Give us the patio for ten minutes. If you keep anyone else from coming out here, I'll double that."

Pocketing the hundreds, he nodded. "Understood, sir. Consider it done." He walked to the door that led inside to the party, closed and locked it, then moved around the corner of the building.

The distinctive smell of peat filling my nostrils, I carried the drinks to where she was looking out over the ocean and set one of the glasses in front of her. "Join me."

"No, thank you."

Facing her, leaning on the railing, I didn't say shit. I waited.

She turned, and her eyes caught mine.

I quieted my tone. "I believe I asked you to join me." I wasn't asking.

For a brief moment, she stared at me as if assessing my mood. Then she turned back toward the ocean, and her hand fell around the tumbler.

"Better." I held my drink up. "*À votre santé.*"

Her eyes resolutely on the waves, she raised her glass to her full lips without saying a word and took a small sip.

I tasted the alcohol. Single malt. Isley by the taste of it. "I'm not sure if you want me to leave you alone or?" Leaning closer, I dropped my voice. "Make your life much more difficult." For five seconds, I held my position. Then I stood to my full height, putting the illusion of space between us. "Then again, I've got one less problem without you." I swirled my glass.

Even in the ambient light from the moon, I could see her cheeks flush. "You seem to have many problems."

I chuckled. "Touché. And how about you? Besides the obvious."

A master at this game, she didn't say a word.

Smiling like she wasn't winning every round, I took another sip of the scotch. "No need to answer, pet. I feel you."

Exhaling, she lowered her gaze and set her glass down. "Mr. Conlon, I think you should go."

"Right. Conlon," I mused, wondering how the fuck I ended up here. "I think I should stay. View's beautiful." I tipped my chin toward the ocean, then I tested a theory. Putting true command into my tone, I issued her an order. "Face me, Sabine."

No fucking hesitation, as if she were made for my command, she turned like a submissive little bird.

"Good girl," I murmured, taking another swallow of the scotch before setting the glass down and stepping in front of her. Caging her in between me and the railing, I leaned as close as possible without touching her. "Do you know what would make a man walk through fire?"

Her hands clasped, her head down, her sexy voice landed quietly, but she ignored my question. "You are here because Joseph hired you."

"Am I?" She should tell me to fuck off.

She hesitated. "Yes."

"Did you like standing next to him all night?" Did I miss the most obvious reason why she would be here, going through with this?

Her gaze met mine. "What are you implying?"

"You tell me." Fuck, maybe I had missed it.

"I did not enjoy it."

I studied her eyes, her lips, the color of her cheeks, her posture. "I think you did."

She slid to the side to escape me. "I think you need to leave."

Grasping her uninjured wrist, I held her with just enough force. "You're probably right." I knew she was submissive. Two seconds in the same room with her and I knew it, but this was something more. Something untapped, and I could fucking taste it. "But first, I think you should tell me if you enjoy having me touch you like this."

"You are out of line."

"I'm well aware." But I didn't give a single fuck. I was going down this path.

"Unhand me," she demanded.

Never. "Ask nicely." Fuck, was I hard.

For the first time since I'd laid eyes on this exquisite creature, a hint of true defiance came out. "You will take your hand off me, or I will tell Joseph."

Reaching in my pocket, I made a calculated move and tossed my cell on top of the railing because I had a theory. "Go ahead." She wouldn't call that fuck. She wouldn't call anyone. She wanted this. But she was in too damn deep in the wrong fucking situation to understand the difference between me and Bertrand, and the difference between asking for what she needed and being ashamed of it.

Her chest rose and fell rapidly as her eyes cut to the phone.

Soft, gentle, I stroked the vulnerable flesh of her inner wrist. "Try again, bird."

Her blue-eyed gaze cut back to me, and something close to fear seeped into her expression. "What did you call me?"

I switched to French. *"Oiseau."*

"Vous parlez français couramment."

I smiled. *"Je parle le français comme une vache espagnole."*

Not biting on my ill-timed joke, she stared.

I gave her more truth. *"J'adore te regarder marcher."*

"You did not tell me you were fluent," she accused, transferring her anger to the least consequential thing between us. "And are you flirting with me, in French?" she spit the last two words at me with indignation.

"No, I'm stating fact." I did love to watch the way she walked. She floated. Like a bird.

"You so easily switch between French and English," she accused again, but this time in rapid speech without holding back any part of her accent.

My mouth tipped up in a true smile because this was her, the real Sabine Malcher. "Is that a question?"

"Who are you?" she demanded.

Someone even I didn't want to know. I switched back to French. *"Tu veux aller faire un tour?"* This time I wasn't flirting or kidding. I was seriously asking. If she wanted out of here, I wouldn't hesitate.

She shook her head. "Stop flirting. What are you going to ask next? If I want another drink? When we already have an open bar?" Her hand waved elegantly but no less dismissively through the air.

"*Non.*" But I would ask her if she wanted to go for a drink. Operative word being *go*. "*Tu veux aller boire un verre?*"

"Stop it. This is not some kind of game, and I am not having this conversation, in any language." She turned to go.

I stepped in front of her. "What exactly are you taking offense at, that I'm speaking French or that I asked if you need to feel dominated?"

Her gaze cut across my stance, but unlike her nervous energy from before, she didn't shy away from the proximity of my body to hers. "I am in America."

"You're French." And fucking gorgeously submissive.

"I am not defined by my country."

I smiled again. "Your country?"

Her gaze, daring and beautiful and yet so fucking vulnerable, focused on me. "What do you want from me?"

Everything. "Why did you really stay with him?" She could have run. Bertrand was so goddamn self-absorbed, he wouldn't have hunted her or her nephew down. "Are you afraid of him or yourself?"

She glanced at my hold on her, and her voice went whisper quiet. "I am afraid of you."

I dropped my hand. "I would never physically hurt you."

Her head still down, her chest rose with an inhale. "I do not let him hurt me on purpose."

"I know, and I wasn't inferring you enjoy pain when I asked if you liked to be dominated." Slow, gentle, I took her hand and threaded our fingers. "May I tell you what else I think?"

Making only a half-hearted attempt to pull away from me, she shook her head, and the intoxicating color of guilt spread across her cheeks. "No, and I have nothing to prove to you."

Ruthless, turned the hell on, I pushed. "Yet you stand here, your hand in mine, with Bertrand not twenty feet from us." Using my hold on her, I pulled her closer. "You're either inviting this in and letting me touch you, Sabine...." Lowering my head to hers, I brought my lips almost to her ear and dropped my voice. "Or you're saying no."

A single tear fell down her cheek.

I gave her one last chance. "Say no if you want me to stop, Sabine."

"I want to hate you," she whispered guiltily.

"But you don't want to push me away." I could feel the connection between us like it was part of my own damn breath.

She shook her head. *"Non."*

"Then stop fighting it." Claiming her mouth, driving my tongue in, I took both her fear and her guilt.

FIFTY

Sabine

IF A THOUSAND LIFETIMES OF PASSION COULD BE HELD IN A MOMENT, this kiss was it. Every nuance of his speech, every move of his sinuous muscles, every ounce of his barely contained dominance—he drew them together and gave me his perfection of insanity.

Obsessive, crazed, desperate, he kissed me with fervor. With the untamed heat of the Florida humidity surrounding our impossible collision, he ignored the guests inside, he ignored the man who held my freedom in his hands, he ignored everything.

Except me.

Wild, feral, but with preternatural skill as if he was made for my pleasure, his tongue stroked, his hands gripped, and his hips moved. He made love to my mouth as his body fucked me with the rhythm of sex as surely as if he were inside me.

I wanted him.

I wanted everything about him.

I no longer cared about what he did in the name of work or what his hands were capable of with a gun in them. His body was his weapon, and his kiss was the ammunition.

I wanted more.

Moaning, I sank my hands into his hair and curled my fingers to hold on to this storm that was all at once Marine, mercenary, protector and dominance. Pressing my aching body against his, I gave.

I gave him the kiss back.

I offered my heart.

I lost my mind.

But as my fingers disheveled the slicked-back orderly chaos of his silky curls and made it as unruly as when I first met him, a crushing thought struck my soul and made me recoil.

My mouth ripped from his, and I dropped my hands.

With a hooded, sexy gaze he stared down at me. "*That* is what a man would walk through fire for."

My heart cowered, and distress slipped out of my mouth. "Sex."

Had he been with a woman before he had walked into Harrington's? Was that why his hair had looked like it did now? Did he have a girlfriend, a wife, a mistress, many women?

Misreading every jealous thought shattering me, he tipped half his mouth up and ran his hand down my arm before resting it possessively on my hip. "Believe me, darling, I'd love to devour every inch of you right now, but this isn't the time or place." He leaned down as if to kiss me again. "And just so we're clear, when I do take you, I promise it's going to be more than merely sex."

I turned my head away before his lips touched mine.

The bartender appeared behind Vance. "Sorry to interrupt, sir, but I have to unlock the door and resume my shift."

Frown lines creasing his brow, Vance grasped my chin and turned me back toward him as he clipped out a reply to the bartender. "Give us a minute."

"That's about all I'll have before my supervisor comes looking," the bartender warned.

"Understood," Vance replied as he searched my eyes.

The bartender walked away.

Still frowning, Vance issued a demand. "Explain what just happened."

As he looked into my eyes and I into his, I knew he was

different from Joseph. There was nothing similar I could grasp at to compare the two men, but I couldn't make the rivulets of fear cascading through my mind stop.

"Sabine," he warned, low and gruff. "We're out of time. Answer the question."

Stupid hope I had allowed myself to feel slipped away. "Why?"

"So I can address it."

"It is not that simple." Nothing would change either of our pasts, just as his words could not change who I had become.

His huge, warm hand cupped my face, and his tone turned darkly soft as his thumb caressed my cheek. "It's exactly that simple."

Did he speak to other women like this? The unbearable thought churned my stomach. "Were you with another woman last night?" I dared to meet his eyes. "This morning?"

His hand stilled. "Were you with Bertrand last night?"

My ugly life seeped out of my mouth like poison. "No, but he was having sex with one of the staff early this morning." Horrified that I had freed the words, giving this man pieces of my toxic life that he could use as ammunition or worse, pity, I stupidly did not stop there. "Vocal and rough, Joseph made sure I heard his anger and pleasure along with her cries of protest. I hear them all, he makes sure of it. So you cannot tell me it is simple. I cannot even piece together my fears enough to tell you that I am broken, and you deserve more than a woman weighted with mistrust."

His eyes no longer hooded, but dark and full of the fury of an incoming storm, stared down at me with gripping intent as his voice quieted. "What, specifically, did you just mistrust about me?"

"Your hair," I admitted.

His frown deepened, but he did not mock me. "Because?"

"This morning, it was disheveled." Shame coated my voice, and I lowered my gaze. "Like it is now from my hands." Already this far, I forced myself to say the rest. "It made me wonder—no,"

I amended, "it made me fearful. That you were with another woman, doing with her what you are doing with me now." Sharp jealousy I had no right to own made the last words slip past my lips in an ashamed whisper. "I do not even know if you are married or in a relationship or have many women, and yet I kiss you as if I know these things."

His hand moved from my cheek to my chin. "Look at me."

I did not want to look at him, because I already knew from the stern tone of his voice that whatever he was going to say next, I would not like it. "*Non.*"

His thumb glanced across my chin in a firm stroke that was both alarming and comforting. "Don't hide from me. Give me your eyes, Sabine."

My name, his caress, the totality of his dominance, it was as if I were not myself when I was with him, but the type of woman I wanted to be.

I looked up.

FIFTY-ONE

Vance

Fuck, her eyes. They were killing me.

The truth was going to kill me more, but I said it anyway. "I was with a woman last night."

Recoiling as if I'd hit her, she dropped her gaze.

Grasping her arms and holding firm, I didn't let her escape. "If I had known you existed, we wouldn't be having this conversation."

Arching away from me, she pulled. "I do not want to hear this."

"I'm not going to be dishonest with you." I didn't want that with this woman. "Whether you want to hear it or not, you need to." Same as I needed to know what I was dealing with when it came to her, not that I needed another reason to fucking kill Bertrand. "I'm not married or attached, but I'm far from celibate."

More agitated by the second, she shook her head. "I am a fool."

Oh, fuck no. "You are not broken, nor are you a fool, and that is the last time you will ever insult yourself in front of me again. Understand?"

She brushed me off. "You call it insult, I call it truth. The same truth that would make me a fool to believe that a man I just met is going to stop being who he is. And for what? Something *more than merely sex*? Am I supposed to stop being who I am?"

"You really want to have this conversation, pet?" She didn't know who the hell she was dealing with. "Because I'm more than willing to go down this road, and for the record, this situation you're in isn't who you are."

Her accent thickened, and her words came faster. "This is insanity. You do not even know me."

"You're right, I don't." But I fucking knew now what my mother had meant when she'd told me and Ronan as kids that love didn't have a timeline. It was or it wasn't, and you just knew.

"Did you know the woman last night?" she threw back.

Half of me, the conditioned part that'd spent seventeen years fighting, wanted to be in the ring fucking shit up. But a new part, something that'd come alive when she'd walked into that office didn't want to be fighting against everything anymore. I wanted to fight for something. But I wasn't going to take shit in the process. "I'm not throwing Bertrand in your face, darling."

"*Darling,*" she repeated, shaking her head like I'd insulted her, but then her tone and posture swung like a pendulum, bypassing submissive and going straight to defeat. "You should throw him in my face. You should blame me for all of it."

I didn't know what was more fucked up, that she'd said that shit to me or that I knew exactly how she felt. "You know my stance on *should*, and I'm not blaming you for a damn thing."

She didn't say shit for a beat, then she spoke so low, I almost didn't hear her. "What if I want to blame you for something?"

"Like?"

Her chest rose with an inhale. "Never mind."

Not a fucking chance. "Answer the question, Sabine," I ordered, using every ounce of dominance I'd been holding back from her.

No hesitation, she fired back her questions. "If I am with you, will we run into this woman? See her around Manhattan? Is she going to look at me with smugness or worse, pity?"

Fucking Bertrand was a dead man. For now, though, I didn't

step around the truth. I owned it. "It was in Miami, and no, you won't see her because I didn't bother asking her name before I kicked her out of my penthouse." The same damn penthouse that still had last night's sheets on the bed because I hadn't had a chance to tell the cleaning service to change them yet.

Which, at this point, was the only fucking excuse I could think of as to why we weren't there, having this conversation in private. Because now, more than ever, I wanted her away from Bertrand and the trail of destruction he'd left in his wake that shit all over her self-esteem.

Ignoring the bartender as he came back and unlocked the door, she didn't look at me as she fired more mistrust. "Not knowing her name means nothing. You could still see her again."

I saw through her. I saw what the hell this was really about. She was fixating on the wrong damn thing, but I wasn't going to insult her by not addressing her fear of some random hookup of mine. "Not knowing the woman's name should tell you exactly what she doesn't mean to me, Sabine. I don't have her number, and I have no intention of seeing her again."

A sound somewhere between anguish and distress escaped her lips as my cell vibrated and the door to the lanai opened.

Ronan stuck his head out and gave me a pointed look. "He's looking for her."

Fuck. "Two options, love. We go inside, or we leave right now." Screw catching Bertrand in the act of whatever bullshit he had up his sleeve, I wanted her away from him.

Her posture stiffened. "I cannot leave."

"Ten seconds," Ronan warned.

"You can do anything you want, pet." But she didn't see that.

"No." She shook her head. "I am going inside."

Dropping my hold on her, I let her walk past me toward the door my brother was holding open. Even now, even with the pressure she was under, she moved with grace and dignity.

Following her back inside, I coasted a hand over her hip and lowered my voice so only she could hear. "We're not done with this conversation, love, but know this, I don't want any other woman."

Before she could respond, if she was going to at all, Bertrand was on us.

Dismissing her, the asshole glanced between me and Ronan. "There're two of you."

Remaining silent, my brother didn't offer his hand or an introduction. If Bertrand was smart or had an ounce of self-preservation, he would've taken notice, but he didn't.

My cell vibrated again as I casually turned my comm back on and chuckled without an ounce of humor. "Two for the price of one."

Bertrand, the fuck, didn't miss a beat. "Good to know I was only getting half of what I paid for." He put his hand on Sabine's shoulder and applied pressure. "We're leaving. Whichever half is Victor, let's go, you're coming with us." He turned her toward the exit like she was a fucking disobedient dog.

"On the move," Alpha said through comms.

"Incoming," November warned a second before a man in a suit appeared in front of Bertrand with three bodyguards behind him, blocking their exit.

Knowing who the fuck it was, I palmed my VP9.

Ronan's hand landed on my shoulder in warning as all three of the asshole's bodyguards reached for their guns.

"Stand down, Victor," Alpha quietly commanded through comms.

"Flanking," Echo's voice came through next. "I've got the two on the left. Twin, you got the third on the right?"

Ronan barely tipped his chin in acknowledgment.

"Joseph." The asshole smiled, waving a dismissive hand toward his bodyguards without looking at them. "Good to see you."

He glanced at me before looking back at Bertrand. "Glad you've upgraded your security. You can never be too careful these days."

The asshole's three bodyguards slowly took their hands off their guns.

Fucking livid, I reluctantly let go of my 9mm.

Then the head of one of the top crime syndicates in the northern hemisphere turned his attention on Sabine. "I don't believe I've had the pleasure." Holding his hand out, the mafia asshole introduced himself. "Massimo Vincenzo."

Sabine reached for his outstretched hand. "Sabine Malcher."

Vincenzo didn't only take her offered hand. Grabbing the other, the gun running, drug dealing, human trafficking fuck brought both of her hands to his mouth and kissed her knuckles before glancing at her left ring finger. "Beautiful piece, *bella*. Your husband has good taste." He dropped her hands and looked at Bertrand. "Apologies for the delayed arrival, a previous engagement ran longer than expected."

Missing pieces of the picture fell together, and I fucking growled under my breath.

Alpha picked it up through comms. "Objective on the target, Victor."

"Fuck that," Echo clipped through comms. "I can drop Mr. Mafia and two of his guards before anyone blinks. Twin can get the third guard, and the spray will hit the auction fuck in the face. Win-win."

"Two more Vincenzo guards outside, two drivers in two vehicles," November interjected.

Echo snorted. "Now you fucking tell us, November. Nice heads-up."

"Don't shoot," I whispered, throwing a warning glare in Echo's direction.

"No one fires near the woman," Alpha ordered. "Echo, we're not starting a war with the Sicilians."

VICTOR

Bertrand gripped Vincenzo on the shoulder and smiled like they were old friends. "No apology necessary. As you know, any of my staff is always happy to give you a private showing."

"Of course." Vincenzo turned his smile on Sabine again. "I hope we will meet again." Glancing back at Bertrand, he nodded. "I see you're heading out."

"Yes, Vienna for the auction," Bertrand answered like the whole damn conversation was choreographed. "See you soon, Massimo."

With a knowing smile, Vincenzo nodded. "Safe travels." He turned to walk out, and his bodyguards followed.

"I'm calling it," Echo quipped through comms. "Auction fuck has the rest of the diamonds, and mafia fuck is buying them. Did you see the way he looked at her ring?"

We all fucking saw it.

"Just found something," November interrupted. "Das Safe in Vienna's eighth district. A safe box registered to a J. Harrington has dual access granted. Second grantee is listed as spouse, first initial C."

Mother*fucker*.

Dropping his bullshit pretense the second Vincenzo was out of sight, Bertrand barked at Sabine. "The jet's waiting, let's go." He walked out in front of her.

"Alpha," I warned under my breath.

"I heard," Trefor replied through comms. "November, target's moving. Victor's with the woman, Echo and I are on their six. Vienna's a go, update Zulu. Status on Vincenzo?"

"Two vehicles loaded and already leaving the premises," November replied. "Bertrand's driver is out front waiting. I'm ten yards back."

"Find out where Vincenzo's heading. Two car follow, use Blade. Stay alert, they'll be looking for a tail," Alpha ordered November. "Echo and I will ride with Victor to the airport. Ronan, you're out. Your wife makes you too high profile on this. Thanks for the assist tonight."

"Good copy," November replied.

"Ten-four," Ronan added before turning off his comm and looking at me. He raised one eyebrow in question, asking if I needed him anyway.

Appreciating the gesture, I shook my head at my brother. "Thanks for tonight."

He tipped his chin, then glanced at Sabine. "Miss Malcher."

"Mr. Conlon."

Ronan turned toward the exit, and I took Sabine's arm. "This way, pet." If we were lucky, her ring would be the only thing that fucking asshole Bertrand sold to Vincenzo.

FIFTY-TWO

Sabine

I DID NOT UNDERSTAND WHAT WAS HAPPENING OR KNOW WHO THE man with the Italian accent was, but anxiety was tearing apart my resolve to stay and see this through as Joseph barked hatred at me.

"The jet's waiting, let's go." Issuing his edict, Joseph strode out of the event.

"Alpha," Vance warned low and angry as his gaze drifted, then he was still a moment as if listening to something being said in the communication device in his ear.

His personality nothing like his identical twin, Ronan touched his ear, then looked at his brother.

As if a silent communication passed between them, Vance shook his head. "Thanks for tonight."

Ronan gave his brother a slight nod then turned to glance at me. Even though his eyes were the exact same dichotomy of color as Vance's, there was a lethalness behind them I had not seen in Vance's. "Miss Malcher."

I barely refrained from stepping closer to Vance. "Mr. Conlon."

Ronan left without another word, and Vance took my arm. "This way, pet."

It suddenly occurred to me that all the men could have been listening to our entire conversation outside. *Oh God*, they could have heard our kiss.

"What's that look, love?" Vance demanded as he ushered me out of the hotel while Mr. Trefor and Echo silently fell into step behind us.

I glanced behind us.

Both men were scanning everything around us as we walked through the lobby of the upscale hotel.

I looked back at Vance and spoke as quietly as possible. "Are they listening?"

Scanning the lobby like the other men, Vance spared me a quick glance. "Who, love?"

I casually touched my ear.

He lifted his chin once in understanding. "Now, yes. Before, no."

I exhaled, but I did not relax. "Who is Mr. Vincenzo?"

"No one good." Vance held the door that led out of the venue, and I caught a glimpse of Joseph's car.

Suddenly I did not want to ride to the airport with Joseph, let alone get on a plane with him. "Are you really coming with us?"

"Just try and stop me, love." Vance's gaze drifted. "November, sitrep." He listened for a brief moment as Joseph's driver held the door of a black sedan while Joseph got inside. Then Vance stopped the driver from closing the door and spoke to Joseph. "There's a potential security threat, Bertrand. I'll drive you and Miss Malcher to the airport."

"Oh for fuck's sake," Joseph snapped at him. "It's a ten-minute drive, and I didn't hire you for security. I have my own. Get in the damn car, or don't." He barely glanced at me. "Sabine, get in."

I stepped forward, but Vance held his hand out, blocking me.

"Mr. Bertrand," Vance enunciated as if fighting for patience. "You may not have hired me for security, but I *am* security. If I tell you there's a potential threat, it's because there is one."

"Then get me some real protection. Tell Trefor to ride with me," Joseph demanded.

Vance glanced at Mr. Trefor, who Joseph had studiously ignored all evening, and nodded once.

Without a word, Mr. Trefor stepped forward and got in the sedan with Joseph, closing the door behind him.

"This way, love." Vance took my left arm, Echo stepped to my right side, and both men walked me to where Vance had left his Range Rover parked in front of the valet stand.

As if choreographed, Echo moved in front of us and opened the rear passenger door, Vance ushered me inside and seconds later, both men were up front with Vance behind the wheel.

We had barely pulled away from the curb when Echo let out a sound of disgust. "Are you hearing this shit?"

"Yeah," Vance answered absently as he scanned the street in every direction before looking in his side and rearview mirrors.

"What is going on?" This had something to do with the Italian man, I was sure of it.

Echo shook his head in disgust. "Bertrand is ripping Alpha a new one. The fucker is yelling loud enough for us to hear every word through comms."

"What for?" I did not ask why. Joseph never needed a reason.

"What do you think?" Echo asked sarcastically before tipping his chin at Vance. "He's pissed at Lover Boy here." Echo touched his ear. "Hey, Alpha, tell the auction fuck we're both hittin' it. Then tell him I have a bullet with his name on it." Echo took his communication device out and pocketed it. "Christ, I can't listen to that shit anymore." He glanced at me. "For real, sweetheart, you want me to shoot him? Leg? Arm? Doesn't have to be fatal, just painful."

"*Echo*," Vance snapped.

The huge man looked at Vance. "Right, pissing in your territory. Got it. I'll leave the shooting to you." He smirked. "That is, if you have any aim left after this afternoon."

My blood ran cold, but before the last words left Echo's

mouth, Vance was violently swerving the SUV to the side of the road and pulling his gun out of his holster faster than I could blink.

Pressing the barrel directly to Echo's temple, Vance issued an order at him. "Tell her I wasn't with anyone."

"He wasn't with anyone," Echo repeated drolly.

"Tell her exactly where I was," Vance demanded.

Echo sighed theatrically. Then, as if he had no regard for the gun aimed at his head, he turned in his seat to look back at me. "Your boyfriend was in the office all afternoon, getting his ass kicked by me because he has anger management issues and started a fight. Then he went home, licked his wounds, and showed up for your party all prettied up for you in his pussy blue suit and thousand dollar wingtips no self-respecting SEAL would ever wear."

"Was. I. With. A. *Woman?*" Vance ground out, still holding the gun to his head.

Deadly serious, Echo did not hesitate. "No."

Vance holstered his gun and pulled back into traffic. "Not a fucking SEAL."

"Exactly." Echo glanced back at me and winked. "Don't worry, sweetheart, I didn't hit him too hard this afternoon. All his essential parts should still be working."

"Every word out of your mouth, I'm filing away," Vance warned with more calm in his tone than I was expecting.

"Counting on it," Echo casually replied.

I did not know if I was more alarmed now or when Echo had insinuated that Vance had been with another woman this afternoon. Anger management issues? Pulling a gun on his friend? But then making him tell me the truth?

My head spinning, I had almost forgotten what Vance had said to Joseph. "What security threat?" I asked.

Vance glanced at me in the rearview mirror before looking back at the road. "No imminent threat. I didn't want you in the car with him."

Echo snorted. "He's lucky I'm not in the car with him. That'd be an imminent threat."

Ignoring Echo, I addressed Vance. "Who was that man?"

Vance took a corner then stepped on the gas. Driving too fast, but also with control, he scanned his side mirrors. "Anything I tell you about Massimo Vincenzo makes you vulnerable."

"The *M*-word," Echo added almost sarcastically and low enough to be construed as a slip.

"Pardon?"

Vance turned onto the road leading to the private airport. Then he clipped out two words that he clearly did not want to say. "Organized crime."

I briefly closed my eyes and inhaled, but it did nothing to calm my spiking nerves. "Joseph knew him." This was getting worse by the second.

"Bingo," Echo commented, but Vance didn't say anything.

The man looking at my ring being associated with organized crime, Joseph insisting I attend the party tonight and the auction in Vienna—none of this was painting a pretty picture. "You think this has something to do with me." I did not know if I was stating it to try to wrap my head around it or asking it in hopes that one of them would tell me I was crazy and imaging all of it.

Instead, neither said anything as Vance drove through the entrance of the Executive Airport and pulled up next to the black sedan that was parked next to two private jets, one of which I recognized.

"What is Joseph going to do?" I asked no one in particular because I already knew it had something to do with the diamonds and my ring.

Vance put the SUV in park then cut the engine. "That's what we have nine hours to figure out."

FIFTY-THREE

Vance

That fuck, Bertrand, went straight to the aft cabin, shut the bulkhead door and took the only comfortable sleeping section of the plane for himself.

I set her suitcase and my bag down and glanced in the cockpit of the older plane before spying the young-as-fuck flight attendant in the galley.

"Take a seat, Sabine. I'll join you in a minute." Without waiting for a response, I made my way to the flight attendant.

She smiled flirtatiously. "Welcome aboard, sir."

"Has the plane been restocked since it landed in Miami?"

Her smile faltered. "Yes, of course. I have—"

"Leave. You're not flying tonight."

Confusion clouded her face. "But I always fly with Mr. Bertrand."

Shocker. "Not anymore. Get off the plane. You have two minutes." I walked back to the cockpit and stuck my head inside. "Gentlemen." I handed the captain a generic business card from AES that didn't give my name. "I'm from Alpha Elite Security. Mr. Bertrand's retained my services, and I'll be flying with you tonight."

"Welcome aboard, Mr. Victor." The captain took the card and pocketed it. "Mr. Bertrand already gave us a heads-up you'll be along for the ride. I'm Mark, and this is my copilot, Jensen."

I nodded at the second chair before looking back at the captain. "Are you the same crew who flew down from New York?"

"No, sir, we're fresh off a forty-eight-hour reprieve. You're in good hands tonight."

"Excellent. Flight time?"

The pilot glanced out his side window at Trefor's new Falcon. "We're not quite as fast as your company's bird, but we'll make good time. We have some minor headwinds. Flight time will be ten hours and fourteen minutes."

I glanced at my watch. That'd put us in Vienna just before eighteen hundred hours, local time. We'd be cutting it close for the start of the auction. "Copy that, thank you. FYI, I dismissed the flight attendant. We won't need her."

The two men looked at each other before the pilot spoke. "Ah, Mr. Bertrand always flies with an attendant."

"Not on my watch," I answered, letting them know I knew exactly why the fuck she was here, and it wasn't happening. "I'll secure the hatch. If you need anything else, ask."

The flight attendant walked past me with her head down and exited.

I closed the main cabin door, grabbed our bags and made my way to Sabine.

She glanced toward the forward cabin. "You dismissed the flight attendant."

"I did." I nodded at her bag. "Do you have something more comfortable to sleep in, love?"

Heat flushed her cheeks, and she glanced away. "I am fine."

"Right. I'll take that as a no." I grabbed a T-shirt and gray sweats out of my bag as the pilots fired up the engines. "It's going to get cold once we're in flight. Put these on. I'll grab us a drink." I held the clothes out to her.

Wide-eyed, she stared up at me from her seat.

"Problem, pet?"

She glanced behind her.

"Afraid to wear my clothes in front of him?" I'd wanted her comfortable for the long flight, but now I wanted her wearing something of mine.

"The restroom," she answered vaguely, not taking my clothes.

"You can change here, I'll turn my back." It wasn't lost on me that Bertrand had closed himself in with the only lavatory on board.

The plane started to taxi, but she still didn't move.

"I doubt he'll notice," I assured.

"He will notice," she replied with a telltale tone.

Making a concerted effort not to show my anger at that asshole, I took the seat next to her and lowered my voice. "Do you know why I dismissed the flight attendant?"

She hesitated only a fraction before shaking her head.

"Because I knew why she was here, and I wasn't going to let that happen on my watch." I picked up the T-shirt. "Just like I'm not going to let anything happen to you no matter what you're wearing." Keeping my eyes on hers, I slipped the T-shirt over her head. "Slide the straps of your dress down your shoulders, love."

Her body trembling, her eyes welled. "Vance."

"It'll be okay," I promised. "We're getting you comfortable, then I'm going to have a drink with you. After, you're going to fall asleep next to me while I keep watch over you. Straps, love. Slide them down." Before I did it for her, which wouldn't end well for either of us.

"You are not going to sleep?"

"No." Not with Bertrand feet away, and no fucking way was I risking a nightmare in front of her on a damn plane.

"You have to sleep," she protested, but not in the judgmental way that my brother or Trefor would've said it. She said it with concern.

Momentarily thrown, I didn't think.

I leaned over and touched my lips to her temple. "Appreciate the sentiment, love, more than you know, but I'll be fine. The Marines trained me well." And my absolute shit decisions took care of the rest.

She stiffened. "What did you do in the Marines?"

Reading her body language, I gave up on my resolve not to touch her right now. Gently pulling the T-shirt down, I skimmed my hand up her arm and slid a strap off her shoulder. "I'm not a killer, darling." Not unless I had to be.

"I did not say that."

"No, but you were wondering it, and I'm reassuring you." Running my hand back down the smooth skin of her arm, all I could think about was sinking inside her. "Before I take this farther than either of us are prepared for right now, I'm getting us drinks. Wine?" I stood.

"Whatever you are having is fine."

"Right." I made my way to the galley as the captain called back to me.

"We're lined up, Mr. Victor, third in queue. Prepare for takeoff."

"Ten-four." I grabbed a bottle of scotch and two glasses and made my way back to her as she was pulling something out of her suitcase. "Need help?"

Flushed, she looked up at me. "No, thank you, but can you please…" She made a circle motion with her finger.

I turned. "Of course, love, but hurry. We're about to take off, and I need you buckled in."

"You do that a lot," she said to my back.

"What's that?" I asked distractedly as I held the bottle under my arm and two glasses with one hand while I fished my cell out and checked the texts that'd come through while we were still at the party.

November: *Call me.*

Then a second one.

November: *There's chatter.*

Fuck.

"You worry about me but not yourself," she replied. "You can turn around now."

Shoving my phone in my pocket, I faced her.

Then, for a split second, I froze.

Wearing my T-shirt under a soft, open-front sweater, she'd put on those black leggings women wore, and her feet were bare. She'd done something to her hair that made it more carefree and loose around her shoulders. Looking younger and more vulnerable than I'd ever seen her, she was so damn beautiful, she stole my breath.

When I didn't say shit, heat hit her cheeks and she ducked her head. "I realize I appear very casual."

Taking the seat next to her, I grasped her chin and brought her face up until she gave me her eyes. "You've never looked more beautiful."

"You cannot say that," she whispered.

"Which part? That you're beautiful or that you don't need a costume to be beautiful?" Setting the bottle and glasses on my lap, I buckled her seat belt then mine. "The clothes don't make the woman, darling."

"Prepare for takeoff," the captain announced.

She didn't reply.

The plane took on speed, and I waited until we were in the air and leveled out before I poured us each a drink. Handing her the scotch, I smiled. "Cheers, love."

She took the glass, and this time she toasted me before she drank. "*Santé.*"

We clinked, and she took a small sip.

I fucking swallowed half my pour. "Do you miss it?"

She glanced out the window. "Miss what?"

"Speaking French."

She glanced back at me before focusing on the glass in her hand. "I miss many things."

From her tone, I couldn't tell if I should touch that, so I let it drop for now. "I'll speak French with you anytime."

"Because you are fluent or because you enjoy it?"

I didn't touch the enjoy part. I'd speak whatever fucking language I had to for this woman. "I get by."

"I think you more than get by." She almost smiled.

I did smile. Wide. "I think you may be right." I downed the rest of my drink and set my glass and the bottle on the table in front of us. "Drink up, love. I want you to get some sleep."

"And alcohol will help facilitate that?"

I took a full beat to study her expression as she continued to stare into her glass. "No. But it's the best I can do for tonight."

"Maybe."

I cocked my head. "Why, Miss Malcher, are you flirting with me?"

"No."

I dropped the playful tone. "Care to explain?"

She tucked her legs under herself and leaned back in her seat. "Maybe you can tell me about her."

Every fucking muscle in my body went stiff. "Her who?" I knew who.

"The woman you made a mistake with."

FIFTY-FOUR

Sabine

EVEN THOUGH HE TRIED TO HIDE IT, I SAW HIS WHOLE BODY STIFFEN. Giving me a half smile that did not reach his eyes, he took his jacket off but not the holster or the gun. "That doesn't make for a good bedtime story, love."

I did not say anything. I studied his face, wondering if maybe, like me, a part of him wanted to talk about it, to share the burden. I accused him of not knowing me, but the opposite was also true. I had known exactly what he meant when he had spoken about meeting someone and feeling like you knew them.

I felt that with him.

Which was why I was almost certain he had never spoken to anyone about what had happened to him when he was seventeen, just like I had never told anyone what had happened to me when I was nineteen—until I told him, Mr. Trefor and their colleagues.

Anxiety was twisting inside me like a churning storm, but I also recognized the thread of difference that had not been there before. It was relief.

Sighing deeply, Vance shook his head. "That tactic is impressive, love."

"Pardon?"

"Your silence."

Worried he was misreading my intent, I tried to explain. "I am not attempting to manipulate you into telling me anything by remaining silent. I was merely giving space."

He smiled tiredly. "Giving me space?"

"*Oui.*"

He gave me his half laugh, but this time it was weighted with the same fatigue as his smile. "All right, love. I'll offer a trade. You do something for me, and I'll give you a complete shit version of a bedtime story. Deal?"

Nerves that were not entirely from anxiety spidered across my skin, but Joseph was steps away behind a door that I knew from experience was not soundproof. I could not make this deal. "I do not know what it is you are asking of me."

"Trust, love."

Two words. The same expression he had sent in a text that had long since disappeared from a phone he gave me. He was not asking me to only trust him. He was asking me to trust him and his ability to handle any situation that might arise.

Knowing I should not do it, I consented anyway. "Deal."

His smile was rare and real, and it made me want so much more than this moment. "Excellent. Be right back." Undoing first my seat belt, then his, he went to a compartment on the plane as if he knew exactly what would be in it and pulled out a blanket and pillows.

Sipping my scotch, I watched his biceps flex and strain the cut of his shirt, and I shamelessly took in the size of his muscular thighs. I also studied how he moved with a gun in a holster at his side and one hidden under his pant leg. He was not only comfortable with them, he was confident in every controlled step he took as if no movements were wasted.

Taking his seat again, he pushed the recline button on mine. "Lift your head, love."

I did as he asked, and he tucked a pillow under my head, then covered me with a blanket. I could not stop myself from thinking about how Joseph had never done anything like this. "Thank you."

"Not a bad deal, is it?" He winked as he took my glass and set it on the table.

"This is all I have to do for you?"

His flirting half smile came back. "Such a loaded question, pet, but for now, yes."

Before I could say anything, the door to the rear of the cabin opened and Joseph yelled out. "Where the hell is the flight attendant with my drink?"

Unhurried, Vance stood. "Not on board. Galley's in front of you. Help yourself."

"What the hell do you mean she's not on board?" Ignoring me, Joseph glanced about before glaring at Vance. "What did you do?"

"Compromised security risk," Vance easily lied. "She had to go."

Joseph's eyes narrowed like they always did right before he was about to unleash his temper. "Sabine," he barked. "Get my drink and get back here."

Every nerve ending in my entire body pulsed then frayed with panic.

Subtle, so Joseph would not see, Vance kept his arm at his side, but he held his hand out behind him, palm flat, silently telling me to stay. "She's already settled for the night."

Focusing all of his anger on Vance, Joseph did not even look at me. "I don't give a damn if she's asleep. Wake her up!"

"Right." Vance's hands went to his hips. "Here's what's going to happen. You can get your own drink, or you can get some sleep. Either way, I'll make sure you're up before we land. You'll have enough time to change, then I'll get us to the auction before the event starts. What I'm not going to do is listen to you berate anyone aboard, least of all Miss Malcher. If I have to run interference, trust me, it won't be pleasant." He sat back down in the seat next to me.

VICTOR

For one unbearable moment, nothing happened.

Then the door to the sleeping area slammed shut.

"You lied," I whispered.

He tucked the blanket tighter around me. "Did I, love? Do you know for a fact that the flight attendant isn't on Vincenzo's payroll?"

Oh God. "Is she?" She had been on our flights for years.

"Let me worry about it. For tonight, all you need to do is get some sleep."

I let out an undignified sound.

His amber-eyed gaze cut to me. "Do you have a problem sleeping?"

"Why?" I hedged.

For a long moment, he did not say anything, he simply stared at me. Then, "Nothing, love. Lean back and close your eyes. You're safe, you can sleep."

It wasn't nothing, and I did not close my eyes. "You made me a deal."

Without a smile or even one of his short laughs that I had already become addicted to, he looked at me with a wary expression I had not seen on him before. "I was hoping you'd forgotten."

"I have not."

"Right." He rubbed his hand over his jaw. "Bedtime story."

FIFTY-FIVE

Vance

"**R**IGHT." I SCRUBBED MY HAND OVER TWO DAYS' WORTH OF growth. "Bedtime story." One I'd never told.

Fuck. This wasn't going to end well.

Sucking it up, I gave her what I'd promised. "I was seventeen, she was sixteen. Her father was physically abusing her. He'd done it to her mother before she'd left him. Then he refocused his efforts on his daughter, and it escalated. One night he went too far. She was badly injured, but she refused to let me take her to the hospital. We both knew the cops would've gotten involved because she was a minor. The problem was her father. He was a well-known criminal attorney, and he had the police in his pocket. He would've twisted the truth to make it look like I'd broken her ribs."

Sabine's hand landed on my arm.

I didn't deserve her comfort, but I didn't move my arm. "The only way out was to leave, but her father could track her car, and I didn't have one, so we took his boat. Except there was a storm that night with hurricane-force winds. She was afraid. I put a life vest on her and told her it'd be okay. By the time we hit open waters, the swells were too high, and the sea was too rough. We capsized. The boat's props hit my back, and I lost my hold on her."

Her hand squeezed my arm.

Choking on the past, I told her the rest. "She drowned. A fisherman found me the next morning, clinging to debris, and brought me ashore." Feeling the tightness of the scars on my back, I shook my head. "I more than made a mistake." I looked at Sabine. "I'm responsible for her death."

Elegant, naturally poised despite whatever thoughts were running through her head, she didn't recoil at my admission. She didn't offer sympathy either. She did the last thing I was expecting.

She gave me understanding.

"To live is to make mistakes, but to love is to make grave mistakes."

I held her gaze for a long moment, then I looked out one of the jet's windows at a night that was as black as the one seventeen years ago. "You've been in love?"

She gave a truth of her own, hidden in ambiguity. "I know love."

"Maybe." Forcing a smile, I derailed the conversation before I had to hit something. "Or maybe you've just never had a bottle of Domaine Armand Rousseau Chambertin Grand Cru on the terrace at sunset at the Villa Belrose."

"You have been to Gassin? To Saint-Tropez?"

I didn't tell her that I'd fucked in Saint-Tropez or that I took out an adversary of one of our biggest paying clients there. "Perfect corner of the world." The kill I remembered, the woman I didn't. "Have you been?"

"Saint-Tropez, yes."

I read between the lines. "But not the Villa Belrose. Would you like to go?" I'd take her. Right now if she wanted. Fuck both our pasts. Fuck Bertrand. I'd restrain the asshole if I had to and tell the pilots to reroute. They could deal with him after dropping us off.

Her hint of a smile was wry. "I almost think you mean right now."

"I do."

"You are trouble, Mr. Conlon."

I didn't lie. "I am."

Her expression turned solemn as her eyes met mine. "I am sorry for your loss."

My first reaction was anger, at myself, at the fucking world, at a man who'd beat his daughter, but as I stared at the gorgeous woman in front of me, I felt a shift.

A goddamn seismic shift.

Suddenly, I wasn't in the past or looking for pain to erase emotions. I was taking in every nuance of her sentiment and tone, and it hit me.

She wasn't judging my past mistake.

She was looking at the man in front of her now.

Taking a breath that felt like my first, I wondered how the fuck I'd gotten lucky enough to be sitting here. "Thank you. I'm sorry for your losses, which far outweigh mine."

"Loss is not measured in weight."

"All the same, love." I brushed a strand of her hair off her face. "Close your eyes and get some sleep. I'll be right here when you wake up."

She turned the tables on me. "Maybe I will be here when you wake up."

Fuck, this woman. I smiled. "A man can dream."

Her voice turned quiet. "How does a man do that when he does not sleep?"

I dropped my smile. "I don't need to be unconscious to dream of you."

Her cheeks flamed, but she held my gaze.

"Right." I wanted inside her. Hell, I wanted to possess every inch of her. "Go to sleep, love, before I do something we'll both regret."

"I do not want to regret anymore."

"I know." I fucking got it. Leaning over, I touched my lips to her forehead. "Close your eyes for me, pet."

Taking a deep breath, she stared at me a beat longer. Then she did exactly as I asked.

For an hour, I watched her.

Her impassive expression gave way to a frown as she started to drift off. Then the anxiety in her features eventually released, and I knew the exact moment this exquisite creature fell asleep. Her breathing evened out, her shoulders relaxed and she turned into an angel.

My angel.

Before I let that thought take hold, I pulled my cell out and dialed.

November answered immediately. "Vincenzo's on a plane heading to Austria. CIA is on his tail, and it wasn't just French Intelligence watching Harrington's."

Fuck me.

I stood and moved to the opposite end of the cabin. "So the Feds are on to Harrington's?"

"Yes. Alpha made some calls with the intent to disclose, but they were already on to Bertrand. Dealing in stolen art and jewels, money laundering for organized crime syndicates and suspected terrorist cells—anything that could fund Harrington's expansion, he took advantage of. They're watching to see what goes down in Vienna, then they'll be waiting the second he lands back on US soil."

"And if he doesn't?"

"Rendition's already in place, but there's more. I got into Das Safe's security feeds and scanned them going back almost two months. Seven weeks ago the safe box in Bertrand's name was accessed by the second user. Three weeks ago, it was accessed by Bertrand himself. I tracked flight logs, and his jet filed a fake flight plan to London, but the pilot didn't cover his tracks at the airport in Vienna. He flew in and out the same day he went to Das Safe."

Jesus-*fucking*-Christ. "He has the rest of the diamonds."

"That's my guess," November agreed.

"We can't let her walk into that auction. I'll take the asshole down before we land and search him for the diamonds."

"And then what? Everything we have is circumstantial. He'd walk."

Fuck. "You said the Feds are waiting for him."

"I said they're waiting for him to make a move."

"She can't walk into this, Rhys," I warned. "Bertrand could have sold more than just her ring to Vincenzo. We both know Vincenzo's family is into sex trafficking."

"I understand, but she has to. If she doesn't, Bertrand will know something's up, and he or Vincenzo will pull the plug. We need her to follow this through."

"Then tell me exactly what the fuck *this* is. I'm not letting her walk blindly into a goddamn massacre."

"It's an auction, not a mass murder. Worst case, Bertrand sold her and the diamonds as a package deal, but usually that's not Massimo Vincenzo's MO. His brother is the one known for trafficking. Best case, it's just the diamonds and they take her ring. Either way, we're there to protect her."

Fucking November and his bullshit emotionless tone. "Do you know that's worst case scenario for certain?"

"I'm as certain as I am about anything else."

Goddamn it. "Okay, I'm trusting you on this. Nothing happens to her." The ring I could give a fuck about if it meant risking her safety. I could always get it back at a later date if it came down to that.

"Nothing happens to her," he repeated before dropping the hard truth. "But I'm not going to be on the inside. You are."

"Right." *Fucking Christ.* "No pressure. Just the Feds, the CIA, French Intelligence, and the head of one of the largest mafia families in the world, all at an auction offloading half a billion in art with a side deal on contraband diamonds. What the fuck could go wrong?" I didn't want an answer to that, and I didn't wait for one. "Anything else I need to know?"

"No, except keep an eye on Bertrand. I picked up intel from a few exchanges between him and his head of security in New York. The rent-a-cops at Harrington's headquarters were there because he thought he was being followed. He was, but as far as I know, he hasn't figured out it's the Feds yet. If he does, he's a flight risk, and the cash from the sale of the diamonds is his ticket to going underground."

"Copy." I didn't give a fuck if he took off, but I didn't want Sabine being left holding the bag on any of his shit. "Do the Feds have anything on Sabine?"

"Alpha says no."

I read between the lines. "And you say?"

"Anything's possible."

FIFTY-SIX

Sabine

Instead of feeling like I had on my armor, the beautiful Naeem Khan beaded column gown I was wearing was weighing me down as if I had a noose around my neck. Standing poised in my Aquazzura metallic heels, I held the fake demure smile I'd had pasted on all evening.

The pieces were selling quickly, and the auction was almost over, but I did not remember any of it.

I only remembered waking up on the plane.

The first thing I saw were his amber-green eyes as Vance looked down at me with a seriousness that would have scared me if I had not understood it.

Except I did understand it.

I felt it.

All the way to my very core.

His voice rougher and huskier than I had ever heard it, he had wished me a good afternoon, then Joseph had come out of the sleeping quarters, and everything had gone to hell. How Vance managed to keep Joseph relatively calm while I had slipped into my dress and heels and did my makeup in the airplane's lavatory was a testament to both his interpersonal skills and his restraint.

I saw every tic of Vance's jaw around Joseph. I knew he wanted to physically harm him. And maybe he would. I no longer cared. Something had happened last night when he had told me about his past, and I was no longer afraid of who he was.

I just wanted this auction to be over.

"You're telegraphing again, love."

With people all around us, I tried to be as casual as possible as I glanced at the clientele paying top dollar for pieces of art I could not describe if you held a gun to my head. All night I had been focused on Vance, Mr. Trefor and Echo as they religiously scanned every client, hired security personnel, and staff, as well as every exit on a continual loop.

"I telegraph nothing," I argued, simply because I was on edge.

His chuckle sounded the same as it always did, like nothing was amiss. "Right. Do you know the definition of courage?"

He did not wait for me to respond, not that I was going to, because I could sense a Vance Conlon trap. His wordplay was mastery level.

"Courage is moving into danger when there's a means of escape." In his black Armani suit and dark charcoal gray dress shirt, smelling of rain-wet cobblestones and masculine musk, he leaned closer. "You have choices, be the courageous woman you are. Trust, love."

I did not know if he was trying to tell me something or simply reassuring me that everything would be okay. It did not matter because it did not work. My anxiety overwhelming me, I reached for the first subject matter aimed to distract and I inappropriately pried.

"You do not get along with your brother." It was obvious in the way they had interacted, and I had been wondering about it since last night in Miami.

He winked. "Not getting along is such a benign term, love."

"Then what would you use?"

His shoulder moved an inch, his head tilted a fraction. "Hate works."

"Why does your brother hate you?" Did I hate my brother for making the choices he had made that had set all of this in motion?

The sides of Vance's mouth tipped up. "It's like this now? I share some details of my past and you've already decided to ask for more?"

I did not react to his disingenuous smile. "Yes."

His expression turned serious as he scanned the ornate ballroom of the historic hotel. "Because he has good reason to."

"What reason is that?"

He stopped scanning the room and looked directly at me. "Because I once let the woman he loves think I was him."

A knot that had nothing to do with what was going on around us formed in the pit of my stomach. "You pretended to be your twin?"

His gaze drifted back to the room. "Yes."

"Why?"

"Because I could."

I studied his strikingly handsome face. "There is more to it."

"Is that right?" he asked absently.

"Yes," I stated with absolute confidence. "But you do not want to tell me." I did not know why that fact upset me. This man owed me nothing, and yet I felt as if he did, same as I owed him, which was why I said what I said next. "You can tell me to be courageous, but you cannot do so yourself?"

"What would you like me to say, pet?" He touched his ear, then his gaze cut back to me, but this time I was looking at dark amber eyes full of intent. "That the scars on my back felt like they'd never heal, and I wanted more pain? That I was a coward, and dying by my brother's hand would absolve me of pulling my own trigger?"

I did not dare react, but inside, my heart broke a thousand times over. Not only did I know this kind of pain, this deep feeling of remorse, but I lived and breathed it as sure as the sun rose and set every day. I did not wish that feeling on anyone, and suddenly, I was ashamed for prying. But I also knew I could not leave this here with words unspoken. He may not realize it, but something else had changed on that plane last night.

There was a difference in his eyes. The heaviness was a lighter shade, and I was only able to recognize it because I had experienced it after telling him and his colleagues my own secrets. Except now that weight was back in his gaze, and I felt responsible for it.

"Right. Of course you have nothing to say to that." He shook his head, then touched his ear again and scanned the room.

I focused on the facts. "This woman mistook you for your brother?"

"Yes," he clipped.

"How?"

"We're identical," he replied dryly.

"*Non*," I argued. "You are nothing alike." This was not about looks.

He chuckled without humor. "We're much more alike than you think."

"You are identical, yes, but it is easy to tell you apart. How did she not know?" The woman should have known.

He focused his stare back on me. "I didn't let her know."

That was impossible. "You do not smell the same. You do not speak the same. Your mannerisms are different."

His expression locked, his voice quieted and he lost his British inflection. "Are you sure, Miss Malcher?"

Startled, I leaned back. "I…" A proper response escaping me, I shook my head. "You still smell different. She should have known." Maybe I would not have known.

"So she says, but it was my fault."

If he could pretend to be his brother so easily, I was sure his brother could do the same. "This is why he hates you? Because you pretended to be him?"

The exit at the rear of the event opened, and Vance

immediately slid his hand inside his suit jacket to where I knew a gun was hidden. "I pretended to be my brother up to and including the point at which his woman was naked and my hands and mouth were on her." His gaze locked on the exit, he issued me a command. "Don't move."

Joseph appeared at my back, grasping my arm too firmly. "Sabine, you're coming with me."

The Italian man from Miami walked into the event with his bodyguards.

FIFTY-SEVEN

Vance

"We've got company," November warned through comms. "Fire exit, two black sedans, two black SUVs, all plates are coming up as a car service."

"November, we need intel from the facial rec software on all these people inside," Alpha countered.

"Still scanning," November replied. "Four men getting out of the sedan. Incoming."

The rear exit that should've been locked was opened, and I palmed the 9mm in my shoulder holster as I replied to Sabine. "I pretended to be my brother up to and including the point at which his woman was naked and my hands and mouth were on her."

"You fucking dog, Lover Boy." Echo chuckled through the comms. "Thousand bucks says you didn't have the guts to stick it in."

Ignoring Echo's bullshit, I clipped out at an order to Sabine. "Don't move."

That fuck Bertrand came up behind us and grabbed her arm. "Sabine, you're coming with me."

Sabine looked at me with fear in her eyes as Vincenzo walked in with his bodyguards.

I didn't think. I moved. One hand went around Bertrand's throat as I shoved my 9mm into his ribs. "You grab her one more goddamn time and I will end you. Let. GO."

"*Victor,*" Alpha snapped through comms. "Stand down. You're drawing attention."

"Fuck that," Echo argued. "Do us all a favor. Pull the trigger."

With half the crowd staring, the other half stepping back, Bertrand didn't let go of her. His face turning red, the asshole spewed more bullshit at me. "You think I don't see what's going on here?"

"I don't give a goddamn what you see." Bertrand was lucky he was still breathing. "You have two seconds to release her and tell me what Vincenzo's doing here."

"November, abandon overwatch," Alpha ordered. "Take up sniper position."

"Copy, moving," November replied.

Bertrand's face twisted with fury. "Did you forget who the hell you're speaking to? I don't need to explain myself or my clients to you." He pulled Sabine closer to him. "She's coming with me, *now.*"

"You take one step with her and it'll be your last."

Indignant, the asshole looked at me like I wasn't capable of killing him in a fraction of a second, let alone making him unhand her. "What are you going to do, Victor? Shoot me in a room full of people?"

Vincenzo walked up with two of his bodyguards flanking him as a gun hit the small of my back. "Gentlemen, I would say it's good to see you again, but my patience has already worn thin with this public display." He looked at me. "As I'm sure you already know, you're now at a distinct disadvantage, and since I have business with Mr. Bertrand, you should holster your gun and let go of him. After I conclude my dealings with him, you can return to whatever—" He waved his hand between me and Bertrand. "—this is."

Catching Alpha and Echo's approach out of the corner of my eye, I didn't let go of Bertrand or holster my VP9.

Alpha took up position behind Vincenzo and his bodyguards as Echo covered the asshole on my six.

"Alpha," I clipped. "Do I like anyone telling me what I should do?"

"No," Alpha stated flatly.

"Let her go, Bertrand," I warned one last time.

Vincenzo smiled at me. "Maybe I didn't explain myself clearly enough. I'll rephrase." The mafia fuck dropped his voice and the pretense like he thought he could intimidate me. "Unlike you and your former military friends here, my soldiers don't worry about minor inconveniences like who'll get hit in their crossfire. So if you would like the *signora* to remain breathing, you will release Mr. Bertrand."

"In position," November whispered through comms.

I squeezed Bertrand's throat harder as a green laser sight appeared on Vincenzo's chest. "*Signorina*," I corrected the mafia asshole. "She is not his wife."

"Massimo," Bertrand rasped, pointedly looking at Vincenzo's chest.

Vincenzo glanced at his chest, then focused his steel gaze on me as a cunning smile spread across his face. "Clever. Who do you work for?"

"Myself." Asshole.

"Joseph, please." Sabine put her hand on Bertrand's chest. "It is okay. Just let go."

Joseph, please? It is okay?

I fucking snapped.

Letting go of Bertrand's throat, I grabbed the wrist of the hand he had on Sabine, and I fractured it with a single snap.

Then all hell broke loose.

FIFTY-EIGHT

Sabine

Vance let go of Joseph's throat only to grab his wrist and violently twist. The snap of breaking bone echoed in the shocked silence a split second before everything happened at once.

Joseph fell to his knees, holding his arm. The Italian lunged for me. Vance aimed his gun at the Italian man's head. The three bodyguards aimed their guns at Vance's head, and Mr. Trefor and Echo aimed theirs at the bodyguards.

Screaming erupted all around us. Chairs toppled, tables were shoved, and glasses shattered as clients ran in every direction while the hired security for the paintings grabbed the last canvas and fled.

A strong arm and even stronger cologne wrapped around my neck. "Still, *bella*," the Italian man ordered in a chillingly lethal tone as cold metal pushed into my side.

His arm extended straight out, his gun aimed at the Italian's forehead, Vance leveled the man with a murderous glare. "Do you know the difference between me and your soldiers, Vincenzo?"

The man pressing a gun into my side as he tightened his arm around my neck laughed. "They have more guns than you?"

Vance ignored his answer. "I do give a fuck about collateral damage, which is why your soldiers will be dead from sniper rounds before my bullet pierces your skull." His jaw ticked. "You have two seconds. Release her if you want to live."

"For fuck's sake, Massimo." Joseph groaned as he cradled his arm and pushed himself to standing. "Tell your men to shoot him!"

"November," Vance clipped.

I did not have time to blink.

One after the other, two cracks sounded like the air was snapping. The bodyguards on either side of the Italian dropped as Echo grabbed the third guard's head from behind and twisted as violently as Vance had twisted Joseph's wrist.

Before the third man dropped to the floor with a broken neck, a stampede of shouting voices with heavy footfalls and the metallic clanking of weapons rushed in from the main entrance. German, Italian, English—orders and threats and warnings were yelled from every direction as the Italian yanked me back from the storming Federal Police.

"Dump her and let's go!" Joseph yelled at the Italian.

"Shut up, Joseph. I paid for all of it." Vincenzo twisted me sideways. "I'm taking all of it."

My heart pounding with fear, my ribs getting crushed, air was stolen from my lungs. My mouth opened to scream, but all that came out was a hoarse cry that was immediately lost in the chaos.

"Let her go, Vincenzo," Vance warned.

"Ignore him, Massimo," Joseph yelled. "Let's go. My driver's outside waiting."

Afraid of the Italian, terrified of the men coming at us with guns, panicked that I couldn't get purchase under my feet as I was being yanked away from Vance, I reached out in desperation.

Except my hands did not connect with the hardened muscles of an amber-eyed mercenary. My fingers did not land in impossibly soft, jet-black curls.

My skin connected to fleshy coolness, and I cried out. "Joseph!"

Gunfire erupted all around us.

FIFTY-NINE

Vance

Mafia soldiers, Federal Police, and CIA stormed the fucking ballroom.

"Exfil, exfil, exfil," Alpha barked through comms.

"*Motherfucker*," Echo swore. "Moving."

"Alpha, Echo, push left. Kitchen, east exit," November clipped. "Victor, I don't have a clean shot. Moving."

Ignoring everyone, I focused on Vincenzo.

Dragging Sabine toward the emergency exit as he jammed a gun into her ribs, Vincenzo yelled at Bertrand. "Shut up, Joseph. I paid for all of it." He jerked Sabine sideways, putting her between himself and the rushing police. "I'm taking all of it."

Keeping my eyes on his trigger finger, I gave the asshole one last warning. "Let her go, Vincenzo."

"Victor, move," Alpha ordered through comms. "Vincenzo's soldiers are almost on you, and the police are right behind them. We can't retrieve her if we're detained."

"Ignore him, Massimo," Bertrand barked, holding his broken wrist against his chest. "Let's go. My driver's outside waiting."

Reaching out, Sabine grabbed Bertrand's hand. "Joseph!"

The Federal Police yelled in German to stop, Vincenzo's soldiers opened fire, and I lost my goddamn mind.

She'd reached for him.

She'd fucking reached for him.

I didn't hesitate.

VICTOR

In a fraction of a second, my aim moved six inches to the left, and I pulled the trigger. The mercy shot blew a fucking hole through Bertrand's shoulder, and I was on Vincenzo before Bertrand hit the floor.

Bullets flying, women screaming, men yelling, my elbow strike hit Vincenzo's face dead on. Blood exploded from his nose, he dropped his aim from Sabine's side, and I grabbed the barrel of his gun. Twisting the 9mm out of his grip, kicking out his legs, the mafia asshole dropped.

Sabine pitched with his fall.

My weapon already holstered, flipping Vincenzo's 9mm in my grip, I ducked.

Catching Sabine at the waist, my arm wrapped around the back of her legs and I put her over my shoulder. Returning fire with Vincenzo's piece, stepping over Bertrand, I shoved out of the fire exit.

I ignored Alpha as he issued orders through comms.

I ignored November's exfil directives.

Fucking seething, I aimed for the first black SUV parked in the alley, engine running.

Yanking the driver's door open, I aimed point-blank at the fuck behind the wheel. "Get out."

The stunned driver swore in Italian as the driver's door to the car behind us opened.

I fired two shots at the opening door and one at the front tire before I trained my aim back on the idiot still behind the wheel. "Last warning."

"*Giuro su Dio che ti ammazzo,*" the driver muttered, getting out.

Keeping my aim on the driver, I dropped Sabine in the driver's seat and barked out an order. "Crawl across, *now.*"

Scrambling over the center console in her dress and heels, her ass hit the passenger seat.

I trained my gun at the ground in front of the driver and fired a round.

The fucker ran.

Getting behind the wheel, I threw the SUV into gear and hit the gas.

SIXTY

Sabine

Radiating anger, Vance yanked the steering wheel of the SUV to get us out of the parking spot and gunned the heavy engine. We shot forward, and he took on speed. Dodging emergency and police vehicles, swerving in and out of traffic, ignoring all lights, he threw the gun he had taken from the Italian on the floor behind our seats and grabbed his gun from his holster.

"Buckle up," he ordered in the same terse voice he had used to tell me to crawl across the driver's seat. The same voice he had used when he had told the Italian man to let me go.

Shaking, my heart pounding, terrified of what was happening, but much more afraid of his tone than everything that had just happened, I managed to buckle my seat belt right before he took a sharp turn way too fast.

Tires screeched, horns honked and Vance cut across several lanes of evening traffic as he put his gun between his legs, touched his ear and pulled out his cell phone.

Dialing one-handed, he then put the phone on speaker and dropped it into the center console before checking the side and rearview mirrors.

A woman's voice answered after two rings. "AES."

"Four-four-five-one-eight. Command center. Secure line." Vance glanced over his shoulder and changed lanes again.

"Transferring," the woman answered.

The phone went silent for a moment, then rang once, and a deep, masculine voice answered. "It's Whiskey, line secure. You're a go, Victor."

"Assignment and location compromised. Comms off, radio silent. I need the nearest available safe house, then a ghost ride home, plus one. Traveling light, ammo low."

"Copy. Location tracked," Whiskey answered. "Nearest safe house to you is Budapest."

"Negative. Border's too difficult without passports. Alternative?" Vance took another sharp turn, and we were on a road with less traffic.

"Northwest three hours. Remote location outside Prague, but it'll take you an hour longer to get there than if you head southeast to Budapest."

"I can get us across the border there without notice. Coordinates?" Vance glanced in the mirrors again.

The man rattled off a series of numbers. "Alpha just checked in. They grounded Zulu and detained Alpha and November for debrief. Echo's clear. He's on standby."

"Copy. Send Echo my way for backup. I pissed off a certain Sicilian, and I'm in a stolen vehicle. How long until Zulu's freed up and we can get an exfil?" Vance glanced over his shoulder and took another turn.

The man gave a short laugh. "I hear you did more than just piss him off. Hold for sitrep."

The line went silent.

I had to speak up. "My nephew."

The man called Whiskey came back on the line. "Alpha says he and November will be a few hours behind you. Echo's en route. In four hundred and fifty meters, turn left, then take the toll road. Echo will catch up to you there. No word on Zulu."

"Copy. Is the safe house stocked?"

"Only basics."

"Have November or Alpha retrieve our bags from Bertrand's plane."

"Done. Anything else?"

"Let November know I need a status update ASAP on the nephew and adult female. He'll know what I'm asking for."

"Good copy. By the way, you and Echo owe me and Kilo for cleaning up this fucking mess in the command center."

"Right." Vance turned left and got on a toll road. "I'll keep that in mind." He hung up and glanced in the rearview mirror.

"Are we being followed?"

"Not yet," he clipped.

"You are angry."

He did not reply. He stepped on the accelerator and moved to the left lane.

I should have been upset he shot Joseph or punched the man who was clearly mafia, or that there had been bullets flying everywhere because he had lost his temper and started this evening's horrific turn of events. I should have even been upset about him throwing me over his shoulder and running away from the Austrian police. Foolishly, I did not care about any of it.

I was upset by his anger.

Resorting to behavior I swore to myself I would never do again if I ever got free of Joseph, I apologized for something I did not intentionally do. "I am sorry. I did not mean to reach for Joseph."

Focused on the road, he did not so much as glance in my direction, let alone reply.

"You said you would not lie to me," I reminded him.

"What have I lied about, pet?" Controlled, distant, there was no warmth in his tone or term of endearment.

With the shock wearing off, everything culminated, and I was no longer looking at a mercenary in the seat next to me who had risked his life for mine. I was seeing a man who had kissed me like a lover kisses his one true love but was now turning his back, and I got angry.

Irrationally, foolishly angry.

"If anyone should be upset, it is me. I am not ignorant. Clearly Joseph had the rest of the diamonds, and he was selling them to the Italian, and they were going to take my ring by force. I was the one accused of spying. I am the one that has been unwittingly in the line of fire. I am the one who should be angry, not you." Fighting tears, I turned toward the window. "You have no right to give me this attitude now."

"*Should*," he mocked. "*Right*."

"Go ahead. Make fun of my words. I do not care. I neither need nor want your sympathy or understanding." Crossing my arms, I lost the battle to keep all my emotions restrained.

Silent tears slipped down my face.

SIXTY-ONE

Vance

SEETHING, AN INTERNAL WAR RAGING IN MY FUCKED-UP HEAD, I caught a glimpse of the tears running down her face.

Silent in her grief, still in her posture, she stared out the darkened window.

I hated that she was mesmerizing.

More, I hated that she was right.

Except she missed one crucial fact. I never claimed to be a righteous man. I wasn't even honest. She was the only woman I'd ever been completely truthful with, but when shit got real, she'd called that fucking bastard's name.

I wanted to hate her for it, but I knew what the hell I was looking at.

"Console," I bit out.

Turning more toward the window, remaining silent, she swiped a hand across her cheek.

A better man would've forgiven her, but I wasn't a better man and I'd been down this goddamn road before. "Console is one of the most useless words in the English language." I despised it almost as much as should. "No one can console anyone."

In direct contrast to the tears she tried to hide, her voice held strong as she brazenly challenged me. "If you believe that to be true, then why are you talking to me?"

"Do you believe I can console you?"

Her attitude held. "What makes you think I need it?"

One chance meeting and this woman had detonated my entire fucking existence. "You don't?"

She didn't hesitate. "No."

"Exactly."

When I didn't elaborate, she glanced at me.

"Grief, regret, pain, none of that is a journey someone can travel for you."

"Spoken like a man who has traveled that road."

"It doesn't matter what I've experienced." I couldn't fucking undo her past. "Nothing changes the fact that no one can take away your pain." I glanced in the rearview mirror at a vehicle that'd come up on us. "Hence the idiocy of a word like *console*." The headlights flashed in a double-tap pattern.

She nervously glanced over her shoulder. "Is that Echo?"

"Yes." Out of goddamn time with her, I tried to tell myself shit was playing out how it was meant to be. That I was no good for her, nor her for me, but I stupidly didn't let it go.

Being a prick, I aimed the first insult I could rationalize that would've made her call out that asshole's name. "Was it for money? Is that why you stayed?"

"Do not insult me, Mr. Conlon."

Decidedly obedient coming from her, I stupidly got off on the mister. "I didn't insult you." I did. "I asked a question."

"One you know the answer to."

I aimed another dig. "If it was for money, or even security, I would've thought a woman like you could do better than Bertrand."

"A *woman like me?*" she asked with well-deserved indignation.

Like a fucking masochist, I kept going. "You're beautiful, intelligent, submissive and loyal. All of it wasted on a man who doesn't know how to dominate you." A fucking bastard of a man who'd not only put her life in danger, but he was going to sell her.

Her muscles stiffened, and her tone went south. "I do not need dominating."

Bullshit. "On the contrary, pet, I believe you do." Every dominant move I'd made with her, she'd responded to. "I think you not only want it, you crave it, but you've told yourself a strong woman doesn't submit to a man. Or that a proud woman wouldn't want a man to make decisions for her, take care of her. You're so damn afraid of the perception of it that you instead chose a situation where the choices weren't only taken from you, they were never yours to begin with."

"You are deplorable."

"Why? Because I want to dominate you or because I'm close to the truth? Or is it that I'm pointing out how you felt so goddamn guilty about your brother and nephew that you put yourself in a situation that punished you every single day. Or maybe you're saying I'm deplorable because I understand that guilt and need for pain. Is that it, Sabine? My actions are unforgivable so that makes me deplorable, but your situation is unassailable?" The sick part of me wanted her to say yes, *fuck, I wanted it*. Then I could walk the hell away and go back to the Annex and break shit and not have to look at my own goddamn life.

"You know nothing about me."

"Don't I?" I knew her worst secrets, and she knew mine.

"I know what you are doing," she accused. "I heard what Echo said about you picking a fight. You are trying to make me the same as you, and you want me to admit to something I did not do. But just as I was not guilty of what Joseph accused me of, I am not guilty of whatever—" She gestured dismissively with her hand. "—impropriety you are accusing me of."

"*Impropriety?*" Echo flashed his headlights again, and I fucking lost it. "Is that what you call reaching for the son of a bitch who let a mafia boss hold you at gunpoint as he attempted to kidnap you? And let me assure you, pet, it wasn't just the diamonds and ring Bertrand was selling to Vincenzo. It was also the woman wearing the ring. You were nothing more than a payday to that piece of shit you called out for." Slamming on the brakes, I pulled onto the shoulder and threw the SUV into park. "For the record, if you'd walked away with me, none of that would've happened."

SIXTY-TWO

Sabine

THE HEADLIGHTS BEHIND US FLASHED AGAIN, AND VANCE BRAKED suddenly, swerving the large vehicle to the side of the road. "For the record, if you'd walked away with me, none of that would've happened."

None of that would've happened.

His words echoing in my mind, my sore ribs pushed against the restraint of the seat belt, I started to shake as I reached for the door just to escape—myself, him, this situation.

But the dominant, alpha mercenary in the driver's seat growled low in his throat and barked an order at me. "Don't *fucking* go anywhere."

Everything instantly suspended.

The spinning in my head, the tightness in my chest, my shaking hands. Breath filled my lungs, and I stopped reaching for the door.

"*That* is how I know you're submissive."

My mind scrambled, and I fought back against everything I thought I believed in. "You threatened me," I accused. "What was I supposed to do?"

"I didn't threaten. I ordered, sternly. And I'm not talking about my goddamn order. Look at your hands."

My gaze dropped to my lap where my previously shaking hands were now calmly clasped.

"Right." He got out of the SUV.

I didn't want to think about what he'd just said, but I could no more stop the reality than I could control the volatile situation that had escalated at the auction. Before I could wonder if everything Vance had said about me was true, my door was opened.

His voice still rough with anger but not as stern, he held his hand out. "Watch your step."

Battling the overwhelming urge to take his hand, I instead fought for independence. I fought for everything he'd just said not to be true. "What are we doing?" I told myself it was not a question, that it was a demand, but even I heard the difference in the tone of my voice that only he elicited.

"Switching vehicles. This one can be tracked. It isn't safe."

Safe.

The word echoed around in my head, and before I could stop myself, I was taking his hand but feeling weak for doing so.

His warm, strong fingers wrapped around mine, and despite his anger toward me, he helped me from the vehicle with both gentleness and dominance.

It hit me as hard and as shockingly as if every star had just fallen from the sky.

I was exactly who he accused me of.

I wanted this man to keep me safe.

I wanted him to protect me.

I wanted to forget about Joseph and what he had almost done. I wanted to forget my entire past, and I wanted to fall into this man's arms and never look back.

I wanted to submit to Vance, and I wanted to trust him.

But trust had to be given in order to be received.

Not letting go of his hand, looking up at his austere face in the moonlight, I gave him the only kind of conviction I had to give in that moment. "You are right."

With his expression locked, he said nothing.

Truth was the only apology I had. "For seven years, I wanted to be safe, but I was a prisoner of my own making. In my mind, I was not calling out for Joseph to save me when the men started shooting. I was reacting to my hand landing on him instead of you, and I told myself that was why his name came out. But that is not the entirety of it." I swallowed down fear and spoke a truth I had not even admitted to myself yet. "I was calling out for what I knew as opposed to what I wanted because nothing I feel when I am with you is safe." Without waiting for a response, I dropped his hand and turned toward the other vehicle.

Before I reached the rear passenger door, his dark voice closed the distance between the two vehicles. "For ten years, I exclusively dated blondes."

I turned to look at him.

Even though I instinctively knew, I asked. "The girl when you were seventeen, she was a brunette?"

Barely tipping his chin, he nodded once. "I learned to live with the guilt coursing through my veins. I embraced it. Using it for fuel and self-hatred, I told myself it was the driving force that ensured I would never make the same mistake again."

Jealousy flared, but I had to let go of both the fact that an innocent young woman who had lost her life seventeen years ago was dark-haired and that Vance had been with many women. Instead, I focused on what he was admitting to. "Did it work?"

For a long moment, he stared at me.

Then Vance Conlon broke me all over again. "Up until two days ago."

My wounded heart took another blow, one I did not know how to comprehend.

As if he knew I was standing there adrift on the side of a road in a country where the language was as foreign to me as this moment, Vance closed the distance between us.

His voice went low and quiet as he reached around me and opened the passenger door. "Get in the car, *oiseau*."

I did as he said, and he shut the door, but then he didn't get in the front passenger seat. He went back to the SUV.

I glanced at Echo. "Where is he going? He said that vehicle was not safe to be in."

Echo smirked. "When you steal the mob boss's ride, nowhere is safe, sweetheart."

Oh God. "The Italian man is going to come after him?"

Echo glanced first in the side, then the rearview mirror as he shrugged. "Who the hell knows what that mafia fuck will do. If we're lucky, your asshole husband won't tell Vincenzo who we are, and Vincenzo will be too busy disappearing to care."

I foolishly thought this could not get worse. "Is Vance in danger?" I watched the taillights of the SUV disappear into the tree line beyond the shoulder of the road.

Echo turned in his seat to give me a look. "Vance, huh?"

Heat flushed my cheeks. "Mr. Conlon," I corrected.

Echo raised an eyebrow. "You're worried about Lover Boy when you were dragged halfway across a ballroom at gunpoint while your jackass of a husband hid behind a Sicilian mafia boss?" He shook his head. "Gotta hand it to you, woman, you got balls." He turned back around and nodded toward the side window as Vance walked out of the tree line. "Don't worry, Lover Boy can handle himself."

Vance silently got in the car.

Echo glanced at him before he pulled back onto the road. "Did you wipe it down?"

"Do I look like an amateur?"

Echo smirked again. "Only ninety percent of the time."

"Right, and the other ten percent of the time I'm kicking your ass. Sitrep on Bertrand and Vincenzo?"

Echo dropped the hazing attitude and turned all business. "Good news—the Federal Police grabbed Bertrand, then CIA grabbed him from them. Apparently the fuck sang like a canary before the proverbial cuffs were even on him. He's already on a ghost plane home, courtesy of the Feds. Bad news—your fucking aim was off, you didn't fatally wound Bertrand, and Vincenzo slipped through the cracks. Alpha's contacts said Vincenzo will go underground for a while, best guess is back to Italy. Zulu's still grounded while the Federal Police scratch their asses. Diamonds are MIA. Harrington's accounts have all been frozen and assets seized pending investigations, and you and your girlfriend managed to walk off into the sunset unnoticed thanks to November erasing all the security footage from the hotel."

"I wasn't aiming to kill," Vance defended.

"Sure, Lover Boy."

"Vincenzo's soldiers?" Vance asked, ignoring Echo's quip. "They can ID any of us."

Echo glanced out the side mirror. "Reverse is also true. Those fuckers like night shade. They won't be the problem."

"No, but Vincenzo will when he resurfaces. Ronan's boss at Luna and Associates used to have Vincenzo's brother as a client. I'll get a hold of Ronan and tell him to have Luna relay a message. Those Sicilian fucks need to know she's off-limits."

Echo shook his head. "All right, but you know that'll cost you. At a minimum, Vincenzo will find out who we are."

"Let him."

Echo smirked. "Your self-preservation sucks. Might want to rein that in."

Vance ignored his warning. "The nephew?"

Echo's tone sobered. "November's sitting on Das Safe's security feeds. It's the only lead we've got."

I leaned forward in my seat. "You cannot find my nephew and his mother?"

Echo glanced at me in the rearview mirror. "No."

"Joseph did not tell the police anything about them?" I did not care what he would say about me as long as Julien and Chantel were safe.

"Affirmative," Echo clipped.

For the first time all night, I exhaled with relief. "Then that means they are safe." If these men could not find them, no one could.

SIXTY-THREE

Vance

FLAT ON MY BACK, ONE FOOT ON THE GROUND, MY ARM OVER MY face, I still heard her.

Not that she made a sound, but I'd become attuned to her brand of shifting air. As effortless as an ocean breeze, the same way she'd floated into the safe house hours ago, she floated into the doorway of the living area. The scent of her perfume long gone, I could still smell the faint hint of exotic flowers and heated citrus.

"Don't take another step," I warned. The mood I was in, I wouldn't be responsible for what I'd do if she came closer. The auction, the evening, three hours in the car where she pretended to sleep, then two hours on patrol outside the safe house while Echo was alone with her inside—I was wound so goddamn tight, I wanted to fuck or fight. Preferably both.

The air molecules stilled. "I did not mean to wake you."

Yes, she did. "I wasn't asleep." The couch was too short for my height, and I was listening for any noise out of the ordinary because my instincts were firing hard. The diamonds were still out there. November and Alpha hadn't shown yet. Zulu was still grounded, and I didn't know where the fuck Vincenzo was. But none of that was what was kicking at my instincts, telling me something was off.

"My grandmother used to have a saying." She paused as if

translating it from French before saying it in English. "The wary never rest."

I chuckled without humor. "Right. She may have had a point."

She didn't respond.

Telling myself I didn't care, I counted seconds.

At one minute, ten seconds, I broke like the fucking pussy I'd become around her. Lifting my arm, I glanced toward the open door.

Looking both exquisite and vulnerable in the evening gown she still had on, she shivered in the unheated space. Completely unaware of the power she had over me, and having no idea how goddamn beautiful she was, she stood in the doorway and submissively waited.

Staring at her, I took the moment like a starved man.

Studying the arch of her neck, imagining my palm on her throat as my fingers wrapped around her delicate skin, I thought about sinking inside her, and I inhaled deep. Crisp air and exquisite woman—a combination I wanted to fucking drown in.

But I wasn't that stupid.

I was rough. She was fragile. Her headspace was on that asshole, and mine was worse. What was I going to do if I did get her under me? Fuck her, then go back to fighting at the Annex and taking assignments for AES? The irony wasn't lost on me that any other woman I was this physically attracted to, circumstances be damned, I would've fucked her by now.

Letting my arm drop back over my face, I settled in for what would hopefully be a short remainder of the night before exfil tomorrow—today if I was being technical. "Go back to bed, Sabine."

"You are still angry with me."

Anger didn't begin to cover the shit rolling around in my head. "Did I tell you I was angry?"

"I wanted to apologize."

"I don't want or need one."

"I am still sorry." Her voice quieted. "I made mistakes."

Mistakes I could handle. The complete mindfuck headspace she'd put me in, I couldn't or wouldn't. Regardless, it didn't matter. The clock was counting down. "Get some sleep. Alpha and November will be here soon." Then I could fucking step back. Or get the fuck out of here and step into the ring.

Her inhale was audible, then her words came out rushed and heavily accented. "You are punishing me for something I cannot undo."

Just like I couldn't undo the image of her in my head as she reached for that prick as it played on repeat like some fucked-up reel of history repeating itself.

"You asked me to walk away." Her voice broke.

I fucking lost it.

Sitting up, I glared at her like she deserved my bullshit. "I didn't ask you to walk away. I asked you to walk away *with me*." There was a giant goddamn difference.

Tears shone in her eyes. "Vance—"

"Don't," I warned a split second before I heard it, but it was too late.

I was too late.

The front door kicked in, and four armed men in tactical gear bled into the space, fanning out in a maneuver I'd done so many times in the Marines I could do it in my sleep. Putting themselves between me and Sabine, they all aimed their rifles at my head.

My hands out, I slowly stood and scanned the eyes behind the balaclavas, but I didn't see any that were a distinctive color of blue. "Gentlemen." Where the hell was he? "You seem to be missing somebody."

"Sit the fuck down," the team leader barked.

I scanned the door, then the four men. Maybe my instincts

had been wrong. Maybe he was dead. If so, we were about to have a bigger problem than missing diamonds.

Stalling so Echo could line up his shots, I forced a smile. "Right. And why exactly would I do that when I'm perfectly comfortable standing with my arms up as you point—" I squinted in the dark like I didn't know what the fuck I was looking at. "—FAMAS rifles at my head?"

"Sit. *Down*," the asshole in front growled.

Any-fucking-time now, Echo. "Let me guess. The lady goes, and I stay." Amateurs. "Although, I should warn you." Catching the telltale glint from the reflection of moonlight hitting the end of a scope, I barely tipped my chin. "I'm not particularly fond of your plan."

Echo fired twice.

Two of the armed men's heads exploded as a third man turned toward the open door and blindly fired. A fraction of a second later, another shot rang out and the third armed man dropped.

Before his body hit the ground, the asshole team leader had lunged, beating me to Sabine. Grabbing her in a headlock, he dropped his rifle to let it hang loose on its shoulder strap as he unholstered and shoved a 9mm against her temple.

M4 aimed, Echo stepped over dead bodies as he walked through the busted-in door.

Fucking tired, my hands went to my hips. "What are you going to do now? Shoot her?"

Sabine whimpered, and Echo let out a growl like the fucking animal he was as he took another step toward the asshole.

"One more step and she dies," the asshole warned.

I glanced at Echo. "Do you believe him?"

"No."

"Me either." I looked back at the asshole. "Before you can think of a dozen different ways her brother will torture you for killing her, Echo will have already blown your head off." I glanced back at Echo. "What do you think? This is pretty close range. You're what…?" I scanned the distance between him and the asshole like I actually gave a shit. "Two meters?" I nodded. "Definitely two meters." Avoiding Sabine, I looked at the asshole. "Do you know what happens when a 556 enters your skull from a distance of six feet? Actually," I amended, "it's what will happen to the back of your skull."

"You shoot me, I shoot her. Reflexive action," the asshole bluffed.

"Total myth, but by all means, keep that 9mm trained on her, and let's find out." This was taking too long. "Echo?"

No hesitation, Echo pulled the trigger.

The asshole's head snapped back from the force of the close-range shot. The back of his skull exploded, and Sabine screamed.

His hand dropped, his gun hit the floor, but his arm stayed locked around Sabine's neck as he went down.

Scrambling to get out from under his hold, Sabine slipped in the prick's blood.

"Stop." I grabbed her by the arms. "You're only making the mess worse." Pulling her to her feet, I avoided the blood and stepped us both back before glancing at Echo. "Patrol. I'll call it in."

"Copy. Clean her up. We're not waiting for Alpha. Exfil, two minutes." Echo disappeared through the kicked-in door.

"Come on, love." I led her to the bathroom as I pulled my phone out and dialed a number I knew by heart.

A benign voice came on the line. "Housekeeping."

"I need service." Grabbing a towel, I turned the water on.

"Of course, sir. Room number, please?"

"Four-four-five-one-eight," I rattled off my AES ID number as I held the phone against my shoulder and brought the wet towel to her face.

"Please hold."

Shaking uncontrollably, she flinched back from me.

"Shh, you're okay, love." I held her arm firmly. "Let me clean you up a little."

A series of clicks sounded, and November came on the line. "Connection's secure. What happened?"

I carefully wiped one side of her face. "Location's burned. I need an immediate assist—cleanup crew, four down, full sweep. Echo's doing a perimeter check, but we're out of time. There could be half a dozen more of these fucks any minute." Folding over a bloodstained section of towel, I wiped down her arm.

"Copy." November clipped as he started typing. "Hold for confirmation."

"Holding." I wiped the other side of her face.

Shaking harder, Sabine stared at the towel. "H-he was going to shoot me."

"I was never going to let that happen, pet."

Outside, three shots echoed in rapid succession.

Sabine jumped, and I tossed the towel.

Palming my piece, I put myself between her and the door. "Pick it up, November. We need an extraction, STAT." Aiming my VP9, I glanced out of the bathroom at the empty hall and living area beyond.

"Alpha and I are fifteen minutes out. Zulu is wheels up. Cleanup crew's en route."

"We don't have fifteen minutes," I warned November, motioning for Sabine to stay behind me as I put her left hand on my left shoulder. "I'm getting her out of here now. Sitrep once we're clear." Hanging up and pocketing my cell, I spared her a glance. "Keep your hand on me, pet. I move, you move. I stop, you stop. Understand?"

Trembling with fear, she barely nodded.

No time to reassure her, leading with my piece, scanning

VICTOR

every fucking inch of the place, I moved us out of the bathroom and aimed for the exit.

We made it one step into the living room.

Weapon drawn, a man I'd only seen in pictures came through the busted door of the safe house. "You're not taking her anywhere."

SIXTY-FOUR

Sabine

"You're not taking her anywhere."

My heart stopped, and my body stilled as all the air was sucked from the room.

I did not think anything could dispel the shock of seeing a man killed in front of me, but that voice...

I knew that voice.

Except, it was impossible.

Too impossible.

My heart in my throat, my legs barely holding me up, I did not want to, but I looked past Vance's shoulder at the man he was aiming his gun at.

Oh dear God. "Henri."

"In the flesh," my brother said in near-perfect English.

"I-I thought...." Everything turned sideways.

"You thought I was dead?" Dressed in all black like the other men who had broken into the house, pointing a gun at Vance as if it were as natural as breathing, Henri stepped over dead bodies and walked into the living room. "I can assure you, I'm not." He glanced at my left hand on Vance's shoulder, then at Vance. "I'm taking it from here. She's no longer your problem. Lower your weapon."

Problem?

Vance didn't budge. "I can assure *you*, she's not the one who's the problem. You lower your weapon."

Henri ignored him and looked at me like the older brother he used to be but was no longer. Then he switched to French. "I'm taking you away from this. No more living under Bertrand. Come with me. You are safe now."

"You died because of me," the horrendous admission I had never said out loud scraped past my throat and bled from my lips. "*I buried you.*"

The man who used to be my brother spoke with zero emotion. "My death was faked. I'm sorry you had to live through that. Let's go."

"Safe?" Vance asked incredulously. "Four of the rogue Legionnaire assholes you tied yourself to are dead, and you have a goddamn target on your back that spans five continents. Unless you're going to have her looking over her shoulder the rest of her life, how exactly do you plan on *taking her away from this*?" Vance mocked in a scathing tone I had never heard from him.

But all of that paled to the one thing Vance had said that was far worse than all of the other words combined.

"Rogue Legionnaires?" No. "Henri?" *Oh dear God, no.* "Tell me you are not a part of that."

Henri's murderous gaze cut to Vance, and he switched back to English. "You speak French."

"I speak a lot of fucking languages, and I can assure you I'll say the same damn thing in all of them." Vance took a menacing step toward my brother. "She's not going anywhere with you."

A muted thud sounded outside, and then everything happened at once.

Echo stormed into the house. Henri jumped through the living room window. Glass shattered. Vance followed Henri, and gunfire erupted in an explosion of bullets. Hitting the front of the house, the side of the house, the broken front door, they whistled past my head. Popping sounds like fireworks rained down all around me.

Echo grabbed the back of my head and shoved me to the floor before firing his giant rifle.

The sound of the gunfight thunderous, my hands flew to my ears, but then I was crawling.

Insanity, fear, I did not know what propelled me on my elbows and knees, but I could not stop.

The window.

I had to get to the window.

I had to get to him.

Blindly moving, my head down, I banged into upholstery. Not thinking, not breathing, I braced my hands on the couch and shoved up.

"*Woman,*" Echo roared in warning. "Get the fuck down!"

Rapid-fire shots rang out.

I reached for the shattered opening where there used to be a window.

SIXTY-FIVE

Vance

THE FUCK JUMPED OUT THE WINDOW.

No hesitation, I went after him.

Landing on top of the asshole, I knocked his gun free and was already swinging with my first punch when a fucking firestorm broke out.

Bullets ricocheting off the house, I slammed my fist into his jaw.

The prick rolled and swung with an uppercut.

Blocking his punch, I kicked him in the gut as he reached for his rifle.

He doubled over, a bullet ripped through my shirt sleeve and I got fucking irate.

Jamming my VP9 into his temple, the asshole didn't even hesitate as he pulled a 9mm from a thigh holster and aimed point-blank at my stomach.

"Vance!" her strained voice cried.

Mother*fucker*. "Get down, Sabine!" Three more shots hit the house beside us, and I gave her asshole of a brother one goddamn warning. "Call them off, or I'll pull the trigger."

"You shoot me, I shoot you."

"Vance, *please*," Sabine cried.

Ignoring the fact that she was trying to protect her asshole brother, I glared at the son of a bitch. "If she gets hurt, you're dead."

"I'm already dead," the asshole argued as two more shots pinged off the house.

"You're only still breathing because you're her brother, but in two seconds, I'll no longer give a fuck who you're related to. *Call them off.*" I jammed the barrel hard against his head.

Sabine whimpered.

"*Cessez-le-feu!*" the asshole yelled.

The sound of tires on gravel echoed in the sudden silence, and I was done. "This is your one free pass. Walk the fuck away, Malcher. But know this. If you so much as step foot in the same country as her again, I will beat you within an inch of your life."

The asshole looked over my shoulder at his sister. "*Viens avec moi.*"

"Don't fucking move, Sabine," I warned.

Car doors opened and closed.

"*Henri,*" Sabine quietly cried as she reached out for him.

Footsteps crunched on gravel.

The fuck didn't hesitate. Not even saying goodbye to his sister, he fled for the shadows of the tree line.

Weapons drawn, Alpha and November came around the side of the destroyed house.

Echo appeared next to Sabine in the broken window. "Some fucking safe house."

Alpha scanned the wooded tree line. "Let's go. Zulu's waiting."

"Echo," I clipped, holstering my weapon and reaching up toward the window. "Hand her down to me." No fucking way was she stepping over the bodies by the front door to get out.

Echo picked up a shaking Sabine and unceremoniously dumped her out the window.

Catching her in my arms, I held her to my chest.

Alpha and November flanked us as Echo jumped out the window and covered our six.

We moved to the SUV as a unit.

Alpha got behind the wheel. November opened the rear passenger door for me and Sabine before getting in front, and Echo took the seat behind Alpha.

Alpha pulled out of the driveway and hit the deserted country road. "How many were there?"

"No fucking clue," Echo answered. "But I got four in the house and three in the woods." He glanced at November. "Let the sweepers know about the ones in the woods. From the northwest corner of the house, straight into the tree line."

"No need," Alpha answered as November opened his laptop. "They won't leave a trail. They'll clean up their own."

Her small body still shaking, silent tears falling, I held her and tried to shove down every shit emotion circling around the fact that two times now, in duress, I wasn't the one she'd fucking reached for. "Shh," I whispered. "It's over."

Alpha glanced at me in the rearview mirror. "She hit too?"

"Who's hit?" Echo asked as both he and November looked at me.

"We're fine," I answered.

Echo glanced at my arm and smirked. "It's barely a scratch. I think Lover Boy will live."

November turned back to his laptop. "With seven down, that potentially leaves four from the rogue unit still alive."

Echo stated the obvious. "None of the idiots tonight could shoot for shit. If any of the original rogue unit besides her brother are still alive, I doubt that was them."

"Victor?" Alpha asked.

"Agreed."

November glanced back at me. "That leaves the brother."

Not only had that fuck run like a coward, he'd run from the only family he had. "He won't be a problem." If he was, I'd take care of him.

Small fingers touched where a bullet had ripped through my shirt and grazed my arm. "You are shot."

"I'm fine." I wasn't anything close to fine. I wanted to kill that asshole Henri and shake some goddamn sense into her. Her brother had come for her ring, not her. The fuck had glanced at it three times when he was lying to her about saving her. "November, any movement on Das Safe or chatter on the diamonds?" Maybe her brother would go after the diamonds and I could take the fuck down, give her the damn diamonds and end this.

"Negative," November answered. "And my contact at Langley says Bertrand's denying everything about both the safe box and the diamonds."

Her voice hoarse, Sabine spoke up. "Joseph will never mention them or admit to their existence. It is over. Let it go."

November glanced at Alpha then me.

I had to inhale twice and grit my fucking teeth before I forced the order out. "If she says let it go, then let it go." I didn't walk away leaving shit unfinished. Ever. But I had to remind myself this wasn't my deal, and this woman wasn't mine. I had no say in her life. All I could do now was protect her decisions. "November, contact that attorney in Miami, Mathew Barrett, and have him prepped for when we get back to the States." This wasn't over for her. Not until Joseph was in jail or WITSEC if the fuck conned his way into a deal.

"Copy." November typed on his laptop.

"Thank you," Sabine quietly whispered.

I bristled. "Don't thank me." Any sane person would've seen this for what it was. I'd walked into her life and fucking destroyed it.

She didn't reply.

Alpha drove us to the airport.

SIXTY-SIX

Sabine

I T WAS OVER.

And the man responsible for it all was holding me on his lap, not letting go.

Emotions ranging from grief to elation, and everything in between, were crowding my mind, and I did not know how to process any of it except for the feel of Vance's arms around me as I inappropriately sat on his lap in front of three other men.

But it did not feel inappropriate, and none of them had so much as glanced twice at us, let alone mentioned the third row of seats behind us that Vance could have set me in.

I did not know if I wanted to run and hide to lick my wounds or grab the man holding me and never let go.

Before I could decide or even begin to think about the blood on my dress and Vance's shirt, Mr. Trefor had turned off the road and was driving along a long stretch of cracked pavement. Hidden in a forest of trees, the makeshift airstrip was closer to a shortly shorn field than a runway, but none of the men said anything as he pulled up next to their private jet.

"November, make sure the cleanup crew takes care of the SUV." Mr. Trefor cut the engine.

"Already handled." November closed his laptop and got out.

"Hold on," Vance roughly commanded as November opened our door.

Before I could protest, Vance had stepped out of the SUV

and was carrying me toward the waiting jet with Mr. Trefor and November in the lead, and Echo trailing behind us.

Almost to the plane, I found my voice. "I can walk."

"I know." Effortlessly carrying me up the airstairs and down the aisle, Vance took me all the way to the lavatory before murmuring, "You're covered in trace evidence."

The comforting feeling of having him hold me instantly disappeared, and my stomach dropped as my muscles tightened.

Still holding me, Vance paused in front of the bathroom door. "What's wrong?"

"Nothing." *Oh God. Everything.* "Set me down."

Searching my face, he did not move as the jet's engines came to life. Then he inhaled, nodded once, and set me on my feet in the restroom. "Don't move. I'll grab your bag."

Like a fool, I stood there.

A moment later, he returned with my suitcase and set it just inside the lavatory. "Dump the dress and shoes in the trash, but be quick. You only have a couple of minutes before we take off. Washcloths are in one of the cabinets."

Reality starting to eat away at the lull of numbed shock, I nodded and shut the door with shaking hands.

Barely glancing at myself in the mirror, I used one washcloth on my face and another on my arms. Then I shoved everything, including my expensive, bloodstained shoes into the small, built-in waste container. Since I was a glutton for punishment, I put on the T-shirt Vance had given me on the way to Austria and the same leggings and sweater because all of it smelled like him.

Slipping on a pair of ballet flats, I zipped my suitcase and opened the lavatory door.

Startled by Vance standing right there, my hand went to my chest.

In the same shirt with the ripped fabric on the sleeve that had bloodstains around it, he tracked the movement of my hand.

VICTOR

Then he dropped his gaze to the suitcase and grabbed it. "I'll stow this. Take a seat. We're wheels up."

Walking past Echo as he stretched out on one of the couches with his eyes closed, I kept my distance from where November sat in the front of the plane with his laptop, and instead took a seat in the middle of the cabin.

The scent of rain-wet cobblestones and musk drifted past my senses a moment before Vance took the seat next to me.

The plane started to move, and I forced myself to ask the hard question. "What happens next?"

"A cleanup crew erases our footprint while we fly to New York. Then you speak to an attorney once we land." Crisp, no emotion, he rattled off the agenda as if nothing had happened tonight.

"Is this what you do?" I glanced around the private jet as it lifted into the sky. "What Alpha Elite Security does?"

He trained his gaze straight ahead. "It's best if you never speak about what happened tonight."

"But you want me to talk to the attorney?"

His amber and green eyes met mine. "I want you separated from Bertrand, Harrington's and tonight. Cleanly," he added. "You can trust the attorney I'm setting you up with. Tell him whatever he asks, and he'll make sure you don't come out of this empty-handed."

I had not been thinking about money, but now I was. I had none. I did not even have a bank account. "I cannot pay for the attorney."

"You won't have to."

"Someone will," I argued because none of this was happening how I expected, and I felt no relief.

Vance inhaled deeply as the plane leveled before leaning back in his seat. "You don't need to worry about paying for the attorney, Sabine."

Sabine.

No pet, no love, no darling—just my name uttered with a tiredness that said more than his actual words.

Fighting foolish tears, I turned toward the window. "Why New York? None of you live there."

"Your penthouse is there."

"It is not mine," I replied with all of the belligerence of a child because I did not want to ever step foot in that space again. I did not want to go anywhere that was tied to Joseph.

Vance exhaled, then he spoke to me as if I were the child I had just behaved like. "Your clothes are there, and a Picasso's hanging in the living room. The painting alone is worth the time it'd take for you to throw shit into a suitcase."

I held on to my stubbornness because I had nothing else to reach for. "I do not want to go there."

"Where do you want to go, Sabine?" he calmly asked.

"Do not call me that," I snapped.

All of a sudden, my chin was grasped, my head was yanked and I was staring into the furious eyes of a mercenary. "Where. Do you. Want to. *Go?*"

Every nerve in my body tingled from his dominant grip, and I could not stop it. I shivered.

His eyes shut, and his nostrils flared with an inhale. "Give me a location."

The command feathered across my skin, leaving an impossible need for something so out of my reach that tears welled. "I do not know." I did know.

"*Tell me,*" he barked.

"Miami," I blurted.

Instantly on his feet, he strode toward the cockpit. "Alpha, Zulu, change of course," he barked at them like he had at me. "Reroute to Miami."

I did not hear their response, but I did not need to.

VICTOR

An angry Marine turned mercenary who had jumped out of a window after my brother, protected me from a mafia boss, and got me away from Joseph and my past, he was coming at me like a cyclone.

Except he did not come at me.

He did not bring me a blanket and pillow.

He did not tuck me in.

He did not even pause.

He barked out another order as he swept past my seat like a gale-force wind. "Get some sleep, Sabine."

Stunned, I watched him stride to the back of the cabin and take the couch opposite Echo. Crossing his arms, he leaned back and closed his eyes.

I turned toward the window and let silent tears fall.

SIXTY-SEVEN

Vance

THE ENTIRE FUCKING FLIGHT WAS TORTURE.

I wanted to fuck her, and I wanted to fight.

I wanted to erase every ounce of fear off her face, but I couldn't.

Her life had imploded in forty-eight hours, and I'd sat in the aft cabin like a fucking pussy because this woman had hit every goddamn trigger I had. I knew if I'd spent one more second in her presence, I'd consume her.

Then I wouldn't stop.

I couldn't.

Which was why I wasn't checking her into a hotel or dumping her at the house in Coral Gables after the ten-hour flight. My masochistic ass was unlocking my penthouse, dumping our bags in the entrance and praying the cleaning service had already come and gone.

Walking in, she glanced around before going to the floor-to-ceiling windows overlooking the ocean, but she still didn't say shit.

In fact, she hadn't said a damn word since we'd landed and I'd told her I'd bring her here, we'd regroup, grab a shower, then she could meet with the attorney.

Except now she was staring at the ocean, and I was staring at her, wondering how many ways I could make her say my name.

Fuck.

Tossing my keys on the counter, I grabbed a bottle of scotch, poured two glasses and walked to her. Holding the drink out, I ordered her around like she was mine. "Drink this."

No hesitation, she took the glass, but she didn't take a sip. "Why am I really here?"

I threw out a bullshit excuse. "We don't know if the Coral Gables house was seized by the Feds."

"That is not what I meant." She turned to me. "You are angry with me, and everything has changed. I am no longer a prisoner of my past, and yet I feel more powerless than I have ever felt."

Bright sunlight and her own painful honesty shining in her exhausted eyes, she was more beautiful than when I first laid eyes on her. Keeping a foot of distance between us, I forced myself not to touch her because she was right. I was still angry. But ten hours had given me perspective. "Do you know the true travesty of pairing *power* and *less* together like they're a goddamn love affair?"

She stared at me with the same haunted eyes I saw every time I looked in the mirror. "*Non*."

"Power doesn't belong to a lesser force." Holding her gaze, holding my goddamn breath like this was my one shot at redemption, I stepped into her and grasped the side of her face. "It doesn't belong to your brother, it didn't belong to Bertrand, and it sure as hell doesn't belong to me." I dropped my voice. "Your power belongs to you."

The fear she'd been holding onto like a shield stayed resolute in her gaze, but the edge of something else flashed.

I took the in. "Take the reins, Sabine." My thumb stroked across her soft cheek. "For once in your life, take control."

"Vance," she barely breathed.

After everything that'd happened, for both of us, this woman had to come to me. "You have the power, beautiful."

She blinked, but then the light in her eyes that'd flashed before shut down. "Why are you doing this? You can have any woman."

I could and I had, but no one was her. She was beautiful, but it wasn't the pretty package staring back at me that was so stunning it was crushing, it was the woman inside.

Unbreakable, graceful and submissive—the holy grail of trifectas.

Like she was made for me, like I had a right to fuck her life up any further, I gave her one last chance to take this moment. "I don't want another woman. I want you. Kiss me or don't, but make the decision you want to make, Sabine." Losing control of something I never had control of in the first place, I brought my mouth within an inch of hers. "I'm not going to offer this again." For my own sanity, I couldn't.

Her lips parted, her breath hitched, and she leaned a fraction closer.

"But know this," I warned. "You touch me, I own you."

SIXTY-EIGHT

Sabine

"But know this," he warned. "You touch me, I own you." Suddenly, everything I had ever wanted became nothing I could handle.

I wanted this man. I wanted every dominant inch of him, but he was right.

He would own me.

He would take me places I was not comfortable with. He would push my limits. He would also give me unparalleled pleasure. I knew he would. A man as dominant as him would be nothing but the perfect lover.

But was that what I traded my old life for?

A perfect lover?

I wanted more. No, I wanted it all. I wanted to be loved. I wanted a partner. I wanted children at my feet and a husband at my side. I wanted summer breezes and, yes, I wanted moody storms.

But Vance Conlon wasn't a simple rain shower.

He was the perfect storm.

One that could destroy me worse than my entire past.

His chest rose with a deep inhale. "Right." Dropping his hand, he stepped back. "Better choice, pet."

"Wait." Oh God. "I did not make a choice."

"You're right, you didn't. Your hesitation did."

"No." *Non.* "Please, I—"

"The lawyer will be here soon. Guest bedroom and bath are past the living room. I'm going to shower." He turned toward a hallway.

Desperate, feeling like everything was slipping away, I barked an order at him as he would me. "Stop."

Pausing, but not turning around, he glanced over his shoulder.

The exhaustion in his eyes hurt my heart. "I was overwhelmed."

"As you should be."

I told him the truth. "I bristled at your choice of words."

"There was no choice in them."

"Please, do not speak in riddles. I do not understand." There was something he was not saying.

"The words were not the choice," he amended.

"I understand that." Or I thought I did. He wanted a choice from me, and I knew my heart. It had already fallen for this broken hero, but I could not be the woman who was a conquest for an evening, a week, a month. I could not give myself to him only to be given away later. I knew it was impossible to hope for guarantees in life, or even happily ever afters, but I still wanted it. I wanted to believe that kind of love existed. It was the one thing I believed was truly still worth living for. But how could I have that with a man who had left his heart in the ocean seventeen years ago?

His gaze stark but unguarded, he asked a simple question. "Then what don't you understand?"

It struck me as fast and as sure as the storm I knew him to be. My hesitation was not that I did not have trust in him, but that I did not trust myself.

I barely whispered the truth. "I do not know how to make choices."

For a long moment, he stared. Then he both broke my heart

and gave me a fluttering of anticipation with his own truth. "I can't do casual with you, Sabine."

Hopefulness surged, but instinct told me not to reach for it yet. "I do not want casual."

"You shouldn't."

The swell of hope waned at the emotionless tone in his voice. "What are you saying?" I was still missing something.

"Your truth."

"Which means?" Maybe this was not only my truth. Maybe this was his.

"If I have to explain, then you're not ready to make this kind of choice."

"I am ready." Was I?

Staring right at me, he inhaled as if he were still here, still present in this conversation, but I saw it in his eyes. He had shut down. "If you were, I would've already been inside you."

Heat flushed both my face and my core, but before I could respond, he had already disappeared down the hallway.

Stunned, aroused, confused, drowning in a need I could not put words to, I stood there.

Then my feet were moving because, while maybe I did not know exactly how to get what I wanted or what I could begin to expect from all of the complicated versions of this dominant, mercurial man, I did know one thing.

Letting him walk away was not the answer.

SIXTY-NINE

Vance

L EAVING MY DOOR OPEN LIKE A FUCKING PUSSY, I YANKED OFF MY torn shirt and tossed it. Before I could aim for the master bath and a shower, I heard her.

Light as air footsteps and the entire fucking atmosphere in my bedroom changed.

Not turning, I inhaled like a junkie just to catch a hint of her scent. "Wrong bedroom if you're looking for privacy, pet."

She was silent a moment. Then, "I did not know what to expect when you told me your back was injured."

Her voice, the closeness of her, having her in my penthouse—*fuck*. I was losing my goddamn mind, and I hadn't even fucked her. "I didn't know what to expect when I walked into Harrington's."

Air shifted and her breath landed on my back. "Do they hurt?" With a featherlight touch, her finger traced one of the scars. "You have so many bruises." Her touch glanced across my ribs, then landed near the graze wound on my arm.

For three seconds, I froze.

Then I was a fucking storm.

Turning on her, capturing the wrist of the offending finger that was still suspended midair, I shoved her against the wall and pinned her left arm above her head.

"Don't," I warned.

"Why?" No pardon, no backing down, she stared at me as I at her.

VICTOR

My heart pounding, on the edge of losing control, anger that had nothing and everything to do with her destroying my judgment, I said the last thing I should have. "You don't touch me unless you're giving permission." *Should.* Fuck, *fuck.* I wasn't on the edge anymore, I was over it.

Pure, innocent, submissive, her eyebrow raised and her voice came out as soft as her touch. "For?"

Every-goddamn-thing. "You know exactly what for."

Her eyes searched my face, my mouth, my eyes. Then her lips parted, and she fucking slayed me. "You touch me, I own you," she whispered, giving me back my own bullshit.

"No." She didn't fucking understand. "I will *own you*," I emphasized. "Every move. Every breath. Every step," I warned. "Control—yours, mine, ours—I'll take it." That was the only fucking way I could do this. "And trust me, I see the glaring hypocrisy. You're the last woman I should be taking control from. I'm not who you want in your life, *oiseau*. I will break you. That's who I am."

"You cannot break what is not whole, and you are already in my life." Her right hand touched her heart, and her voice went soft, submissive, but resolute. "You are already in here." She switched to French. *"Vous allez le nier?"* Are you going to deny it?

"Not the point," I ground out.

"Then what is? You brought me here. You are afraid to touch me back? Afraid of what you will feel?" Her voice turned alarmingly quiet. "Do you think I will hurt you?"

My nostrils flared, my jaw locked and my hand was on her throat. "You think you can hurt me?" Irrational anger flared, and I threw down my last warning. *"Tu es un oiseau fragile."* You are a fragile bird.

"I am only as fragile as you make me in your imagination."

Jacked up, mind fucked, no outlet—hard guilt dripped on me

like fuel on a flame. "Fragile." My hand tightened on her throat. "You think that's only in my head?"

"I think your warnings do not have my attention yet."

What the fuck? "Is that right?"

"Yes."

"Bullshit."

"Then prove it," she taunted before her voice dropped to a seductive whisper. "Try to break me."

I fucking lost it.

Shoving her hard against the wall, my leg went between her thighs, and my hips pressed into hers. Dominating, controlling, overbearing, I glared down at her. "You want me to break you, *oiseau?*"

No self-preservation, she didn't hesitate. "Yes."

My mouth slammed over hers, her head hit the wall and I sank my tongue in with unhinged desperation.

Then I fucking levitated.

She tasted like redemption for every mistake I'd ever made. She tasted like forbidden fruit. She tasted like fucking exquisite beauty.

I didn't deserve her.

But I took.

My hands on her face, my fingers in her hair, I angled her head and slanted my mouth over hers, but it wasn't enough. I needed more.

"Say yes," I demanded, pulling back as I ground my knee between her thighs.

Her lips wet, her eyes hooded, she moaned. "Yes."

My cock pulsing, need strangling my fucking lungs, I gave her one last warning. "Say it and know what you're saying yes to." There was no going back with this woman.

With her eyes focused on mine, she gripped my waist and pulled me against her. "*Yes.*"

I spun her.

Then I was barking out orders as I shoved my own goddamn T-shirt up her back and gripped the hem of her tight pants before yanking them down. "Face against the wall, arms above your head."

With instant compliance, she did as I said, but she didn't stop there. Arching her back, she thrust her hips toward me.

Staring at her perfect ass in a black lace thong, I couldn't unzip my pants fast enough. "You have no idea what I'm going to do to you, pet." I stroked myself once, then pulled her thong to the side.

The scent of her desire driving me insane, I drew two fingers across her already wet pussy, then pressed against her clit and circled.

Her hips jerked.

Fuck yes. "Do I have your attention now?" Dragging my cock through her slick desire, I didn't wait for an answer.

I drove into her with one single thrust.

Jesus Christ.

My head fell back, and I lost my goddamn mind as the tightest cunt I'd ever felt gripped around my cock in pure fucking ecstasy.

Fighting not to come, I pulled back, then I drove deep and bottomed out. Her body shook, my cock pulsed and her sweet cunt gripped me even tighter.

She didn't make a sound.

Lost in everything I never knew I needed, I drove into her three more times, and a groan ripped from my chest.

Her hips met my thrusts, her pussy quivered around my cock, and her hands stayed flat against the wall above her head.

But she still didn't utter a single sound.

Gripping her hair, I yanked her head back. Blind with lust, I sucked her neck and thrust harder. "Is this what you wanted, *oiseau?*"

"No."

I fucking froze. "What?"

"*Non.*"

My thoughts plunging, my cock pulsing, guilt slammed into my chest, and I jerked out of her wet cunt. No goddamn air in my lungs, I threw blame at her. "You asked for this." Fuck. *FUCK.*

Trembling, my T-shirt falling back down over her ass, she turned. "I asked for you."

I was staring at blue eyes, not green, but the look was the same, and suddenly I was fucking drowning all over again.

"You had me." Guilt filled my lungs, and I hurled my own disgust at everything I'd become in her face. "I told you—I touch you, I own you." Adrenaline surging, hands fisting, I dug my own goddamn grave. "This is who I am. You wanted me to touch you, *break you?*" I didn't warn her with my next words, I threatened. "Then this is what you get."

Not waiting for a reaction because I fucking knew what it would be, what any sane woman's reaction would be, I walked the hell out.

Grabbing my keys off the counter, I yanked open the front door. As it slammed shut behind me, I heard one word.

"*Menteur.*"

Liar.

SEVENTY

Sabine

My body shaking, I burst into tears.

He was a liar. That was not the man who had iced my wrist or tucked me in on a private jet before telling me his most painful experience. That was not even the man who had shot Joseph.

The man who turned me toward the wall and thrust into me without consequence, that was only a part of him. The part who thought he needed to scare me away.

I was not afraid, but I did not want only pieces.

I wanted all of him.

I knew I was right for saying no, for telling him what I had wanted. But now I could not breathe, and everything was falling apart faster than the bullets flying in Austria and a house that was not safe in Prague.

I had no money.

I had nowhere to go.

And I had no way to leave.

Oh God.

What had I done?

My hands trembling, I pulled my leggings up just as a doorbell sounded.

Moving on autopilot with my ballet flats still on, I tried to ignore the space between my legs that was now both sore and feeling so empty I wanted to curl into a ball. Swiping at my tearstained cheeks, I opened a front door that was not mine.

A very tall, very handsome, black-haired man with black-framed glasses and a messenger bag over his shoulder peered down at me. "Miss Malcher?"

"Yes."

"I'm Mathew Barrett, your attorney. May I come in?"

He looked like a movie star, one I could not remember the name of. He also seemed too young to be a lawyer.

Wishing I was not in rumpled clothes and bare-faced with no makeup to hide behind, wishing I did not even need an attorney at all, I silently stepped back.

As if he knew his way around, he walked into the spacious penthouse and set his bag on the kitchen island. "Is Mr. Conlon here?"

"No."

The attorney stared at me a moment. "Are you all right?"

Valiantly fighting tears, I managed to nod, but English did not come out. "*Oui.*"

He frowned. "I'm afraid my French is limited to a few high school courses, and even that will be rusty at best. Are you comfortable speaking in English? If not, we can wait for Mr. Conlon to return."

Oh, God. Would he return? Did I want to be here when he did? Did I have a choice? Having nothing to my name but a ring on my finger and the clothes on my back, it was seven years ago all over again.

"Miss Malcher?"

Startled out of my own thoughts, I flinched. "I am sorry. Yes, I speak English. My apologies. Thank you for coming."

"My pleasure." The handsome man who smelled clean and fresh and had more muscles under his dress shirt than any lawyer I had ever met, calmly nodded as if he dealt with near-hysterical, desperate women every day. Opening his bag in a crisp, controlled movement that was reminiscent of another man with jet-black hair, the lawyer took out a pad of paper.

The question was out of my mouth before I could stop it. "Were you in the military too?"

"Not something I'm usually asked by clients, but yes, I served." Giving me only a hint of a smile and no further details, he directed the conversation back to why he was here. "I just have a few questions, and then I'll download what information I have so far for you."

I could not help my surprise. "You have information for me?"

"Yes. AES filled me in, and I did some preliminary work before I came over." He glanced at the expansive dining table I could not image Vance eating at. "Shall we sit? Can I get you something to drink?"

Completely out of my element, I realized all at once how very sheltered I had been these past years. Joseph may have given me a position at Harrington's and took me to fancy restaurants and entertained clients in the penthouse, but it was suddenly glaringly obvious how little I had been involved. With the exception of dressing pretty, smiling and familiarizing myself with the art world so I could converse, I had never done something as simple as cook a meal.

"It is I who should be offering you something to drink, but I am afraid I do not know my way around Mr. Conlon's home."

The attorney frowned again but then quickly hid it. "It's all right. Please, have a seat." He pulled a chair out for me.

I sat.

Taking a pen from his bag, he set it on the pad of paper but then pulled his own chair out. Instead of facing the table, he sat sideways and focused on me as he laced his hands and rested his arms on his thighs. "Why don't you start at the beginning?"

Remembering Vance's directive, I did not hold back. I told

this stranger everything, including the horrible things Joseph had done to me.

With the exception of inhaling sharply twice and writing down three dates, he respectfully listened to every word.

When I finished speaking, he stared at me a moment longer, then his gaze drifted over my head. For several seconds, he said nothing.

Then he inhaled and nodded as if to himself. "Okay. Here's the truth." He met my gaze again. "You have no legal rights to any of his assets in New York or otherwise because you are not legally married and the state does not recognize common law marriage. However, given the circumstances, the details with which you can recall them, and the fact that Mr. Bertrand put you on the board of directors gives me a very good basis for going after Harrington's, which I strongly suggest we do."

"For what?"

"I'm going to argue multiple points, but in effect, this will be for monetary compensation for everything you've been through in addition to a settlement in exchange for early termination of your board position." He jotted something else down on his pad of paper before looking back at me. "I'm assuming you do not wish to remain at Harrington's?"

"I want nothing to do with Harrington's or Joseph ever again."

"Understood." He wrote something else down, then looked back at me. "Based on the annual compensation for serving as a board member, along with the payout package at the end of the term of service, and adding in the duress I am going to argue you suffered, I believe we should propose a settlement of fifteen million."

I blinked. "Pardon?"

"It's a safe amount. If we go higher, I think we'll risk a drawn-out lawsuit, and I'm assuming you want to avoid that?"

"Fifteen million?" I asked, my voice barely forming the words.

"Yes. Based on the annual salary of seven hundred and fifty thousand dollars and the final payout of three to five million, minus what you've already been paid, plus undue duress, sexual harassment and physical abuse in the workplace, I think fifteen million is fair, but I will present a higher amount if you wish."

Oh my God. "I have received no salary."

The attorney's jaw ticked as he nodded. "Mr. Conlon relayed his suspicion that you may not be aware of the fact that you had been earning a salary for seven years."

Shocked, I barely whispered the truth. "Joseph controlled everything."

The lawyer stared at me intently, then his voice came out rough. "Now he doesn't, and he won't ever again. Understand?"

No. "Okay."

"Say yes," he demanded.

"Yes."

"Good."

I had to ask. "What will happen to Joseph?"

The lawyer stared at me a moment. "Are you asking as my client?"

I did not understand. "Yes?"

"I don't know," he quickly replied, looking down at his pad of paper.

"What if I am asking as a friend?"

He gave me his blue-eyed gaze again. "As my friend, I would tell you that we are not having this conversation. I would not tell you that I heard a rumor about a deal that was struck in exchange for witness protection. I wouldn't even reassure you that you're safe because he's already gone and you'll never see him again. As my friend, I would simply tell you to let the courts worry about it."

Trying to wrap my head around everything, I nodded my thanks. Then I asked what I had been avoiding. "Am I in trouble with the police or any other agency either here or in France or Austria?"

Mr. Barrett set his pen down. "Technically, no. I've spoken with the FBI, and they're after Bertrand. They know his history, and they know the evidence on your laptop was planted. I'm trying to avoid you having to give a statement in person, so I'll type something up and have you sign it and hand it over to them. That should suffice." He leaned back in his chair. "Informally, I highly suggest you keep the events of Austria, Prague, and Paris seven years ago to yourself. I would not attempt to ever contact your brother, and I would not travel to Austria any time soon. Speaking confidentially, even though I believe you're already aware of this information, your presence in the country was wiped clean as far as a digital footprint, but I would still avoid the area."

"Understood, thank you." Since he was being so forthcoming with information, I decided to ask about the one last thing I was worried about. "Do you know if I can keep my ring, or if there will be consequences if I do?"

The attorney slowly nodded and seemed to think a moment before answering. "I cannot divulge confidential information I receive from other clients, but let's just say that I have no doubt AES will secure both you and your ring's safety. You will not be in any danger from a certain Italian organization. As far as the ring, I believe it to be yours. However, if you attempt to sell it, I cannot guarantee what will happen."

"I understand."

"Good. Okay, do you have any other questions or issues you'd like to discuss before we move on to the last order of business I have?"

Shame colored my cheeks. "Until I receive a settlement, I do not have any money or anywhere to live."

"I understand your concern. Unfortunately, Mr. Bertrand's residences were in his name only, and legally I can't do anything about that. However, I believe you'll find solace in the last thing we have to discuss."

"Which is?"

"Your bank account." The lawyer who looked like a movie star gave me a full smile as he pulled a piece of paper from his bag. "Since the account is in your name, the Feds did not seize it. You have complete access, and this is the balance." Setting the piece of paper on the table, he turned it to face me.

I looked down.

Shock slammed into me and I stared. "This—this is mine?" Six *million* dollars? I glanced at him. "This cannot be true."

"It is and it's yours." His smile held a moment before he turned serious. "There is a local branch of the bank here in Miami. Go in person, show your ID, and ask for a new bankcard, checks, whatever you need, and make sure you have them help you change the password to the account. I'd also suggest you reassign a new beneficiary."

"Pardon?"

"Bertrand set himself up as the beneficiary on the account."

Of course he did. "I am speechless." Joseph was going to keep this money for himself. I owed the attorney and everyone at AES more than I could possibly repay. "Thank you."

"You're welcome. I'm glad I was able to help, and I'm confident that Harrington's will settle quickly and quietly. Once we receive the settlement, I'll deposit it into your account." The attorney put his pad and pen back in his bag. "One last thing. Would you like me to arrange to have your personal belongings from the Manhattan property or Coral Gables house packed and shipped here to you?"

I barely had to think about it. "Can you donate them?"

His frown came back. "You don't want your clothes?"

"I want nothing from that life."

"Of course, my apologies, and understood. Consider it

done." He held out a business card to me as he stood. "I'll be in touch, but if you need anything, don't hesitate to call. Both my office and cell numbers are on the card."

Taking the card, I barely held my emotions back. *"Merci beaucoup."*

"My pleasure, Miss Malcher. I'll let myself out. Have a good rest of the day." The attorney who had just changed my life smiled politely and walked out.

For a long moment, I sat there trying to wrap my head around the fact that I now had choices. I could go anywhere. Live anywhere. Do anything.

But the longer I sat, the more it became strikingly clear.

There was only one thing I wanted.

But first, I needed to shower, change and go to the bank.

Going to my suitcase, I pulled out what would have been a casual outfit for New York. After a brief shower, I dressed and shoved a change of clothes into my purse along with some travel toiletries. Then I went into the hall outside Vance's penthouse and found the trash chute.

Opening the small, levered door, I threw away the rest of my past, listening until the small suitcase hit the bottom, twenty-five floors down.

Then I pulled out a cell phone that had no contacts and no history on it, and I called for a cab.

SEVENTY-ONE

Vance

TOO LATE, I SAW HER EYES FROM ACROSS THE GYM. THEN HER LIPS, her hair, her face, and every other fucking inch of her. I didn't know who'd told her where to find me, but I could guess, and I was going to kill my brother.

The young prick who had something to prove caught my split-second of distraction and threw a perfect uppercut.

Taking the blow square to my jaw, my head snapped back, and I stumbled.

Then I was doing exactly what I came here not to do.

I fucking fought.

Moving with lightning-fast speed, I was on the prick. Punch after punch, hit after hit, I rained holy fucking hell down on him because it was all I had left.

I'd told her every goddamn thing about me. I'd saved her. I'd spared her piece of shit brother's life, and I'd gotten her out. I kept my fucking word. I did every goddamn thing I said I would, and she'd called me a liar.

The worthless prick went to his knees, but I kept fucking swinging.

Every judgment in her haunted expression made me want to get hit harder, punch faster, feel the pain deeper. But this useless prick was no match for my fury as I drove my fist into his face again and again. Enraged I wasn't the one taking the blows, I didn't notice he was unconscious until I was grabbed from behind.

Arms locking around mine, pinning them to my back, I was yanked off the pathetic fuck.

"Enough," a voice I knew like my own ordered.

With my brother holding me back and the woman I'd given everything to standing speechless ringside, I fucking snapped.

Spitting my blood-soaked mouth guard to the mat, I glared at her. "Couldn't get enough of me, pet?" Like a fucking bastard, I winked. "Coming back for more?"

"Is this what you do?" She didn't ask, she accused, complete with repulsion and fear in her tone. "All those bruises you had, this is what they were from? This is what you were doing? Beating and hurting people?"

The fuck on the mat groaned and rolled to get up.

I lunged.

"*Vance*," Ronan clipped, stopping me from head-butting the asshole, but not fast enough to stop my kick.

My foot connected with the asshole's jaw. His head snapped back, and Ronan dropped me. Slamming me onto the mat face first, his knee hit my back, and he yanked my arm to the point of breaking.

"Stop," Ronan ordered. "Last warning."

The air knocked from my lungs, my shoulder about to dislocate, my gaze hit hers, and I fucking sank my own goddamn ship. "Am I lying now?"

Horror locked in her expression, she turned and fled.

Waiting until the door to the gym shut behind her, Ronan spoke. "Luna made the call you wanted. It's handled. Vincenzo's backing off her, but he had a condition. AES now owes him a favor. Open ended. He'll collect when he's ready."

"Fuck you, that wasn't the deal."

"That was the only deal. Let Alpha know." Ronan released my arm and pushed off my back. "Get up."

Shoving to my feet, still fucking enraged, I got in my brother's face. "You fucking brought her here."

No remorse, he didn't hesitate. "Yes, I did."

I swung.

Blocking my punch, grabbing my arm, spinning me and taking me down a second time, Ronan shoved my head to the mat. "I told her where you were because she asked. Then I drove her here because she was going to come alone. Now I'm leaving to take her wherever the hell she wants to go, and I sure as fuck am not going to tell you where that is." Shoving my face into the mat one more time for emphasis, he released me. "You're fucking losing it. Last time I'm saying this. Get your shit together."

My brother stepped out of the ring and walked out of the gym.

I fucking laid there.

Echo leaned on the ropes and glanced at the exit. "Gotta admit, that fucker has balls." He looked back at me. "What the hell happened to yours?"

A woman happened.

Getting to my feet, I stepped out of the ring and turned toward the locker room.

Echo tipped his chin at the unconscious prick on the mat. "You gonna clean up your mess?"

"No." All the fight in me gone, I headed to the showers.

SEVENTY-TWO

Sabine

Tears streaming, I blindly ran out of the gym.
 Except it was not a gym. Ronan had lied. His brother had lied. My brother had lied. Everybody had lied.
Vance was hitting people.
Why?
Why?
Is that what he did? Is that who he was? Just like Joseph, he liked to abuse people and hurt them? As soon as I thought it, as soon as I had said those words in the gym, they had tasted sour on my tongue, and they felt wrong in my mind, but I could not ignore what I had seen.
Could I?
For seven years, I had taken abuse, and now I was chasing a man who liked to do the exact same thing?
How could I do this to myself?
How could Vance do that?
I wanted to take back every minute of this afternoon and undo going to Luna and Associates to look for his brother so I could ask where Vance was. I wanted to unsee Vance in that gym. I wanted it all gone.
But my heart hurt for more than what this meant for me.
My heart hurt because I had seen the look in his eyes.
I knew that look.
Pain. Grief. Guilt. Rage.

I knew that recipe and the warring cocktail of emotions it made.

"Sabine." Short and clipped and nothing like how Vance said my name but in a voice so eerily, exactly the same, Ronan called after me.

Running down the sidewalk, no direction, not daring to look back or stop, I kept going.

Vance was hurting. I saw it in his eyes.

"*Sabine.*"

How much of that hurt had I put there? Was I the one hurting him instead of him hurting me?

"I know your history, and I'm not going to put a hand on you, Sabine. Stop walking. The SUV's behind us."

I was not walking.

I was running.

But just like his brother, his dominant command made me stop.

Turning, I was struck all over again by how he looked exactly like Vance. Except he didn't. His eyes, while the same color, looked different. His demeanor—dark, ominous, quiet, like the calm before a threatening storm—he was the polar opposite of his identical twin. And yet he was the same.

"Why does he do that?"

Ronan's eyes scanning everything around us, he did not look at me. "Let's get back to the vehicle."

"I asked a question."

"You've asked me several today, and I've been more than accommodating, but we're not going to stand here on the street, in this neighborhood, and discuss it. SUV, Miss Malcher. *Now.*"

"You are demanding and controlling, just like your brother."

That did it. His gaze zeroed in on me, laser-focused, and he leaned toward me without actually moving. "I am nothing like my brother."

"Why do you hate him?"

"Why do you?"

I did not say anything. I started walking back to the SUV.

Ronan fell into step beside me, but he had moved to my left side, putting himself between me and the street.

"You are wrong," I accused.

Scanning the street, Ronan said nothing.

"You are like him. You are protective."

Vance's twin remained silent until we got back to the SUV. Then he opened the passenger door and looked at me. "He fights so he doesn't have to deal with his emotions."

I knew that, I did, it made sense. It was logical, and emotionally I could understand it, but seeing it happen? That frightened me. Not for my own safety, but for his, for what he was fighting inside that I could neither help nor fix. "Why did you bring me here?" When I had walked into Luna and Associates, asking for Ronan, I did not know what I was expecting him to do, but I certainly had not anticipated his single response, *come with me*, followed by a completely silent drive to a warehouse district in Miami.

Ronan stared at me with the same eyes as his brother, but everything behind them was different. "Why did you come looking for him?"

Because I no longer knew how to breathe without his presence. Because I had wrongly accused him, because I could not bring myself to walk away. But none of that I spoke out loud. Instead, I gave a different truth. "Because I judged him."

"Easy to do." Ronan closed the door.

A moment later, he was behind the wheel and we were driving in traffic that was different than the kind of traffic in New York or Paris but still made me glad I was not driving myself, not that I knew how.

"Where can I take you?" Ronan asked.

VICTOR

It was eerie how the tone of his voice, the pitch, was exactly the same as Vance's, and yet they sounded so different. I missed Vance's voice, and the last thing he had said to me in the gym as he had bled from his fight made me want to cry.

Suddenly feeling so trapped that I could not breathe, I made a rash decision. "Can you possibly get me a plane?"

Ronan glanced at me, but I could not read a single thing in his expression. "A plane?"

"I mean a flight. Preferably private." I did not want to wait for a commercial flight to be available. "I can pay for it." I had money now.

"AES has company jets," Ronan replied.

Just the thought of Vance's work made my heart hurt. "No thank you." I looked out the window. "Can you please take me to the nearest public airport?"

"You have no luggage."

"I do not need any." I had my passport and my wallet, and I was still holding on to the phone Vance had given me even though the number he had had me memorize was no longer in service. I had tried it twice after I had visited the bank before giving up. Then I had gone to Ronan's work out of desperation, not only hoping he would be there, but that he would tell me where to find his brother.

"Where are you going?"

Ronan's question, asked so casually in his quiet voice that was just like Vance's, but was also different, sounded almost as if he were hiding something. Maybe these two brothers were more alike than either of them wanted to admit. The thought making me even more despondent, words were coming out before I had enough sense not to interfere. "Family is important. You do not always get second chances with them. You are lucky you have a brother."

Ronan said nothing for a long moment. "Are you lucky you have a brother?"

"I was." Now I was not, and that was a hurt I had not yet begun to process, so I was doing what I could to not think about it.

"Now you're not lucky," Ronan stated.

I did not reply.

Ronan pulled the SUV over, and without further comment, he made a call through the SUV's speakers.

A man picked up on the first ring. "Roark."

"It's Conlon."

"I know."

"I need a favor."

"You need one or Luna needs one?"

"This is personal. You busy right now?"

I glanced at Ronan, but he did not look at me.

"I'm always busy," the man replied.

"I have someone who needs a ride to…" Ronan finally looked at me.

"France," I answered.

"France," Ronan repeated.

"You do realize I fly a seaplane?"

"You fly all sorts of planes," Ronan calmly countered.

"So does AES. They have a whole fleet. Call Trefor or your brother."

"Conflict of interest," Ronan clipped.

The man exhaled. "Is that Sanaa?"

"No."

"Who is she?"

Uncomfortable and not wanting to be in the middle of this conversation, I spoke up. "My name is Sabine Malcher, and I would like to go home. Anywhere in southern France would be appreciated. I can pay you for your time there and back, and of course, the flight. I prefer not to wait for a commercial airline flight." Or fly commercially because it could be easily traced, and not that anyone was looking for me now, but recent events had altered how I approached everything.

Silence.

"Roark?" Ronan asked.

"I'm thinking. You in Miami?"

"Yes," Ronan answered.

"Level of urgency?"

Ronan glanced at me. "Between fade out and double-take."

"All right. Give me an hour to get up there, find an available bird and get a second chair. Have her at the Executive Airport in an hour."

"We're on our way there now. I'll see what's available."

"Copy."

"See you when you get here, and thanks, I owe you."

"Add it to the growing list." The man called Roark hung up. Ronan pulled back into traffic.

My heart racing, I leaned back in my seat.

SEVENTY-THREE

Vance

Trefor walked into my penthouse unannounced as I stood at the kitchen sink with an ice pack pressed to my lower face. "Do you ever knock?"

"No." He tipped his chin at my jaw. "Is it broken?"

Picking up the tumbler of scotch next to me, I drained the three-finger pour in one swallow, wishing I couldn't still smell her in my place. "Would I be talking to you if it was?"

"Unclear." He leaned a hip on the island counter and crossed his arms like he was settling in for a goddamn chat.

"What the fuck is that supposed to mean?" I adjusted the ice pack as the hard alcohol hit my empty stomach.

"You like pain."

"Fuck off. Door's behind you." I poured another drink.

Trefor ignored my bullshit. "Vincenzo's handled. When he collects, it will no doubt cost us, but the woman's safe. My contacts say Bertrand cut a deal with WITSEC. I'd be surprised if he isn't already off the radar."

Fucking great. "The asshole got off easy."

Trefor didn't comment. "Want another assignment?"

I wanted to undo every goddamn move I'd made on the last one. "Do I get to shoot people?"

"No."

"Then no." I took another swallow of scotch.

Trefor nodded once, but he didn't leave, and he didn't say shit else. He stared out at my view.

I flipped the ice pack over. "You need something else or you just bored?" We both knew he was here for a reason.

"Mind if I ask a personal question?"

"Since when do you dance around shit?"

His stark gaze landed on me. "Did you kill her?"

I fucking froze. "Her who?"

"Annabeth Stephens."

Rage hit. "Get out."

"COD on her official autopsy report was drowning, but she had broken ribs." Trefor dangerously kept fucking talking like he knew what the fuck he was getting into. "Could have been from the boat capsizing, but I have a different theory."

"Leave," I fucking rasped, anger choking my goddamn throat.

"You know what I think?"

I dropped the ice pack in the sink. "I'm not going to tell you again. *Leave.*"

Trefor didn't fucking move. "I think the string of ER visits for broken bones Mrs. Stephens had before she walked away from her husband and left her daughter weren't accidents. I think Stephens focused his aim on his sixteen-year-old daughter after his wife left him. You had five classes with Annabeth your junior year of high school, and I think you figured out what the fuck was happening. I think that's why you started running guns when you were seventeen—because you needed fast cash. I'm guessing Stephens beat the fuck out of his daughter the night she died, and you tried to run with her, the boat being your only option, but it capsized in the storm. The unknown male that showed up at a walk-in clinic a day later with lacerations on his back that required one hundred and eighteen stitches was you." He pushed off the counter. "You didn't fucking kill her, but you blame yourself."

"Get. *Out.*"

"Did you join the Marines to learn how to be a sniper? Because Stephens was dead twenty-four hours after your first leave post Scout Sniper School graduation. Cops ruled his death a mob hit, assumed one of his disgruntled clients got to him."

I glared at Trefor.

"The storm wasn't your fault. Stephens is dead. You got justice for her," he calmly ticked off his list. "When are you going to forgive yourself?"

My hands fisted. "You don't know shit."

"You're right, I don't. I'm just putting together what I dug up on your past when I hired you and sizing it up against the man I'm looking at now, and I'm speculating. I'm also weighing it against the assignment I unwittingly sent you on that turned out to be a domestic situation."

"Domestic situation?" I fucking seethed. "Is that what you call a man beating a woman? *Domestic?*"

"No, I call it fucking unconscionable, and I would've shot Bertrand, too." Trefor walked toward the door. "But it wouldn't have driven me to the Annex after I got the woman out because I'm not living with your past." His hand on the door handle, he glanced over his shoulder. "Forgive yourself, Conlon. No one else can." He walked out.

I picked up the glass tumbler and threw it at the door.

SEVENTY-FOUR

Sabine

"YOU SURE YOU WANT TO DO THIS?"

A humid night breeze swirled around my bare legs and pushed my hair into my face. I glanced at Ronan and lied. "I am sure." I was not sure of anything, but I could not stay here, not right now.

Vance's twin brother scanned the Executive Airport tarmac and surrounding airplanes that were parked for the night before glancing behind us at the private jet with open airstairs that he had somehow managed to procure for his friend Roark. "He'll ask where I took you."

My muscles stiffened. "I do not think he will."

Ronan spared me a quick glance. "Don't underestimate him."

"What will you tell him?" I would not ask him to lie for me, not to his brother.

Ronan scanned the entrance to the airport. "It's not what I'll tell him, it's what I'm going to tell you." He turned to me with his amber-eyed gaze. *"Mieux vaut être seule que mal accompagnée."*

I blinked. "You speak French." Without an accent. And he was insulting his brother. "Maybe I am the one who is not good company, and he would be better off without me."

"Chacun voit midi à sa porte." Ronan tipped his chin toward

a black SUV coming across the tarmac and switched back to English. "They're here."

I did not have time to ask him how he was familiar with French proverbs.

A giant beast of a man got out from the driver's side, immediately followed by a beautiful golden dog as an equally large, equally overmuscled man with a trimmed beard got out of the passenger's side. Both men and the dog walked toward us.

Ronan stepped forward and held his hand out to the man who had the dog at his side. "Thanks for coming, Roark." He nodded at me. "This is Sabine Malcher."

The giant man with huge muscles lifted his chin. "Roark MacElheran." He glanced at the man next to him. "This is Harm."

The bearded man barely looked at me before glancing at Roark. "I'll start prechecks." He moved toward the plane with a slight limp.

Ronan waited until he was out of earshot. "I didn't know Harm flew."

"He does." Roark glanced at his dog. "Missy, hurry up."

The dog thumped her tail, then ran off to a nearby patch of grass.

Ronan glanced after her before looking back at Roark. "Thanks again."

"Welcome." Roark turned his attention to me as the dog came running back and sat at his feet. "Specific destination?"

"Saint-Tropez?"

Roark nodded at me before sparing Ronan a glance. "Conlon." Then he issued another command to his dog. "Missy, plane."

The dog ran ahead and went up the airstairs as Roark followed.

VICTOR

Ronan studied me for a brief moment. Then his voice quieted. "Be at peace, Sabine." Without waiting for a reply, he walked toward his SUV.

Peace.

I wondered if Vance was at peace.

Glancing up at the tropical starry night, I inhaled deeply. Then I walked toward the plane.

SEVENTY-FIVE

Vance

LAYING THE WHITE LILIES IN FRONT OF THE HEADSTONE, I STOOD back up.

"I'm sorry." My apology hung in both the humid morning air and my throat. "I never came to tell you that. I should have." *Fuck*, I should have. "This was my fault." I glanced at the headstone to the left that was dated four years after the one in front of me. I didn't tell her that it was his fault. He didn't take her on the goddamn boat.

Squatting, I put my hand over her name. "You deserved better than me, Annabeth." My voice broke. "I'm so fucking sorry I robbed you of your life."

Memories of her flooded my mind. They were distant and vague compared to the last breath we'd shared, but I still remembered her soft voice and gentle touch. She'd been so pure of heart, so damn innocent. She'd always wanted to believe the best in people. Part of me wondered if I could ask her, if she'd forgive me. But the rest of me refused to acknowledge whatever the answer would be.

I'd done this. I didn't deserve forgiveness.

All I could do was apologize and say what I came here to say.

"Happy birthday, Annabeth." I fisted my hand against the warm granite and dragged my pinky across her name. "Always and forever." Standing, I turned.

The sun blocking my view of her face, a tall, thin brunette

stood a few paces back and for a split second, my heart fucking dropped, thinking it was a different brunette before the woman took a step forward.

Older, eyes haunted, she looked at me with an expression I immediately recognized. "It wasn't your fault. I know you loved her."

Jesus fucking Christ. "Mrs. Stephens." She was alive.

"Hello, Vance." She looked past me at her daughter's grave. "She would've been thirty-four today."

Fucking shook, I shoved my hands in my pockets. "I know."

The woman who gave her daughter her green eyes looked at me with drowning guilt. "It was my fault. I left her with that monster."

Fuck, fuck, *fuck*.

All the shit I'd done, all the times I'd pulled the trigger, used my fists, or put Peter Stephens six feet under, this was it. This is what would take me down, and for one goddamn heartbeat, I only had a single regret.

Oiseau.

I hadn't apologized to her.

But Sabine wasn't here, Mrs. Stephens was, and it was time. Past time.

I owned my mistake. "I was the one who took her on the boat that night. It wasn't you. It was me. I killed your daughter, Mrs. Stephens."

Without even a blink, as if she already knew, she didn't hesitate. "And how many times had he hit her before you tried to take her away?"

"That night?"

She looked back at me with a pained expression. "So it was more than once?"

I didn't answer. I couldn't fucking do that to her. Instead, I turned back to face her daughter's grave. "She wasn't angry with you for leaving. She only hoped you were alive and okay."

A pained sound escaped her throat. "That was my girl. So pure. So strong. She was braver than me." She swiped a tear from her face. "But I think it's time we both took a page out of her book, don't you think?"

"I'm sorry?"

"We can live with guilt and regret forever, or we can forgive ourselves. Neither of us took her life." Her gaze fell on her husband's grave. "That monster did. He was responsible for all of this." She choked back a half laugh, half cry. "The irony? Annabeth would've forgiven him too in the end."

I didn't disagree, but I was too fucking thrown from seeing her, from this whole damn conversation, to utter a single word, so I stood there.

A minute, an hour, I didn't know how much time passed as we stood there, but eventually Mrs. Stephens put her arm around my waist and rested her head on my shoulder.

"Thank you for loving my daughter," she whispered.

I said the only thing I could. "Thank you for not blaming me for her death."

She glanced at her husband's grave. "Accidents happen."

On a fucking roll, I admitted the whole goddamn truth. "His wasn't an accident."

"I know." She looked up at me with the same green eyes her daughter had. "That's why I don't blame you, not for anything." Going on tiptoe, she kissed my cheek. "Thank you, Vance Conlon. I hope you find love again." Without waiting for a response, she turned and walked away.

I stood there until I could fucking breathe again.

Then I pulled out a burner phone because I'd smashed my last cell and dialed as I walked back to the SUV.

November answered on the first ring. "Do you need me to call the lawyer?"

"No, I need a favor." Wait. "Why the fuck would I need Barrett?"

"Because I know where you are, and I know who was there with you."

Fucking hell. I paused as I opened the driver's door. "Who else knows?"

"I didn't tell anyone."

"How do you know?"

"That flight to Miami from New York. I heard you say something, and I did some digging. Then I saw where your vehicle was going today and put it together."

Goddamn it, now both he and Trefor knew. "You frequently monitor the company's SUVs?"

"Yes. Especially when one particular company vehicle hasn't gone anywhere except between your penthouse and the Annex for three weeks, then suddenly deviates from the norm today."

"So spying on everyone at AES is part of your daily responsibilities?"

"No comment."

Christ. "And the company I had here? Do you have a comment about that?"

"Hacked the security camera at the cemetery's front gate, ran the plates." November paused a beat, then he asked a question I'd never heard him ask anyone. "You okay?"

Stalling, I got in the Range Rover and turned the engine over. My first reaction was to tell him to fuck off. But as I cranked the AC, I thought about the past three weeks. I'd tried like hell to beat my past out in the ring. Then I'd tried to forget about an exquisite woman who'd seen me for who I was. Neither had worked.

I remembered what Zulu had told me about November. "Not being a dick, but honest question. Would you ever tell a woman about Bosnia?"

"No."

I glanced back one more time at Annabeth's grave before I drove out of the cemetery. "Because you can't or won't?"

"Both."

I understood where he was coming from, but I already knew I needed a different path forward. "I need a favor."

"Already on it."

"I didn't ask it yet."

"She's in Saint-Tropez," he answered.

I paused. "At the Villa Belrose?" I'd purposely stayed off my computer for the past few weeks. I knew if I'd opened the damn thing, I wouldn't have had any self-control, and I wasn't ready to see her.

"Yes."

Now I was. "Text me her room number?"

"Copy. Two of the Gulfstreams are at the Executive Airport, fueled up, ready to go. Zulu just came off an assignment, but I can call him."

"I'll do it. Thanks, Rhys."

"Chardonnay," he stated. "Her preference according to her room service charging history."

"Right." I chuckled, realizing it was the first time in three weeks I'd laughed. "I think I can do better than that." She was getting a Domaine Armand Rousseau Chambertin Grand Cru. Hanging up, I made another call.

Zulu answered on the fifth ring. "I'm sleeping, Conlon."

"Saint-Tropez is calling."

"Not interested."

"Not work related."

"Fuck." Zulu sighed. "I'm going to regret this, but go ahead. I'm listening."

I laid out my plan and made him an offer he couldn't refuse.

SEVENTY-SIX

Sabine

A HAND CLOSED OVER MY MOUTH, AND I JOLTED AWAKE TO PITCH dark.

"Don't scream."

It was instinct. I grabbed the arm, rolled and kicked with my legs.

My feet made contact, and a soft grunt sounded, followed by a curse in French as my legs were pinned down.

"Sabine," the distantly familiar voice growled. "Stop it, it's me." The bed dipped. "Can I let up, or are you going to kick me again?"

Henri.

My heart pounding, my breath short, I lay still as my eyes adjusted to the dark room.

My brother released me. "Good. I see you still have some sense," he criticized.

"What are you doing here, and why are you speaking in English?" He was taking a big risk coming here. I remembered every one of those horrible pictures November had shown me. If the authorities knew Henri was alive, they would surely arrest him.

Sitting back against the headboard of the big bed, keeping one booted foot on the ground, the ambient light of the moon cast shadows on his tired, unshaven face. "Aren't you American now? Isn't that what your passport says?"

The way he said it, I could not tell if he was insulting me or not. "Where are Chantel and Julien? Are they safe?"

His gaze drifted. "I hope so."

I hoped so, too. I wanted to ask more, but I did not. I desperately wanted to be a part of my nephew's life but not at the expense of risking him or Chantel. I knew I was not responsible for the situation they were in. Henri had created this, but that did not mean I would selfishly add to their problems.

"What are you doing here, Henri?" I did not ask how he had found me. I had seen firsthand how no one's movements were ever completely invisible.

Inhaling deep, then letting it out slowly, Henri's laugh was haunted and without humor. "You wouldn't believe me if I told you."

"Probably not." He had lied to me about everything. Maybe he thought he was protecting me, or maybe he just did not care. Either way, the betrayal was still fresh.

Turning to face me, tucking his arm under his head, my brother suddenly looked like the disheveled boy I knew when we were young. "I'm sorry, Sabine."

A pain in my heart that spread deep into my soul stretched around words I did not know how to respond to, so I simply nodded.

Always so much taller than me, my brother did what he had done my whole childhood. He reached out and put his hand on top of my head. *"Mon p'tit bout."* He ruffled my hair. *"Je t'aime."* He switched back to English. "Thank you for taking care of my son and Chantel."

"I did nothing to take care of them. Chantel did all of that on her own." Everything I thought I had been doing had been a lie.

His eyes softened. "You gave her money and stayed with a man who mistreated you to keep them safe."

"I am no saint." I looked up at the ceiling. "I could have done many things differently."

His rough hand caught mine, and his voice turned weary with exhaustion. "So could I, *mon p'tit bout*, so could I."

"I want to ask you something but I do not know if I want the answer."

Henri snorted. "Then don't ask."

"What happened to the man who came after me for the diamonds? The man I…" I could not say the rest aloud.

My brother stiffened. "I don't know what you're talking about."

"Henri."

Inhaling deep, he let it out slow. "No one will ever know."

"Did you—"

"Stop," he barked, his voice and his entire demeanor changing. "You do not ask questions and you do not speak of this," he warned. "Not ever again, not to anyone."

His non answer was answer enough but I would never know the exact truth, and I no longer wanted to. "You probably do not have much time before someone finds out you are here." He was risking both of our lives by coming to see me.

For a long moment, he said nothing. Then he spoke so quietly, I almost did not hear it. "I blame myself for everything."

"Then fix it." He could turn himself in, maybe trade information for his freedom. But even then, I did not know if that would keep his son and Chantel safe. There was so much I did not know about my brother. I did not even know about the diamonds, and I did not want to.

Henri laughed a quiet, haunted laugh, and suddenly I realized who else I knew who had a laugh like that.

"Believe me, *mon p'tit bout*, if I could, I would." Slow, as if years of fatigue were weighing down on him, my brother got up. "I have to go." In a dark, opulent hotel room I never would have imagined us to be in, my brother looked down at me and said words I did not want to hear. "I do not know when, or if, I will be able to see you again."

My heart ached for so much loss, and all of a sudden, I did not want him to go. "You have choices." I could call... him. I could ask Vance to help my criminal brother. I told myself that for Henri, I would call. "I can help you."

Henri's smile was placating as he leaned down and kissed the top of my head. "I know you would, *mon p'tit bout*. Live well. You will be fine."

Tears welled, and desperation leaked out. "Do not go. I cannot do this. I do not want to be alone." Anxiety swelling into an insurmountable panic, I was on my feet and fear was tumbling out of my mouth faster than I could rationalize. "What if I lose you for real? What if I never see you again? Please, do not do this. Do not leave."

My last word struck me as hard as the pitying look on my brother's face.

He was not leaving. My brother was already gone, and I was doing exactly what I swore I would never do again. I was begging.

"Sabine—"

"Never mind." I held my hand up. "I am me. You are you." I was on my own, and that was going to have to be okay. "I am alone, and I accept that." I had to. Maman had always said life was for the living. "Just tell me one thing."

"If I can."

"Am I safe from your past, from anyone who may be looking for you or the diamonds?"

"*Oui*," he replied before reiterating himself in English. "You have nothing to fear."

I did not know if I believed him, but I nodded anyway.

Pulling me into his arms, my brother hugged me tightly. Then he took my hands and held them in his, right over his heart, as he whispered his lies. *"Tu n'es pas seule, mon p'tit bout."* Releasing me, he moved through the shadows toward the terrace.

"What about your son?" I asked as he reached the glass slider doors.

Pausing, a gun tucked into his waistband, he did not look back at me. "He will grow to be a better man without me in his life."

My heart wept for the child. "No boy thinks that about his papa."

Henri looked over his shoulder. "No boy besides him ever had to have me as his father."

I let my tears fall freely over my past.

"Je t'aime, Sabine." His voice was quiet, but my brother's escape into the night was silent.

"Je t'aime, Henri," I whispered to the empty room as the curtain blew in the breeze. "Be safe."

It was not until I turned back toward the bed that I felt it.

I glanced down at my left hand.

The ring was gone.

SEVENTY-SEVEN

Vance

THE BOTTLE OF WINE IN MY HAND, THE STEMS OF TWO GLASSES hanging between my fingers, I stopped short and stared. She was stunning.

The Mediterranean breeze tousling her hair, the sun kissing her long legs, she hid behind dark sunglasses as she looked out at the sea from her lounge chair. Exquisite, solitary, strong, sad, peaceful—I had a hundred adjectives to describe her, but none did this moment justice.

I wanted to capture her, just like this, in a picture I could have forever in case it all went to hell in the next minute.

Fuck it.

Now or never.

Striding across the terrace, I stepped in front of her chaise and blocked the late afternoon sun from falling across her gorgeous body.

Cocking my head toward the bottle in my hand, I smiled. *"J'aime les vins subtiles et élégants. J'ai choisi un Domaine Armand Rousseau Chambertin Grand Cru. Je vous sers?"*

Stock-still, hiding behind her sunglasses, she stared at me.

I switched to English. "Hi."

"Hello." Quiet, subtle, reserved—even her voice was exquisite.

"You look beautiful." I was right, Saint-Tropez suited her.

"What are you doing here?"

"You're speaking English in France." I winked. "I like it." Turning the bottle slightly, label out, I presented it to her like a sommelier would. "I'm bringing you a proper wine for the view."

"A subtle and elegant wine?" she asked, repeating what I'd said in French.

I laughed. "A shamelessly ostentatious wine, *oiseau*. One that I hope you'll enjoy." I nodded at the chaise next to her. "May I?"

"As you wish."

Thrown by her less-than-warm reception, holding my smile, I took the chaise and set the glasses on the small table between us before pulling a wine opener out of my pocket. "Interesting story about Armand Rousseau. He was among one of the first producers in Burgundy to bottle his own wine. He—"

"Is this what you do?"

Twisting in the corkscrew, I glanced at her. "Do what, exactly, love?"

"What happened to 'bird'?"

It hit me like her beauty had the first time I saw her.

I was fucking nervous.

Me.

Vance Conlon—Marine, mercenary, murderer, sometimes pilot, real estate speculator, hacker, and all-around playboy. I was fucking sweating as I sat in front of one of the most spectacular views of the Mediterranean with an unparalleled beauty by my side, and I was goddamn tense from nerves.

"*Oiseau*," I murmured, tasting the term of endearment in a new light before I pulled the cork out and set the bottle next to the glasses. Leaning my arms on my knees, I folded my hands together for the exact same reason I'd done it a dozen times before around her—so I didn't reach for her.

Focusing on her gorgeous face, I hated that I couldn't see her eyes. "Do you know why I called you that?"

"No."

Fuck this. Leaning forward, I quickly grabbed her sunglasses before she could protest and tossed them on the small table. But when I looked back at her, I froze.

Her beautiful ocean-blue eyes were red and swollen.

Quickly scanning her from head to toe for injuries, I noticed her naked ring finger and rage hit. I was on my feet, scanning the property in every direction, cursing myself for not seeing this coming. "Where the hell is he?"

"He who?"

"Don't lie to me, Sabine." Grasping her chin, I swept my thumb across her tearstained cheek. "He was here, and you're not wearing your ring." Barely holding it together, I issued her an order like the asshole she'd given seven years to. *"Where is he?"*

Pulling out of my grasp, she reached for her sunglasses and put them back on. "If you're referring to Henri, he's long gone. And no, I do not know where Chantel, Julien, or the diamonds are either, and I probably never will."

Shoving down anger, I compartmentalized.

I was fucking this up. Epically. And this woman didn't deserve that.

She deserved the three-thousand-dollar bottle of wine and perfect sunset, not an angry asshole.

Doing what I should have when I first saw her eyes, I sat on her lounge and took her hand. "I'm sorry."

She pulled away. "For what? Missing the opportunity to beat Henri within an inch of his life?"

"Admittedly, I deserved that." It was true. I was going to lay the fucker out if I saw him again. "But I was apologizing for your loss." I meant it sincerely, but I had my limits. I wasn't going to call that fuck her family.

"Thank you."

Refraining from taking her in my arms, hell, taking her back to her suite, I poured two glasses of wine. "Would you like me to look for Chantel and Julien?"

"*Non.*"

Setting the bottle back down, my hand paused for a fraction of a second before I let go of it. "May I ask why?"

In a sheer white dress, barely concealing the sexy white bikini that tied at her hips, she sat with her long, tan legs stretched out, ankles crossed as she focused on the ocean and the setting sun. "You could."

"But you won't tell me."

"You did not tell me why you call me *oiseau*."

"Forgive me," I replied dryly. "I wanted to see your beautiful eyes when I told you, but I got distracted when I saw your face and the fallout from your encounter with your brother."

"Fallout," she repeated as if she didn't understand the term.

"Consequences," I amended.

"I know the term," she stated.

"Right." Nothing was right. Fuck this. "I'm sure you do, but I didn't fly across the Atlantic for this." Scooping her up, I stood, straddled the chair, then sat back down with her in my arms.

The second my ass hit the cushion and hers landed between my legs, she was aiming for escape.

"No," I barked, tightening my arm around her nothing waist.

"Let me go," she hissed in a furious whisper as she glanced at the few other guests lounging by the pool. "You're causing a scene."

"Darling, if you make one more move to get up, I'll cause the biggest damn scene you've ever witnessed."

"You do not have your gun," she snapped, unleashing a feral anger at me that made my dick hard.

"You're right," I stated calmly. "So considering you've seen me in a firefight, imagine what I can do that would be worse than that before you attempt to take your gorgeous ass away from me again."

"I did not take anything away from you to begin with!" she whisper-yelled.

"On the contrary." She'd taken everything. Every damn piece of my sanity, every waking thought, every second of escape I used to get from fighting—she took it all.

Now I was taking it back.

Holding her close, I reached for one of the glasses. "The first time I saw you, you didn't walk into that office, you glided." Pulling her back against my chest, I held the wine to her lips. "Take a sip," I quietly ordered, tipping the glass. "Let it sit on your tongue."

With a slight tremor in her hand, her back stiff as hell, she wrapped her fingers around my wrist.

Dropping my voice, I leaned to her ear. "Close your eyes and taste it, *oiseau*."

Tilting her head back to my shoulder, her other hand grasped the wineglass, and she drank.

I gently removed her sunglasses. "Feel the heat of the setting sun. Taste the wine. Inhale the Mediterranean." I spoke with a reverence meant only for her. "Feel all of it, love." I brushed my lips against her temple. "You're free as a bird."

SEVENTY-EIGHT

Sabine

Rain-wet cobblestones and heated musk held me as summer berries burst with life on my tongue. I tasted velvet and spice and peonies and oak. Succulent and seductive, resonant and soaring, my senses were all at once overwhelmed but rejoicing.

Both flying and grounded, I was soaring above the deep blue Mediterranean Sea, and I was running between rows of vines heavy with grapes. The ocean breeze kissed my skin, and the sinking sun warmed my face. Leaning back against the solid strength of a dominant, complicated, haunted man, I finally knew what this was.

Homecoming.

Life, living, feeling, tasting—this was exactly what he had described. Sunset on the terrace at the Villa Belrose with a wine as extraordinary as the view.

But none of it would have had meaning without him.

My walls breaking, my soul reaching, I spoke my heart. "I feel it." I felt him.

His full lips coasted across my temple again, leaving the gentlest of kisses. "You're free, *oiseau*."

Both hands on the glass, my heart too vulnerable to speak, I took another sip.

Then I reached for the courage he had spoken of in a historic hotel in Austria that felt like a lifetime ago. "Are you free?"

His short laugh was without humor.

I looked up at him.

His expression sobered. "I thought I was. Then a blue-eyed brunette with a sexy French accent took everything from me."

I started to protest again. "I did not take—"

"Hear me out." His thumb glanced across my lips in both a gentle caress and display of dominance. "I owe you an apology."

I looked back at the disappearing sun. "I am not asking for one." We both made mistakes. "If anyone owes an apology, it is me."

He grasped my chin and tilted my head back up. "You have nothing to be sorry for."

Yes, I did. "I am sorry I called you a liar." It was unfair.

His chest rose with a sharp inhale. "About that."

I held my hand up. "I do not wish to discuss it." Or what happened leading up to that moment. It was both the best and most terrifying sexual experience I had ever had, and it still scared me. I could not close my eyes without thinking about him inside me and feeling the heat between my legs. But I was also ashamed at how much I had liked losing all control to him. That was what had frightened me the most. I would have done anything he had asked of me in that moment, even if it hurt me. And that complete submission felt dangerously close to losing myself in him and his perfect storm.

Forcing myself to let that memory lie, I said what I should have long before today. "You gave me everything you promised." There were no criminal charges against me. Joseph was gone. Harrington's board of directors had given me the settlement the attorney had asked for. I was free because of him. "Thank you," I whispered as the sun dipped below the horizon.

"We've already been over this, pet. You don't need to thank

me for anything." He reached for the second glass. "Unless you'd like to thank me for dinner." He took a sip of his wine.

"We have not had dinner."

"Hm." He took another sip. "I do believe you're right." He casually glanced at his watch. "Maybe we should remedy that after we finish our wine. I have a place in mind."

The glass to my lips, I smiled for the first time in as long as I could remember. Of course he had somewhere in mind. I may not know the intimate details of him, but I did know he was a man who would have a restaurant already picked out before he asked me to dinner. "Is that so?" I teased.

"Yes," he answered without any playfulness to his tone. "But we need to discuss something first."

My smile disappeared. "I asked not to."

His hand slid leisurely up my arm in both an electrifying and comforting touch. "We need to, Sabine."

"You used my name," I accused, suddenly feeling defensive.

His chest expanded with a steady breath. "I did."

My courage disappeared into a whisper. "I know what that means."

"Then you know I'm not letting this go."

Day slipped into night like a clandestine love affair. *"Je sais."*

"I need to know what happened." His touch on my arm stilled. "You said you wanted me, then you backtracked. Why?"

Heat flamed my cheeks. "I was not saying I did not want you."

Perfectly still, his voice deepened as it got quieter. "You were afraid of me."

"Non." I was not.

"Expliquer," he demanded, easily switching to French.

All of a sudden, the world beneath my feet shifted.

For seven years, I had straddled French and English. My native language in my mind, my adopted one on my lips, there had always been a disconnect between my thoughts and my words. But now, here, with him, a man who could straddle that divide as easily as breathing, I realized I no longer had to fear the translation of my thoughts or how they would be interpreted.

I could simply speak.

And I was choosing English. "I was afraid of myself," I admitted. "Of what I was feeling."

Effortlessly switching back to English, he asked the one question that conveyed just how much he understood me. "Losing control?"

"Yes," I whispered.

With his fingers applying pressure, he ran his hand possessively up the length of my arm before grasping my throat in a hold meant to convey dominance, not fear. "I would never hurt you." His lips brushed against my ear. "Not unless I am also giving you pleasure."

Fear seeped under his dominant hold. "You like to do that?"

"Not necessarily, but you are fragile, *oiseau*, and you've seen me in the gym."

Oh God. "That was not a gym." That was a place where men were hurting each other for sport.

He said nothing.

I had to see his eyes. Looking up at him, I asked what I did not want to hear the answer to. "Do you need that?"

The night breeze blew at the last of the setting sun's warmth, mingling the scent of ocean with rain-wet cobblestones as a man I both knew and did not know stared down at me. His gaze unreadable, his eyes turning colors as day became night, he studied me like he was weighing his words.

VICTOR

I could not take his silence. "Please, do not shelter me from the truth."

"I'm not." His thumb stroked my cheek.

Anxiety and the gentle evening wind made my skin pebble. "But you are not saying anything."

For three beats of my heart, he did not reply.

Then he took my glass, set it down, gently pushed me forward and stood up from the chaise.

He held his hand out. "Come with me."

SEVENTY-NINE

Vance

I WAS DONE TALKING.

There was nothing I could say that would alleviate the fear in her eyes. I needed to show her exactly what I wanted to do to her.

Offering my hand, I didn't issue an order or demand, but it wasn't a request either. "Come with me." I wasn't going to let her float away from me again, not without erasing the last memory she had of my hands on her.

She searched my face with a wary gaze.

"Trust, love."

Her hesitation fled, and she took my hand. "I am not dressed to go anywhere."

I pulled her to her feet. "You're gorgeous and perfect as you are."

She stepped into a pair of casual sandals I never would've imagined her wearing when I first met her and shouldered her bag. "*Merci*, but where are we going?"

Somewhere we wouldn't be interrupted. "It's a short drive."

Holding her bag in front of her like armor, she turned toward the villas. "I will change first."

Shoving my hands in my pockets so I didn't reach for her and ruin this entire fucking plan, I stepped in front of her. "Do you trust me right now?"

The early evening light making her eyes as dark as the

Mediterranean after sunset, she stared up at me with warring emotions. "I don't not trust you."

I forced a smile. "Double negative, darling." *Fuck.* "I was hoping for something a little less reserved."

"I am who I am."

I sobered. "I wouldn't have you any other way. Will you trust me enough to come with me this evening?"

"You know that I will, but I prefer to change first."

"Right." I'd seen this woman dressed to the nines, I'd seen her with blood splatter all over a designer gown, and I'd seen her casual. I knew her enough to recognize clothes were a defense mechanism for her, and right now, she was still afraid. She could walk into half the restaurants in Saint-Tropez dressed how she was now, but she wouldn't. She wanted her armor on, and I understood it. Her fear would make this more difficult, but there wasn't a single thing about this woman that wasn't worth it. "About that." I smiled.

She frowned. Then she turned her gaze toward the water. "For seven years, I was told what to wear."

Fucking Christ. That asshole Bertrand was lucky he was in WITSEC, and I was a complete bastard. "I did not know that."

"I think you are implying more than a short drive and dinner."

"You're right." I was. "Will you look at me?" Jesus, I'd fucked this up.

She immediately gave me her eyes.

I took her momentary show of trust and gave her as much honesty as I could without giving away my entire plan. "I am implying more than an evening. I'm hoping for much more, actually. But right now, all I am asking is for you to trust me because I would like to surprise you. I would like to show you a side of myself you've not seen, and in no way does that have anything to do with controlling what you wear." Not intentionally.

With a crisp nod as if this were a business transaction, she acquiesced. "All right."

I exhaled. "Excellent. This way, love." I turned toward the front of the hotel.

Not following my lead, she aimed for the private villas. "I will quickly change and meet you in the lobby."

Fuck. *Fuck.* "You can't do that."

Lines creased her brow. "Pardon?"

I could've come clean. I could've told her I'd checked her out, that this was all prearranged, that she had nothing to fear. But I didn't.

For this to work, I needed her to walk to the goddamn car.

I needed her to walk away with me.

My hands fisting in my pockets, testing the fuck out of her, hoping like hell she would choose me, I tipped my chin toward the lobby. "Car's waiting."

A dozen emotions crossed her face, none of them good.

I held my fucking breath.

Every molecule of air between us went stock-still.

Then this exquisite woman that I didn't deserve nodded her head once.

EIGHTY

Sabine

Tension making his shoulders stiff, he kept his hands in his pockets, carefully not touching me as he stared at me with the same stark, haunted expression as when we had first met.

This was a test.

He needed me to go with him, no questions asked.

God help me, I wanted to. I wanted it more than I wanted the freedom of the large bank account balance with my name on it

I just did not know if I walked away with him now, if I would be able to keep walking away with him because that was what this was.

That was Vance Conlon's test.

He was not Joseph. It was a betrayal to even think of him in the same thought as Joseph, but make no mistake, Vance needed control. I knew his lack of words for what they meant, and going straight to the car with him was synonymous with giving him the reins.

Could I do that?

Could I give this man my heart and my hard-earned freedom?

If I was being honest with myself, I would admit he already had the former, and for three weeks, I had thought of nothing else except the latter.

Knowing this man could hurt me far worse than Joseph ever had the potential to, my heart had already made the decision.

I would give up a lifetime for one evening with this man. Not trusting my voice, I nodded.

His expression holding his austere seriousness, he merely leaned forward and touched his lips to my forehead before his hand landed on the small of my back. "This way, love."

That time, I heard the rough edge in his term of endearment, and I knew he meant it.

My nerves sharply edged since he had shown up, I inhaled his rain-wet cobblestone and musk scent that I had missed so badly, I had yearned for something he had worn simply so I could breathe him in.

But now that he was here, butterflies were dancing in my stomach along with the nerves prickling across my skin, and his touch made me shiver.

His hand moved to my shoulder, and he wrapped his arm around me as he ushered me up the terrace steps and into the lobby. "We'll turn on the heat in the car, darling."

"I am not cold. I am underdressed." I felt naked despite the almost sheer dress I wore over my bikini. I knew I was in appropriate attire for walking through the hotel lobby or for some of the casual seaside restaurants, but I was not in evening attire, and I did not think for one moment Vance would take me somewhere casual.

Guiding me to a waiting sports car that was already running as if he had timed all of this, he paused before the opened passenger door.

Taking my face in both of his hands, he looked down at me with his amber-eyed gaze. "You are perfect. I promise you are not underdressed."

Suddenly, every inch of my body remembered exactly how he had felt inside me, and a need twisted low in my belly. "I am trusting you," I barely whispered.

"I know." His eyes briefly closed, and he inhaled sharply

before he focused intently on me again. "It's killing me not to touch you right now and show you how much I appreciate that." Abruptly stepping back, he dropped his hands and held the door. "Get in."

I slid into the fancy car, and he shut my door.

Getting behind the wheel, his movements both fluid and precise, the muscles and veins in his exposed forearms where he had his shirt sleeves rolled up, bunched and moved. Expertly handling the sports car as we left the beautiful hotel grounds, he maneuvered the winding road that led down to the sea like he had driven it a hundred times.

I did not ask where we were going, and he did not offer an explanation.

As we turned toward the Port de Saint-Tropez, he broke the silence. "Did your brother take your ring?"

Shame flared, but I did not hide the truth. "Yes."

Vance's voice turned low and threatening. "By force?"

"By deception," I admitted.

A man whose honor I had never questioned glanced at me. "Just so we're clear, I'm filing away this piece of information."

"You seem to do that a lot."

"It keeps me honest," he clipped. "Tell me how he deceived you."

"I think it keeps you from getting angry in the moment because you equate anger with losing control."

"We're talking about your brother right now, not me. Did he hurt you?"

"Only my pride." I was still angry I had let my guard down. "He came to see me under the pretense of saying goodbye and apologizing for his past actions. Then with a sleight of hand, as he hugged me one final time, he slipped the ring off my finger without me noticing until it was too late."

"I'll get it back for you."

"I do not want it. I have already mourned its loss and what it represented." Under the protection of my sunglasses and on a near-empty pool terrace overlooking the Mediterranean, I had cried all day over it. "I also realized after it was gone that I was truly free."

"As a bird, *oiseau*."

The flutters low in my belly returned in full force. "Of all of your terms of endearment, that is the one I like the most."

"I know."

"How?"

His stark amber eyes met mine. "Because you are the only woman I call *oiseau*."

EIGHTY-ONE

Vance

PARKING THE BORROWED LAMBORGHINI, I CUT THE ENGINE. She looked out at all the anchored yachts. "This is not a restaurant."

No, it wasn't. "Trust, love." Fighting the urge to touch her, I reached for my door. "Wait." Getting out, I rounded the front of the car and opened her door. Too fucking spun up to smile or banter, I held my hand out.

Her small hand landed in mine and she gracefully stood.

Suddenly I was acutely aware of every fragile inch of her. Her small waist, the curve of her hips, the easily breakable bones in her hands—she was a head shorter than me and so damn vulnerable in her trust, I owed her better.

Full disclosure, I told myself. Warn her.

Right.

Fuck.

Caging her in, bracing my arms on either side of the open car door, I pulled the pin. "I'm about to take your flight, *oiseau*."

Goose bumps broke out across her arms and she blinked. "Pardon?"

"Like a one-winged dove." No escape.

"Vance—"

Still holding the proverbial grenade, I let it drop. "Your next steps, if you take them with me, you'll be giving up control."

I didn't do water.

I didn't sail.

I didn't step foot on any goddamn watercraft.

I fucking hated boats, and open water was worse. I wasn't going to be on edge in the next ten minutes, I was going to be over it—with her.

Fucking purposely.

At my most vulnerable.

Stripping her bare.

Her quiet voice floated. "I am already here."

Her tone too damn reserved to give me any clue, I searched her eyes, her face. Looking for tells and finding none, I didn't know what the hell I was looking at. "I can't read you right now." Maybe it wasn't her. Maybe it was me.

"Could you ever?"

"Yes."

"When?"

When I wasn't losing my shit. "Every time you were afraid."

She nodded as if she understood what she was walking into. "I am not afraid now."

She should be. "Last chance," I warned. "You can go back." I wouldn't let her go after this. Not if she stayed.

Her gaze briefly cut to the docks. "Will you come with me?"

"No."

She stared.

The wind blew. Water slapped against the pilings. Ocean air filled my head.

I fucking waited.

Her chest rose with an inhale, then she asked the right question. "I come with you now or never again?"

"Yes." I couldn't do halfway with her. I couldn't just fuck this woman. She was already so deep in my head, I only had two options. Open the door I'd closed seventeen years ago, or walk the hell away.

Ever so slight, she nodded.

My chest tight, gripping the fucking edge of the Lamborghini and my sanity, I asked. "Trust?"

"*Oui*. Trust."

I took her hand and led her down the docks to the very last slip.

The two-hundred-and-thirty-eight-foot luxury yacht lit up the night sky as the captain met us at the lower deck. "Good evening, Mr. Conlon, Miss Malcher. Welcome aboard. It's a beautiful night to be on the water."

I tipped my chin. "Thank you."

"Solace?" Sabine whispered.

I didn't make a joke about the irony of the name of the boat. "Yes. Watch your step."

Her feet planted, she gestured toward the water. "This is—that is the ocean."

I glanced at the captain. "Give us a minute."

"Of course. We'll depart once you're ready." With a polite nod, he disappeared.

Alarm written all over her face, she looked at me like she could see right through me. "You own a yacht? After everything?"

Suddenly defensive, I tried to rein it in. "Do you cross streets? Ride in cars?"

"That is not the same, and you did not answer my question."

I took a deep breath and forced my tone to normal. "No, I don't own it." I wasn't in the habit of throwing a hundred million at a floating deathtrap. "I borrowed it."

"From?"

"A friend." Of a friend.

She looked away. "A woman."

Grasping her chin, I brought her face back to mine. "Yes, a woman owns Solace. She's a friend of Zulu's. I never slept with her, nor had any desire to. We met through AES, and that's all I can divulge on the matter."

Her hand waved dismissively toward the Turquoise yacht. "So, your friends are on board and you want to what? Take me from the hotel in my swimsuit at night and *depart?*"

I saw her jealously, I saw her insecurity, and I saw the same damn thing in her that I saw in myself. Solitude, by design.

"There are no other passengers aboard," I reassured. "I asked for a minimal crew. There's the captain, an engineer, a chef, a housekeeper and one extra crew member. We won't see any of them unless we want to."

"Why do we need a crew?"

Under any other circumstances, I would've smiled. "It's a two-hundred-and-thirty-eight-foot super yacht, pet. It needs a crew." I brushed my lips against her forehead and took her hand. "Come." I turned toward the boat.

"Why?"

Glancing back, seeing her beautiful face in the moonlight, I was reminded of every reason why I wanted to fuck her under the stars, conquer my fears, and redo every damn second of the last time I was inside her. "Trust, *oiseau.*"

"Trust," she repeated, glancing at the Solace before looking back at me. "Have you been on a boat… since?"

I held her gaze for a full beat. "No."

With a slight nod, she stepped in front of me and boarded.

The captain appeared. "All set?"

"Yes." I put a possessive hand on her back. "If everything's ready, we won't need anything else tonight."

"Understood. Have a good evening." The captain glanced at Sabine before retreating. "Miss Malcher."

"This way, pet." I took her through the main cabin to the upper deck.

Glancing all around, she murmured one word. *"Magnifique."*

"It's better out here." Opening a slider door to one of the two private balconies off the master suite, I led her outside as the Solace left the marina.

Looking back at the docks before glancing at the full dinner spread on the table in front of the lounge chairs, she pulled her hand from mine before giving me her eyes again. "I was right."

I hated not touching her, and I couldn't read her expression. "About?"

Her hand skimmed along the back of one of the lounge chairs as she walked past it and briefly looked up at the stars. "This is more than dinner."

Sea air filled my lungs. "It is."

Her gaze meeting mine, she didn't miss a beat. "I gave you my trust."

I didn't miss how she was standing five feet away from me. "Come sit."

She didn't move. "Why are we here?"

Fuck. We were doing this now. "Short or long version?"

"The true version."

"Right." I wanted my hands on her before I said more, but I wasn't going to do her like that. Owning it, I laid out the truth. "Seventeen years ago, I couldn't control a woman, and it cost me my sanity. I fought to get it back." Literally. "Swearing I'd never lose control like that again, I made myself a promise—no attachments. Until a few weeks ago, I'd stayed in line. Then I met a beautiful brunette I couldn't walk away from."

The Solace easily cutting through the water, wind blowing her hair from her shoulders, she said nothing.

"The irony? Fate was throwing my past in my face. I'm not now, nor will I ever compare you to her, but it wasn't lost on me that I couldn't convince you to walk away from Bertrand any more than I could a sixteen-year-old from her father. Unresolved shit surfaced, and I lost my fucking mind. Again. Except this time, every single step was different. *You* were different. I didn't want to control you. I wanted to own you. The problem? I don't own women. I never did, and I sure as hell don't let them in. But you?" *Fuck.* "I wanted to let you in. I wanted you to see the real me. I even convinced myself it could work. All I had to do was get you away from Bertrand. Then the bullets started flying, and you reached for him."

"I told you I did not mean to."

"It wasn't your fault, and I'm not blaming you. I own what I did in Vienna, including the impossible situation I put you in. Experiences mold us, and I'm not perfect, not even fucking close, but I'm done hiding." And done losing my mind over shit I couldn't control. "I meant what I said. I don't want to control you, Sabine. I want to own you—every beautiful, exquisite, submissive inch."

Closing the distance between us, I cupped her face. "You said you didn't know me. This is who I am. I'm the man who was rough with you in my penthouse. I'm also the man who made a promise that it would be more than sex. If you trust me, I'll show you."

Her voice went soft. "How?"

My cock pulsed, and I tipped my chin starboard. "Go to the railing."

The sea air blowing her hair, her dress, she turned and floated on the wind.

For a beat, I stared not at my past, or the regret and guilt that ate at me for almost two decades, but at her—ethereal, resilient, beautiful.

I stepped behind her.

Lowering my mouth to her ear, grasping the hem of her dress, I ran my fingers up her thighs. "This is what I want with you, *oiseau*. The good, the bad, the fear, the joy, the grief. All of it."

She shivered.

"No half measures," I warned.

"*Non.*" The wind ate her whisper.

"Say it," I demanded.

"All of it." Her head tilted back on my shoulder, and her eyes met mine. "No half measures."

Pulling her dress off, I issued my first true taste of control with her. "Grab the railing."

Like the submissive bird she was, her hands wrapped around the cool metal.

Bringing my lips to her neck, untying the strings at her hips, I dragged the material purposely between her legs. Nipping the skin just below her ear, I swirled my tongue over the sting. "Do you know what I'm going to do to you, pet?"

"*Non,*" she moaned.

"I'm going to fuck you against this railing, then I'm going to take you inside and make love to you."

EIGHTY-TWO

Sabine

IN OUR OWN PRIVATE OASIS IN THE MIDDLE OF THE MEDITERRANEAN, under a blanket of stars, he reverently undressed me while whispering his brand of dominance. "I'm going to fuck you against this railing, then I'm going to take you inside and make love to you."

Every nerve in my body tingled.

Pulsing between my legs, never feeling more empty than I did in that moment, I begged for what he was offering. "Yes, please."

"*Tu es belle*," he murmured, as his hands skimmed over my bare hips and curved around my thighs before he cupped me. "You want me, *oiseau*?"

More than anything. "*Oui*."

Slowly dragging his fingers between my legs as the boat glided across the water, he kissed my shoulder and groaned low in his throat. "Already wet for me, pet." His finger barely touched my clit before his palm spread across my lower stomach and I heard a zipper. "Do you know why we're out here?"

"*Non*." Oh God, I wanted to feel him inside me. "*Peut être*."

His huge hand palmed my hip as he dragged the tip of his hard length between my legs. "Which is it, love? No or maybe?" Pressing against my opening, he just barely breached me then froze.

"*Oui.*" Oh my God. "Yes, yes, yes. Don't stop." I pushed back into him, but he held me firm.

"Then tell me," he demanded.

"The ocean," I blurted in desperation.

The tip of his huge, hard cock sank only a fraction deeper. "What about the ocean?"

I did not notice his voice was like jagged edges of rock. I did not feel the cool night air. I was heat and need and desperation. I wanted him inside me as much as I wanted to forget every moment of the last seven years.

"*Oiseau,*" he warned in a deep growl.

Reasons flew from my mouth and caught on the wind. "Because this is where you lost yourself. This is where your mistakes and grief and guilt live." Letting go of the railing with one hand, I reached back for his soft, inky hair and sank my fingers in. "Now you are erasing them with courage."

Just like in the penthouse in the tropical Miami sky, he slammed all the way into me in one savage thrust.

His fingers digging into my hips, his hard length pulsing, his invasion stretched me beyond my limits as he roared in denial. "*No.*" Pulling back only to thrust deeper, he buried the shattered pieces of my heart. "This isn't courage. This is me fucking you, pet." He drove into me again. "This is you forgetting every other man except me." He thrust harder.

My core pulsing, my body trembling, I had already forgotten. "Vance." He was my new high ground, threading tendrils of hope through my heart.

"Say it again," he demanded, fisting my hair.

My head yanked back, my scalp tingled, and my core throbbed with need. I got closer. "*Vance.*"

"Who owns you?"

Amber eyes, rain-wet cobblestones, and the darkest ocean of complex dominance owned me. "*Tu me possèdes.*"

"In English," he ordered.

My nipples hard to the point of pain, my knuckles gripping the railing tighter, my legs began to shake. "You own me."

His mouth against mine, his breath full of masculine dominance, he made his own law. "In both of your languages, in any country, on land, on sea, I own you." Thrusting deeper, he touched a world I did not know.

"Oh God." My fingers fisted in his hair as a sharp pain flared into blinding ecstasy. As if knowing exactly what he had just done to me, he did it again and again until the shake in my thighs built and everything tilted. "Vance, *please*."

"That's it, *oiseau*. You come for me." He thrust harder.

My body not my own, I exploded like a sky full of cascading stars.

"*I own you*." He slammed his mouth over mine.

I cried. I fell. I flew.

My core pulsed, my body tightened, and I came apart as every fracture of my past faded into nothingness.

His tongue, his hard length, they drove into me two more times. Then he thrust deep, his hips stilled and hot warmth pumped inside me.

A second, agonizing, too intense wave shuddered through my core.

"Fuck, *oiseau*," his carnal roar carried on the wind as his chest shook with a tremor.

I came again.

My legs giving out, my hand slipping from the railing, we sailed across the water as a cry ripped from my heart and I slid toward the deck.

"It's okay." A huge, muscular arm wrapped around my waist and caught me. "I got you, love."

Reduced to the addictive quiver between my thighs, I had no words.

Slow and gentle, he started to pull out of me, but I flinched at the tenderness. "Shh, shh, you're okay."

Emotions slipping down my cheeks, I was not okay.

Picking me up, unconcerned about the heat leaking between my thighs, he cradled me to his chest and carried me inside.

Leaving the slider open, striding toward the huge bed in the middle of the master suite, he laid me down. Rising to his full height, his stare intent on me, he shed his clothes and stepped out of his shoes.

Then he did the last thing I was expecting.

Grasping my thighs and spreading them wide, he ran his thumbs through the mess of his own making and pushed his seed back inside me.

His touch, his intent, his fingers inside me, I could not stop the moan as I bit my lip and my head fell back. Already aching for more, I desperately grasped at the soft bedding.

"*Eyes on me.*"

His sharp retort in direct contrast to the gentle swirling of his thumbs, I immediately did as he asked.

"Good girl," he softly praised as he reached with one hand and pulled the tie from my bikini top.

The fabric fell away and cool air hit my already aching nipples. Sucking in a sharp breath, I fought not to touch myself as his warm hand coasted down my neck and over my breast. Pinching my nipple, then smoothing his rough palm over it, he repeated the caress on my other breast as his thumb made slow, agonizing circles over my clit.

"Exquisite," he murmured, his gaze drifting from my breasts to my bare core.

I needed him again. "Vance."

His intense amber-green gaze cut back to me. "Are you on the pill, *oiseau*?" Rough and intent but tinged with a tenor I had never heard, his voice wrapped around my soul and heated a longing deep inside me.

"*Non.*"

"Good." Hard, huge, dominant, my mercenary all at once came down on top of me and thrust to the hilt.

EIGHTY-THREE

Vance

Her back arched, her legs came up and she moaned like a goddamn vixen.

"Fuck, *oiseau. Je veux te baiser de toutes les manières.*" French, English, I didn't know what the hell was coming out of my mouth. I was buried in the sweetest cunt I'd ever felt, and I never wanted to pull out.

I drove into her deep, and her hands fisted in my hair.

Goddamn. "That's it, love, hold on to me." I could stare into her eyes for the rest of my life.

"I am holding."

I fucking smiled. "I know." Caging her in, I rocked deep and ground against her hips. "Do you know how amazing you feel?"

Her cheeks flushed. "*Non.*"

I kissed her hard. Then I pulled back enough to see her eyes. "You feel incredible, but I'm bareback."

Her gaze drifted down my chest, and her voice turned quiet. "You already came inside me."

Feeling the weight of her response but not the tone of it, I tipped her chin. "Do you want children?"

Her expression shut down. "Do you?"

Fuck. "Not what I asked, and it doesn't matter what I want. Answer the question, pet."

She frowned. "Why would it not matter?"

Measuring my intent against her first reaction and the look

on her face now, I calculated my next move. I hadn't planned on doing this tonight, but fuck, I wasn't waiting anymore.

Snaking one arm under her hips so she didn't go anywhere, I kept her against me as I grabbed what I needed off the nightstand. Setting the two boxes on the bed, I issued her an order. "Arms around my neck, pet. Hold on."

No hesitation, she did exactly as I said.

Staying inside her, I cradled her back and sweet ass as I flipped us over and sat against the headboard. Grasping the backs of her thighs, I brought her legs up until she was straddled over my hips.

She sucked in a sharp breath at the new angle, and my cock pulsed as I seated deep inside her. "That's it." Fuck, she was tight. "Right there, *oiseau*. Feel me inside you."

"*Non*." Her hands braced on my chest, she trembled. "You are too much like this."

"Breathe," I commanded, grabbing the first red box.

Shifting, she tried to lift off me.

"Stop." I caught her hip. "Take a breath. I'm already inside you, love."

Still trembling, she gave me only a shallow inhale.

"Again," I ordered.

Deeper this time, she took a full breath and the trembling eased.

"Good girl." Vulnerable as hell, brave for trusting me, she was so damn beautiful, I didn't deserve her, but I was taking her anyway. "Now, am I truly hurting you?"

Her face flushed, and she shook her head.

"Sore?"

She half shrugged.

"Words, pet," I demanded.

"*Non*, not hurting. But sore, *oui*, a little."

Sliding my hand across her hip and down to her sweet

cunt, I slowly rubbed her clit until she started to constrict around me. Then I eased back on the pressure so she didn't come yet. "Better?"

The flush on her face took on a whole new shade as she dropped her gaze to watch my hand before giving me a sexy whisper. "Yes."

Her shyness was fucking intoxicating, but I wanted to see her. "Look at me, Sabine."

She lifted her head, then without preamble she dropped her brand of honesty on me. "I have never felt this before."

I fucking stilled.

Then I had to inhale. Twice.

The man I was a month ago would've dismissed any woman who said that to me with a thinly veiled caustic retort followed by a smile. I didn't fucking smile. Nor did I brush it off. "I'm selfish enough to tell you that if you had, I would've been pissed."

"Angry?" she asked in her sexy accent.

"Very. But that's not the point." I wanted to be in her head and her body when I answered her previous question. "I want to be inside you right now, *oiseau*. You good?"

Shy, seductive, she whispered, "Yes."

Still stroking her clit, keeping my gaze intent on hers, I opened the first box one-handed and quickly grabbed the two items, concealing them. Then I kissed her once before taking her left wrist in my hand. "Do you remember what I said on deck?"

Briefly glancing at my hold on her, she nodded. "Yes, but you said many things. I do not know which part you mean specifically."

Fuck. This woman. No pretense, giving me her trust, she was so goddamn perfect.

I brushed her hair back from her face. "The all-in part."

Her expression giving nothing away, she gave the red boxes a fleeting glance before looking back at me. "I remember."

"Good." I put the bracelet around her wrist and grabbed the small screwdriver. "Do you know what this is?"

Her throat moved with a swallow as she stared at the yellow gold and diamond band I was putting on her. "Cartier," she whispered, before her voice went completely hoarse. "The love bracelet."

"Yes, it is." Tightening the screw all the way until the piece was secure on her wrist, I tossed the gold screwdriver on the nightstand and took both the bracelet and her wrist in my hand. Bringing them to my chest, I held her hand over my heart as I cupped her face. "I love you, Sabine Malcher. It doesn't matter if I want kids. Whatever you want, I want."

Tears welled in her eyes. *"Je t'aime moi aussi."*

Her admission hitting me like a blast wave, I let go of her hand, grabbed the other box, and set it on my chest. "Then mean it."

Staring at the new cuff on her wrist, she inhaled sharply and her sweet cunt constricted around me.

"Oiseau," I warned. "Open the box." She had thirty seconds before I was flipping her back over and driving us both over the edge.

With shaking hands, she opened the box and stared at the matching bracelet, but this one was larger and in white gold.

As she traced a finger over the piece, a single tear ran down her face.

Swiping my thumb over her cheek, I brushed her tear over her full lips. "You gave me your trust. Now I'm giving you mine." Purposely dropping my hand, I rested it on my chest. Then I held my fucking breath.

My exquisite bird, she didn't hesitate.

Taking the bracelet, she put it on my left wrist and secured it.

Before she had time to drop the screwdriver, I was on her.

Taking her face in both of my hands, plunging my tongue into her mouth, I fucking kissed her like I owned her—because I did.

She was *mine*.

Every fucking inch.

Growling into her mouth, flipping her over, I reared back only to plunge deep.

Her gasp filled the cabin, and I did it again. I wanted to fuck her, I wanted to claim her, I wanted to make love to her in every imaginable way, but I also wanted more.

I wanted it all with this woman.

Driving into her one more time, I ground against her clit, but then I held still. "You didn't answer my question."

Her eyes hooded, her breath short, she gripped the back of my neck and pulsed around my cock. *"Please."* Her hips moving, she was so fucking close. "Do not stop."

"Oh, pet, I love to see you beg, but you're not coming yet." Not until I knew how deep she was with me. "Do you want it all?"

Her sweet cunt constricted, and she bit her lip. "All?"

Fuck. "Children," I ground out.

She stilled, and I saw it in her eyes.

"Don't answer me with a question," I warned. "Tell me what you want, *oiseau*, and tell me now." Because I was barely holding it together.

Her eyes, her face, her entire expression softened, and for the first time I saw a different version of her. My wounded, resilient bird dropped her guard, and with one look, she crushed me.

Showing me what hope looked like on her, I got a smile.

"*Oui.* Yes." The shy tilt of her full lips transforming her entire face, she spread her wings. "Many children. With ink-black hair and two-color eyes and mischief in their smiles. *Please,*" she added.

    I didn't smile.

    I didn't tell her I loved her.

    I didn't say I wanted every goddamn piece of what she'd said.

    I fucking surged and took her mouth.

    Then I devoured her, every inch, and drove us both to the edge. Her body meant for mine, she detonated at the exact moment I let go.

    "*I own you,*" I growled, coming hard inside her.

    The woman who was my entire fucking world grasped my face with her small hands. "You are free with me."

EPILOGUE

Vance

Navigating the Songbird away from the dock and shallow waters, I gave her some speed and my cell rang.

My gaze locked on the woman who was my entire reason, I took the call. "I'm busy." That bikini was coming off Sabine the second we hit open waters.

"She surfaced," November stated cryptically.

My focus shifted, and my gaze drifted. "Did you get it?" I didn't ask about her. If she'd surfaced, she was breathing. That was all I needed to know in that regard.

"She didn't have it."

Not that I thought she would, but fuck. "She in trouble?" November never randomly called.

November paused. "No."

"Then why are you calling?"

"Look to your right."

I scanned the turquoise waters off the coast of Miami as we approached the Gulf Stream. "What am I looking for?" We were in the middle of the fucking ocean. "No one's out here."

"Closer right."

Christ. "Not in the mood for games, Rhys. I'm with my woman, and I don't have shit to do today except her." Easing back on the throttle, I cut the engines. "Speed this up. I'll be out of cell range soon."

"Look where I told you."

"Right," I muttered. "I used to appreciate that you were a cryptic fuck." Glancing around again, I scanned the entire starboard side of the Carver yacht. "Now I'm changing my mind. There's nothing here."

Static hit the line. "It wasn't clean... nothing... come back...."

Shit. "You're breaking up. What wasn't clean?"

"I'll... off the grid... starboard...." The call cut out.

I immediately tried to call him back, but I didn't have any signal. Tossing the cell aside, I checked starboard again. Nothing.

"Everything all right?" Oiseau called out.

I glanced at my exquisite bird. "Remind me again why we're out here, pet?"

Her smile was always reserved, but she used it more now than she ever had. "Because you are a mercenary Marine who secretly pretends to hate the water, but in truth enjoys being on it because it is a rush that you no longer get since you quit going to that gym where grown men beat each other."

Fucking hell, she had my number. "First of all, not a mercenary, love." Some details, she didn't need to know. "Second, there's no pretending." I really did hate being on the fucking water. Unfortunately, she loved it and I loved her, so here I was, in my brother's Carver, playing captain and catering to my woman's want of all things ocean and sun.

My one consolation was her nothing bikini that tied on the sides of her hips for the easiest access known to man.

Her hand waved dismissively through the air. "You are driving. That gives you control. You love it."

"I'll show you control." I wouldn't. "Take that bikini off and come here." I'd fuck her rough the first time, probably the second too because I had no control around this woman. Two months of being with her, taking her every day, in every way imaginable, and my obsession was only growing.

"Non." She glanced over her sun-kissed shoulder. "Are we there?"

"Close enough." I wasn't going farther out. The Gulf Stream was thirty-five miles wide. "Since when do you say no to me?"

"Since you are driving the boat and need to pay attention." She looked east. "I do not see the blue."

"You're in the middle of the ocean, pet." It was all fucking blue. "And technically, this is a yacht. Also, for the record, I can fuck and drive at the same time."

She looked over the port side of the Songbird. "I meant the deeper blue I can see from your penthouse. Where the ocean changes color from the clearer, greener hue to the darker, cobalt blue." Her voice turned to a shade of quiet I instantly recognized. "And I am not commenting on any particular multitasking skill of yours that I have no knowledge of."

Fuck, I loved that she got jealous, I fed off it, but it was a double-edged sword. Upsetting her was the equivalent of taking a knife to the gut.

I fessed up. "Just so you know, darling, I was referring to fucking and driving this yacht, which is only the third time I've driven a boat and the first two times I wasn't fucking. So while my statement is technically theoretical, I'm positive it's no less true. But just in case, why don't you come join me and we'll test my theory."

"Why don't you take us to the darker blue and come join me?"

"You're portside, darling. Look starboard." I grabbed a bottled water from a cup holder on my right. As I pulled it out, I heard it.

A slight ping.

I glanced down and a telltale glint caught in the bright sunlight.

That *motherfucker*.

"You have got to be shitting me," I muttered.

"Pardon?"

November, the fuck, left a half-million-dollar diamond in a goddamn cup holder, on a boat that wasn't mine, which I hadn't asked Ronan to borrow until this morning.

I didn't know if I should kill November or fucking thank him.

"Vance?"

Distracted, I answered her as I surreptitiously pocketed the ring. "I promise, darling, we're in the Gulf Stream."

"We are floating, yes?"

"We're not anchored." It was too damn deep.

"*Bon*. Can you come join me? I want to ask something."

Even with the ring weighing me down, I still saw through her. "My answer is no."

"I have not asked yet."

"Doesn't matter. Nothing good comes after that statement, pet." If she had to ask, it meant I wasn't going to like it.

Her hands went to her hips. "Come here," she demanded.

Fighting a grin, I shoved my sunglasses up and raised an eyebrow. "Oh, pet, are you trying to unleash me?"

"I unleash nothing. I want to talk. I am being serious."

"I know you are." She wasn't ever not serious. "But my answer's still no. The last time you said you wanted to ask me something, it was to tell me you gave away your entire settlement from Harrington's and you weren't moving into the beach house." It wasn't the money I gave a damn about, I had enough for two lifetimes. It was the fact that she wouldn't even consider moving out of the penthouse and into the new place I'd bought.

"It does not have views."

"It's an oceanfront house, *oiseau*." One that would be a clean start for both of us.

"You know what I mean." Her hand waved dismissively at the water all around us. "No views from the sky."

"It's hurricane safe," I argued.

"The penthouse is safe. Are you coming down to talk to me?"

"We're already talking." If I got within two feet of her, we wouldn't be talking anymore. And now that I had the ring, a whole new layer had been added. No way was I giving it to her without being inside her.

She stared at me.

I stared back.

Water slapped the side of the boat, a slight breeze blew and suddenly it hit me.

I wasn't shoving down my past. I wasn't angling for a refuge from the shit in my head. I wasn't fighting or fucking or getting off on an adrenaline rush from an op, mission, or assignment.

I was staring at a woman who I didn't have to pretend with, and this was it.

I was living.

A peace I never thought I would have settled around me, and I smiled. "This isn't a standoff, love." Holding up my left wrist, I winked. "I already own you. Come here."

Glancing at her own bracelet, she shook her head.

Then my exquisite bird gave me her reserved smile and came up to the bridge. "You are impossible."

I wrapped my arms around her and kissed her neck. "I love you."

She melted into me. "*Je t'aime.*"

"I know." I tugged at the tie around her neck and kissed

her shoulder. "What did you want to ask me?" Her top fell down, and I latched on to one of her nipples. Biting softly, then swirling my tongue, I sucked away the sting.

Her moan floated across the ocean as she tangled her fingers in my hair. "This is not fair."

"Life's not fair." I moved to the other nipple and sucked harder as I pulled at the ties on her hips.

Her bikini bottom hit the deck, and she went on tiptoe to grind her hips into my already hard cock. "I cannot concentrate when you do this. Take your shorts off."

Dragging my hand between her legs, already feeling her slick desire, I chuckled. "You don't need to concentrate, and you're very demanding today." I sank two fingers inside her and stroked deep as my thumb circled her clit.

Her sweet cunt pulsed hard, but she didn't fall into my touch like she usually did. Instead, her entire body stiffened. "I demand nothing."

I slid my fingers out and grasped her chin. "What's going on?"

Her gaze hit my shoulder.

"No," I barked sharply. "You don't do that with me, Sabine. I already told you this months ago. We're not backtracking. You never need to look away from me. I don't give a shit what you have to say, I'll never hurt you."

Tears filled her eyes. "I know."

Alarm hit. "Then look at me and tell me what's wrong."

Panic all over her face, she met my gaze. "I gave all the money away."

I cupped her cheek. "You didn't want it and you don't need it. I already told you, what's mine is yours."

"I do not have money," she whispered.

Searching her face, I tried to read between the lines. "How much do you want? I'll put it in your account."

VICTOR

Pulling out of my grasp, she turned her head. "I do not have an account."

"What happened to the six million you had in the bank, Sabine?" I asked as calmly as possible.

"Do not call me that."

"It's your name."

"It is only my name when you are angry with me."

"I'm not angry with you." I was going to kill Barrett, though. "That six million wasn't part of the settlement. That was money you earned. What happened to it?"

Her voice barely a whisper, she looked at her feet. "I gave that away too."

I inhaled.

"See?" Frantically trying to cover her breasts with her untied top, she turned away. "You are angry, I have no money and everything is wrong." She reached for her bikini bottom.

I grabbed her left hand, spun her, and put both our bracelet-clad wrists against my chest, dead center. "I'm not angry at you, and I don't give a shit about the money. You know that. I'm just trying to understand why you're upset now." And what she needed money for.

"You are angry," she accused. "I see it in your eyes."

"Right." Fuck. "Okay, so I admit I'm considering how much bodily harm to inflict on Barrett. I know he helped you give the settlement away to that women's shelter, but he wasn't supposed to touch your account. That was for you, for a rainy day." She'd fucking earned every penny of it.

Something close to guilt crossed her features. "There was more than one shelter that needed help."

Christ, I loved this woman. "How many more?"

"Seven," she whispered before pausing, then blurting out the rest in a rush. "Three that were in New York and four in Paris."

Grasping her nape, I brought my forehead to hers. "You don't need money, we have plenty, and I understand and respect your generosity." I more than respected it. I was fucking humbled by it. "Tomorrow we'll go to the bank and open a new account for you. I'll transfer ten million and you won't have to worry about money ever again, okay?"

She burst into tears. *"Non,"* she cried, pulling away and rapid-fire aiming her panic at me. "Don't you see? Everything is wrong! I do not have money. I do not have a job. I have nothing of my own. This is like seven years ago all over again. I cannot take care of—" stopping herself, she inhaled sharply, then she spoke with quiet defeat. "I am not nineteen, but I still have nothing."

"Not true." I reached in my pocket, then took her hand. "You have me, and you have this." I slid the ring on her finger.

Her mouth gaped, and she went stock-still as she stared at her hand.

Fuck. "I know you said not to—"

"I'm pregnant," she blurted.

The earth shifted. "What?"

Her head came up, and she looked at me with tears falling down her face. *"Je suis enceinte."*

Barely keeping my shit in check, I spoke. "That's why you need money?"

"Oui." She nodded. "To take care of the baby, in case… in case you don't…." She shook her head. "You never said. You never said if you wanted children too. You only asked what I—"

Grabbing her, I slammed my mouth over hers and stood to my full height. Her feet came off the ground, and I kissed the fuck out of her.

Her legs wrapped around my waist, and her hands grabbed the back of my neck, but she pulled her mouth from mine. Lips wet, panic gone, she looked at me with hope. "You want children? This is good?"

I fucking grinned. "Better than good." I dropped the smile. "But don't ever pull that money shit on me again, *oiseau*. I meant what I said before I knew you were carrying my child, and I mean it now. All in means all in."

"Okay," she whispered.

"Say it," I demanded.

"All in."

"Again."

She pressed closer to me. "All in. *Je t'aime*."

Fuck. A kid. *My kid*. "I own you." Holding her up with one arm, I shoved the front of my shorts down with my other hand and fisted myself. Dragging the head of my cock through her slick cunt, I positioned myself but didn't sink inside her yet. I paused. "We're getting married. Tomorrow," I added.

"*Oui*," she barely breathed, rocking her hips. "Tomorrow."

Drifting in the fastest current in the world, I sank inside my woman and gave her the truth. "You own me, *oiseau*. Forever."

Prone, my right eye sighting through my scope, I exhaled.

The new burner in my pocket vibrated.

Keeping my finger on the trigger and my eye on the target, I pulled the cell out. Answering the call without looking at the display, I held the phone to my ear, but I didn't speak.

"Rogue team's down."

My target moved six inches to the left as he turned in his chair to look out his window. "Not quite."

"Then you know one member's AWOL."

I calculated wind speed, distance and elevation. "Affirmative."

"Charlie mike?"

I adjusted my aim. "Who the fuck do you think you're talking to?"

"A dead man if this shit gets out," he answered honestly.

Taking a breath and letting it out slow, I pulled the trigger.

My target's head exploded.

Pushing to my knees, I stowed the TAC-338 in its case, and snapped it shut.

"You still there?"

Pulling my baseball cap down low over my face, I headed for the stairwell. "Do your job. Continue the mission."

"Or?"

"I'll find you." I hung up and removed the SIM card.

THANK YOU!

Thank you so much for reading VICTOR! If you are interested in leaving a review on any retail site, I would be so appreciative. Reviews mean the world to authors, and they are helpful beyond compare.

Turn the page for a preview of ROMEO, the next exciting book in the Alpha Elite Series!

ROMEO

Pilot.

Handler.

Marine.

My first memory was in the cockpit of a plane. My second was of a uniform. All I'd ever wanted was to be a pilot. The Marines gave me wings, and I gave them my all.

Half a dozen deployments, countless flight hours—I knew the controls in the cockpit better than I knew my own name. I never made mistakes. But war didn't care how good you were. One surface-to-air missile and my career was over.

Thinking I'd left dangerous missions and adrenaline rushes in my rearview, I was piloting a seaplane in the Florida Keys when a beat-to-hell, dark-eyed blonde washed ashore. In nothing but a bikini, she asked me for help. Help I couldn't give without an assist from Alpha Elite Security. Except AES wanted a favor in return… one that would put me right back in the line of fire.

Code name: Romeo.
Mission: Rescue.

ROMEO is a standalone book in the exciting new Alpha Elite Series by *USA Today* Bestselling author, Sybil Bartel. Come meet Roark "Romeo" MacElheran and the dominant, alpha heroes who work for AES!

NOVEMBER

Airman.

Hacker.

Mercenary.

Hacking one of the government's top agencies when I was seventeen, then covering my tracks before telling them about it was my first mistake. My second was thinking they'd want to know that if I found the opening, anyone could. Nineteen hours later, five armed men in uniform kicked down my door.

I had a choice. Prison or recruitment.

The Air Force took me in and trained me to be the best Cyberspace Operations Officer they'd ever had. Being the gatekeeper for the military's strategic operations intel was an honor, but it put a target on my back. I never traveled without security—until I made my third mistake.

Four days and twenty-two hours later, barely able to stand after events that I wasn't at liberty to discuss, I erased my past, changed my identity, and went off the grid. Then I joined Alpha Elite Security. I was invisible, exactly as I'd planned… until she found me.

Code name: November.
Mission: Extrication.

NOVEMBER is a standalone book in the exciting Alpha Elite Series by *USA Today* Bestselling author, Sybil Bartel. Come meet Nathan "November" Rhys and the dominant, alpha heroes who work for AES!

ECHO

Navy SEAL.

Mercenary.

Ghost.

Joining the military wasn't a choice, it was survival. It was also the last place they would think to look for me. Hiding in plain sight, I lived in the shadow of deployments… until an off-the-books mission put me in the crosshairs of my past.

My cover blown, I walked away from the SEALs and sought refuge at the one place where I'd be more invisible than on the Teams—Alpha Elite Security. As a Black Ops government contractor, AES was the world's leading provider of security solutions. High stakes, higher price tag, and complete anonymity. Trained to kill long before the Navy put a gun in my hand, I fit right in.

Legally aiming my rifle, taking any AES assignment that guaranteed action, I lived to fight. But then I made a mistake. One single misstep and I was face-to-face with the only woman who could kill me faster than a bullet.

Code name: Echo.
Mission: Evade.

ECHO is a standalone book in the exciting Alpha Elite Series by *USA Today* Bestselling author, Sybil Bartel. Come meet Echo and the dominant, alpha heroes who work for AES!

ZULU

Navy SEAL.

Sniper.

Mercenary.

The Navy trained me to be the best, but the Teams turned me into a deadly weapon. Every mission honing my tactical skills, I never missed a shot. Living for my brothers and the Trident I'd earned, I didn't look past my next deployment.

Then my friend and former teammate made me an offer—private sector, government contracts, combat missions and the chance to fly my own jet. Retiring from the Teams, but not the mission, I joined Alpha Elite Security.

As second-in-command at AES, I demanded precision because I didn't do things the wrong way. Until a mysterious brunette walked through the door and everything went FUBAR.

Code name: Zulu.
Mission: Exfiltrate.

ZULU is a standalone book in the exciting new Alpha Elite Series by *USA Today* Bestselling author, Sybil Bartel. Come meet Zane "Zulu" Silas and the dominant, alpha heroes who work for AES!

ACKNOWLEDGMENTS

As I write the last line in VICTOR, it is exactly one year to the day that my only child, my son Oliver, passed away tragically and unexpectedly in his sleep from an undiagnosed birth defect in his heart. My Sweet Boy was only fifteen-years-old.

Oliver was my entire world. Born with an autoimmune disease, he overcame every obstacle life threw at him, and he not only survived, he thrived during his time here on earth. Intelligent beyond comprehension, he was a straight A student (with a 4.45 GPA!). He was an incredibly talented cello and piano player, a black belt in Karate and Jiu Jitsu, and a compassionate friend to everyone he met. He had the biggest heart of anyone I've ever known. I was blessed with a gift beyond words the day he was born.

Oliver taught me about unconditional love and perseverance. He showed me what determination looked like, and he showed the world how someone so young, yet so wise, can handle life's obstacles with grace and humbleness. Oliver made me a better person. He brightened every single day. His smile was my joy, and he truly made this world a better place.

I will never understand why he was taken from us, and I cannot imagine a day where the grief isn't so punishing that it robs me of all breath. I would give anything to have just one more minute with him so I could hold him and tell him I love him. But life, for all its beauty, cruelly doesn't work like that. So this is me, holding my son the only way I know how and telling him I love him more than words. This book is me doing my best to honor the memory of my beautiful son.

My Sweet Boy—you were, and will forever be, my most treasured gift.
I love you, Oliver Shane.
I love you more than anything.
XOXO
Mom

ABOUT THE AUTHOR

Sybil Bartel is a *USA Today* Bestselling author of unapologetic alpha heroes. Whether you're reading her deliciously dominant alpha bodyguards or alpha mercenaries, her page-turning romantic suspense, or her heart-stopping military romance, all of her books have sexy-as-sin alpha heroes.

Sybil resides in South Florida and she is forever Oliver's mom.

To find out more about Sybil Bartel or her books, please visit her at:
Website: sybilbartel.com

Facebook page: www.facebook.com/sybilbartelauthor

Facebook group: www.facebook.com/groups/1065006266850790

Instagram: www.instagram.com/sybil.bartel

Twitter: twitter.com/SybilBartel

BookBub:www.bookbub.com/authors/sybil-bartel

Newsletter: http://eepurl.com/bRSE2T

The Oliver Bartel Memorial Scholarship Trust:
sybilbartel.com/Oliver-Bartel-Memorial-Scholarship-Trust.html

Made in United States
Orlando, FL
12 January 2022